RIVENWILDE

Cover design by St Jupiter

Interior illustrations by

Ireen Chau https://www.ireenchau.com

Grace Crandall @krasnetigritsa

EK Belsher http://www.ekbelsher.com

Victoria van Herckenrode @vicsdrawss

EmberMarke https://www.embermarke.com

Silversteampunk @silversteampunk

Seda Coşkun @artofseda

Beriz Art @berizart

Teresa Vu https://www.peachiemochi.com

Marta García Navarro @margana_mgn

Myrthena @myrthena

THE RIVENWILDE SERIES

MELISSA WRIGHT

BEYOND THE FILIGREE WALL

PROLOGUE

The good king-fearing people of Westrende held a single faith without question: *magic isn't real*. Stories of fae were only constructs designed to explain away the sort of unpleasantness no one wished to examine overmuch—unpleasantness like the madness that struck when the moon was full, when a maiden went lost, a child fell ill, or perhaps when a king's gold was stolen and the wheat stores turned foul. That sort.

Myth, superstition, and deception were what the tales were made of.

Etta, neither unreservedly good nor especially king-fearing, knew the truth was far simpler. Beneath their willful ignorance and outright denial rested a dark secret, depthless in its desire for vengeance. Indeed, the people of the kingdom had no notion that they were only a single misstep from plummeting over a deadly precipice. They liked it that way.

Lady Antonetta Ostwind, sole daughter and heir of the great General Ostwind, had kept that vile secret since she was a girl. *Tell no one*, her father had warned in whispered threats. Tell no one of the monsters who'd come for her mother while Etta had watched from the darkness beneath her bed. *Speak of them, and they shall come again.* She had bitten down on the words until she tasted blood. She had not spoken, had not screamed, had not uttered a single word of the fae in all the days which followed.

It had not stopped their coming because the fae had been there all along.

Antonetta could see through their glamour. Her father's fear and the king's council may have kept Etta from shouting the truth, but it could not take her sight. The fae, magical beings intent on doing harm, walked among them. Lesser fae may have seemed harmless if not for the shadows—beings like those who had taken her mother, darker in both intent and form. Shadows, they were called, because to acknowledge the existence of the high fae of the Riven Court was to meet a disagreeable fate.

Etta had been forced into a secrecy meant to protect her, but it had protected only the monsters. She understood precisely the ruin they caused because she could see a truth at which no one else dared look. The fae were worse than any imagined tales. And her silence had kept them safe. Her hands had not spilled their blood.

All that was about to change.

CHAPTER 1

"Nearly there," Nickolas chirped. Blond, approaching five and twenty, and apparently entirely at ease being cramped inside a juddering cabin for days, Nickolas Brigham—Etta's escort, onetime childhood friend, and several-time nemesis—had been unashamedly vying for her attention for the entire trip.

Etta stared out the window of the carriage. There was nothing particularly outstanding beyond the cloudy glass, but there was equally nothing outstanding about her, and she wasn't fool enough to believe his attentions were genuine. Nickolas was tall and handsome and had the sort of crooked smile that made many a knee go weak. Though passable in many respects, Etta was little different than the other ladies at court, of which he surely had his pick. She understood full well that his attention—like nearly all attentions she'd been paid since she was young—came not from any special beauty or grace but from her standing.

As head of the council, Etta's father was the most influential of a dozen men and women who directed the fate of the kingdom and all those within it until a king was returned to power—which, at the rate things were going, would not be anytime soon. It was no secret that the current prospects were all a good decade short of meeting the age and education requirements to become king, and two of those prospects had recently been stricken ill.

Furthermore, in a matter of days, Etta herself would become marshal, head of law and order in the kingdom and responsible for overseeing the guard. She was not about to cock it up for a boy like Nickolas, who would get no further than captain without an advantageous marriage. She drew in a long breath, comforted by what was to come once she was finally installed into the office of marshal. The position was significant in that it alone allowed freedom of movement beyond the council. She'd be tied no longer to their foolish rules and society games. They would be unable to stop her from crossing the Rive.

"You must be excited to return after all these years," Nickolas said. "Eager? Relishing the tingle of anticipatory glee, perhaps?"

She continued her regard of the unkempt grass beyond the carriage window. The seemingly endless expanse of sky had been overcast most of the day and was beginning to color with a tinge of pink to herald the coming sunset. The trip had been planned in exacting detail to allow for the carriage's timely arrival—even if that arrival was two days prior to her father's expectations—because none were allowed to cross the border once night had fallen.

The kingdom gates, twisted dark iron topped with deadly barbs, tucked neatly between walls of the finest stone, came into view. A line of kingsmen stared down from the parapets, surely aware even from such a height who warranted the pomp of the approaching caravan. She would be scrutinized regardless. They would make her wait outside the gates while her documents were verified, even with Nickolas and his ilk at her side. She glanced back to the rest of her escort, kingsmen of varying status perched in full regalia atop prized horses. More than one of her protectors seemed to have an eye on the line of trees in the distance. Even Nickolas seemed a bit fidgety in the dying light.

It was telling that the people of Westrende denied the existence of fae and magic, yet not a soul seemed comfortable with a wait outside the gates so near where the dark forest loomed. As if the Rive might reach out and snatch them.

Etta scoffed. "Nickolas," she said, finally giving him her gaze. "Tell me what I have missed."

His smile was golden, a great, glowing, ridiculous thing that seemed to light up the carriage. By the wall, he had always been so mulishly oblivious. She wasn't certain he'd ever been able to read a person's mood—or maybe he'd simply not bothered to care if, in the end, doing so didn't further his cause. One more trait it seemed he'd not outgrown. She gestured for him to get on with it.

"Little has happened that was not relayed in your reports, I'm sure, my lady." His smile hinted that he in fact knew exactly what she was about—mood and all—and intended to toy with her.

She gave him her flattest expression.

His grin shifted into something a bit more tenable. "Lady Yates is having a torrid affair with a barber's son. Theo's carpenter was caught using funds meant for suite furnishings to procure an absolutely obscene collection of crystal urns, which were discovered by a maid while freshening the mattresses." He waved a hand vaguely near the curtain, as if drawing the memories from air. "A pair of scribes was caught desecrating the king's garderobe, and the magistrate had them pilloried in their small-clothes for a week."

She managed not to wince. Castle gossip wasn't at all something she'd missed about being away, and certainly not the information she'd been after from Nickolas. "What of the new chancellor?"

The answering spark in his eyes teased something that Etta did not like at all. He leaned forward on the seat, his long fingers woven together only inches from her knee, the scent of roses and sandalwood wafting off him. "Ah, yes," he said. "Gideon."

Gideon. He was going to be hideous. She could tell already. "Yes."

"Nephew to our great steward."

Etta had never met the new chancellor but had heard well enough: he was a brutal tactician with no regard for new ideas, no interest in improvement to their ancient laws and inter-kingdom protocol, and not a whit of tolerance for those who crossed the wall. "He's a traditionalist," she said.

Nickolas chuckled. "You could say that."

"I did. What would *you* say?"

He leaned back, tossing his hands a bit before sliding them over the slick blue fabric that covered his knees. "I'd call him a raging cumberground. An absolute saddle-goose. Ineffective as a boat full of holes." He shrugged. "But that's just me."

Well, now he was just trying to buy her with flattery. Etta nodded. "We shall see."

The man had been installed after she'd gone away—been sent away —for her training. In the nearly four years since, he'd risen to the head of chancery with unlikely speed. It was a position that rivaled hers. There was every expectation he would become the marshal's mortal enemy.

Etta intended to crush him.

AFTER THEY HAD BEEN PERMITTED through the gates and winded their way through the kingdom under a sky that had turned turbulent, the carriage, at long last, drew to a stop before their destination. Said destination was not the front entrance of the castle to a grand reception, as would surely have been planned by her father's staff. Etta had demanded that Nickolas both keep their arrival confidential and deliver her to the service entrance. She needed to prepare for her reintroduction to the council and courtiers on her own terms, and in time to suss out what else they might have planned for her. Besides, she wanted greatly to wash the days of travel from her person before meeting a single soul.

Shoving a lock of her chestnut hair behind an ear and sorting her disheveled skirt into order, she drew a fortifying breath of stuffy cabin air.

When she glanced up, Nickolas was watching her, a sly grin on his stupid charming mouth. "Ready, my lady?"

She would not reward him with a glare, never mind that his tone had been loaded. They both knew she was walking blindly into a lion's den, against the general's orders. "Nickolas," she said, "I am always—"

His bark of laughter broke the stillness she only then realized had come over them. He placed a hand over his heart and slid forward in his seat. "Yes, it is not as if you have ever let me forget." The door opened, and his long legs carried him past her in one graceful motion to land outside the carriage and between a waiting pair of umbrella-wielding ushers. He leaned in and adopted a conspiratorial tone. "The lady Ostwind is always ready."

Despite the dread that sank in her belly, Etta took his proffered hand. "Yes," she said. "Always."

Etta was not ready. A single flash of her reflection in the ornate metal trim that lined the carriage door made her state painfully clear. She stepped out regardless, just as the murky sky let loose and poured rain onto the fine cobbled drive.

Nickolas glanced at the deluge, taking hold of one umbrella while leaving the second for the ushers. "Portentous."

She resisted the urge to jab an elbow into his ribs. The space between the carriage and the entrance was excessive and scattered with mounted kingsmen eager to return their charge. Until the general's daughter was safely inside, their duty was not complete. Etta took hold of the umbrella with Nickolas, and they weaved swiftly between the beasts with their clattering hooves and the castle staff converging on the carriage to retrieve the pair's many trunks.

Beneath the overhang at the entrance, Etta stopped to shake the umbrella and draw another breath. Her apprehension was nearly under control when a black dog shot from beyond a column to dart past her skirts. She shrieked—an absolute embarrassment she would dwell on when she wasn't thusly occupied—leaping back into Nickolas, who brushed off the arms of his embroidered suitcoat.

Clearly not expecting the collision, he barely caught her before they both tumbled to sprawl on the rain-soaked cobblestone. As it was, his boot splashed into an impossibly fast-forming puddle, splattering wet filth up the leg of his fine trousers and half of Etta's skirt. She did not bother with explanation or apology because in that moment, she became aware that the creature had been no dog at all.

It had been a lesser fae. Etta said a curse, gritted her teeth, and took tighter hold of the closed umbrella. Stomping through the door on its trail, she dodged two serving men and a downstairs maid before she caught sight of the dark mass of fur sliding around a corner. She was after it without another thought.

Etta had made a promise to herself while she'd been away: not a single fae would pass her sight without coming to regret it. Her silence was over. They would pay for what they had done.

The thing darted into a storeroom, turning to give her a savage grin made of too many teeth before the door slammed closed behind it. Etta picked up her pace, shoving through after it, rain-soaked weapon in hand. The door snicked shut behind her, throwing the narrow room into near darkness. The creature had disappeared, but she could feel its eyes upon her and almost sense the horrid glee vibrating through it.

A drop of rain fell from her umbrella to splat loudly on the pantry floor. In the shadows, something giggled.

"Come out, you filthy—"

A solid slab of wood smacked into Etta from behind, Nickolas and the light of the main room coming along with it. The creature shot across the space, and Etta took an off-balance swing just as Nickolas grabbed her in some dramatic and entirely misplaced heroic gesture that she made a note to discuss with him at a later date. The swing missed, the umbrella thwacked into a sack of flour, and Etta was quite suddenly covered in a matted, pale paste. The creature shoved her to land face-first into the sack then darted out the open door.

Etta lay there for a moment, swallowing words she'd sworn she would never eat again. A lock of hair was wedged into her mouth. Her knee throbbed. And the beast must have gotten a swipe in on its way through because she felt the thin stinging line of the cuts she'd grown accustomed to as a girl. Several cuts, it seemed, began to burn near her ankle.

"By the wall," Nickolas murmured, staring down at the mess in apparent awe.

"The wall indeed," she said through gritted teeth then flopped to her back so she could glare up at him.

They came out of the storeroom to an audience of at least a dozen kingsmen and castle staff. Etta slapped a hand to her skirt, which puffed what flour had not yet caked on, then threw the umbrella to the floor. "Ladies, gentlemen, so good to see you once more." Then she tottered off on flour-caked heels without a single look back.

Nickolas found her in the first empty corridor she'd come to, pounding her fists on the wall with a curse entirely unseemly for one of her station.

"Etta," he said, his voice low, careful, and not at all in a tone he'd used in their many days of travel.

"No. Don't. Just—I need to return to my rooms."

"Absolutely," he answered with not a single question about why she had just attempted murder on a rangy dog. "Only"—he glanced over his shoulder—"let me be certain word of this doesn't leave the, uh..."

Etta groaned.

"Right," he said. "One moment."

She turned to lean against the wall of the empty corridor, jerked her wet gloves off, and threw them to the floor. The narrow passage was used by staff, poorly lit, sparsely decorated, and unlikely to be occupied at the current hour. Not that it mattered. She'd been planning her triumphant return to Westrende since the day she was shipped off to school. And there she was, all her care and caution exhausted within minutes of her arrival.

She unbuttoned her lace-trimmed jacket and yanked her arms free of the damp material, tearing seams by the sound of it. It went in a pile with her gloves. Bending over to ruck up her skirts, she cursed again when she saw the damage the thing had done to her leg. "This is why I hate dogs," she muttered, as if in reply to all the remembered comments she'd been unable to answer to honestly since she was a girl. "Cannot trust a single one not to be fae."

She snapped the skirt down and wrapped her arms around her middle, wondering if she might succeed in navigating to her rooms without Nickolas there to clear a path. By the sight of her, it was probably best she didn't try. She sighed, closed her eyes, and leaned back against the wood-paneled wall.

Door, her mind corrected just as it fell open behind her. She fell with it. Her arms went out, scrabbling for purchase, and caught only one side of the frame. She felt more than heard the intake of breath of the person she'd pitched into and drew herself up to turn and look. It was a dark-haired man in his early twenties, impossibly near. His square jaw had gone slack in an improbably perfect face, everything else about him entirely buttoned up. He wore a high-collared black shirt beneath a well-fitted black suit, not a lick of fanciful trim upon him. Against his chest was clutched a sleeve of parchment, his long fingers curling more possessively around it as she watched.

Then her eyes rose to his, dark beneath thick lashes and soft with something akin to bewilderment. That was when she remembered, quite suddenly, that half her clothes were strewn across the floor.

"Oh," she said, searching for anything at all she might say to the poor man. She drew herself up. "Lord—" She stopped and cleared her throat, unsure of his identity. He seemed vaguely familiar, but she had been gone for four years. People changed.

"Lord Alex—" he started almost automatically then abruptly cut himself off to stare back at her. He did not appear to have the same sort of trouble with recognition Etta was experiencing. His tone changed. "What precisely are you about?"

Her mouth came open without a single answer in mind just as Nickolas burst back into the hallway, announcing, "Done, we're covered. Saved you from a spanking no doubt—" His words fell off, his wink and stride stuttering to an awkward halt as he took in the scene.

He decidedly did not look down at Etta's clothes on the floor or her person, which gained him a point in her tally, but neither did he explain what they were about, which, to be fair, seemed unlikely to be believable in any case. He cleared his throat, not unlike what Etta had just done.

The new arrival glanced between them, apparently making his own assumptions. "This behavior is entirely unseemly for persons of your station."

Nickolas ran a hand over his chest, seeming to fight a smile. "Quite." He stepped forward, resuming his casual posture as he approached the pair. He held an arm toward Etta. "My lady. Perhaps we shall take this kind advice in the spirit it was given and remove ourselves to your rooms."

Etta's gaze darted between Nickolas and the other man. She felt her cheeks heat, but she was not sure precisely where to direct her ire, had she even the energy to unleash it. She decided she didn't have to. She was an Ostwind. Without a word in farewell, she bent to pick up her things then turned and strode away, Nickolas's chuckle echoing behind her.

CHAPTER 2

Etta stopped at the door to her rooms, a sense of familiarity twisting in her gut. Her hand was frozen, unable to touch the lever that would let her inside. Angry at herself for being incapable, she turned her back and leaned on the finely carved wood to shoot a look at Nickolas. "This has been a disaster."

He grinned. "Entirely." He handed over a flour-caked glove she'd apparently missed in her hasty escape. "And it's barely begun."

The dread in her stomach turned to lead. He was right. She still had to face her father and the council, never mind that she'd not yet conquered her childhood rooms. "Well," she managed, her tone making clear she would not be inviting him inside. "I suppose you've some advice for me in that matter?"

His bright eyes stayed on her a moment too long then flicked briefly to her mess of attire. "No, I think you have it well in hand. May luck be in your favor, my lady." Nickolas inclined his head toward her in something of a bow then turned to go, merrily twirling a ribbon that she was fairly certain had been attached to her gown not a quarter hour before.

Etta let her head drop back to the door. It hit with a rather solid *thunk,* and she sighed. When she finally went inside her room, the hopelessness only became worse.

Drapes rested over the furniture—her room disused in the years she'd been gone. Had she returned when she was meant to, the space would have been set to rights, its decorations polished and shined, windows opened, tapestries beaten, the tables topped with generous bouquets. She had not returned when she was meant to, and not solely because she was a coward.

Etta had been tired of waiting, tired of pretending all was well. She'd been eager to come home because she'd been afraid that if she didn't come back on her own, her father might take his chance to stop her.

In the darkness, she ran a hand over the drape that covered a side table, her fingers brushing the carved trim through the fabric as it caught on a familiar nicked edge. It didn't matter that the furniture was hidden. The memories remained. She did not search for candles. She had no tinder. Across the sitting room, she opened one side of the double doors to her bed chamber. The room was dim, lit only by the occasional flicker of far-off lightning through the windows and what moonlight made it past the storm. Rain pattered against the glass in waves.

Do not speak of them. Tell no one.
Speak of them, and they will come again.

There, by the narrow door that led to her closet, they had wrapped their hands around her mother's arms. And there, where sunlight would make a pattern of squares on the fine wood floor come morning, she had dropped her dagger. Etta moved forward, her feet silent and her breathing slow. There, beneath the bed, Etta had waited, watching it all without a word.

Lightning flashed in the same moment when something moved in the room behind her. Etta spun, hand to her side, but here in Westrende, she wore no sword. Weapons were for the training yard, for uniform dress. Etta had been relegated to a mere lady home from school, traveling beneath the protection of her father's guard. Just because she'd learned how to use a weapon didn't mean her father would allow her to wield it in his domain.

"My lady." The maid carried one end of a trunk and gave a little curtsy, tugging the burden and, in turn, the arms of the footman on the other end. "Sorry to have startled you. The storm must have drowned out the sound of my knock."

Etta waved the apology away as two more footmen came inside. They moved through the space in a practiced flurry, efficiently removing the furniture drapes and lighting candelabra.

"A shame we were not warned ahead of time," the maid remarked as she started opening Etta's trunks. "We could have had your rooms ready if we'd known."

"Please." Etta leaned down to stay the woman with a gentle hand on her arm. "I'll have a fire and water for a bath, but the rest I can do on my own."

The woman gave her a narrow-eyed look but made no comment on the state of Etta's wardrobe. "Very well. But be warned, we'll be in for a full cleaning tomorrow." She snapped her fingers at the footmen. "You heard the lady. Send up Greta with water and have someone from the kitchens bring a nice dinner. The lady looks as if she could do with some local fare." She shifted, facing Etta full on. "You'll remember where the bell pull is, my lady."

Etta smiled. "I believe so, yes."

She nodded. "Very well, then. Good to have you back."

At the maid's command, the pack of footmen exited the room in an order that would have made any general proud. Etta stared down at the row of trunks in the warm light of the candelabra, not particularly eager for the task of unpacking. With any luck, a hot bath would ease her stiffness from the days of travel.

When she heard the door open once more, she assumed it must have been Greta with her water. She glanced absently toward the entrance, her heart catching in her throat at the sight of the figure in the doorway. *Not the maid.*

"How dare you?" Her father's words were low and even, but Etta felt them like a slap. Her mouth snapped shut, her expression level as she straightened to face him in the manner he'd always expected—the manner that had been drilled into her further during the past four years of training.

He closed the door then crossed the space in a few brisk strides. Standing before her, he was as imposing as ever, despite that Etta had grown in the years she'd been gone. It was difficult not to flinch, but she stood tall, shoulders back and bearing proper.

"Do you have no care for the risk you have taken? No concern for how your disobedience casts shame on the Ostwind name? You have not only defied a direct order but blackened the reputations of a dozen trained men. It is not you alone who will pay for your transgressions."

Etta drew a sharp breath. "You cannot punish those men. They acted under my orders. They've done nothing at all but—"

His response was swift and forceful. "I cannot? I cannot, you tell me. Here in the domain of the kings of Westrende, under the protection of the king's army, an unbanded girl tells the commander of it all what he may or may not do."

"Father, I—"

"Father, is it? Not General now, not when it is convenient for you to forget my responsibilities to council and kingdom?"

She swallowed hard. She had known he would not be pleased when she'd subverted his plans, but she hadn't intended to bring punishment upon the kingsmen who had helped her. "I didn't think," she said sullenly. She could not say the truth, could not admit that she'd felt as if she had no other choice. "The blame rests solely on my shoulders."

"Your shoulders." He shook his head, as if she'd not heard a word he'd said. "I had hoped that the years away would have helped you grow out of reckless actions and impudent notions. I see that it has not."

"You shipped me off for four years, as if I mattered not at all. Three kingdoms away, as far as you could manage."

His voice was ice. "I would send you off for another four if I could."

Etta felt herself blanch. Her insides twisted into a tortuous knot. He had confirmed all her fears in a single blow. Then something else rose in her, wild and hot. "Reckless, you say. Impudent." She leaned forward, almost daring him to act. "I watched them take her from this very room—"

General Ostwind was a formidable man. Etta understood that. He commanded armies, was head of the council that, as he was so fond of reminding her, ran the kingdom. But the speed in which he closed the distance, palm slipping over her mouth in a move that might prove deadly with a different motive, stunned her. Her arms dropped limply at her sides, her heart beating like a rabbit's.

She stared at him with wide eyes. Short, sharp breaths puffed through her nose where it brushed the side of his hand.

He did not let go of her. "I forbade you to speak of them."

Etta was very still for a very long moment. When he did not let go, she nodded beneath his grip.

Her father watched her, possibly considering punishments, possibly making certain she understood him clearly. Etta might never know.

When he spoke, it was in a cold whisper. "Your mother was taken for the same foolish impudence. Remember that when you invoke her memory." The warning settled in the bare space between them, slow and tumbling like a stone through water. It would remain there forever, Etta knew, piled upon its brethren, too far beneath the surface to ever pluck free.

Finally, he stepped back. "Council is meeting at cockcrow. You will attend. Homecoming celebrations will be canceled. Your work begins now."

She swallowed, unable to quite form a response.

He turned without another word, but when he reached the door, he looked back. "If I hear a single utterance more of this nonsense, you will be removed from consideration for the post of marshal. Indeed, from any post at all."

The door shut behind him like a punch to her midsection.

ETTA HAD LIVED with strangers in a distant kingdom for four long years, waiting for her return with the constant fear that it might never happen, that she'd been sent away to be dealt with—and not as a true threat, but merely an inconvenience. *That cannot be his purpose,* she'd told herself. *It is nothing so nefarious as that.* She had been lying to herself.

Removing Etta from Westrende and its fae with the greatest distance possible had been no accident.

There was no room for taking chances. Etta needed to secure her spot as marshal, the only thing that might gain her solid footing. The meeting with council was paramount. And she was running late.

Her feet moved silently through the corridor, her lips running with wordless curses for the nightmares that had kept her awake. She'd dressed in a trim gown and coiled her hair hastily at the nape of her neck. A splash of cold water was all the attention she'd paid her face before blotting it dry, the dark rings beneath her eyes unheeded.

She had no time to spare, but when her steps faltered, it was of their own accord. In the long corridor outside the council chamber, an endless row of paintings was strung high on either wall.

Her mother's portrait was among them. Her father's, too, but Etta had seen him in the flesh. In the darkness of her room at school, Etta had longed to stand so close to the familiar strokes of color, the soft curve of amber hair, the warm plane of cheek that met a small crescent of shadow near her mother's deep rosy lips, an ever-present hint of humor that even the artist could not bear to hide. The entire corridor was lined with paintings of Westrende officials, a tribute to agents of the kingdom.

Etta's would be installed next. Before she took her position, she would be painted in the fine uniform of marshal, the highest level of law enforcement in Westrende, and given the band that marked her as an agent of the kingdom. Etta would head the branch of law that, unlike chancellor or magistrate, would be allowed free rein beyond the castle walls. Freedom to move through the entire kingdom would be hers.

In a matter of days, she would be appointed to the post, and her portrait would be hung in the same hallowed hall as her mother's in a ceremony for all the courtiers to see. Etta's father would be unable to remove her from the post or to force her from the kingdom ever again.

The sound of a gavel echoed from beyond the chamber doors down the corridor. It was the call to order. She cursed, breaking into a sprint that had her winded by the time she reached the entrance. She took one steadying breath, swiped back a loose lock of hair, then strode into the chamber.

Every set of eyes in the room turned toward her. *Steady*, she reminded herself. Her victory was assured. The previous marshal was set to retire, and no one else had vied for the position with an Ostwind trained and ready. Whatever else her father had done, sending her away for her studies had ensured she would be prepared. It had guaranteed the spot was hers.

"Lady Ostwind."

Etta found Louis, owner of the voice that had greeted her and a man she'd known since she was a child, and gave him a friendly nod. He gestured toward the side of the room. "Session has just begun. Please take a seat."

If color rose to her cheeks, at least her expression remained calm and pleasant as she made her way past the half dozen kingdom officials on her side of the table. She took a seat in one of the many chairs lining the wall, great carved wooden things with embroidered cushions and a poor view of the table's proceedings. If nothing else, it gave her time to survey the crowd.

Her father stood at the head of the table, a long, wide monstrosity that held permanent stations for the twelve members of the king's council. The council members' positions were permanent as well. Over half of the members were silver-haired, and two had been doddering along even before Etta had gone away. It did not mean their minds were not sharp, however. Each held impressive skill of both wit and weapon. At three and sixty, Louis still wielded a sword as well as any younger man, and the lady Cerys had deadly aim with a dagger despite that she was barely able to see across a room.

A clerk and two scribes sat further down the same row of chairs as Etta, and several more figures watched from seats near the opposite wall. She was blocked from seeing precisely who the others were, as the lady Maura's assistant stood at his mistress's side, passing ledgers and notes as they were requested and obstructing a decent view.

For nearly two hours, the council heard reports from each bough of the absent king's rule, arguing over much of it then pushing proposed changes off until another meeting. Nothing had changed. She supposed she should have expected no less. They moved on to petitions, and as each was processed or set aside, the attendants around Etta thinned to none. Her father stood once more, as if to dismiss the meeting, and Etta was on her feet before she could stop herself.

"Yes." He frowned. "One more item to address before we withdraw."

Etta moved nearer the table at the end opposite her father, where no chair blocked her from view of the dozen members. She gave each one her gaze, direct and proper. Despite how much a girl her father made her feel, Etta was ready to take on the post.

"Ah, yes. The lady Ostwind is to be nominated for marshal." Stefan —warm eyes, warm complexion, cool disposition—watched her for a moment before his brow drew down. "I believe this was on next week's agenda. Come back early, have you?"

The general gave Etta a hard look. "Indeed. You all know the candidate's capacity. She has returned as primed as any candidate before her." His words were not spoken with the glowing pride one might expect. In fact, his tone was rather lacking in enthusiasm.

Shoulders back, Etta addressed the council. "As the general says, it's as if I've been trained in conflict since I could toddle." The chuckle that ran through the onlookers was gratifying, but she kept on. "I have met all requirements, including age, education, and military training. My studies since childhood have focused at length on law and history. I am prepared and well able to fulfill the duties of my post."

"Agreed," Maura said. "I see no reason to rake the coals with Lady Ostwind. I move that we bring the matter straight to vote."

"Seconded." Louis glanced down the table, apparently deciding the nays would be the easier vote to count. "Any opposed?"

There was a moment of silence in which Etta's heart swelled to the very walls of her chest. Not a single concern had been brought against her. It was no small thing—the office of marshal held considerable weight, and she'd only proven herself in her studies and in the training yard, not by working through the lower ranks. Her sacrifices had paid off. The years of brutal toil were about to be paid back in manifold abundance. She watched with deep pride as Cerys raised the gavel.

"Hold."

The voice came from the far wall of the chamber, an unsteady echo that shattered Etta's swollen heart. She stared, jaw slack, as Cerys's hand lowered the gavel to its side and a quiet rest.

Etta's eyes slid slowly from the gavel, past her watching father, to the wall from which the voice had come. A throat cleared, then a figure rose to stand tall in a long black robe, arms crossed before his waist. Recognition came immediately, as Etta had stared at the same face in the empty corridor only the night before. He looked slightly different, though he still wore the familiar disapproving frown. She suspected the difference was the robe of his office and, she saw now, that he wore the band that marked him not as some scribe or cleric, but an officer of Westrende.

A long silence followed, during which the man said nothing more, his gaze on Etta. One of the council members shifted, and Etta realized her expression was not what one might consider polite. She smoothed it out as Louis spoke to the man. "You have something to add?"

He stepped forward, his attention on Etta. "I—" Abruptly, he looked to Louis. "Perhaps we should discuss it privately."

Louis's fingers flicked irritably against the parchment beneath his hand. "This is a council matter. Surely, it is not that she's the general's daughter, not in a kingdom that's been known to install a king's heir even as master of coin. It cannot be her age, not with you only a season or two older. Whatever your concern, out with it."

"I understand," the man said. "It is just that it's of a... more delicate matter."

Etta stiffened, as did several other council members. A pall fell over the room. "Speak up if you've seen something untoward. And do it now." Louis's tone felt like a warning.

The man seemed to take a steadying breath. "I have, in fact, witnessed behaviors most inappropriate from Antonetta Ostwind. I believe it incautious to allow her appointment."

The words hit Etta like the war hammers they'd used in training, swift and heavy and as if they meant to knock her to the ground. "What?"

General Ostwind stared on, his expression grim.

The man asked, "Do you deny only yesternight acting in a manner unbecoming of a person of your station, let alone the post to which you aspire?"

An outraged gasp tore from Etta, not particularly suiting the demeanor she was trying to present. There was nothing for it. She leaned forward. "I have done nothing of the—"

A telling stillness followed as Etta recalled what the man had seen. Etta, wet through and coated in flour, her jacket and gloves, and—oh yes—everything down to her bodice tossed in a pile on the floor. And Nickolas sauntering toward her, saying... *what had he said?* Right, that he'd saved her from a spanking. By the wall, there was no talking her way out of that one. Not in front of the council and her father. She wet her lips.

The look the general gave her was pure disappointment but not a hint of surprise.

Etta's jaw went tight, even as her dreams were crushed by a studious man in a drab robe. "You know nothing of the situation," she told him. "Why would you even consider this your concern?"

He stared at her, somber, staid, and a little as if she'd said something nonsensical. "Because I am chancellor. My very duty relies upon a marshal who is above reproach."

Her chest felt as if it had caved in, as if that swollen, shattered heart had fallen to her gut and taken with it the air that she might breathe.

Lord Alexander. Etta suddenly recalled the man starting to say the words, just before he'd given her a stern reproof about cavorting in the hallways. *Gideon. Alexander.* The single man who might bring her difficulties in her post.

She was going to murder Nickolas Brigham with her bare hands.

CHAPTER 3

"Antonetta, do you dispute Lord Alexander's testimony?"

Etta bit back the "yes" that tried to leap from her tongue at Louis's question. Disputing the word of an official of Westrende was all but a criminal act. She'd not been installed in her post—she was still a citizen—and it would not be her word against his. It would be her word against the kingdom's. She wet her lips. "Not his testimony, only that it does not take into account the circumstances surrounding my actions."

Gideon Alexander stared at her. She could not precisely argue the details of the matter, so she gave her attention to the council instead. "Will none of you speak for me? You know well that my reputation has been above reproach." Even if she'd been gone for four long years, they had known her since she was a child.

"And yet, here is your reputation under reproach."

Louis's mouth had moved into a hard line. Emotion swelled hotly in Etta's throat. *Please*, she wanted to beg. *Please, don't do this*.

"Gideon," Cerys began, "do you care to elaborate on your concern?"

"I prefer not."

"Very well." She sighed. "It seems a great waste to allow the years Lady Ostwind has put toward service to the kingdom to no use. And yet, we cannot in good conscience allow a potential weakness in our defenses, given the importance of this post." Her cloudy eyes shifted toward the head of the table. "I propose a probationary period, during which Lady Ostwind will be under the watch of our chancellor. If she can perform to his satisfaction the duties his office assigns her, we will bring the nomination to vote once more. If not, then other candidates will be considered for the position. Say, by the next moon?"

A chorus of murmurs rose along with nods of approval around the council table as Etta's vision swam. Gideon had gone a shade paler. The general's lips turned down in displeasure. "Seconded," said someone at the far end of the table. Not a word rose in dissent when the vote was called.

"The ruling stands." Cerys's voice echoed through the chamber, followed by the terminal bang of gavel striking block.

Etta stared dumbly as figures moved around her to gather documents, break off into small discussions, or quit the room. One discussion in particular seemed more intense than the rest. Lord Alexander had cornered Cerys and Louis—seeing how quickly he might toss her from candidacy, no doubt, or trying to duck out of the second chance they'd offered her. She went for him, her feet moving without conscious thought, but Maura's assistant backed into Etta's path, landing a presumably unintentional elbow against her midsection. The assistant made a sound of surprise, fumbled his stack of documents, and caught them only by coming directly into her path. Another council member made to help the assistant, and by the time Etta found her way past the commotion, Gideon's drab robe was disappearing through the chamber door.

Etta rushed into the corridor, jaw clenched. The space was filled with loitering courtiers hoping to win a moment of the council members' time. She caught sight of her prey again just as he turned the corner into another corridor. It was a lesser used passage, a bit narrow and dark, but no one blocked her way, and she reached him before he made it to the final exit. He moved as if unaware of her presence, so she seized hold of his sleeve.

Gideon stopped abruptly, and Etta's momentum brought her a step too near. He seemed somehow taller as he stared down at her, his expression conveying nothing more than being taken aback. There was a moment of recognition after the instant of softness, then his gaze lowered deliberately to her grip on his arm.

She snatched her hand away, but her fingers curled into a fist at her side. She leaned toward him, keeping her voice low. "How dare you—"

"Lady Ostwind." His tone was detached, only serving to illustrate how out of control she'd become.

Reckless, her father had said. *Impudent*.

"How dare you," she started again. He only blinked at her, and her rage heightened to dangerous levels. She might actually have pummeled him with her fists. "Incautious? You're not certain? You do not even *know* me."

She all but spat the words, and something in his expression drew back as his shoulders suddenly became more square. He was no longer the meek clerk she'd nearly collided with the night before. He was no clerk at all—he was chancellor—and his bearing was that of a formidable man. In the dim light, he was all hard lines and shadows, a man who not only outranked her but outweighed her by half. "Were you not in a state of semi undress in a public corridor of this very castle only hours ago?" He did not need to add "with a known rakehell" —it was implied by his tone.

Her mouth snapped shut. She couldn't explain that she'd been chasing fae, not if she wanted to ever hold a position in the kingdom. That was the very point—no one else would believe. No one else would fight to keep them away.

"And have you not proven by your actions this very instant that you are incapable of the composure required to perform the duty you so zealously pursue?"

"Zealous? I have worked for this since I was no more than a girl. I have held my tongue against my father's expectations, against this council's rules, and against every slight ever paid me. All so I might one day—this day—*today*—finally be able to set right their ridiculous laws."

His brows lowered. "Do you hear yourself? You stand before a chancellor of Westrende and declare our laws absurd." He seemed to shake himself. When he took a step back from her, it became painfully clear how close they'd been standing—or rather, how far she'd come into his space. "Lady Ostwind, I intend to do everything in my power to prevent your nomination from returning to vote. It would be a dereliction of my duty to do otherwise."

Etta had been waiting her entire life to be free—free from her father, from the secrets, and free to seek justice for her mother. She opened her mouth, either to find a way to explain that to the man before her or to make a vow of her own—she hadn't decided which—when the sound of a throat clearing brought her up short.

"Lady Ostwind?" One of her father's assistants stood halfway down the corridor, looking concerned. The worry wasn't for her, she knew, but rather that if he'd been sent to find her, as with any task named by the general, he had better do it quickly. "I'm afraid your appointment still stands."

"Appointment?"

He inclined his head. "The portrait. Your father had us arrange the artist last night when the homecoming celebrations were being canceled. I realize that now, it may be unnecessary—"

"It is not unnecessary," Etta snapped. "Do not postpone it. I'll be just a moment."

She would be marshal by the next moon, by whatever means required. That was her vow and what she would tell Gideon Alexander. But when she turned back, Gideon was already gone.

CHAPTER 4

Nickolas was waiting for her in the connecting corridor, leaning casually against the wall in a long blue jacket. The rose in his hand was as bright as the golden embroidery on his vest. When she came into view, he straightened, smiling as if she'd accomplished something grand and twirling the rose stem between his fingers as if he was not a man about to meet his death.

His smile fell as she came to a stop mere inches before him. "The moment we are out of earshot of the council members in the next corridor, I am going to rip out the best of your entrails and feed them to Narine's raptors until the next moon."

He made a face. "The bird lady? You know I'm terrified of her."

"Precisely."

His nose scrunched. "Is this because of the Gideon thing?"

"The Gideon *thing*?" She stepped nearer, dangerously close to grabbing him by the lapels and shaking him like a rag doll. "You made an absolute fool of me."

Nickolas only pursed his lips as if biting down a smile, and Etta had to turn and leave to avoid attacking the man in the hall and making her situation even worse.

He rushed to catch up with her, tossing the rose into a tall urn near the wall. "Etta, please. It can't have been that bad. You excel under pressure. Always ready and all that."

"You're right," she said. "You didn't make a fool of me at all. I made a fool of myself." She glared sidelong at him. "He says I'm unfit to be elevated to marshal because of cavorting in the hallways with you. They refused to hold the vote."

Nickolas's step faltered, but when Etta kept on, he took a longer stride to reach her. "No."

"Yes. If I don't perform what I'm certain will be an impossible task, my chances of being anything—ever—are out."

To his credit, Nickolas looked as if he might be ill. It was all that saved him from a fist to the gut. "I thought it would be funny, that's all. I knew he was an ass, but I didn't think he'd actually contest your appointment. Did your father not stake his name for you?"

"No! He's furious that I've come back."

Nickolas frowned. "Come back *early*, you mean?"

Etta pressed hard against the urge to cry. She could not see how things could become any worse. She'd let her frustrations boil over to the very man she'd vowed to crush once she'd become marshal. He now held her fate in his hands, and her father wanted nothing more than to be rid of her.

She stopped outside a door near the gallery entrance and turned to face Nickolas. "It's over. There's no way he'll approve of me in a mere thirty days." It wasn't as if Etta could find a way around it or sully his name. Despite that the man had clearly never even tucked a collar out of place, she needed him in good standing as chancellor in order to bring back her vote. A shaky sigh escaped her. "I'm a fool. Look at me, about to sit for a portrait in the uniform of an office I can never gain. I might as well have them paint over the coat and sword with a leather apron and the tools of an armorer's apprentice." She barely held back a sob. "Or a mobcap and broom."

Nickolas grabbed her by the shoulders and straightened her to face him. "Stop this right now. You're going to march through that door as if you've already won the post. You're going to get painted in that awful jacket that's all the wrong color for you, and you're going to give them the terrifying marshal face I know you practice in your looking glass every night before bed."

She stared at him.

He let go, straightening his own shoulders. "And when you come out, I will be right here, waiting for you. We will commence stealing back what you've earned." She opened her mouth, but he shushed her, pointing a finger in what could only be assumed was a wildly off-precision imitation of a military command. "Not another word. Go."

She did, but only because she was too exhausted to argue.

CHAPTER 5

The entrance hall was dim with only a few candles burning fitfully near the far wall, their light flickering strangely off a row of mirrors. Etta stood quietly for a moment, listening for sounds to indicate the painter was in a connecting room. She heard nothing but the flicker of the candles and the sound of her own breathing. The space was decorated with rich, warm colors, without a single window in view. She walked forward through the narrow room and past her many reflections as they jumped from mirror to mirror alongside her.

Unease niggled at her, and she began to doubt that she'd heard the directions from her father's assistant correctly. If she were late again, for another official appointment... But the thought fell away as the scent of powders and artist's oils met her at the doorway to the next room. She paused inside the entrance, taking in the large, open space cut by shadow and light. The room was littered with props and setups. High windows let in the morning sun, bright and clear over everything it touched. Centered in one square of brilliance was a carved wooden stool, and on the floor around it, various pillows in shades of sapphire, plum, and red. A tasseled scarf was tangled around the legs of the stool, as yellow as one of Lady Narine's birds.

In another square of light stood a valet rack with a dignified officer's coat resting over its arms. Etta walked closer, her eyes tracing the lines of the garment as her footfalls echoed off the far walls. She caught the scent of orange oil and something a bit like musk, but when she glanced through the space, she was still alone. "Lord Barrett?"

No one answered her call, despite the presence of an easel beside a table scattered with what appeared to be freshly prepared paints. She took a final look through the room before her attention was recalled to the coat. The material was dark with red trim and fine gold stitching at the collar and hem. The thing looked as if it might hang off her, as if perhaps it had been a spare sewn for the tall and stoutly built man who currently held the post. A prop for the artist only, and yet, her fingertips trailed reverently over the material. Etta pressed a thumb against a gold button embossed with the office's emblem. *Marshal.* Her dream was so close, she could taste it. But her own actions had driven it from her grasp.

She'd been afraid of her father, afraid he would not let her return. She never should have attempted to outwit the man. She should have faced him in the manner of an officer, one of his own.

She'd wanted to contend with him on her terms. As if such a thing would ever have been possible.

She carefully lifted the coat from its rack, doubling the bulk of it over one arm to straighten a bit of gold stitching.

"Lady Ostwind," came a voice from behind her.

She startled and spun, expecting the portrait artist but instead finding a young man with sandy hair and a freckled nose. At her replied, "Yes," he held forward a letter.

"From Lord Alexander."

Once the message was in her hand, the young man gave a sharp nod and left without another word. Etta shifted the coat to unfold the parchment. A precise script met the heavy dread in her gut, spelling out in detail the task that had been set by the office of the chancery.

Etta stared at the text. The task was a monumental undertaking, impossible for anyone to compete on their own. And yet, the entire kingdom had already attempted it. Every kingsman under her father's command, officer in the current marshal's force, and council member who had a hand in law and order had taken as their responsibility the duty of investigating the noted crime. All had failed.

Etta had been gone from the kingdom for years. She was not yet marshal and had not a single soul under her authority. She'd no chance at all. Gideon knew that and had intentionally given her a task that could not be completed.

The ridges of the chancery's seal caved beneath the pressure of her grip.

Etta stepped backward, leaning heavily upon the stool. Gideon's terms were impossible. She was going to fail and be ruined, and then her father was going to ship her off somewhere far worse than school.

"Antonetta."

The voice was unsettlingly quiet and held a purr, and Etta's gaze snapped up to find its source. A slender man with dark, untidy hair stood in the shadows.

"Lord Barrett?"

His lips tilted up as his head tilted downward in an angle that implied she'd guessed correctly.

She stood.

"No," he replied in a tone just as smooth as his approach, "stay."

She glanced at the high windows, which threw their brightest light solely over her and the rack that had held the coat, then back at the man. He'd moved to stand by the easel, half hidden by its bulk, his hollow eyes on her. Sitting felt suddenly unnatural. She straightened, shoving Gideon's letter into a pocket of her gown then squaring her shoulders.

"Yes," he said, "just there."

She slid on the oversized jacket, raised her chin, and composed her face in the most esteemed expression she could manage. Her eyes found a spot on the far wall and focused on a bit of cut marble trim that evoked none of the horrible emotions she'd shoved away with the chancellor's letter. There she would sit, Antonetta Ostwind, daughter of the great General Ostwind, as unflinching as her mother, as deserving of the office of marshal as everyone knew she was.

She would make Gideon Alexander eat the parchment his words were printed on.

The artist made another sound like a purr, apparently approving of whatever the posture conveyed from his view. He picked up a brush from the table and began his work without another single word for either Etta or her pose.

ETTA SAT SO until the shadows had slid near her slippered feet, until the sun had angled well past noon. She had not asked once for a break, had not shifted more than a breath as the artist worked. She would sit so for days if that was what it took.

"There." Lord Barrett put down his brush, leaning back to survey the canvas.

Etta blinked, uncertain what precisely *there* meant. "Is that all for today?"

"Come," he beckoned. "It's finished. Tell me what you think of the piece."

Etta stood slowly, surreptitiously stretching limbs that had gone numb. Surely, the portrait could not have been entirely complete, not so quickly, unless he'd used a model for her body, someone sitting for the bulk of the work so that he'd only had to finalize the face. She wasn't certain if artists even did such a thing. She wished she'd paid closer attention, that she'd asked or looked at the canvas before the process had started. But the coat had already been in the room, and she supposed that the man had painted enough official portraits and knew what he needed from her.

She crossed the distance to Lord Barrett, her eyes slow to adjust to the change in light. He gestured toward the canvas, the tilt to his lips widening into something Etta did not quite like. "Your honesty," he told her. "This piece may be the most consequential of your life."

She flinched, snapping her gaze away from him. She'd been so distracted by her anger at Nickolas, what had happened standing before the council, and Gideon's horrendous terms that she hadn't noticed the way the man's teeth did not seem to sit quite properly inside his mouth. It was as if they meant to escape and... well, *bite* her.

Her body shifted as if it intended to move back from him without her command, but her eyes caught sight of the portrait, and she stopped cold.

Etta felt the breath of the man beside her catch. "Stunning, is it not?"

She stared at the portrait, a canvas that rose taller than her. The colors were subdued, a light gray mist covering a backdrop of castle walls and ancient tapestries. The torso and head of a woman centered the image, the coat of marshal fitted well to her straight shoulders and lean form, her hands positioned delicately before her chest. Etta's own eyes stared back at her, her own face bright and hopeful in the center of the frame. It was all that made sense in the portrait, as the rest was... was...

It was absurd. Someone was playing a jape with her, surely. It was why the painting had been completed so quickly. There was no logical reason, no rational excuse for what she was seeing otherwise. Official portraits were so far removed from what was before her that her eyes could not quite decide where to land, what to look at. It was as if a circus had exploded onto the canvas, a troupe of entertainers costuming the figure to gain the most preposterous response possible. A fox peeked out from behind a column in the background, and a shiny red apple rested in the hand of Etta's likeness. Whimsical birds nestled in the cape at her shoulder, and *by the wall*, a black ribbon threaded through her lips, its ends tied into a precise bow.

Lord Barrett sidled closer. "Well," he prompted. "What do you think, Lady Ostwind?"

"There's a goose wrapped about my shoulders and a ship in my hair!"

"Yes," he answered, quiet delight unconcealed in his tone.

"No!" Etta shouted. "This is—it's untenable! Asinine! You've made me look a complete fool!"

The words slipped out before Etta had a moment to realize that they could have been more diplomatic. She couldn't—she just couldn't fathom what had gone wrong. She had to fix it. She had to convince the painter to make it right, to make her look reasonable before anyone saw and she was laughed out of her last chance at the post she so desperately needed.

She glanced at the painter to gauge his response.

He was watching her. After a moment, he asked, "You do not like it?"

Etta swallowed. "I—apologies, my lord, but I feel that the painting..." She pressed her lips together. "Is it possible to remove the more... playful elements of the work to allow the portrait to better fit with the others? You've seen the other portraits, have you not?" He would surely have painted every single one installed in recent years.

"I have." His expression was hiding some emotion that Etta could not make out while the shadows obscured his face. "They do seem very dull in comparison."

"Yes," Etta told him enthusiastically. "Dull would be perfect. Can you make this more... dull?"

His eyes narrowed on her. "How important is this to you, Lady Ostwind?"

"It is of grave importance. My lord, I would never ask the additional work of you if I did not consider this a matter of utmost urgency. This painting is... well, it's my life."

A rumbling, gratified sound came out of him, somewhere between a laugh and a cry of rejoice. "Indeed," he said. "Do I have your accord, then? It's a bargain?"

"A—" Etta felt her brow draw together in confusion, but at his expectant and encouraging gaze, she nodded vaguely. "Yes, please, my lord. As soon as possible."

Lord Barrett clapped his hands once, the sudden movement and sharp bark of it in the silence startling her a step backward. He did not seem to mind. He hummed delightedly as he turned to the table and unlatched a wooden box inlaid with pearl.

"Here we are," he whispered, attentively drawing a brush from inside. He turned to Etta. "All will be done as agreed. The portrait will appear just as dull as every other that lines the council corridor, and all who look upon it with their dull eyes will see only General Ostwind's daughter, for as you say, this painting for your life."

Etta's mouth came open to reply, but the man stepped closer, the light catching on his face in a way it had not done before.

"Just one thing more," he murmured as if deep in thought. He raised a hand, and the brush he'd taken from the case brushed her cheek like a feather, the movement fleeting and too quick to escape.

Etta stumbled away from him and tripped over a stack of pillows on the floor. Her face was hot, seared from the touch, and her heart raced. Outside, the screech of a hundred birds rose, their wings and feet battering against the windowpanes as they took frantic flight. Etta caught her fall, steading herself to stare at the hollow eyes of the man before her.

A familiar unease slid through her, followed by a cold, dark surety. He had touched her. And when he had, something had been taken. She couldn't say what, precisely, but she could feel the absence of it. It was thievery, to be sure, and nothing natural.

Etta's body had ordered her to flee before the realization of what was happening had time to settle. Instinct, memory, and the sense her sight gave her that no one else seemed to be willing to accept, those things knew. They understood her mistake.

"Fae," she hissed.

The painter gave her a look that said she was an utter nit.

"What did you do to me?"

He dropped the brush into its case and snapped the lid closed. Then he fastened the clasp, tucked the case under his arm, and gave her a careless glance. "I have taken what is no longer yours."

Fear hit her first, followed swiftly by anger, but it was the fear that drove her to attack. The fae could not be left to escape. Once they crossed the border to their home, one would never be able to reach them again, to steal back what they had taken.

Like when they had taken her mother.

Etta rushed at the man, but his hand went up, and she slammed into a wall of magic as hard as any stone. The impact bloodied her nose. She drew back, her pulse racing in her ears, her fury palpable despite the threat of a powerful fae before her. She wanted to end him.

"What have you taken from me? Give it back, or fates save me, I will destroy you."

His mouth turned into something crueler, something far less human, and she could see that his glamour had been fooling her all along. Her sight had failed for just a few brief glimpses, but those short moments were all it took. She tried frantically to recall what she had said, what words had passed between them.

"A bargain," he answered. "You have traded your life, Lady Ostwind. If you want to see it returned, call his name."

"Who? Whose name?" She needed to know who had done this to her. She could hear the terror in her own voice.

Beneath the beating of her heart, she could hear the answer the painter had not bothered to speak before he turned to go. *Him. It's him.* Not the painter at all, but the fae behind everything, the one they all bowed to, the shadow she had seen as a girl, the one who had taken her mother.

The prince of Rivenwilde.

CHAPTER 6

Etta could see all of him, the artist who was most certainly not Lord Barrett. The creature who'd turned his back on her to walk from the room had let the glamour fall away, his long fingers and smooth gait all that remained of the lord she'd seen before. Something dark like the color of old blood stained the tails of his coat. He was leaving, and she could not let him. Her life, he had said, was in the hands of the fae. The figure shifted into the familiar shape of a shadow, just as it slipped through the door.

He could not be allowed to escape.

Etta made to chase him, but her foot slipped in something slick and dark in the shadows. Among the pillows at her feet, was a form she had not seen. The shape of it could only be that of a man. *Lord Barrett*. Bile rose in Etta's throat, then she picked up a discarded sword near the body and ran.

The entrance hall was no longer dim, as every candle burned hot. The flames blazed, bright and steady, illuminating the mirrors lining the wall in a way that felt endless, as if she were falling. She stumbled once more, off balance, the coat she'd worn hanging from a shoulder. Chest heaving, Etta moved helplessly toward the looking glass, her task forgotten. It might have been a well, its water deep below the rim of stones, calling to her, begging her to fall within.

Magic, some part of her whispered. But the sensation was not caused by the looking glass at all. The magic was closer, hot like the flame of the hundred candles burning around her, alive and stinging on her skin.

She stared into the reflection of a girl in the same dress, the same shoes she'd donned that morning, the same hair. Her hand rose to touch a cheek smeared with paint. Etta's fingers were soft, familiar, so very like what they had always been. She pressed them to the flesh of her cheek, and the glass before her snapped, a long crack splitting the surface in two.

The face—not her own, too round, too soft, too much like a vague and nameless facade, an illusion of glamour like so many the fae wore —stared back at her. A sound somewhere between a sob and a wail crawled from Etta's chest. Her knees gave, but her feet pushed her forward. The next mirror offered another try, and she rushed toward it, saw the girl who was not her, and stared in disbelief. Again, she brushed the flesh of the face with the lightest skim of her fingers. Again, the looking glass shattered.

Etta swore, a vile and ugly string of words that said just what she thought of the fae, that called them out by name. At her shout, every mirror in the room split. Noise crashed through the space as Etta cowered in the center of it, her hands over her ears and her head down to protect a face that was not her own. When the room finally fell quiet, she glanced up. A thousand jagged reflections stared back at her from the floor.

"By the wall," she whispered as Nickolas burst into the room.

He staggered to a stop in the doorway, taking in the shattered glass and Etta's hunkered form before his gaze landed on hers. There was no sign of recognition in him, not a single whit.

She pushed to her feet. "Nickolas!" Whatever she might have asked of him, whatever she might have said, was swallowed by the way he looked at her like a stranger who had no right to know his name.

Her life, the fae had said.

In the endless reflections watching her, she saw a stranger. Realization fell heavily upon her. All the years in which she had seen the cruel tricks of the fae made understanding the depth of their power impossible to ignore.

She hadn't merely been touched by fae magic—it was not some passing jest. Etta had been cursed. Everything that had been hers was, in that brush of fae power, carried off with the monster who'd walked from the room.

Nickolas pushed past her. "Where is Lady Ostwind?" His demand unanswered, he yelled, "Etta!" He rushed into the main room without a backward glance.

Here, her heart whispered. *I am here*. But the words died in her throat, swallowed like all the screams she'd meant to loose as a girl.

The vows she'd made had not gone silent, though. Her fingers curled around the hilt of the sword she'd dropped to the floor beside her. Etta rose, steady on her feet. She would take back what they had stolen. This time, the fae would not win.

CHAPTER 7

The sun, too bright and too hot, was angled in an afternoon sky. Etta had tossed off the marshal's coat outside a castle door, running in slippered feet with no more at her aid than a sword and absolute surety that she had only one chance to stop this catastrophe. Shouts rang out behind her, deep inside the castle walls. She was beyond the notice of the royal guard—she'd escaped by routes few knew of. Her eyes were on the forest ahead.

At the edge of the trees, something chittered, followed by a high-pitched cackle that sounded more like a laugh than any sound an animal should have made. She ran faster, leaping over the stone edging that warned of the encroaching forest then splashing through the narrow creek that wound between the stone and brush. She shot into the tree line, and sweetbriar snagged her hair and dress. Flipping the sword downward, she shoved herself farther past the edge of the woods, snapping limbs and crunching vines and making no secret of her pursuit.

In the distance, a shadow shifted.

"Stop, fae!" The shout echoed through the forest, sending birds to flight and scattering small prey. She ran beneath the cacophony, the chaos of limbs and brambles thinning as she went deeper into the

55

woods. She had her feet again, and she did not waste the advantage, running as fast as she was able toward a creature who had no need of haste.

The fae strode through the forest without looking back at her. What little light filtered through the canopy dappled his form and revealed glints of color with every new step.

"Halt!" she shouted, furious that the word held no true weight of command.

The shadow did not stop but moved deeper into the woods, forcing Etta to follow. She was gaining on him, but he turned too swiftly, and she nearly lost him between the trees. She struggled past a thicket of spiny shrubs then turned to free whatever had snagged on her skirts. It was not a branch, as she expected. A low, slinky, furred *thing* smiled up at her, its teeth a row of spikes like shards of glass. She shrieked, raised her sword to strike, and nearly came off balance as it sprung at her. Its claws were dug well into her skirts, and the horrid thing was too close to get a good swing in. Faster than should have been possible, it scampered up her body, drawing the length of her caught skirt on its way then tumbling them both backward over a log.

Etta landed on her back with a grunt, swinging her sword arm up just as the creature launched itself free and took a hunk of her skirt with it right over her head. She smacked the fabric down from her face, rolled onto her knees, and jumped to her feet. She went after the thing, bruising a shoulder on a tree before breaking through to a dark clearing.

She froze, chase abandoned, to stare up at a massive structure that seemed to stretch the length of the forest. Her mouth gaped in awe, and her heart did a strange little dance in her chest. Magic thrummed through the ground beneath her, as if she stood on the bank of a river and could feel its current, as if the mud beneath her feet might fall in at any moment to be swept along with the flow.

Rising from blue mossy earth before her was a wall as ancient as Westrende. Like so much tied to the fae, it appeared as lovely and harmless as the common pale stone it mimicked. But Etta could see the truth. Beneath the flowering vines that appeared to roll softly over its surface waited bloody thorns as sharp as blade. Where one might have seen the face of the stone as smooth, Etta could make out delicate curves and twists of iron, the metal ties that bound the fae.

The wall sat upon the Rive, a boundary between the fae wilds and Westrende. Those ancient knots of metal were all that kept the fae out—all that was *supposed* to keep them from coming through and all that kept an unsuspecting human from stumbling into the fae realm.

Some small thing bounded from a tree behind her, and Etta's gaze swung down the wall. Not thirty paces from her stood the shadow who had posed as her artist, the man who had taken her face.

He was as still as the stone, glancing at her only briefly before moving to step toward the wall.

Etta launched herself at him, her grip firm about her raised sword.

His attention came back to her, revealing in its true form the same wicked smile he'd given her in the castle. "Call his name," the fae reminded her, "and discover what trade it might take to see your precious life returned."

The echo of his laughter was all she heard as her sword struck where he had been, the wall as solid as if he'd not just walked through.

"No!" she screamed, pummeling the stone with sword and fist. She'd had one chance, one single hope of regaining her life.

It was gone. Once the fae she'd just lost delivered the box that held her curse to the prince of Rivenwilde, Etta was doomed. She did not need to hear his taunting laugh to understand that. There would be no trade at all that she could make with fae royalty, and calling the prince would only bring him to retrieve the box that much sooner. Etta knew better than to believe they would give her a chance. She swore, the wall flickering beneath hands she realized had gone bloody.

She snatched her fists back, watching as the magic seemed to sap her blood. It crackled icily, a flower blooming at the site of one drop, its petals unfurling in the short moment Etta held her breath. Stepping back, she watched as more vines expanded like metal skeletons. But through the glamour, they appeared as elaborate carved stone. Pale fingers rose from the smooth surface, a sculpture unsettlingly like Etta's own hand. It wrapped about the newly formed blossom, grasping in a manner so desperate it made her heart ache.

She took another step back, her stomach turning. Fates protect her, she was standing unguarded before the Rive. Her gaze flicked down the facade, the horror of what each carving meant becoming painfully clear. Just beyond the flowering vines, a half-formed figure of smooth stone had risen, the shape of a man who appeared caught stepping through, frozen in time and only partially emerged, his features as finely formed as any sculpture in the castle. His hands were wrapped around the reins of a horse, its stone head thrown back and nostrils flared. Tendrils of the animal's mane curled outward, catching in the vines and thorns that fell over the top of the wall.

Etta blinked away the images and swung back toward the forest with her heart pounding. Lesser fae watched her, perched in trees and tucked beneath piles of earth. None wore glamour in the safety of the woods. Unafraid, eager, they waited for her next move.

A hasty swallow stuck in her throat. She gripped the sword tighter. A long vine reached out from the wall and brushed her shoulder. She jerked away from it, tearing another piece of fabric. She ran, full force, into the trees.

ETTA'S LEGS did not want to carry her farther, but she had little choice but to keep on. It had not been a long walk from the castle to the wall, but she wasn't foolish enough to misunderstand how she'd found it so quickly.

She had no shadows to follow anymore. She could not trust whatever lesser fae interrupted her journey to see her out of the forest—they would have led her deeper, forcing her to become more entangled in the mess and the magic of the greenwood. She couldn't stop to rest. She had to get out, return to the castle before nightfall, make a plan, and find some way to cross through the wall. She had to get her life back.

"There you are."

The voice jolted Etta so profoundly that she was swinging her sword before she realized she knew whose voice it was. Nickolas ducked, and her blow missed him by a hair. He grabbed hold of her, but it was not the embrace of a friend.

Nickolas was holding her captive. He stared down at her, his hand twisted in the material at the shoulder of her gown. Etta was so taken aback by his manner that she let him remove the sword from her aching hand.

"Where is she?" His tone was remarkably cold.

Etta opened her mouth to reply but could not find a single word. She could barely fathom what she had just been through.

"Lady Ostwind," Nickolas demanded. "Where is she?"

Etta's mouth snapped closed. She recalled Nickolas having found her among the shattered glass outside the portrait room. When he'd gone inside to search, Etta had not been there. "She's—Nickolas, it's me. I'm her."

Something passed over his expression as he leaned closer. "I don't know how you know my name, but if you have hurt her—"

"Don't be ridiculous. I'm telling you, it's me. Etta." She was yanked nearer and smacked at his hand—ineffectually, it turned out, because she was quite tired and Nickolas was quite strong. "Let go of me."

He turned, tugging her toward what she abruptly realized was the edge of the forest. She sagged in relief, and he turned back again, evidently deciding she meant to resist his capture. He drew a strap from his pocket then yanked her nearer to snatch her wrist.

She gasped, twisted, and spun free of him, only to fall face first to the forest floor when her torn skirt was ripped further by his grip. He leapt on top of her, pressing her into the earth. She growled, wrapped a leg about his ankle, and rolled them both. Off balance, Nickolas was a much easier opponent to manage, but he still outsized her by half. His cursed lanky arms trapped her in a solid hold before she could escape.

"I'm too exhausted for this!"

He stared down at her.

"Get off me, you lout." Limbs going limp, Etta sighed. "Fine. I'll explain it from here."

"Do," he said, "and quickly."

The afternoon sun was nowhere in sight. If Etta had to guess, they had less than an hour before sunset, and they were still on the wrong side of the tree line.

"It was a setup. The portrait artist was not Lord Barrett at all. I was a fool. I should have noticed. But I was so distracted, and so"—she shook her head—"he put me in the painting somehow. Touched me with a brush, and I knew it was magic and what—what did he say? *The painting for your life*. Then my face was gone. I felt it. I just didn't know what had happened until I saw the mirrors. I chased after him, but I wasn't fast enough. Now, he's gone, and I'm gone, and I just need to go home so I can get into my father's study, search his books, and find a way over that blasted wall."

Nickolas only blinked. After a moment, he stood and shook his pant leg straight before tugging Etta to her feet. "All right," he said. "Time to go."

Go. He meant to take her—as what, she wasn't sure. A prisoner, perhaps, if he truly thought she'd done something to the missing Etta.

"Nickolas, why am I in restraints?" she demanded.

His expression said he was entirely done with their conversation, and maybe that he wished she would stop calling him by his given name. "My lady, it appears you were the last known witness at the scene of a heinous crime. It is my duty, as a citizen of the great kingdom of Westrende, to hand you over to the marshal."

A boulder dropped in Etta's stomach. Her knees felt as if they might not hold her weight. "Lord Barrett," she whispered.

"Indeed. Now, you can come along willingly, or I can drag you to the edge of this forest and whistle for a guard to haul you back, strapped like luggage to the rump of his horse. I recommend the former."

"No. It's not what you think. Please, Nickolas, just listen to me. Just"—she cursed. "I did not murder Lord Barrett."

His blue eyes, as earnest as she'd ever seen, met hers. "The truth is, whoever you are, I care not at all about the lord in that hall." His voice lowered. "I care about finding Lady Ostwind."

"Nickolas."

Her word was barely above a whisper, her heart warming until

Nickolas tugged his lapel straight and added, "She needs to clear my good name."

Something horrid rose in Etta, that same boiling, awful heat that she felt toward the fae. Whatever nasty word that slipped free from her mouth, Nickolas only had time to look momentarily appalled before she took him to the ground. "You dirty, self-serving, absolute boor of a man! I swear to the wall, I will gut you and string your insides out for the birds, you no good—"

Beneath her, Nickolas's grappling suddenly stilled. Etta froze, too, afraid for a moment that they'd waited too long and the forest had come alive. But it was only her words—that Etta had threatened him with the birds.

"Yes," she whispered. "Nickolas, it's me." She shuffled off him, trying fervently to explain it all again. It took longer this time, though her mind was a tangle and Etta herself could barely believe it was real.

"The painting," he repeated. The disbelief was so plain in his voice that she might have thrown up her hands in defeat. But she needed him. To add insult to injury, her hands were bound.

She needed someone, just one lousy soul to believe her. Nickolas was that lousy soul.

"Exactly. The painting. It was hideous. I said so." She wiped a lock of hair back from her face with an arm. Her fingers were trembling, her wrists burning from the cord. "And he turned to me and..." And she had seen. She had known. By the wall, she should have run when she'd had the chance. "It was him." Her voice had gone tremulous. There was nothing else she could say. If Nickolas didn't believe her, if someone didn't come to her aid...

"You're saying he was fae?"

Etta's head shot up. "Yes. Oh, saints, Nickolas, I'm so glad you believe me. I can't—"

He held up a hand to stop her. "My lady, I feel that we are both overwrought. Perhaps you believe entirely what you are telling me, but the truth is, it's impossible to credit. Magic does not exist in Westrende. Fae don't walk the castle halls, pretending to be lords. You may have been involved with Lady Ostwind's disappearance, but you most certainly are not her."

"I can prove it."

He crossed his arms. "I don't have time for this nonse—"

"You have a scar on your right thigh."

Nickolas gave her a patronizing look. "That's not exactly a state secret, is it?"

Etta leaned closer, voice dropping to something mean. "It's long and narrow. A slice that skinned you of your trousers while you shimmied not from Lady Asha's balcony in a hasty escape, as you like to boast, but from your own mother's garden wall because you thought she was after you with a switch."

His mouth went flat.

"There's another on your hip. No one sees it, not these days, but when you were two and ten, you jumped from the roof of the old smokehouse, trying to catch a pig. You caught him. He pummeled you and took a bite out of your haunch. You couldn't wear your sword for a week. Made up a tale about it when the other boys saw you swimming bare-cheeked in the watering hole beyond the west gate."

He went pale.

Etta took a step forward. "And your left ear." She raised a brow. "It's smaller than the right."

Nickolas drew a breath as if he'd been slapped.

"That's right," she told him. "I can do this all day."

"You cannot be seri—"

"Try me," Etta said.

The look on his face was utterly unstable. Wearing her own skin, Etta had never pushed Nickolas so far—it did little good, as he knew her weaknesses too. But this girl, this crazed, disheveled mess of a thing, she was something that Nickolas didn't understand.

"You owe me." Etta's voice was as hard as steel. "You owe me, and you agreed to help me." Her finger found his chest, poking him right over the gilded trim. "You didn't tell me the man I stumbled into in the corridor upon our return was Gideon Alexander, when you knew full well that I would be facing him at the council meeting that would decide my fate. You let me fail, Nickolas. And for that, I call in my due."

He shifted nearly imperceptibly, something like guilt rising in the softness of his expression, threatening to overtake the disbelief.

She moved in for the kill. "You will help me, or I will report to the council the thing you did on Harvest Day."

His jaw went slack, his sharp eyes snapping to scan the clearing as if someone might have overheard.

Etta leaned back, hands on her hips as if she'd already won—hands that she'd freed from his tether without his notice and right beneath his nose. He looked at her again, clearly noting the set of her shoulders and the tap of her finger on her side. *You*, she made certain the posture said, *have been beaten*. It was the manner in which Lady Ostwind had often stood.

"You," he breathed.

"Yes," Etta answered. "Me."

CHAPTER 8

"You can't just walk back into that wing of the castle." Nickolas's words held a hint of lingering disbelief.

She didn't have time to finish convincing him of everything she understood about fae and magic. "What else am I supposed to do? I need to sort this out, Nickolas. I have to get that box, end that fae, and return with my own face in time to..." She sighed. "In time to fail at completing the chancellor's task."

"One failure at a time."

She gave him a look. He winced, apparently put off by her mannerisms on someone else's face.

"The chancellor wants me to discover what's behind the string of misfortunes and illnesses that have befallen our prospects for king," she said.

Nickolas gaped at her.

"I know. It's inconceivable." She picked a thorny twig from the material of her skirt. "The only thing I can do is gather the existing evidence, make a thorough report of every prior inquiry's failures, and hope that it's enough. Hope that he recognizes the work I put in and sees that I'm serious, capable, and not a fool cavorting with a known rake in the staff corridors."

Nickolas placed a hand on his chest, opened his mouth as if he might defend his reputation, then apparently thought better of it. "Will that be enough?" he asked instead.

"I don't know." She ran a hand over her face. "It's all I have."

He shook his head. "I think I can help but... I'm not certain what —by the wall, I cannot believe I'm considering any part of this. I must have lost my mind."

"You haven't. It's me beneath this mask. That's my disappointment in your character you're seeing, just like always."

"Shrew."

"Lout."

His mouth twisted thoughtfully. "The groom's entrance. There's a corridor that lets out near the south end of the chapel."

"Perfect."

It was not perfect, but it had done. They'd managed to deliver Etta to her rooms without drawing notice from a single kingdom official. Then Nickolas had run like the coward he was, which was fine. She had much to do.

The door snicked quietly closed behind her, and Etta let her gaze sweep the room. Castle staff had already been in, lighting candles and leaving a dish of food on a table in the sitting room, despite that she'd gone missing. She grabbed a roll before even washing her hands then paced farther into the room. Beyond the doorway, evening light spilled in through the window of her bedroom, illuminating the floor in the spot where she had watched the fae prince seize hold of her mother so many years before.

Do not speak of them. Speak of them, and they will come again.

The bread turned to ash in her mouth. She dropped what was left of the roll onto the mantel and knelt before her trunk. She'd meant to gather a clean gown, but a glint of metal caught her eye. She reached into the pocket that held her jewelry, taking hold of the chain that had worked free during their travels. It was her mother's locket. Inside were two tiny paintings, one of a young Etta and one of her father.

She stood and crossed to the vanity table, where she settled atop the fine cushioned stool, still in a torn, filthy gown. She turned the looking glass toward the face she wore. A stranger's features stared miserably back. It was fairly torturous to look upon oneself as someone else, and Etta felt downright wretched, overall. But she was back in her rooms, among old memories, and she would use what she'd learned to dig her way out. She was ready. *Always ready*.

The glamour flickered over her skin. Its illusion would fool any single human who looked at her—any human, Etta supposed, who was not able to see through the magic like she could.

Etta wasn't certain when she'd realized others could not see the truth, some whispered word, probably, or some warning from her father. Her flesh was still her own, which was a comfort, but only she would be aware of that. The magic couldn't change her actual form and couldn't make her someone else, but it had changed how others would see her. The fae had taken as much of her identity as they could.

Glamour was not their only tool. Since she was a child, Etta had watched fae walk through the halls of the castle, unmasked, their magic diverting the attention of any who passed. But to interact, they needed more, something that convinced the public that they'd seen only a common man, nothing out of the ordinary. The illusions were always as plain as a human might come, purposefully forgettable.

Etta recalled her mother saying long ago that too great a beauty came with unpleasant rewards, the sort of attention that got in the way. "You, my darling girl, are the precise amount of loveliness that means many will look upon you with admiration, but not so much that the beauty inside of you will not also be allowed to shine. Whatever it is that you set your heart on, it will be yours. I'm confident of it." She had smiled, brushing a thumb softly over Etta's cheek. In the looking glass, she saw her own hand rise and brush a cheek that wanted others to see nothing of that girl at all.

The mirror shattered. Glass clinked against the table in shards, a scattered mess so much like the one in the hall outside the portrait studio.

She cursed the fae. She cursed their cursed curse.

Behind her, the door to the room swung open. Etta turned to find a maid standing in the doorway, taking in the scene with apparent shock. "All is well," Etta began, forgetting for a moment that she did not have her own face.

She was not allowed to forget for long. The maid shouted, picked up a candle holder, and rushed at Etta.

"I couldn't just walk back into that wing of the castle."

Nickolas crossed his arms, giving Etta a flat look.

She shrugged. "A maid tried to have me arrested for breaking into to the lady Ostwind's rooms. I barely escaped. She was absolutely vicious. 'How dare I sneak into the room of the venerated general's daughter and steal her bread rolls.' Nearly ended up in chains. Thank the fates for the hours of running they put me through during training. Can you imagine the incoming marshal being put into irons?"

Nickolas blinked.

She moved past him to flop onto a chaise in his absurdly extravagant sitting room. "I need a place to stay."

"No." He shook his head, his finger, and apparently the thoughts right out of his mind, because he only stood there, staring at her as she sprawled over his furniture.

"You owe me," she said.

He pursed his lips.

"Oh, I see. As Lady Ostwind, I'm perfectly marriageable and all you ever wanted, but suddenly, I have nothing, and you won't risk being caught with me in your rooms."

"You're a fugitive," he reminded her.

She kicked her earth-smeared feet up onto his table. "You're the only witness that this face was even there. For all we know, *you* killed Lord Barrett."

His eyes narrowed. "No. Nay. Certainly not. This isn't happening. I will find a place for you to stay, but that place is *not* here."

Etta drew her feet down, sitting up to look at him. "So I've convinced you fully, then? You believe at the very least that this is me?" He did not quite believe the fae were in Westrende, but she chose to ignore that.

He squeezed his eyes shut for a long moment. "Yes. You can stop your bullying and acting the tormentor. I yield."

A relieved breath slid from her. "Thank all that is agreeable. How do you tolerate being so indecorous all the time? It makes my neck twitch."

Nickolas's head dropped back to stare at the ceiling. "It's a gift."

She was quiet for a moment, letting him adjust to their new reality. Eventually, he came back to center, dropping his arms to his sides in defeat. He leaned against the arm of a puffy embroidered chair. "What is the plan?"

Her expression might have been sober, but Etta felt the first bubbles of hope rising in her chest. "I need access to my father's study. One book in particular. Clearly, that won't happen with me looking like..." She gestured vaguely to her face. "His rooms are far more protected even than the king's suite."

"That's because there's no king in them."

"And beside the point. I need that book to find a way through the wall."

Nickolas stood. "No! Why—what is wrong with you? Have you entirely lost your senses? You plan to go through the wall?"

"They *stole my face*, Nickolas. My life. If don't get it back—" A sound of pure misery crawled out of her chest. "If I don't get it back and soon, I'll not only never be Antonetta Ostwind. I'll never be marshal."

"It's disturbing the order of importance you've put on those things. You realize that, do you not?"

She frowned. "I do. It doesn't change anything."

He paced back to the chair then sat to perch on its edge, his thinking face firmly in place. "So you need access to well-protected documents, and you also need to complete the chancellor's task."

"Yes. And quickly."

"Without the use of your own face."

She pressed her fingers hard against her temple. It did not make the headache go away.

Nickolas nodded. "Feasible. You'll need fresh clothes. But—and I can't believe I'm saying this at the state of you—don't clean up."

CHAPTER 9

"Yᵒu'll see." Nickolas had told her of his plan that she go to the chancery's office as bedraggled as she'd come into his rooms. He'd allowed her to sleep in his suite but had tucked her into a closet on a blanket, the door nearly closed. It wasn't much more absurd than anything else that had happened since the dawn before, but as Etta stood outside the office of chancery with a forged letter of reference from Nickolas's distant cousin, she had serious doubts that she would succeed at anything outside of being arrested.

A waif of a girl with an arm full of scrolls rushed past, nearly knocking into Etta as if she'd not noticed her at all. A few steps beyond, though, and the girl froze, her shoulders straightening as she turned to face Etta head on. One of the scrolls tumbled from her arms, rolling across the floor before knocking into a door frame.

"May I help you find something?" Her hair was slightly disheveled, her big brown eyes earnest despite that she was clearly in a rush.

Etta managed not to out with her standard introduction of "Antonetta Ostwind," but only barely. Moving a step forward so that her voice was less likely to echo through the chamber beyond, she began, "I'm here for—" She had to stop, clear her throat, and force a lesser confidence into her tone. "I was told there was a position available as secretary?"

"Secret—oh, well. That's unexpected. The prior secretary has just left us, as a matter of fact. I'm surprised word is already out, frankly. It all happened in a bit of a rush. But yes, she's to be married, so there will be no more flitting around the stacks for her."

"She was removed from the position for becoming engaged?"

The girl's cheeks colored. "Oh, no. Not at all. No one minds if staff is married. I blame her fall from the library ladder."

Etta blinked.

"Broke her leg in several places. The doctor informed her she was not to climb another ladder as long as she was under his care."

"It never healed properly?"

The girl looked at her as if she were slow-witted, and Etta was beginning to feel as if she might be. "She's to be married to the doctor," the girl explained.

"I see," Etta said, though she did not. Her confidence in Nickolas's plan was taking a hard dive into murky water. She wasn't certain she'd get into the chancery at all.

Shifting her burden into one arm and consequently dropping two more scrolls, the girl added, "I'm Jules. Clerk's assistant, notary's assistant..." She waived a hand, as if to encompass all the assisting not theretofore mentioned. "Come along, and I'll get you to the proper desk."

The proper desk, it turned out, was vacant.

"Robert," Jules called. "Where is the clerk?"

A freckled, sandy-haired young man popped his head out from behind a tall shelf. Etta's stomach flipped in recognition—he was the boy who'd delivered her message from Gideon, right before things had gone so horribly wrong.

He barely glanced at Etta, his eyes skimming over her with no sign of recognition. It was precisely how the fae illusions were meant to work.

"Out for the day," he said of the clerk.

Jules nodded briskly then led Etta through the next room.

The chancery's office remained in an older wing of the castle, likely because no one was interested in relocating the sheer volume of records it held. Every wall supported shelf after shelf of books, and every flat surface was stacked with more. Document carts and scroll baskets scattered a space that smelled somewhat of rusk and leather beneath slightly musty air. It was strangely charming and intimate, despite the grandeur. She'd been sent to fetch books from the stacks as a girl, her history tutor claiming he no longer had the legs to make the trip. It had seemed so much larger then. Now, her task loomed impossibly higher before her.

"My lord," Jules called as they came into a new chamber.

"One moment," a voice replied from somewhere beyond another rack of shelves.

"I've found a lost soul," Jules said toward the voice's general direction. "She's looking to apply for the position of secretary, if you can believe it."

Etta came to a dead stop, unease crawling up her neck.

"Secretary? Jules, you know we no longer need someone for that post." The face that peered around the rack was perplexed, then at the sight of Etta, suddenly became distressed. The chancellor opened his mouth as if to shout a warning, and Etta's stomach pitched.

She was certain he saw through the fae glamour, and she could feel the last chance at the only thing that might win her life back slipping from her grasp. And again, all because of *him*, the stupid fool man with his stupid dark eyes and—she screamed when a giant beast leapt from the darkness, knocking her straight to the ground. It was massive and hairy and wiggling, and by the fates, it had too many arms. Shouts rang through the room as she struggled beneath the monster without sword or weapon, her own limbs ineffectual as its reeking mouth found her face, hot and wet and—

A sound like *oof* slipped out of her when it slammed the full weight of its bottom half right atop her gut. The other end settled firmly on her chest and shoulders, its gaping maw inches from her nose.

"Clara!" one of voices scolded, closer this time, and the great vigorous beast was hauled off Etta's chest.

She gasped for breath, unable to move outside of a generalized shaking.

"Please, Jules, please just take her outside."

Etta caught sight of Jules, stock still with her slender hands covering her mouth. Her eyes were wider than ever, her cheeks gone pale.

The dark-robed figure of Gideon Alexander held the collar of what Etta realized was an enormous dog. He passed possession of the beast to Jules, despite the girl's diminutive frame. The dog hopped once, excitedly trying to lick at Jules's face, then was led from the room as if such was an everyday occurrence.

Etta stared after them, still prone and with no intention of rising.

Gideon moved to stand beside her, and for a terrifying moment, Etta expected a declaration that he recognized her, that the whole ordeal had been some sort of jest. But he only leaned down, taking hold of her arm to help her to her feet. His grip slid down her forearm as they straightened, and he did not immediately let go of her trembling hand.

"Are you well?" he asked, his gaze remaining solely on her eyes.

"No," she answered automatically then swallowed and shook her head. "I mean yes, I'm unharmed."

"Please, allow me to apologize. Clara is only—well, she adores meeting new people. I keep her tucked away in a spare office when we have visitors, but with Jules and the others..." One of his shoulders raised in the slightest shrug. "She's used to them. They're used to her. She meant you no harm. She's a darling, truly."

Clara. The beast that had mauled her had the sort of soft, sweet name that sounded as if it belonged to someone's favorite aunt.

Gideon's other hand came to rest beneath Etta's elbow. His head tilted as he examined her face. "Are you certain you're well?"

Etta realized she was still shaking. She realized he was still holding her hand. She snatched the hand back, running her palms over her borrowed skirt, a garment that Nickolas had said made her look properly indigent. "I'm sorry. I must seem a fool. It's only that I really needed the post."

The post that was no longer available. The man before her, the man who'd just held her hand, had given her a task that would have been impossible even as a general's daughter. It would be unimaginable with a stranger's face and no ties to the kingdom. Nickolas had been right. Taking a post in the chancery's office was her only way out. She needed access to her father's documents, and she needed to be close to Gideon to complete his ludicrous challenge. There were no second chances with council beyond the one they'd given her.

And it seemed she'd just failed.

"My lady." Gideon's voice was soft, and Etta realized she'd been silent for far too long while he contemplated her.

She tugged the sleeve of her gown to cover the scratches on her arm from the fight with a lesser fae and a half dozen brambles.

The chancellor pretended not to notice. "Did you tell me your name?"

"Etta." Something like a flinch went through him, and she stuttered. "For Margaretta. It was—my grandmother—it was her name." She dipped an awkward quarter-curtsy to hide her flush. "Please, call me Etta."

He didn't seem to mind that she was flustered as her eyes rose again to his. He only watched her calmly, his lips pressed together. Saints protect her, she wanted to hate him. She wanted to want to smash his perfect pensive face.

"Margaretta," he said, "perhaps I can find something for you to do."

CHAPTER 10

Come evening, Etta was settled into the staff lodging for the chancery's office with Jules in the bunk opposite her and young Robert and another man in an adjoining room. She'd been aware, growing up with so many tutors and in proximity to her father, that many who worked inside the castle did not live among the luxury of Etta's personal rooms. But she'd always assumed anyone who worked for the kingdom lived well. She had grossly over-supposed.

"It's perfectly lovely, isn't it?" Jules smiled as she wrapped her arms around a threadbare pillow and leaned back against the dark-paneled wall of their room. Her booted feet were curled beneath her, her posture so at ease that it was clear she felt the statement to be entirely true.

Surrounding them was ancient wood, spare of trim, none of it polished and oiled but worn with age. The room held no fireplace, no window, and would be as black as pitch when Jules put out the single light, never mind that it smelled a bit too much like the dull-gray bird whose cage was perched on the nightstand against Jules's bed.

Etta's throat felt tight. "I've never been more pleased." It was true, but only because of the immense relief flooding her after coming so close to missing a post in the chancery. Her fingers curled into the scratchy blanket covering her bunk. She had not a single possession aside from the locket she had taken from her trunk and Gideon's letter detailing her task. Even her gown was borrowed, a fact she'd been too distracted to follow up on at the time, though she was sure Nickolas had managed a delightful excuse for whomever he'd borrowed it from.

Jules tugged a chunk of bread from her pocket and carefully fed pieces of it to the squawking bird through the bars of its cage. Her fingers no more than slid free of its reach before the thing's frantic flapping started up again.

"There you go," Jules cooed, passing over the last of her supply. "A few more weeks, and you'll be as good as new."

The creature's wing was at an angle that did not appear to support the promise, but Etta held her tongue. "So up at cockcrow to ready the rooms, meals in the back office, and casual dress. Is there anything more I need to know?"

Jules's dark eyes met hers. "Robert and I will ready the rooms. We've no need of your help for that. You can get started a little later, as the chancellor prefers a bit of private time in the mornings."

"What does that have to do with me?"

"You'll not want to disturb him." She waved a hand as if the details were inconsequential. "You'll catch on soon enough. I've confidence in you, my lady. It won't be long before you have free run of the place. I'm sure of it. Get some sleep now. I'll lend you a gown so you might get that one washed. No worries this evening, I'll lay it out for you when morning comes."

Etta glanced down at her dress. The seams pulled in two spots where she'd hastily tied it on inside Nickolas's closet. Her fingers were twisted in the ribbon at her waist, hands scratched from the fae, and nails dark with earth from her tussle with Nickolas on the forest floor. By the wall, she'd too much to do. She needed to find a way out of the chancery's wing and into her father's office. She hoped Jules was right that she would have a bit of freedom soon. She glanced up to ask another question and found Jules fast asleep, her dress still bound to her slender frame, boots laced tightly where they stuck out from beneath her hem. The bird sat silently, head tucked into its neck, the occasional twitch the only sign it was aware of Etta.

Etta stood, carefully lowered the drape over the cage, then snuffed out the light. In the darkness, she stepped cautiously back to her bunk. Her shin bumped against the edge, as it was impossibly near. She sighed, untied her gown, stripped down to her shift, then crawled into bed to stare up at the darkness. She would not tell Nickolas she preferred his closet. She would not think of how easily she might sneak in and smother the head of chancery in his sleep.

"What do you mean?" Etta hissed. "The secretary doesn't work directly with the chancellor."

Jules grinned at her with that same pleasant smile that could not have been as consistently genuine as it seemed. "Normally, no. But you've no experience as a secretary, now, do you? He can train you. Besides, I think you should give Lord Alexander a chance. You might like him."

"Like him?"

"The work, I mean. Chancellor is certainly a more interesting post than secretary. Experience it while you have the chance. And he's the only one who has time."

Etta's eyes narrowed. The girl had left her a decent gown, as promised, and had come into their room as chipper as a new chick, eager to usher Etta to her station. But every word that came out of her mouth felt as misleading as the last.

"You're saying the head of chancery has more time than—"

"Off you go." Jules shooed Etta through the doorway, leaving her with no more than a little wave and a wish of luck as she hurried in the opposite direction. "Don't fall off any ladders!"

Etta stood silently inside the door to the chancellor's office, staring after Jules. Then quite suddenly, she recalled the giant dog Gideon had said he kept locked inside. She spun, expecting at any moment to be laid out once more, and found the chancellor of Westrende, dressed not in the robes he so often wore but in the official coat of his station.

It was fitted to his form with square shoulders, the high collar done all the way up, and the buttons gleaming and polished despite the sparse light. At his side, a slender sword hung. In his hand, he held a piece of parchment.

"My lady."

Etta's gaze jerked back to his face. She wasn't certain whether she was meant to curtsy. She didn't think she would. He was her last chance at freedom, though, so she dipped her head. "Lord Alexander."

"Gideon."

She gave a brief nod, hating the way polite familiarity tasted in her mouth. "Gideon." He stood there a moment more, and she had the sense that he'd forgotten entirely that he'd offered her a post. "Where shall I get started?"

He made the smallest little head shake then took a breath. "I was on my way to a meeting. But I'll just"—he held up the document—"let me send this with Robert, and I'll be right back. We'll figure something out."

He walked past, a whisper of woodruff hitting Etta before it disappeared among the scent of stale documents. *We'll figure something out?* She prayed he would not change his mind. Of course he hadn't had the time Jules had promised. She couldn't understand why he had even let her stay.

Etta walked farther into the room, taking in a well-loved desk stacked with layers of official-looking correspondence and a neat pile of blank parchment beside wax and seal. She ran a finger over the edge of the quill feather, black as his robes and its vane just as pristine. Her gaze trailed up a wall of books beyond the desk and down another beside it. Records and rules. Every law the kingdom had ever known. He spent his days surrounded by the code she, as marshal, was meant to uphold.

Etta turned slowly, memorizing the space.

When she noticed Gideon's return, she straightened, waiting for him with a posture she realized too late was probably overly militant for her stint as Margaretta. She wasn't sure how to soften herself but made an effort.

Gideon stopped inside the room and looked around, the edge of his lip tucked beneath his teeth. His eyes landed on a stack of crates by the far wall. "There we are." He gestured toward the mess, not hiding the that-should-keep-you-occupied-for-a-day-or-two note to his tone.

He intended to keep her toiling away at busywork, then, not train her as secretary. And there, inside his office. Her carefully laced fingers tightened, but she managed a civil smile. She had to be grateful for any chance to win back her life, even if she would have to do it right under his nose. "Of course. I'll get to work right away."

He nodded, apparently satisfied, and went back to his desk. Etta moved a chair closer to the crates to begin her work. She would sit pleasantly, looking as busy as he wanted, but the moment Gideon left her alone, her true tasks would begin.

CHAPTER 11

They sat in easy silence until Etta's eyes were sore and her fingers covered in dust from the sorting. Gideon had not left his post once. When Jules fetched Etta for a brief meal with the rest of the staff, Gideon took the opportunity to run off for a meeting. He was back before the others had let Etta out of her sight. It was as if they didn't quite trust her, despite that they'd taken her on without a single check of the poorly constructed background she and Nickolas had thrown together or of her character.

The afternoon went similarly, the quiet shuffle of paper the only sound for so long that when Gideon finally spoke, it came almost as a surprise that she wasn't alone. She glanced up at him behind his desk, much more put together than she was with documents strewn across her lap and in newly made piles on the various crates and shelves around her.

"Enough for today," he said. The light coming in through the windows had faded, evening apparently having arrived without her notice. In the candlelight, the gold of Gideon's collar gleamed—still done up to the neck, not a stitch out of place on his person—but there was a little twist to the lock of hair at his temple, which curled down to brush his skin. She drew her gaze from it when his tone became a dismissal. "It looks as if you've made good progress. You can start again in the morning, same time."

She began the next morning, the same task in the same chair. She was certain the chancellor had other duties to perform, that he would not normally spend all day hunched over his desk. But by midafternoon of the third day, Etta felt as if she'd been a problem forced upon him, that her presence had somehow changed the entire chancery staff's schedules.

They'd made room for her. She needed less of it.

"Robert," Gideon called from the corner of the office. He was in the coat again, his shoulders set in the way of a person who had far too much to do and no time in which to do it.

"He's gone out," Jules answered, peeking her head around the doorframe with bundles of rolled parchment in each arm. "Won't be back for hours."

"Tobias, then."

Jules shook her head. "Not feeling well." Her eyes flicked briefly to Etta. "Nothing serious, but I've sent him to his rooms for a bit."

Gideon frowned. "That's twice this month."

"He'll be all right." Jules's voice was firm, but her grip on the rolled parchment, not so much. One fell to the floor and rolled into the distance. "What is it that you need?"

He sighed. "It's only a letter for the exchequer. I'll not trouble you with it."

Etta stood. "I can deliver the letter."

They both glanced at her, Gideon's expression almost offensively uncertain.

"It's no problem. I know precisely where his office is. I can have it delivered before Robert even returns." When he didn't immediately reply, she added, "And it will get me out of your hair for a bit." The smile she gave him was probably not quite as self-deprecating as she intended, but she did try.

His thumb slid over the parchment. Eventually, he held the letter forward. "It's not entirely vital. I'm sure you'll do well enough."

She took the proffered letter, hoping he meant it wasn't important enough to merit someone with a higher level of security delivering the thing and not that he fully expected her to cock it up. She didn't have the luxury of being offended, in any case—she needed out of the chancery wing, and running messages might be her only way.

Gideon gave her one final look before turning back to his work. Etta didn't wait for him to change his mind.

ETTA'S ROUTE to the exchequer's office took her down the corridor outside council chambers and through the long, wide passage that was strung with portraits of Westrende officials. It felt strange to be back in the council wing, but no one's eyes stayed on her long, thanks to the fae glamour. So she let herself slow, taking in the endless row of paintings of officials who had performed their duties for decades, men who had worked with her father when Etta had been barely old enough to swing a sword and women who had children as old as the general and still served alongside the kingsmen they had trained. And others, younger, but still clinging to the traditions of their forebears. Etta stopped, turning to face the wall.

The hall's newest portrait stared down at her with a plaque beneath that read *Gideon Conrad Alexander, Chancellor of Westrende.*

"Conrad," she murmured, thinking of a Lady Conrad she'd met as a girl. Perhaps the woman had been a ship's captain. Etta could not quite recall, but as she examined the lines of Gideon's face, she felt the hint of recognition at first seeing him fall into place. In the portrait, Gideon wore the same style coat as he'd donned that very morning, and Lord Barrett's depiction of him contained not a single scrap of whimsy. Something dark and determined lurked in the chancellor's eyes, something that spoke of the resolve he meant to put to task. It seemed to swear a vow and proclaim his dourness all at once. Behind Etta, a pair of ladies passed, their eyes skirting hers but their lips turned up at her gawking of the young lord. She paid them no mind, as they could not have known who she truly was. She no longer had a reputation to uphold—not until she broke her fate forsaken curse.

Gideon's figure in the painting was angled not toward the other portraits, but to the empty wall beside it, a bare space where Etta's own portrait should have been.

She walked on, taking each of them in. Her father stared down at her from the greatest height, his shoulders drawn back and his mouth in a hard line. He was proud and stern, holding the bearing of a general, through and through. Etta's mother had said once that it had been difficult for the general to come back from war and have to behave in a civilized manner. Etta wasn't sure one could be civilized and still command such battles. She suspected a person was one or the other and that her father only thrived when there was a war to be fought. Such had certainly been the case in his relationship with Etta.

She let her gaze roam over his coat, the epaulets and trim, a dozen metals of honor. Etta had no metals. Her father had been right—she'd not earned a band marking her as an official of Westrende, but she supposed she'd been in somewhat of a battle, herself, in her four years of training. She had felt strong and capable then, at the top of her class, only to return to the rules her father had set for her and to do as she was told.

Since she was a girl, Etta had been forced to make judgments, to advise and council and possess an opinion on every little matter. It was all part of her training, drilled into her so that she might someday take a post among the kingdom's most powerful. Now, she would not be heard if she screamed from the top of a tower. She was a lowly assistant, an expert in nothing. The chancellor barely trusted her to deliver a letter.

A muttering man passed behind her, and she moved down the wall to stand before the portrait that most touched her. Etta's mother hadn't been especially beautiful in the lines of her face, her figure, or the sheen of her hair, but everyone who knew her instantly became enamored. It was something in the spirit that sprung from her, in the way she tossed her head when she laughed and the sly tilt to her lips as she smiled. When she told a story, the entire hall would fall silent just to hear. She had been made of life. She had positively glowed with it.

The fae had taken that from her. The fae had taken it from all of them.

"They will not take it from me, too," Etta whispered. "Whatever the cost, I will steal it back."

A trio of guards walking by gave notice at her words, and Etta moved on, head down as she strode toward her father's wing.

THE GENERAL'S OFFICE WAS ONE of the most secure areas of the castle. But Etta was the general's daughter and had learned a few of his tricks by mere proximity, having gone through a stage in which she had reveled in uncovering his secrets.

Experience had soured her on the desire to discover things her father kept hidden and on frivolous adventure. But Etta had not forgotten how her father operated. It was little work to find her way outside his chambers, to the narrow space secreted between his office wall and the next. The desire to spy on his visitors had left the general vulnerable to the same, though he would likely suffer an apoplexy, should he discover his own daughter using it against him. Etta waited quietly behind the wall, listening as footsteps came and went, eager for her chance to enter her father's office alone. He had always been a busy man, but the bustle seemed unusually lively, and Etta's intense impatience was tested. In the corner, the shadows seemed to breathe, but Etta held her place.

Inside the office, the door closed again, followed by muffled noises and a pair of booted footfalls. Voices floated through the room—kingsmen, by the sound of them. She leaned against the plaster, her gaze turned away from the darkest corner. Sweat beaded on her temple and beneath the neck of her gown. She did not recall the space being so stifling as girl.

"Already?" a low voice said. "The lady Ostwind has only been missing a day."

Three days, Etta corrected. Surely, the kingsmen Nickolas had said were looking for her had spread word of that. She straightened to shift farther down the wall, her steps light and measured in the dimness, her ears pricked for any movement behind her.

Another voice grumbled, "We can't go on like this, not with this sort of misfortune coming more frequently. It's not just potential kings any longer. What happened with the general's daughter only proves that."

The first man made a grunt of approval. "It's a shame. A marshal with her disposition is just the sort of enforcement the kingdom needs."

Etta stilled to wonder precisely what he meant. The lightest movement echoed through the space behind her.

Outside, the other man chuckled. "You think her temperament was fitting now, imagine how she would have grown into the post."

Both men's laughter abruptly cut off, followed by the sound of a closing door. In the silence, Etta held her breath. There was a muted string of footfalls, sure and steady, then the nearly imperceptible protest of a chair shifting against the polished marble floor.

"General," the men said in unison. Etta could picture their matching salutes, the way their shoulders tensed with her own, an instinct drilled into them over years.

Her breath was stuck in her chest. She knew she'd held it too long but could not convince herself to release it. She could not fathom what her father had thought of her disappearance or whether he had been laughing it off like the other men. "Only been missing a day," the guard had said. As if it were all a jest to them. As if she'd never returned from training, had not been slated to take place as their marshal, a kingdom official whose rank surpassed their own.

"Report," her father snapped.

There was a shuffling of paper, a short silence, then a slight scrape as her father's chair moved again. "Unacceptable. Get out of my sight with this. If I see you again before she is found—"

He did not need to finish the order. He'd likely not even stood.

Heavy footsteps hurried from the room, the two who'd been laughing and an apparent third kingsman, whom Etta had not heard speak at all. She was grateful she'd not had a chance to attempt entry, because the silent man would have seen her caught.

The door closed, and there was a soft sound as something settled onto the desk. His hand, perhaps. It was too hot inside the space, too narrow. The shadows were too close. She leaned against the wall, pressing her palm to the dusty plaster. She could only picture him, alone at his desk, just paces away from the thin panel she hid behind and from a truth he refused to acknowledge, that remaining silent could not keep the fae from hurting them.

Her father sighed, the sound a knife to Etta's resolve. She had meant to wait for him to leave, to steal the book that would help her cross the wall. To do it all on her own. To face the fae. But he had an army of men at his command, a kingdom that might be able to save her... if he would only let them.

Etta's heart was in her throat, hot and hammering and preventing even a swallow. He had sent her away. *I would send you off for another four if I could.* But when she came back, he'd let her stay and stand before council. She was the one who had failed. And now, she was missing. His daughter was gone, nothing in her place but the body of the man who'd been hired to paint her. He might have thought Etta was responsible, that she'd killed Lord Barrett and run off to save her skin. Or worse, that she'd been stolen, taken by the fae for the sin of speaking their name.

Taken, as Etta's mother had been. Seized by the prince of the fae.

It was her fault, he would assume. If only she had behaved and done as she'd been told.

Her father didn't have the sight, but he knew the truth about magic. He understood there were fae who crossed into Westrende. If anyone would know her, if anyone could truly see...

A strip of light cut through the darkness as Etta's slick palm pressed the secret panel open before she'd had time to think it through.

She realized her mistake in an instant.

SOMETHING CHITTERED in the darkness beside her. In the room beyond the doorway, General Ostwind was standing, sword in hand, before Etta had even a moment to speak.

"To the floor!" he ordered, her father no longer. His was the voice of a man trained in battle and who would make no hesitation in cutting her in two.

"Father," she said anyway, "it's me."

He was moving toward her, as agile as any beast, his grip sure on the sword.

Etta held her hands forward in surrender. "Please. Just listen."

The tip of his sword cut off her plea. It pressed to her neck in one smooth gesture, only the brief flash of metal catching her eye before a trickle of warm blood slid down her skin. She'd not yet felt its sting.

"Who sent you?" he asked in a low voice, offering a warning. He'd no need to call the guard, not with his blade at her throat. The gesture showed he intended to kill her, just as clearly as any word he might have said. He did not need a witness to slay an intruder. Not as a general.

"It's me," she choked out. "Etta."

Her voice had not changed—surely, he could at least know that. But his eyes were cold, bearing no hint of recognition. His weapon remained steady. "You dare speak her name."

The fae, she wanted to scream at him. *The fae did this*. But Etta could not. The last thing her father would accept would have been the invoking of them by a stranger, a girl with an unfamiliar face.

"Don't believe what you see," she begged.

He stepped forward, his blade digging deeper. *Last chance*, the gesture warned.

"Yes," she answered aloud, because Etta knew it was true. She'd been a fool to ever believe he might listen or to think that her disappearance would mean enough to change things. One more word, no matter what it was, would be her last. So she moved slowly, easing the necklace from the pocket of her skirt. She held it forward, letting the chain that held her mother's locket drop from her open palm at his eye level, because a man like the general would never look away from an opponent, should she have tossed it.

The flinch didn't show on his face, but Etta felt it through the tip of his sword. It was her one opportunity. Her only opening.

She rolled backward, away from her father and into the narrow space from which she'd come. He was on her in a moment, but from the darkness shot the ball of dark fur that had been watching her all along. It pounced at the general, drawn by her blood, and that single moment of hesitation was all Etta needed to land a hand on the panel to her escape. The general's curse echoed off the walls behind her, but she didn't waste time by closing the door or attempting to shove furniture in front of it. She needed only three paces, three good steps toward the next doorway, and she'd be in the hidden walkways used by staff.

He would never find her, not with a maze of options from which to choose. Etta burst through the doorway and slammed bodily into a woman a solid head taller than her. A huff of breath escaped them both, then Etta was up, tumbling forward though a passage at random, not precisely to her plan. Behind her, she heard the woman spluttering an explanation to Etta's father, but the thunder of his chasing footsteps never came. Etta could not wait around to discover why. He'd had no change of heart, despite that she had handed over her mother's token, she was sure of that. More likely, he'd only decided not to chase after her like a fool.

He would tell his kingsmen, put them on alert. He would not have accounted for the glamour on her face, the way it would turn a man's gaze no matter how he tried. In truth, her father may have forgotten already the very details he would need to identify his intruder.

She would not be grateful to the curse, even for that. Etta flung herself through the next doorway, pressed the panel closed behind her, and leaned against its wood. Chest heaving, hands slick, she pulled the kerchief from her pocket to wipe at the blood streaking her neck. The wound hurt but not badly. There was something to be said for a sharp blade. But it smeared, already thick, and she counted herself fortunate to have landed in an empty study. She found a decanter, poured water over the kerchief, then drew a chair out before the small writing desk to pen a message of her own.

If her father refused to see her for who she truly was, then she would act as herself in the only way she could.

CHAPTER 12

Bloodied and sweating, Etta had taken the letter for her father to Nickolas, who'd been entirely put out by her reappearance, let alone that she'd ordered him to deliver a message to the very man who might implicate him in a crime. But he had eventually agreed, and Etta had returned to the chancery's wing in time for a meal, a bath, an hour's research to catch up on the task Gideon had set for the marshal, and a solid night's sleep. All should have been well by the next morning, except that in a fresh gown, standing beside the chancellor as he examined a parchment clearly not meant for his eyes, Etta was starting to suspect more than the fates were playing against her.

The script on the letter she'd had delivered—not to the chancellor but to her father—was entirely her own, the signature intact. No one could have disputed that. But clearly, someone had. Gideon's desk was spread with documents Etta had signed years before, personal correspondence and public contracts. His expert chancellor's gaze traced the lines, studying their curves as he held each beside the one she'd penned just the night before, yet he did not seem convinced. Etta had eased closer through the morning, finding reasons to sort and file ever nearer to his desk.

Finally, she broke. "You think it is not her? That someone delivered a forgery?"

Gideon's head snapped up, and Etta realized she had leaned more closely than a mere assistant ought. She caught the scent of him, that hint of woodruff and soap, but it tangled with something else, familiar and warm. The scent was her own, she realized, the parchment in his hand having come freshly out of the possessions in her trunk. He slid the documents into a single pile, apparently assuming she was interested in gathering gossip to trade among castle staff. It was better, she supposed, than having him think she was sniffing his person.

She straightened. "It's only that it seems unlike the lady Ostwind, from what I've heard. What would she gain from bludgeoning a poor artist to death? He was to make her portrait, after all. And the years of work she'd put toward becoming marshal... it makes no sense that she'd throw it all away without reason."

Gideon's lips pressed closed. "That is not for me to judge. But a single message does not clear her name, not when it was first in the hands of her father."

"Her father? You believe him—what? That he somehow may be covering for her? You truly think so badly of the general and his kin?"

Gideon pushed away from the desk to stand, the documents—her documents—pressed to his chest in the way he'd held a stack of parchment the first time she'd seen him. But the man could not have been mistaken for a simple clerk any longer, not by the manner he carried himself or his tone.

"Continue the filing, my lady. I've a few errands to tend to. I'll send Jules in to assist you."

It was a reminder of her place. He'd given her a position as his assistant, and the business of Westrende was not hers to weigh. Gideon didn't trust her alone in his office. The chancery did need to remain secure, but Etta was part of its staff.

She didn't know why she'd expected him to trust her as his assistant when he hadn't trusted her as Lady Ostwind, but it rankled her. He thought Etta's letter was a fake, that she was a fraud who had kingdom officials lying for her. Etta's father was the general, head of council. She didn't know what more the man wanted. It was fine, then.

If Gideon needed more than a letter passed to General Ostwind, she would give him one from Antonetta Ostwind herself.

"My lady?"

Etta glanced up to find Jules in the doorway, her focus on the crumpled document in Etta's hand. Etta cleared her throat and offered a weak smile. "Just keeping up with this filing."

It took her most of the afternoon to get away long enough to write a few measly words, not counting the quarter hour she'd spent attempting to locate parchment that would not give her ruse away. The chancellor had proven he would inspect whatever she sent him to the finest detail, so paper pulled from his own supply would never do. When she finally had it folded and ready to leave on his desk, she became aware of another issue: no one in the office would be able to attest to how the missive had been delivered.

Her savior came in the form of Nickolas Brigham.

"My lady," Robert said from the doorway. "Lord Brigham is requesting a word with you. He insisted that he not reveal his name, but everyone knows who he is." He pushed a piece of sandy hair from his brow. "Shall I send him away?"

Etta blinked up at the boy from her sorting. "No, thank you. I'll take care of it myself." As she stood, brushing her skirts, Jules gave her a speculative glance. "All's well," Etta promised. "He's a friend of the family." Then she hurried from the room before she had to invent an entire battalion of relatives to befriend the man.

Nickolas lingered in the shadows outside the entrance to the chancery's office, glancing about as if involved in something illicit.

"What are you doing here?" she hissed, taking hold of his sleeve to pull him farther from the doorway. "You're the one who insisted we reveal no ties to one another."

"The letter to your father didn't work," he snapped. "No one believes it's real. Furthermore, the fact that a missing person sent a message at all is suspect. This does not look good, Etta, and you should know that once they've ruled you out for being too missing to blame, I'm the next closest witness to a man's death."

"Quit being a coward." At his outraged expression, she stepped nearer. "I know the letter didn't work. The chancellor himself was tasked with verifying it. But I have a new plan that will buy us both time."

His eyes narrowed. "Why do I not like the sound of this?"

"Because I need you to deliver it."

He leaned closer and kept his voice low. "I may owe you, Antonetta, but not so much as this."

"It's this or an investigation into your private dealings by the entire office of marshal. Which do you prefer?"

Something that sounded like a curse ground out of him, just as movement caught the corner of her eye. Gideon was crossing through the corridor on his way to the chancery entrance. He met her gaze.

"Margaretta, a word, please."

She swallowed, taking a step back from Nickolas before giving Gideon a small nod that she hoped he understood meant she would be along shortly.

"Margaretta?" Nickolas murmured.

Etta rammed an elbow into his stomach, watching until Gideon was out of sight. Then she turned. "I cannot very well claim to be Antonetta, can I?" He opened his mouth, likely to remind her it was not the name but the familiarity he was pointing out, and she shoved the letter into his hand. "Get this delivered. As soon as possible."

"Must you keep tangling me in your—"

"You are all I have," she said in a harsh whisper. "The fae stole the face of the general's daughter right beneath the council's watch, and no one will even acknowledge their existence. It's up to me to fix this. The only way I ever will is if I break this curse and become marshal of Westrende. I have to, Nickolas. And the only help I have is you, whether either of us likes it."

Etta did not wait for his reply, but his words at her back stopped her cold. She'd barely gone three steps.

"They're replacing the marshal. Council had a special meeting this afternoon. They sent Lord Alexander the letter that was addressed to your father, and he would not confirm its authenticity. With you missing and another prospect for king taken ill..." His words fell off, but Etta could not make herself look at him. "That's why I've come. At the turn of the moon, a new marshal will step into the post, whether or not you have cleared your name."

"Thank you for telling me. I-I appreciate what you've done, Nickolas, and the risk. I won't ask anything more of you aside from the letters."

Her heart heavy, Etta forced her feet to carry her forward. She did not look back. Whatever Nickolas thought, whatever her father and council did, it would not change the outcome. Westrende's marshal was the one person who could stop the fae. If Etta ever meant to succeed, it had to be her. She owed it to her mother. She owed it to the kingdom.

When she came back into the chancellor's office, Gideon was not sitting at his desk. He was leaned against the front edge of it, arms folded over his chest, his expression grim. She had quite forgotten he'd caught her in the corridor with Nickolas. He tilted his chin toward a chair that waited across from him.

Etta crossed the space slowly then sat. "My lord."

He stared down at her. "As chancellor, my reputation rests on the shoulders of those associated with this office. My duty is to uphold the sanctity of law and ensure justice is carried out in every instance so that the kingdom remains safe and its people prosper."

It was difficult to keep the frown from her face, but despite the effect of the glamour, Gideon's focus on her facade did not waver, so Etta managed. He uncrossed his arms. "As such, we all risk a great deal when a new member of staff is taken on. For it is not only my reputation that might pay the price for a poor venture. It is the entire staff of this office, every soul you have and have not yet met who has found a place within these walls."

"My lord?"

Gideon reached behind him to retrieve a crumpled parchment from his desk. He held it forward, and in the light, Etta could see that its edge was smeared dark, a color that Gideon might not recognize as day-old blood.

The exchequer's message.

He clearly took note of the realization sinking in, as Etta recalled that instead of delivering it as she'd promised she would, she had not. He couldn't have known that she'd snuck into her father's office instead, been chased through the staff passageways, and delivered her own missive to Nickolas's rooms. But she could not believe she had forgotten the reason she'd been let out of his sight in the first place.

Gideon dropped the letter back to his desk. "I cannot in good faith keep someone on staff who cannot be trusted, Margaretta."

Saints, he did not know the half of it. Even the name was a lie. "Please," she started, but Gideon left her no room.

He sighed, turning from her to round his desk. "It is not my place to warn you of personal matters, my lady, but I feel I should not leave it unsaid." He sat, drawing his chair forward to position himself in the most officious manner he might, plainly uncomfortable at what he intended not to leave unsaid. "The"—he stopped then started again, and Etta realized the word he'd abandoned was "gentleman"—"the *lord* with whom you were meeting outside—"

Etta stood so abruptly that it startled them both. Wherever the cool calm had gone from her years of training, she could not find it. "You cannot dismiss me. You mustn't. It was only a misunderstanding. I truly was on my way to deliver the letter when—I was—I had an accident, and there was—" She stepped forward. "Lord Brigham is only a family friend. He notified me of-of the accident, and—" Her hands found his desk, clinging in a way she would not be proud of when she looked back on it later. "Please do not dismiss me. I need this post more than you could possibly understand."

Gideon had gone silent, his expression blank. He stared at her with such open expressionlessness that she had no idea what his next words might be.

"Please," she begged. "There's nowhere else for me." *Let me stay*.

"My lord." Jules's voice rang from outside the doorway, breaking the tension so thoroughly that Etta jumped.

His gaze was on hers only a moment longer before he glanced at the door. "Yes?"

Jules's face popped into view. "I have those documents you—" She looked from Gideon to Etta. "Oh, I apologize if I've interrupted."

"No." Gideon cleared his throat. "Just leave the documents here,

Jules. Thank you. And, if you will, won't you take Margaretta to the archives so that she might help your search for the records of the Richards plea."

THE NEXT MORNING, Etta was up well before dawn. Jules lay sprawled on the bunk opposite, limbs akimbo, braid slung across her face, and one booted foot wedged between the mattress and wall. Beneath the drape of its cage, the bird purred. Etta had mended her borrowed gown the night before and hurriedly slid into it so that she might have time to find more current records of the prospects for king and Gideon's task. Time was spending faster than she had imagined possible, and it was getting no easier to live the life of someone else.

She needed to complete a report that would prove to council, if not to Gideon himself, that Lady Ostwind was up to the post of marshal, steal back into her father's office to retrieve his book, and get over the wall to win back her face.

Her forehead thunked against the door at the very thought of all that standing between her and success, but Etta took a deep breath, tightened the tie of her dress, and opened the door to leave the room.

She'd nearly waited too long to retrieve the records of the incidents involving the prospects for king and the various investigations, but Gideon had given her a second—*third?*—chance. She would not waste it. At least if she had possession of the records, being thrown out of chancery would not hurt quite so badly.

The clerk's desk was empty, no one in the entire office moving besides a humming Tobias tucked away in the stacks of a back room, as he so often was. Jules had explained that Tobias sometimes took ill, so when he felt well, he caught up on work, whether night or day. *As long as he's out of the way, it doesn't bother anyone,* Jules had noted in a tone that made clear it wasn't to bother Etta. It hadn't, but Etta was beginning to appreciate the uncommon protectiveness among the chancery staff.

By the time she was able to locate where the reports should have been, only to find the space empty, the others had stirred, and Robert began heating the water for morning tea. Etta had no idea when Jules might let her out of her sight again, but she was forced to end her search before she was caught. Tidying her skirts, she made her way into the chancellor's office so it might appear she'd been working only on the task of sorting.

Gideon had not yet arrived. She walked quietly around his desk, sliding open two drawers to nothing of interest before finding a third locked. It was the contents of the fourth drawer that stopped her cold, the narrowest one and closest to his seat. Beneath a few folded documents rested a missive she recognized as her own. A ribbon of the lightest blue clung to the broken wax seal of the house of one of her oldest friends. The girl had been shipped away to another kingdom, well before Etta had gone off to a separate kingdom for her own training. Her father had refused to let Etta visit, and once she'd left Westrende, their messages had been fewer and farther between.

The only letter from her they might have found when searching Etta's rooms would have been the one stashed in her traveling trunk. She'd held onto the message because it had been one of the last and because it had spoken of the dedication Etta had shown and how proud Etta's mother would have been. *Taken*, the message had said. Taken from Etta in a manner far too cruel.

Etta had wondered about the wording of the letter and whether leaving the kingdom had allowed her friend to accept the truths of Westrende. She had not asked, though, because she'd feared the answer might be no, that the reference had only meant taken from the world while unfairly young.

The drawer slid quietly closed beneath Etta's palm. Gideon had received her personal correspondence in the line of duty. Etta could claim no such excuse. She was not marshal yet, and had she been, Gideon was not the man she was meant to be investigating.

He'd given her a reprieve and let her stay on at the chancery, but he hadn't trusted her enough to leave her alone, so she would not riffle through the rest of his things, even if it was tempting. Getting caught would have been the end of her access to the entire wing.

Instead, she drew her chair toward the endless stack of documents she was meant to sort and file, but before she settled in, she heard a muffled sound from beyond the far shelf of books. Etta glanced toward the empty office door then at the hint of dawn light visible through the high windows.

The sound came again.

She stood, smoothed her skirt, then crossed to the shelf of books. It rose tall, overflowing with bound volumes, its wood thick and dark. Behind it waited more shelves, just as sturdy, making a maze of sorts that led to the office's far wall. Etta should have turned back, but another dense thud sounded in the room beyond, followed by a low grunt.

She moved through the darkness, her hand on the lever before she could talk sense into it. The door slid open to reveal a large, nearly empty room. A few scattered candles burned unsteadily on untrimmed wicks, lighting the space enough to reveal that a small number of furnishings had been slid to the outer walls and a bare wood floor, worn with age. A lean figure clad in trousers and shirtsleeves centered the room. He moved with the ease of a practiced swordsman—*step, swing, back, spin, thrust*—just as Etta had done for years. But there was no master swordsman battering him with a rod, no sparring partner taunting his swings. Only Gideon, alone, his blade polished and grip steady, the flash of metal mesmerizing as he moved. Beyond him waited a post and dummies, apparently the source of the muffled thuds.

Etta could not draw her eyes from Gideon, though she knew she should. Jules had said the chancellor had private business to attend each morning, but this was not what Etta had expected. Hair tousled, temples damp with sweat, the buttoned-up man she'd come to loathe was gone. Even the laces of his shirt were undone halfway down his chest. Beneath the thin fabric was lean muscle, shifting with every graceful strike. He moved through the room at a steady pace, his form that of someone who had been practicing even longer than Etta. He tossed the blade from one hand to the other, and the motion that followed was nearly as smooth. The turn of his blade took him partially out of her view, and Etta inched forward to see.

Her shoulder bumped a garment rack by the doorway, and something metal fell from its coat to clatter to the floor. Etta froze. Gideon's head snapped in her direction, his stunned gaze cutting into hers for one long moment before his expression shifted.

"I was... I just—" was all she managed before a wet, hairy beast knocked her to the floor.

CHAPTER 13

"Clara!" Gideon yelled, his footsteps pounding ever nearer as Etta tried to roll away from the dog. By the wall, the thing was unbelievably massive. It had to have had too much fur.

Etta had only half a moment to consider whether a dog could possess less fur without being more offensive before the clamoring beast was hauled off her.

"Down," Gideon commanded. The creature was led to another room, and Gideon was back at Etta's side, kneeling with a hand out, presumably to help her to her feet.

Flicking her hands vigorously, Etta moaned. "Why is she so wet?"

Gideon's mouth pressed together as he made a sound of what might have been chagrin but that could not be ruled out as a repressed laugh.

Etta narrowed her gaze at him, just in case.

If it had been humor, he managed a sober enough reply. "We go for a morning swim."

"We?" Etta asked, horrified.

He did smile then, if just a little. His face wasn't perfect, she realized. Up close, she could see that the bridge of his nose bore a small crook, as if it might have once been broken. And there, by the corner of his eye, was a tiny white scar, faint with age. His lips... no, they were perfect.

"We go," he said. "Clara swims."

"And then you practice swords. Every morning."

A hint of color rose to his cheeks. "Are you injured, my lady?"

Etta glanced down at herself, her fresh dress littered with hunks of wet fur. "I—" She looked back at him, too close, too concerned. He did not know who she was, not truly. But something in Gideon's gaze said that he saw her, that even if his eyes did not linger on her face, they connected with hers, the only recognizable part of Lady Ostwind that remained. "I wanted to say thank you for yesterday. And I-I only meant to get an early start."

Her voice was soft enough to encompass both shame and an apology, and Gideon simply nodded before he reached for her dog-dampened hand. He pulled her with him to stand. "It's early enough, indeed. You've time to run back and change into a fresh dress if you'd like."

Etta sighed. "I've only the two. Better make do as is."

His brow drew down. "I'll have the clerk issue your payment this week. You've done a few days' work already, and I'm certain he'll release just that if nothing else."

"Oh, I don't mean to make trouble. I've done quite enough of that already. I'll just wash up and let you get back to..." She glanced at the open space across the room where he'd been practicing.

"What?" Gideon asked softly.

She met his gaze, direct and sure, the way she might have done as Antonetta Ostwind. "Would you like a partner to spar with, my lord?"

OFFERING to spar with Gideon had been the most advantageous move Etta could have made. He'd been stiff at first, too careful, and she wasn't normally one for showing off, but it was clear he would not lean into the match until she'd proven her skill. One quick move had his sword batted aside as she sprang forward into his space, the tip of her own weapon hovering threateningly near the soft bits beneath his ear. His eyes widened almost imperceptibly when he realized he would have to back away to ready another strike. Etta did not give him the chance. She spun, pressed, and struck again, keeping him on the defense until he was backed against the dummy.

"My lady," he said mildly, "it appears I've underestimated your ability."

"That can be forgiven," Etta said, "as long as you hold back no longer."

The hint of a smile crossed his lips before he moved for her, and something in Etta's belly flipped. He was quick. Precise. A match to Etta in agility. But he had her in speed.

His technique was confined by his training, but Etta had learned countless fighting styles to prepare for the post as marshal. She relaxed into the motions of a style that fit his, and soon, it was as if they'd practiced together for years. Gideon seemed truly to be enjoying himself.

Etta relished it, too, the muscles she'd not used for days as she'd sat hunched over documents in a thinly padded chair, sighing with relief at finally being able to move. Nickolas had refused to spar with her on their journey despite his fancy sword, citing a fear of being trounced in front of the king's guard, but Etta suspected it had been more because she was the general's daughter. A misstep might have meant something different when a man had to answer to the head of council.

But Gideon had no idea. She was only Margaretta to him, a new assistant who seemed unnaturally skilled with a blade. And once he had warmed to her, his guard began to come down, the staid expressions and steady posture a show put on for all of Westrende. If she were to guess, he'd had to so the council and the others would take him more seriously. Because Gideon, it turned out, had quite the boyish grin.

"No," he said with a laugh at Etta's stories. "It cannot be true."

"It is. I swear by it, my lord. To this day, I cannot heft a sword without recalling the sound of that costermonger's oath as his fruit tumbled streetward at the hands of a girl no more than four. My first and only criminal act. I was given a tutor the same afternoon and warned that if I meant to wield a sword, I would without question know how to use it."

"My lady, I would never have guessed." Gideon drew his sword back, coming to rest as he shook his head.

Etta chuckled, flipping hers so that she might offer him the grip. "Enough for today?"

"Indeed. For there is much to be done." His eyes remained on her a moment longer, then he came forward, taking possession of the weapon before moving to stow them both away.

"And what are we working on this morning?" she asked as casually as she might manage.

The levity fell from Gideon's being. "Nothing so enjoyable as this."

Etta stepped closer. "Is it Lady Ostwind? Have they discovered where she might be?"

"No." He ran a palm up the back of his neck. "In fact, the entire ordeal has become more complicated."

Etta could not have stopped her sharp gaze if she'd wanted to, but she kept her voice low. "How so?"

Gideon's lips pulled down in a true frown that felt entirely appropriate as he picked up his chancellor's shirt. He glanced at her then gestured vaguely with the garment as he stepped behind a screen. Etta waited impatiently. One arm and a bit of his shoulder stuck out from behind the partition as he drew the thin white shirt over his head and tossed it aside. The muscles of his back shifted as he leaned forward to grab the fresh one, and an unexpected flush of heat shot through her at the sight of lean muscle flexing beneath bare skin. But the clean shirt was one of the slim black versions that he wore as chancellor, and she forced herself to look away.

Behind the partition, Gideon said, "This morning I received another letter, directly from the Lady Ostwind herself."

"So it's true," Etta said breathily in mock surprise, thinking that Nickolas had taken his time in delivering the letter. "She's really out there?"

Gideon stepped out to face her, still fastening the shirt at his neck. "I can't be sure. But the message says that she is performing her duty to the kingdom."

"Her duty?" Etta prompted, unable to let his consistent disbelief go unchallenged. Two letters from the lady herself. She didn't know what more the man could need—perhaps a vow before a king or a contract signed in blood.

"She claims to be hunting Lord Barrett's killer and says that she will prove her innocence when she returns."

"So she's coming back. Thank the fates. You should send a note to council. They'll want to cancel their plans to replace the marshal, posthaste."

His gaze cut to hers.

"Because she's coming back," Etta explained.

"We shouldn't be discussing this, my lady. Best we return to work. The both of us."

"But she must have the chance. If she can prove that it wasn't her, that all along she was pursuing justice, then she possesses just the sort of character the office of marshal requires."

Gideon's palm slid over his chest as if the very idea pained him, though perhaps he was only straightening his shirt. Perhaps Etta was spending far too much time examining his expressions and following his hands and attempting to force him to see the issues from a side he so adamantly refused to. Perhaps she should have knocked him out with a sleeping draft and spent the morning rummaging his files in search of the reports she needed.

Certainly, she should stop having thoughts of both kinds, unfit as they were for a marshal.

"If she returns, if she completes her task satisfactorily, then all will have been done fairly. I will stand by my word." He gave her one final look before gesturing toward the door. "You can trust in that, my lady, if nothing else."

Etta followed, forcing whatever else she might have said to stay on her tongue. The events of the last fortnight had thrown her off balance, and she'd forgotten her training. Fear had driven her to disobey her father's orders and return home early, and anger had seen her caught half-dressed in a public corridor with Nickolas. Emotion had failed her in her encounters with council, with Gideon, and with the fae who had set a curse upon her. She knew how best to play the situation to her advantage.

It was time she did so.

Gideon paused at the doorway to remove his officer's coat from the garment rack, and Etta glanced down at the bit of metal that had fallen earlier as it flashed on the floor. It was a signet ring, gold and garnet, and as she bent to scoop it up, she realized it did not belong to the chancellor of Westrende, despite that it had escaped a pocket of his coat.

Gideon glanced back at her, and she tucked the ring inside her boot, pretending to secure the lace. "Ready?" she asked, coming to stand just as he pulled the lever.

"I'll be right in," he told her. "I only need a moment to release Clara from her prison."

Etta gave him a look. "You say that as if she has not committed a crime against my person."

Gideon bowed his head, a hint of the smile he'd worn that morning flashing over his lips. "She seems particularly fond of crimes against your person, my lady."

Etta stepped closer. "An incident that does not need repeated to Jules, I trust."

His hand moved solemnly to his heart. "You have my vow."

CHAPTER 14

The door came open to a frowning Jules, arms crossed over her chest and eyes on her employer.

"Jules," Gideon said. "Good morning."

Her gaze moved purposely to Etta. "Is it? I wouldn't know because I've spent the last hour looking for..." Her words trailed off as she took in the state of Etta's hair and her fur-spotted dress. "I just had this washed."

Etta winced. "I'll clean the mess myself. It's not your burden."

Jules uncrossed her arms then reached past Gideon to drag Etta through. "It's not the burden I'm concerned about. It's the reputation of this office." She threw a glare over her shoulder at Gideon. "And what might happen to poor Clara if anyone realizes there's a dog terrorizing the entire wing."

At the sound of Jules's condemnation, a muffled whine came from behind the other door. But Etta was led to a small storage room, where she could brush fur from the front of her gown with a tool Jules apparently kept at the ready. Before the woman had a chance to scold Etta for taking off unannounced and interrupting the chancellor's morning routine, Robert came searching for Jules, and Etta was set to task with more busywork and a warning that Jules would quickly return.

The morning carried on much the same, and eventually, Etta glanced up from her documents to realize that the last time Jules had hovered nearby with an eye on her was much longer than it should have been. She stood, stretching her legs, then crept into the storage room to which Jules had disappeared, only to find it dark. Inching forward, she pressed the door wider to let in light from the next room. Tucked neatly between the shelves on a small, padded seat, Jules's petite from was curled so that her head rested against her knees, her back and boots holding her upright as she appeared to sleep. Etta stared for a moment, unsure, but a deep, easy breath lifted the woman's shoulders, so Etta eased out of the room.

Closing the door carefully behind her, Etta glanced about the main chamber. She'd been left alone, finally, for whatever brief span of time it might be. She did not waste it. Scouring the crates and cabinets, Etta searched for any sign at all of the investigations into the prospects for king. Not a single document was present in any of the places she might have expected, and when Jules—appearing as if she'd not just been taking a midmorning nap—returned from the storeroom to check her progress, Etta—appearing as if she'd not just ransacked the room—inquired about the filing system in any way she could.

The day passed with no progress in the matter, though, and Etta was beginning to suspect that the reports were locked somewhere she would not have access to. She was itching for progress in any matter, especially given how difficult it would be to return to her father's office since he'd caught her—or rather, Margaretta—behind his walls. When night fell, the chancery staff sleeping soundly with it, Etta could not seem to lie still in the narrow bunk of their dark room. She dressed quietly then sneaked into one of the smaller offices, where the castle guards might not catch her moving about after hours. Climbing onto the wide ledge of a window, she leaned against its cool glass and tucked her legs close to her chest. The night sky stared back at her, a sliver of moon warning that time was running out.

She'd wasted too many days already, days she could never get back. Whatever game the fae were playing, Etta's chances of saving herself were slipping from her grasp. She tugged the ring from the hidden pouch at her waist, twisting it in the dim light. It had fallen from a pocket of the chancellor's coat, she was sure. And yet she could not for the life of her understand why. Gideon had dealings with her father's office—a chancellor would sign and verify and file any number of documents a general and the council might need. But to have possession of another man's ring, a man who was head of the council and important to the kingdom... Etta could not make it make sense.

Without question, the ring belonged to her father. It had his colors, his insignia, and was a piece he'd worn for years. The general's name might as well have been inscribed upon it. How it had ended up among Gideon's things was a mystery.

Etta slid the thing over her thumb, unable to stop herself from thinking about the mystery that was Gideon. He'd been so stiff and formal every moment she'd worked across from his desk. But at play, Gideon had moved with easy grace, his eyes lighting with laughter, his usually stern mouth soft in a smile.

He didn't know this Margaretta well enough to trust her. He and Jules had barely left her alone since she'd come on staff. But when she'd stood with him after their swordplay, he'd confessed details about the lady Ostwind that made clear he was conflicted about giving Etta a chance. Why a stranger might have warranted repeated chances when someone well known in the kingdom did not should have been plain— because as he'd said, a marshal must be above reproach. But it felt like something more. It felt as if he'd not trusted her even before she'd returned.

Never mind that she had vowed to crush him before they'd even met. Whatever she was, Gideon was not. He was as straight-laced and by the book as they came.

Except for the ring.

Her finger idly spun the metal over her thumb, the starlight winking out as clouds moved overhead. Maybe she had been mistaken. But Gideon was entirely by the book—at least that much, she was certain of. She would have to complete his task by the next moon, as he had vowed. And he, trustworthy and loyal chancellor that he was, would have documents of such importance secreted away, where he would not have to worry about who he could trust not to find them. Etta needed a better way to retrieve the reports.

And she had just the plan to make it work.

A muffled *whuff* sounded from through the glass, and Etta glanced toward the courtyard. Among the shrubbery, Clara bounced, limned in moonlight as she darted to and fro, sniffing various topiaries before circling the choicest landscape. Beyond her, near the overhang of an upper-floor balcony, stood Gideon in his most drab robe. His hair was wild, his posture resigned, and he looked on at that horrible dog with nothing but devotion. She had to fight the smile that tugged at her lips.

"My lady."

The voice jolted Etta from her reverie, and she shoved the ring into her pocket as she turned. The voice belonged to a kingsman, one of the guards set to patrol the castle corridors in the chancery wing. The kingsman would report directly to Gideon.

"Best not to wander this late," he told her, his gaze moving slowly from Etta to the scene outside.

Etta stood, brushing a hand now empty of her father's ring over her skirts. "Of course. I'll get back to my rooms. Couldn't sleep, is all."

"Aye," he said. "Takes a bit to become accustomed to a new place. But you'll find your rhythm soon and settle in for the long years."

Etta could only hope not, but she gave him a smile then slid a piece of blank parchment off a side table on her way out of the room.

EARLY THE NEXT MORNING, Etta slipped the letter for Gideon in among a pile of others Robert had retrieved at dawn. Jules had returned her to Gideon's office to continue sorting the crates she'd started on her first day, under Gideon's supervision. When he opened the message, he made a strange sound that Etta assumed was an intake of breath, but she dared not look up, lest her expression give her away.

He stood, pushing back from his desk then crossing to the door. "Robert," he called. "Where did you pick up this missive?"

Robert came closer to examine the letter, mumbled something

about not recalling seeing it at all, then apologized profusely. Gideon disappeared into the main office for what must have been a quarter hour before he finally returned. He strode to his desk with such purpose that Etta let herself look up with an attempt at concern.

Gideon sat heavily, elbow resting beside the stack of unfolded messages, fingers woven helplessly through a mess of hair. His other hand pressed Lady Ostwind's letter flat, his gaze pinned to her words.

It was a request for the records she required in order to complete his task. A demand, more precisely, that he deliver them to her assistant by the authority granted her by council and kingdom. It had been written carefully in her own hand, signed by her full name, and sealed with the emblem from her father's ring.

It felt a little cruel to have done it as she watched from her seat across the room. But he'd left her with little choice. She stood. "My lord, is something amiss?"

Gideon raised his face to look at her.

"Is there anything I can do?"

He shook his head. Etta moved closer. He folded the parchment and slid it aside, though she did not miss that it became determinedly pinned by his elbow. The document that had rested beneath it on the stack was a standard recognition of title, nothing worthy of the look Gideon was giving it. His other hand smoothed his hair back into place with a single swipe.

"Thank you," he said. "But you're free to take the afternoon to assist Jules or..." He glanced up at her again. "You say—"

Etta stepped forward, only the desk between them. "What is it?"

Gideon's gaze slid briefly to the door. "You say that Lord Brigham is a family friend."

"Yes." Etta shrugged. "Can't be helped, I'm afraid."

He did not laugh.

Etta pursed her lips. "Is there something you need, in regard to Nickolas?"

"How well do you know him?"

"Well enough to know that he's mostly harmless, whatever your assumptions."

Gideon's shoulders straightened. "Right. My apologies, Margaretta.

I meant no insult to you or your family by voicing my concerns before."

Etta waved him off. "It's true, he has no sense of propriety when there's someone he means to charm. But his intent is rarely ill, and he has a good heart somewhere in there."

"I shouldn't pry."

"My lord, tell me what it is that you want to know."

Gideon sighed, leaning back in his chair to take the letter from Etta in hand. The parchment slid between his fingers as he spoke, his expression grave. "Can he be trusted?"

CHAPTER 15

Nickolas could not be trusted with state secrets, but Etta hadn't been about to confess that when he was the only ally she had. Instead, she'd convinced Gideon to deliver a set of highly confidential reports regarding the prospects for king, as the Lady Ostwind had demanded. And so, on Margaretta's day off, she sat on a chaise in Nickolas's suite, pouring through reports while the rake of ill repute paced nervously before her.

"You said the letters were all. You said you'd involve me no further."

She did not look up, as they'd been having the same conversation for the past hour. "You're not involved. I just need your suite for a few hours. Leave if you want. Go out with that pack of beasts you call friends."

He flopped onto the chair opposite her. "I call you a friend. And here, you're the beastliest of all."

Etta had fallen silent in her reading, and Nickolas sat up. "Antonetta," he said. "What's wrong?"

Her face had gone pale, she knew, but she couldn't manage to play it off as nothing. She'd paged through dozens of reports, accounts of how and when the prospects had fallen ill, been involved in regrettable accidents, and suffered a host of general misfortunes. But suddenly, the investigation had taken an unexpected turn in the form of an unlikely connection to a single individual.

Etta met Nickolas's gaze. "What do you know of the prospects for king? The investigations."

He shrugged. "Only rumor, and a bit about the interviews. My mother and that lord—what was his name? Richard? Randolf?" He shook his head. "The marshal had called them in to inquire whether they'd witnessed anything suspect at the winter ball."

"The ball?"

Nickolas leaned forward, his elbows resting on his knees and his fingers laced. "Yes. The eldest of the prospects had taken ill that night. Apparently, no one else had symptoms of anything outside of a bit too much punch."

"You were there?"

"Of course. I go every year. Wouldn't miss it."

She wet her lips. Took a breath.

"Etta?"

She stared at him, hating that she had to ask. "Was my father present?"

Nickolas's brow shifted. "I don't—yes, I suppose. He usually is."

"You've heard nothing else?"

"Saints, what is it? The face you're wearing is utterly—" His words cut off at the realization that the face she was wearing was not hers at all. His voice dropped. "Your expression, is all. I meant your expression."

"Paper," she demanded. "And your best quill and ink."

Nickolas gestured toward the writing desk against the wall, a grand station that appeared to be little used. "My best is all I have. You're welcome to it."

He leaned closer, and Etta snatched the reports out of his view. She had the irrational urge to toss them into the hearth, but it would do little good. The words on them had already passed from the marshal's hands. And besides, if Gideon discovered that she'd destroyed kingdom property...

"By the wall," she whispered, her grip on the documents going limp. "That's why. It's why he's never trusted me. It's why he has the ring."

Nickolas stared up at her.

A helpless laugh escaped Etta's chest, ending in something of a sob. "Do you know what this means?" Not only would she have to redeem herself. Etta would have to clear her father's name as well. If he was branded a traitor, she would never receive her post.

"I do not know, as I have reminded you twice. What did you find, Antonetta?"

She marched to the writing desk. "It means you'll need to deliver another letter." And Etta would be sneaking back into her father's rooms.

THE GENERAL OF Westrende was many things, but incautious was not one of them. Traps had been set in every conceivable manner at every single access point surrounding his office. The number of guards had been increased, and only a portion of them were in uniform dress. At various positions throughout the corridor were men and women who appeared to clean, to be on their way to some other destination, or simply to be in conversation while standing conveniently in view of his rooms.

If she had been the betting sort, Etta would have placed the king's jewels that her father had told no one why he had organized the additional guards. But she was not the betting sort, and she knew her father well enough to know that the presence of so many kingsmen meant he was nowhere near his office. He would be in his rooms, and anything of real value to him would have been removed to his private vault.

She walked past a pair in cleric robes as they discussed in great detail the tapestry that hung on the opposite wall. Each glanced at her, eyes skirting her face in evidence of the fae glamour doing its work. The general's office was several corridors away from his private rooms, and with evening came the lull of activity between dinner and lights out. The halls were quiet, the few passersby seemingly uninterested in what Etta was about. It helped, no doubt, that she'd borrowed the uniform of a maid—one that she had no interest in knowing why Nickolas had on hand.

Etta's father would be in his study at that hour, the same as always. Etta would not be attempting to stroll anywhere near the place. The glamour might prevent him from recalling her features, but she could not be sure he wouldn't recognize her again, particularly if he was waiting for the return of a young female intruder. He was, surely, or he would not have loosed so many kingsmen in the corridors outside his office.

Head down, she entered the staff areas where those responsible for care of the general's wing gathered. Etta had been away for several years, but turnover was slow, and she would still know most of them by name. With a stranger's face and an Ostwind's knowledge of their own rooms, Etta would be able to get close enough, under the guise of performing staff duties, that she might slip unnoticed to the place where her father kept his most prized possessions. She might get close enough to find her way into his chambers and the vault in which he kept things he meant for no one else to see.

She fell into step with a pack of footmen, picked up a bucket along with a group of maids, then shuffled behind a slender woman who was deftly trimming wicks and preparing rooms for the evening. Eventually, Etta was at the door to her father's sitting room, one short evasion away from the bedchamber and the vault. But as she waited for the other maid to turn away, Etta sensed movement on the opposite side of the room.

Her eyes tracked a shadow at the base of the wall near the wide fireplace, and she watched as the shape skittered into something unnatural. Etta shifted, pretending to wipe dust from a chair back as she followed its movement. It darted toward the far door, a cackle of glee erupting from the creature as it disappeared, impossibly, beneath the narrow strip between door and floor.

The maid glanced at her as if she had made the noise, but the woman's gaze skirted the glamour on Etta's face. The woman stood for a moment, as if having forgotten herself entirely, before finally returning to the task still in her hands. Etta moved closer to the door but froze when muffled voices sounded on the other side. Heart in her throat, she listened then swallowed a curse. It was her father, not in his study but in the room just beyond, a small private space that connected his suite to the one that had been her mother's.

No one should have been with him in that room, not when he'd sealed his wife's chamber from their own daughter.

Etta could not help herself, as unsafe as it was, as much as she risked. Her feet moved closer, ears pricked to pick out the second voice. It was male. Smooth. Measured in word and tone. Not at all familiar.

Etta leaned closer to the wood, her palm pressing against it while her feet remained well away from where the shadow had slipped through.

"No," her father said. "That will not do."

The other man was silent. There was a sound too light to be certain of, and Etta's ear found the door next to her palm. *Paper.* It was the sound of rustling paper and... something else. She could not be sure what.

"I refuse." Her father again.

And the other. "Tell it, then, to the prince."

The prince. The words were a sword that cut Etta down the middle, half of her pinned to the door, the other half falling into that pit of dread and despair like so many stones her father had tossed to the bottom of a deep, dark well. She couldn't settle on a response. He could not, would not, be standing in the next room with a fae.

He was the general. An Ostwind. It was impossible.

Etta leaned back, her palm coming from the door to slide down the bare skin of her neck. The choking sensation might have been fear or anger, but she could not let it out. She could not let herself be caught. Fingers trembling, she glanced at the maid, but the woman had moved to another section of the room.

Beyond the door, Etta's father said, "And for that, you would give me your true name?"

The other voice was quiet a moment too long.

Fae, Etta's mind screamed. *It's because he's a fae.*

"A name has more value than your question implies."

The general made a dismissive sound. "Many a name would." At the noise that followed, Etta imagined her father stood. "But not yours."

Etta's racing heart froze. He could not have been fool enough to challenge a fae. But the thought was more foolish than his action. Etta's father was a general, battle trained and with an army at his back. Etta's father was the one man who might have been able to stand against all fae. Except he never had, not for her and not for her mother. He had all but vowed he never would.

"You," a voice called from inside the room, and Etta turned, feeling the blood drain from her face as a footman in the doorway stared her down. "What are you about?"

He clearly had no idea the general was inside the next room, or a kingsman would already have been summoned for her eavesdropping. Spying on a man like the general would amount to treason.

Behind the doorway, Etta's father—the highest official of Westrende—made a deal with a Rivenwilde fae. A bigger crime, she could not imagine, aside from maybe poisoning a king. In a muffled tone, the fae spoke his side of the bargain, revealing his true name.

Etta straightened to face the footman. "A mouse."

He gave her a look.

"I thought I saw one, but.... Possibly, I only feel faint."

There was surely a more believable excuse somewhere, had Etta's mind the space to spare it, but the man only flicked a gesture that ordered her to him. He was not a small man. She supposed she could take him, but things would go much better for all involved if she could talk her way out of it. Lying was admittedly not one of her stronger skills. Shoulders dropping, she crossed the room in the least confrontational manner she could manage.

He guided her by the upper arm into the corridor. "Wait here."

Etta wondered if the face she wore looked like enough of a half-wit to lie in wait for her punishment, but she did not say so. "Of course." She clasped her fingers before her waist, head down in meek remorse. The footman strode away, likely to get a higher up and have the snooping maid who'd lingered by a restricted doorway removed from service. The book she'd come for would be permanently out of reach. Worse, her father was... had just... saints, she couldn't even think it. Her hand slid into the pocket of her gown, beneath the borrowed apron, and found her father's ring.

It was cold and hard, and so much like the truth she'd just discovered. She wanted to be sick. She wanted to turn around, stride into his rooms, and... she had no idea. But she would decide once she faced him.

Down the corridor beyond her came the echo of a quiet *snick*, and Etta glanced up in time to see a tall, dark figure exiting through one of the barred doorways to what had been her mother's rooms. The man strode away without a single look in Etta's direction, but his form flickered as his glamour revealed itself to her sight.

It was the fae who had met with her father, the fae for whom Etta had overheard a true name.

Something wild rose from her stomach to her chest, and she was moving before good sense could stop her. The maid Margaretta had no weapons—staff caught in the general's rooms with a blade would bring a far swifter response than what the footman had delivered—but Antonetta Ostwind had not been trained with sword alone. She crouched to the floor and reached inside the general's doorway to retrieve a drapery brush from the maid's supplies.

Etta's steps were silent and swift, her moves a graceful dance, her palms curved firmly around the brush as she snapped it in two.

The fae had not heard her coming and only glanced back at the sound of snapping wood.

Its jagged edge was at his neck before a lick of magic had risen to strike, Etta's words a whisper against his ear from behind him as she invoked his true name. He stilled, and she warned, "If I scent a bit of power, if you make one single flinch, so help me, I will bleed you out right here on this priceless carpet, even if your screams cost us both our lives."

Her words were a vow, and the man beneath her was as silent as a statue. Etta was not certain he had even drawn breath.

"Why were you meeting with Ostwind?" she whispered. "What business do you have with a general of Westrende?"

She felt his jaw shift in a smile. "I know who you are, Lady Ostwind. There is no need to pretend with me."

Etta pressed the stake harder against his flesh. "If you know who I am, then you know I speak the truth. Your life is worth nothing to me. Less than nothing, for it would bring me great pleasure, in fact, to rid the world of every single fae." She punctuated her last words with a deeper press of her makeshift weapon. Had it been any less dull, his blood would already have spilled. It would have been a far slower death than with a dagger, but she could not make herself care. The fae had taken everything from her, and if that was not enough, they now meddled with Westrende's general.

"Every life is worth something." His voice was calm, but Etta felt the truth in it. He believed he had something to give.

"Tell me, then. You know what I want. You know what they did to me."

"I cannot tell you that."

"Then you have nothing for me."

She braced herself, but the fae said, "Wait."

Her hand stilled, trembling, eager to be through with what would have been an especially unpleasant task.

"I cannot tell you what I am bound by edict not to speak."

But that did not mean he was bound not to speak at all. Etta had little idea what to ask of him, aside from whatever business was between Rivenwilde and her father. She didn't know what good an answer would do if she had no valid question. She would not waste the risk of a bargain if nothing useful would come of it. "Tell me what it is that you cannot speak of."

He laughed. "That would give the very game away. Do not ask me what you have asked already. Nothing of kings and princes, nothing of generals, but anything else."

"How do I cross the wall?"

"As with any curse, speak his name, and he will come to you. The price he gives, once paid, will return what you once called yours."

She yanked him closer. "I am not fool enough to fall for that." Summoning a fae prince into Westrende was a sure way to end up regretting all she'd ever done. But the words were an echo of the painter, and while Etta may not have been able to ask a bound man what deals her father had made or what precisely the fae was about, it might gain her the power to ask it of another, someone closer to the curse that obscured her true face. "The painter."

Beneath her hold, the fae tensed.

Etta's mouth flattened into something of a grim smile. "Give me his name." The man did not respond and did not move for so long that she began to wonder if he *had* turned to stone. But he was only considering, giving thought to the bargain in the unhurried way so many fae adopted. "Time is almost up. It is this or it is nothing. His true name for your life."

A slow breath released from the form beneath her, and with it, a single word: "Elsher." As if that breath were a wind, the bargain made, the figure of the fae was gone with it, his hair sifted through her fingers like sand, his flesh no longer beneath her weapon. There was nothing but the girl who had once been Lady Ostwind, holding her broken shard of wood.

Nothing but a curse and a faceless maid who had possession of a fae's true name.

CHAPTER 16

Etta returned to the chancery wing well past dinner to find Robert quietly reading, Tobias methodically sorting a jar of buttons, and her roommate sleeping facedown on a narrow bunk. Jules had left a plate of bread and fruit beneath a thin napkin on Etta's bed. Etta sat heavily beside the plate and unlaced her boots before carefully dropping them to the floor. She'd rinsed her hands in a basin before returning, but the sensation of fae magic still felt too recent. She brushed her fingertips lightly over her face. The shape of it was the same as ever.

The bird watched her from its cage, so Etta pinched a hunk of bread from her roll and tossed it through the bars. The animal did not seem hale, but she wasn't about to stick her fingers inside to find out. It pecked at the bread as any other bird might have, and Etta went back to undressing. Likely she was too tense for sleep, but the only way she might sneak off alone was to be up well before dawn.

Lying back on the bed, she let the fae name repeat through her mind. Come morning, she would say it, dagger in hand, and Margaretta, the assistant, would have one chance to win back her true life. The lady Ostwind was ready.

Hours before cockcrow, Etta bolted upright in bed, her chest heaving with sharp intakes of breath. The room was dark as pitch, and no amount of blinking could erase the images of the fae from her nightmares. She grappled blindly for her clothes, not bothering to attempt donning them until she made it to the corridor. Were she to run into any guards, they would just have to accept seeing her in a shift because waiting—or waking Jules—was out of the question. The dreams had made Etta feel trapped and alone in a way she'd not felt since she was a girl pinned by fear beneath her childhood bed as the prince and his men took her mother.

With shaking hands, she tied the dress snug to her form then stepped into her boots and laced them carefully. In her left pocket was her father's ring. In her right palm, she held the dagger she'd taken from Nickolas's rooms.

He would be delivering another letter for her at dawn, one for the chancellor from Lady Ostwind herself. With any luck, Etta would have more than a single fae name. She'd have answers. Evidence. A way to get free.

She strode down the corridor, toward the most isolated and insulated storage room nearby. Not a single guard found her on the walk, but should one hear a struggle once the fae had been called, as a staff member, Etta could easily claim she'd been dragged from her rooms and that the man was trespassing on chancery property. He would be arrested. An iron-barred cell, she decided, would be as good a place as any to keep him until she had a way to prove who he was.

Edicts were not an easy thing to unwind—otherwise, she might use the power of Elsher's true name to force him to confess. But the prince's power would supersede such a command. Etta would have to ask of the man something he would be free to give.

She lit a taper, carried it into the storage room, and placed it on a narrow ledge before she locked the door. The key went into her pocket opposite the ring, and she took one slow, deep breath as she adjusted her grip on the dagger.

Do not speak their name, her father's voice said. *Speak of them, and they will come again.*

Back against a wall of shelves, Etta whispered, "Elsher."

THE FAE FORMED like the shifting of shadow. The candle flame guttered then swelled, throwing light over the flesh of painfully familiar shapes. Dark, hollow eyes stared back at her from beneath a sharp brow. His hair was mussed—not from sleep, Etta thought, but as if he never bothered grooming it into a style. The same scents of orange oil and musk rose from him, along with smoke and roasting meat.

His mouth slid into a hard line, his gaze never leaving hers. "Lady Ostwind. How good of you to ruin my night."

She held the blade forward. "I call you to bargain. A true answer in exchange for your life."

He scoffed. "My life belongs to another. Good luck winning it back."

She tipped her chin toward the door. "Your freedom, then, for without that trade, you cannot escape."

He crossed his arms and scowled. "What business have you with me? I no longer possess your trade. I'm bound in more ways than either of us could count. There is no threat you might offer me that others have not already."

Etta flicked the dagger tip to his chest above his crossed arms. A gold button *tinked* against a jar on the shelf beside them, and the fae gasped in outrage when he realized she'd cut it from his coat. She raised a brow. "What is happening between the prince and my father?"

"I cannot answer that. I am bound."

"Why has he come for me? Because of my mother? Because we can see?"

His arms dropped to his sides. "You think so highly of yourself. A great Ostwind, as lofty as your father."

Another button clinked off the shelf then clattered to the floor.

He huffed. "Call his name if you want your answers. I have nothing for you."

"We both know I cannot do that." Not until she had the upper hand—any hand, even a stake in the game. The dagger shifted in her grip. "Why you? Why not him? Why not face me himself?"

He turned up a palm. "I have a talent for glamour."

"And the prince knows I can see. Was he testing you or testing me?"

Elsher chuckled.

Etta moved closer.

He held up a hand. "You're wasting time for the both of us, Antonetta. Might as well get some sleep." He leaned in. "The sands are spending. Best to enjoy what days you have left."

A weight settled in the pit of Etta's stomach. "What do you mean?"

His mouth twisted into a cruel smile. "Did you think the curse had no limit? That you might live forever in this state of in-between?"

"There's a clock? You told me nothing of the sort."

He shrugged, sliding a hand over his chest where the row of buttons once was. His brows drew together as he picked at a loose thread. "Why should I? I left it right there for you to see."

She stuck the tip of the blade to his chest, not gently.

He glanced up at her.

"Tell me," she ordered, "in plain words."

"The painting, of course." He reached into his pocket and drew out a bright-red apple. He tossed it into the air, but Etta did not catch it. It smashed onto the floor, cracking open to splatter bits of pulp up his trouser leg and Etta's skirt. He frowned. "That was all the fruit I had with me. There's no call for—"

His words cut off as her dagger slid from his chest to the soft bit of flesh beneath his chin. "You're still here."

"Yes," he managed despite the clearly uncomfortable angle of his head with a knife at its base. "That one was free."

"Because you were meant to tell me days ago, when you first set the curse."

He did not respond. Etta swore.

"There is nothing more you can ask me tonight," he told her. "Why not just let me go?"

Etta's dagger inched higher. "You have given me nothing." It meant she could call on him again, whenever she wanted. But if she did, the next time, he would be ready. "What does the prince want with Westrende?"

A sound like a laugh moved his chest. "That is no secret, either."

"And yet, somehow, no one here seems aware." She jerked the blade away from his jaw.

His depthless eyes met hers.

"What does he want with Westrende?" she asked again. "Why us?" Her mother, her father, and Etta herself... it could not have been a coincidence. "Why does he send his men here to meddle and curse while he sits so easily on his throne? What is his goal?"

Elsher's teeth flashed in something that was not a smile. "Why, to unrend the kingdoms, of course."

Etta's insides went cold. She unlocked the door and set the fae free. With the bargain unmade, he would be forced to walk back through the castle grounds, into the forest, beyond the filigree wall, and past the Rive, the ancient boundary that had split the kingdoms in two.

Unrend, Elsher had said.

Fates protect us all.

She strode through the chancery corridors, fuming that the fae had done her so wrong. She'd not been warned of a clock on her curse and had no idea where the painting might be.

"Why, I left it with you," he'd said when she'd asked. "As part of the curse, it will never stray far."

All along, it had been right there, beneath the guard of the chancery. It had found its way there as evidence, no doubt, in the case against whoever would be blamed for the death of Lord Barrett.

The corridors were still dim as she slipped between one office and the next, on watch for patrolling kingsmen. Dawn light had not yet begun to peek through the widows when she finally came into the records room where Tobias spent so many of his hours, toiling away. Stepping past racks and shelves, Etta held her candle high.

A canvas-covered easel stood among stacks of crates and boxes. She crept forward, hating the fear that crawled over her skin. She knew what was beneath the drape of fabric, even before she reached to pull it down. But once she did, the fear grew worse. The portrait that stared back at her, though it was hers, was not the same as it had been the week before.

Narrowed eyes glared out from a face that had lost all hint of the hopeful expression Elsher had painted into it. Instead, the visage spoke of vengeance. It held a horrid sense of loss, anger, and a fruitless desire to undo what could not be changed. The hidden fox now showed its teeth, its shadow long in spiky strips of black. The ship in her hair had sails that appeared weathered, and the goose was missing patches of feathers. The ribbons laced through Etta's mouth remained, as if tying her from speaking—of what, she didn't know. From revealing fae secrets, perhaps, or from convincing a soul of who she truly was.

Etta moved nearer, standing so close that she might have reached out to brush her fingertips over the paint. But she did not touch it, not when she could not pull her eyes away from the apple in the figure's hands.

Young and hale, the painted fingers cradled their prize in the way they'd done before, but instead of the bright, shining shape it had been when Etta had first seen it, the apple was dark, withered and rotting, its skin and flesh decaying even as she watched. The paint was crazed over its surface, fine cracks spreading from it like shattered glass.

It was her clock. And time was running out. When the apple was gone, so would be Etta, snatched across the Rive as a prisoner to the fae and their magic, never to see the light of day again. No one would ever know what had become of her.

A sound echoed from the main office, and she glanced up, surprised to find that dawn light was rising in a gray haze through the windows. Having no idea how long she'd stood mesmerized, she blew out the flame of her candle then set the holder on the floor at her feet. A tendril of smoke rose between her glamoured face and the more familiar one on the canvas.

Easing a hand around the grip of her dagger, she stepped closer still. The portrait seemed to pulse with magic, with the strange sense of falling, as if she stared into the depths of a well and she might tumble weightlessly in at any moment.

She knew what waited on the other side.

Etta drove the blade into the canvas, her loathing for the fae and their curse pushing her to destroy everything they had ever done. She would shred it to ribbons and burn the remains. The dagger cut effort-lessly through the paint and cloth, but the magic was not destroyed. Heat worse than any pain she had ever felt seared through her arm. She stumbled backward, knocking into a crate before her back hit a sturdy shelf.

Palm wrapped about her forearm and eyes on the painted girl in the marshal's coat, Etta slid helplessly down the shelf to sit on the floor. Her feet splayed out before her as she stared at the portrait, Nickolas's dagger on the floor beneath it, and morning light shining through the slice of canvas in the center of the figure's arm, just where Etta's own arm was flayed and bleeding.

A gasp sounded from the doorway. Tobias, stock-still, watched in horror. Jules was suddenly beside him, her hand on his shoulder and her quiet assurances in his ear as she pressed him aside.

Once the boy was gone, Jules rushed to kneel at Etta's side.

"Let me," she murmured, prying Etta's fingers away from the weeping wound. Jules winced, made a sound of dismay, then followed Etta's gaze to the portrait of Lady Antonetta Ostwind. An unusual expression—too quick to make out—crossed Jules's face. In a blink, her attention was back on the wound. She tied a handkerchief tightly around it and urged Etta to her feet. "Come now. We need to get this washed and stitched. Hurry," she added, and Etta tore her gaze from the portrait to truly take in Jules. "Before anyone else comes and tries to make a fuss," she said, as if the justification made any sense at all. Someone would absolutely make a fuss. Lady Ostwind's portrait had just been stabbed, and Etta was bleeding all over herself.

"There goes another dress," Etta said numbly as she stared down at the mess.

"Come," Jules said again.

Etta did go, if for no other reason than she couldn't stomach one more moment in the presence of the portrait. But before they left the room, Jules crossed to the easel and tossed the drape over the canvas once more. Without a single look at Etta, she kicked the dagger beneath a shelf. When she returned to Etta's side, Jules spoke not a word of what she had done but only led Etta from the room.

SETTLED on a low bench in a quiet storeroom, Etta stared at the narrow gash that crossed her arm. It still felt strangely hot, not unlike the stinging cuts and scrapes the lesser fae had given her as a girl and, more recently, in the forest outside the kingdom borders. Jules wrung a cloth out over a basin before pressing it to the wound with a click of her tongue.

"You aren't going to ask what happened?"

Etta's tone had been cagey, but Jules's reply was subdued. "We all have our moments. If you had wanted to tell me, then you would have."

Etta watched the gentle pressure and graceful movements of Jules's practiced hands. There was something too delicate and deliberate about it, something very unlike the girl who fumbled scrolls and napped like a drunken sailor. "Where did you learn to care for wounds?"

The pressure from Jules's ministrations stilled, but only for an instant. One of her shoulders shifted in a shrug. "I had a half dozen brothers growing up. One was always in a tumble of one sort or another."

"Where are they now?"

Jules's gaze met hers. "Would you like to discuss our pasts, my lady?"

"No," Etta answered truthfully.

"Something else, then?"

"Do you mean the lady Ostwind?" Etta asked.

Jules's eyes went back to her work. "If you wish."

"Yes," Etta said after a moment. "I would like to talk about Lady Ostwind."

Jules tugged the needle through Etta's arm and tied off the first suture.

Etta released her gritted teeth to ask, "Why does the chancellor hate them?"

The needle missed its mark. "Them?"

"The general and his daughter. He's pitted himself against the family, has he not?"

"My lady," Jules started, but Etta cut her off.

"The truth would be helpful."

A strange quirk tilted the edge of Jules's lip before her mouth went into a thin line. "And yet you're the one who drove a dagger though a portrait of an Ostwind."

"It's hideous."

Jules made no reply.

Etta shoved a loose lock of hair behind her ear with the arm that wasn't being prodded. "The chancellor believes her a criminal. Unfit for office."

Jules worked in silence for a long moment. When she finally spoke, her tone was careful. "Gideon wasn't raised in the way a person might expect."

She cut another suture, one more in a very neat row of small, close ties over a dark line that made Etta's stomach turn. Etta had seen blood often enough, but it was somehow worse when a wound was formed by magic. Worse still was to know that anyone might cut her in two just by slicing up a cursed bit of canvas.

Jules said, "He had to work very hard to get where he is."

Etta bristled. "Every Westrende official works hard. They give up everything just for the chance."

The needle stabbed a little fiercer into Etta's arm. "Some start with much less and lose much more."

"His uncle is steward. His mother captained a ship. He'd have been raised in luxury, with the best training." She frowned. "It's not as if a man like that has ever missed a meal."

Jules gave her a look. "You truly don't know?"

"Know what?"

Jules wiped a towel over the skin surrounding the wound then shifted the bowl of supplies out of the way to settle beside Etta. "Lord Alexander was raised by his mother's cousin. His parents were gone before he'd turned one and ten. He may have possessed the title of lord, but a sailing mother and a military father did not make for a stable home life. Once they were gone, their estate was seized by an uncle on his father's side. Apparently, Gideon's parents made no arrangements to protect their sole heir. I take it there were a few years where he struggled in ways difficult to imagine." She gave Etta a pointed look. "Ways that he refuses to discuss. The relative who finally took him in was a clerk of sorts, an assistant to the magistrate. He was in need of a strong set of arms, most likely. He was a... difficult man, by all accounts. But with time, he became something of a mentor to a young boy who had no one else. When one has very little, any scrap of security can feel a great deal more valuable than it appears on paper."

Etta had known nothing of the sort. Only sparse bits of information had reached her at school, and Nickolas had clearly left out the most pertinent facts.

Jules folded the cloth into a neat square. "Two years back, that man was killed."

Killed. Not died. Murdered. Etta's voice was barely above a whisper. "How?"

"He happened across information that cost him his life." At Etta's intense look, Jules shrugged. "Something he reported to the magistrate. An investigation followed. The evidence disappeared before charges could be brought. It was all very hushed." She stood.

"Wait—"

Jules bent to pick up the bowl of supplies and tossed a gauzy wrap to Etta. "That's all I know. But had you given the man a chance, you would have found that our chancellor has reason to operate on such a hard line."

"I don't—it's not about giving him a chance." It was impossible to defend her situation, not when she was meant to be Margaretta, family friend of Nickolas Brigham, who had no higher connection to the Ostwinds or the law. "I only wanted to understand and to see that the lady was treated fairly, given her own chance."

At the door, Jules gave Etta a fleeting glance over her shoulder. "My lady, you will not find a man more honorable than Gideon Alexander."

CHAPTER 17

E tta awoke with a splitting headache and a stinging throb in
her arm. After washing up the night before, she'd fallen into
bed, but no amount of sleep could undo what she had done.
Jules served her black tea and fresh biscuits, but her sympathy did not
extend far enough to release Etta from the day's work.

She had so much to do, not the least of which was to find a way
across the wall without calling a deadly prince. Whatever business the
fae had with her father, whatever was behind the misfortunes of the
prospects for king, those tasks would have to wait. Etta's time was
running out. She had to break the curse.

"More sorting and filing today," Jules said over an armful of scrolls,
"in the chancellor's office."

"Right." Etta rose to her feet without a single swear at the fates
that had her tied to a job when she had more important things to do.
She needed to find a way free of the chancery's watch, and it could not
wait until her next day off the following week.

She tugged her dress back into place, making certain the gauze
covering her wound was well hidden. As her mind rummaged through
potential plans to retrieve her father's book and possible questions she

might trade the fae whose true name she held, Etta strode through the main office with her head held high.

Her feet stumbled to a halt when a shadow crossed her path.

Etta gaped, and her hand moved automatically to her waist. But she wore no blade. Around her, time carried on, as if not a soul was aware of the danger they were in.

Hurrying past with a stack of boxes, Robert bumped into Etta's shoulder then stopped to apologize. "I didn't see you." His gaze followed hers. "Oh, my lady, this is the clerk, Eldon. Have you not been introduced?"

A pair of dark, hollow eyes rose to hers. *Fae*, Etta's mind screamed even as the man offered her a wicked grin.

"No, Robert, the lady and I have not been formally introduced. Though I've heard much of her."

Etta's mouth snapped closed. She managed a single, sharp nod. The fae's gaze remained on hers, the face beneath his glamour as plain as pikestaff in the well-lit room. His true form was wild and beastly, despite the drab robe and neat haircut the others would see.

"My lord," Tobias said from across the room, "the delivery you asked about has just come in."

The fae's attention shifted to the boy. "Ah, yes. Thank you. I'll be on my way." He inclined his head to Etta. "My lady."

Her feet were moving before he had a chance even to gather his things. She would not stand in the middle of the office when it was clear he meant to move past her. She shot into the chancellor's office and slammed the door behind her.

Gideon glanced up from the rack of bound documents he'd been searching. She crossed the distance in a few long strides, grabbed hold of his sleeve, then yanked him with her around a tall shelf. She glanced at the closed door then shoved him another step back to peer around the corner, watching.

"Margaretta." Gideon's tone was firm, chiding, and more than a bit confounded.

Etta spun, covering his mouth with a palm and making a hushing sound before she could think better of it. His eyes went wide, and she snatched her hand back. They stood in silence for a moment, Etta's heart racing and Gideon by all appearances baffled. She grabbed hold of him again, this time by the wrist, and drew him through the door to the room where they'd sparred.

The latch no more than clicked behind them before the massive head of a sleeping Clara snapped up in attention. She was on her feet, coming at them so fast all Etta had time to do was turn and grimace. The dog slammed into Etta's back, shoving her into Gideon's front and knocking them both against the closed door in her excitement. Gideon's hands were on Etta's waist as if by instinct, steadying her before his fingers shifted into a softer grip. Etta was still, her entire body pressed to his. Her cheek brushed his neck as the dog danced against the pair enthusiastically, Etta's pulse still racing hard from her encounter with the fae, and Gideon surely having no conceivable idea what she was about. His throat moved in a swallow. His fingers flexed. Etta dared not look at him.

"Clara," he finally commanded. "Down."

The dog did not sit down. Instead, at the sound of her name she wriggled closer, rapturously licking toward Gideon's cheek with her paws heavy against Etta's back. She held her arms rigid. Fighting a creature was all well and good, but she could not deal with... *this*.

Letting go of Etta's waist, Gideon reached past her to shove the dog away. Etta pressed her face into the crook of his neck to avoid a hot, wet dog muzzle from becoming intimate with her nose and mouth. When the beast snuffled her ear, she made a sound of distressed revulsion, and Gideon spun the pair of them so that Etta's back was to the door and he could settle Clara down.

Etta watched, shaking her arms in an attempt at composing herself as Gideon led the dog to the next room and shut the beast inside. He stood at the closed door, his palm on the wood for a very long moment before he turned suddenly back to Etta, apparently having recalled that something had gone wildly wrong.

"The clerk," Etta explained. "Eldon. How long has he been on staff?"

Gideon's brow drew together. "What has that to do with—"

"How long?" Etta stepped forward then froze before moving back once more to press herself to the door. She couldn't decide which might be worse, if the fae man were to come through after them or if he stood outside, listening. There was no way to know where he was.

She rushed toward Gideon, pulling him by the arm as she moved to cross the room. He was apparently becoming accustomed to being handled, because he followed without dispute as Etta led him to a cabinet and wedged them both into the narrow space behind it.

"What has he been doing, this Eldon? What work has he shown interest in? And who did he replace?" By the wall, first, the fae disguised as her painter, then the one meeting with the general, and now, a third posing as clerk. It was as if they'd infiltrated the entire kingdom while she'd been away. The memory of Lord Barrett's body in a dark pool on the polished floor made her stomach turn. It was impossible to say how many other men they'd done away with to take their place.

Gideon's expression made clear he had no idea what she was on about. Then, softly, he asked, "My lady, has the lord done something to you, acted in a way that has made you feel unsafe?"

Unsafe was precisely how Etta felt. The fae had taken residence inside the castle and maneuvered themselves near positions of real power. She didn't know if she would ever feel safe again. "Yes," she said. "But not how you think."

Etta couldn't let Gideon accuse him of anything that she might actually have to prove. No one could see through fae glamour but her, and unless the clerk had left a trail of whatever bad things he was up to, an investigation would only reveal that Margaretta was not a real person, that she and Nickolas had forged documents and inserted Etta into the very office of the man she had accused. Her head hurt. Her wound throbbed. The magic on her skin tingled hotly, sharply. Fae brazen enough to lay a curse on a general's daughter was beginning to seem the least of Westrende's problems.

Gideon's expression had gone deadly serious. He made to reach for her then apparently thought better of it. He stepped closer, despite that she was near enough to hear his heartbeat—though that might have been her own. Saints, it was too warm behind the shelf. Maybe she could crawl out of a window.

Gideon's voice was low. "I understand that you might be hesitant to say. But whatever he has done, my lady, it will be handled discreetly."

Etta ran a palm over her face. "Do not remove him. Do not tell him I've spoken a single word against him, please. I'll handle it. I just need..." Time. She needed time, and she needed the cursed fae to give her a break.

Gideon gave a swift nod. "Whatever you need, it is yours. But until then, you're to stay at my side."

"What? No."

"I insist, my lady. If he is a danger to you—"

"What about Jules and the others? Will you have the entire chancery constantly at your side as well?"

"Jules is protected."

Etta's protest drew up short.

Gideon apparently had no intention of explaining the remark. He took hold of her elbow. "I've a meeting, in fact, if you'll—" His words cut off at her wince, and he glanced down, finding the edge of gauze that peeked from beneath her sleeve.

She tried to jerk her arm away, but Gideon held fast. He slid the fabric up to reveal the bandage. His gaze met hers.

"It wasn't him. Saints, I only cut myself, that's all. It's nothing."

"Etta." His voice held the edge of something painful. "This is not a minor wound." His fingers hovered over the bandage, the fabric wrapped as wide as his palm. She had the sense he wanted to tear it away and see what hid beneath. He looked at her. "If you're in trouble, you need to tell me so I know how to help." His gaze was intent.

Etta tugged her arm from his grasp. "You can help me by saying nothing of the clerk and by letting me go about my work as if this never happened."

"I can do the first. The second is not negotiable." He glanced at the light through the windows. "I'll be late for my meeting. Come along, and bring something to take notes. It needs to appear that you are needed."

Etta pressed her fingers to the bridge of her nose, refusing to consider what her life had become. "Where are we going?"

He straightened, adjusting the lay of his chancellor's coat. "To the council chambers. I've a private meeting with General Ostwind."

"General Ost—" Etta's words cut off as she realized she was speaking to Gideon's back.

He refused to hear her objections, walking away from her as if she were a dog meant to follow.

She did follow.

"I've received another letter from Lady Ostwind," he said.

When he turned to look at her, Etta had to force the expression from her face. She'd forgotten about the follow-up letter she'd sent with Nickolas.

Gideon's voice dropped. "You might as well know, now that you'll be privy to the general's complaint."

"His complaint?" Etta whispered.

Gideon picked up a bound book from his desk. "He hasn't taken well to the knowledge that his daughter has been in contact with a mere chancellor more than she has him." He handed her a book of blank pages for her to note whatever of import was said.

"Of course she's written you," Etta said. "She has a task to complete."

He turned to stride toward the office door, and at his gesture, Etta followed. She took a hasty extra step to catch up to him.

"Lady Ostwind is very driven, is she not?"

As he passed through the doorway, Gideon gave her a sidelong glance. "I suppose that's one way of putting it."

"How else?" Etta asked. "How would you put it?"

Gideon did not answer, his attention on the room. Searching for the clerk, no doubt. The man had no earthly idea that he'd been working with a fae all along.

"He's gone out," Etta said coldly. "Something about a delivery."

Gideon minutely adjusted his stride, but only a fool could have missed that he was suddenly walking shoulder to shoulder with her like a kingsman on guard. He gave a small nod to Jules, whose surprised gaze tracked them crossing the room, but Gideon made no explanations. He didn't have to. He was the chancellor.

They stepped through the wide entrance doors into a busy corridor, and something dipped in Etta's gut. She had to get out of this. There was no way she could sit in a room with her father and—fae glamour or no—he not realize that she was the girl he'd seen in his office.

She considered faking an illness, but one look at Gideon's dark eyes subtly searching every face in the corridor made clear he would not let it go. She didn't know what she'd been thinking. She never should have asked him about the clerk, not when Jules or Robert or any of the others would have given her whatever they knew without risk of—whatever this fresh abyss was.

Training had given her the tools she needed. She'd been in Gideon's presence for more than a week. She knew what would make him respond. There was nothing she could offer to stop him outside of something more urgent than his meeting with the general. Something that would be important enough to tempt him to break his word.

Something that would allow her to kill two birds with one stone.

"I can give you information about General Ostwind."

CHAPTER 18

G ideon stopped in his tracks.

"It's something of great import to the kingdom"—she hesitated and lowered her voice—"with regard to the wall."

He took hold of her elbow and ushered her into a lesser-used corridor, waiting until no one was in sight before speaking again. "What are you saying?" They were face to face, his hushed whisper barely echoing off the walls.

"I can show you. I can give you evidence, but it has to be now—while the general is occupied with council business."

Gideon stared at her, the cogs clearly turning in his mind. "You're asking me to—" He shook himself, apparently unable to even think it. "This goes against my every duty, the very order of precedence."

Etta leaned closer. "The marshal hasn't managed it. You know that. He's had years to uncover secrets. What's he done? Filled your office with useless reports?"

Gideon's eyes narrowed. "I knew not to trust Nickolas Brigham."

"Enough already with Nickolas. He didn't show me the reports. What is your problem with the man, anyway?

"He's a rake and a gossip and apparently trades information for..." His angry hiss cut off at Etta's expression.

She inched closer still. "You think I would be so easily fooled? That I would fall apart over a few pretty words and a man who did nothing more than give me his gaze?"

Gideon was petulant. "I've seen it happen."

Etta crossed her arms, furious that he was still on about the scene he'd caught in the hall. "Truly? You'll judge him so harshly when you yourself were pressed up against me not a quarter hour ago?"

His face went pale, guilt washing every feature. He didn't know she was Lady Ostwind. He thought she was a member of his staff.

"My lady, I—" He made as if to reach for her then snatched back his hands. "You have my sincerest apologies. I never meant to—if I have made you feel uncomfortable..." He frowned. "Of course I have. I've put you in the worst sort of position, and I'm sorry. I vow that I'll never again—"

Etta held up a hand. "Please. It's been clear since the moment we met that you're not the sort to become impassioned enough to cavort in a public corridor. I doubt you've ever been infatuated in your life."

He stared at her dumbly.

Glancing at the connecting corridor to be certain no one might overhear, she said, "I can show you." Her gaze came back to his just as color rose in his neck. "The general," she snapped. "I can show you what I meant about the general."

Gideon took a step back. "My lady, I think we need a moment to... No, I'm already late to the meeting. Let's go. We can discuss this later." Giving her a look, he added, "Maybe." He shook his head, as if to dispel the thoughts that must have been racing through it.

Etta reclaimed the distance he'd made. Facing her father would be a disaster. She would be arrested and thrown into a cell, offered no chance to break the curse before time ran out. She needed to give Gideon something he wanted. "Trust me with this," she vowed, "and I will tell you about the clerk and what happened to my arm."

She had him. She could see it in his eyes. As chancellor, he had to discover if his clerk was a danger, and Etta knew he bore a great distrust of the Ostwinds. Two birds, one stone.

"No," Gideon said as they stood outside the general's private suite. "Absolutely not."

"Would you keep it down?" she hissed. "If we get caught before we have the evidence in hand, not even a chancellor will be able to talk his way out of it."

"Do you understand how many laws you're about to break? Have you no shred of decency or, saints protect us, self-preservation?"

Etta blew out a long breath. "I do not have time to debate this. If you care about the kingdom at all, if you have any loyalty to your post and to your mentor, you'll do this. You'll see what I have to show you, and you'll understand things you wish you'd never known."

"My mentor." His tone was level.

"Jules told me. I can see now why you don't trust the general. He does look guilty, after all, does he not?" When he didn't reply, Etta glanced back at him. She was being a bit crude, but there wasn't a moment to spare. "You believe he's behind all of it—that he wants to keep his position as head of council and that someone you cared about was killed for getting too close to the truth." Etta swallowed hard, praying that whatever evidence the chancellor had already gathered was false, that it had been put in place by the fae to make him look guilty. But if her father truly was involved, she could not save him. No one could, not if he'd bargained with a fae prince for the security of Westrende. "You think that General Ostwind is responsible for what's been happening to the prospects for king. We are paces away from the truth. If you follow me inside, I'll give you what you need. You have only to trust me." She placed her hand on the lever to her father's room. "And if not, then I suppose you'll just have to ask our current marshal to throw me in a cell to rot."

Before he had time to respond, Etta opened the door and stepped through. A relieved breath slipped from her as she saw the lavish room was empty. Had there been a kingsman on guard or even a maid present, she'd no idea what might have happened.

As it was, Gideon was trying desperately to snatch at her gown and drag her back. "Etta," he demanded.

It only made her feet move faster. She had needed him in order to get closer to the general's rooms unsuspected, but he was only a liability moving forward.

A low oath escaped him as they entered the general's bedroom,

Gideon's entire posture making clear that he could not believe he'd allowed himself to come so far. But Etta worked quickly, rolling the edge of carpet up beneath the bed.

"Help me with this," she said, shouldering the weight of it to slide the secret floor panel aside. It wouldn't budge, so she raised up to rummage through the items in her father's nightstand while Gideon knelt at her side.

"You have to stop," he said.

Etta found a comb and tried to pry up the board. It wasn't thin enough. She turned to Gideon and yanked one of the metal bands from his coat. As he reached for it, clearly hesitant to grab her bodily after the conversation they'd just had, she shoved the metal between one plank and the next and levered the wood up with the weight of a forearm. Before Gideon had changed his mind about taking hold of her, Etta had opened the vault and was reaching inside among her father's things: a master key, private letters, and an ancient leather-bound book.

Gideon made a sound and shifted backward, but Etta could not focus on him. Flipping through the pages, she nearly crowed when she found the passage she was looking for. No time to celebrate one small victory when her battle had just begun. She turned to face Gideon, both of them kneeling on the floor beside her father's bed. She would have to be fast, but the look on his face said she'd shocked him enough with the fae-marked book to gain a moment's head start.

"Trust me," she said. "You do not want him to know how you've found this. Speak nothing of me, of Margaretta, or you'll look as guilty as the rest of us in the eyes of the law."

His mouth opened in question, but in one fluid motion, Etta stood and tore out three pages before tossing the book to the floor at Gideon's knees.

She was running before she'd taken another breath. The bedroom door slammed behind her, and she turned the key, but she wasn't free —inside the sitting room was a footman, his shocked gaze swinging to hers at the sound of the door. She didn't waste time by confronting him but took the shorter route to her mother's rooms instead of the exit. The footman gave chase then rammed into the door as Etta shut it behind her. Her father's key was already in the lock, and she was on her way to the next room. She had seconds before the call went up. Kingsmen were everywhere inside the castle and on the grounds, and one alarm would be all it took before she would have nowhere to turn.

She burst into her mother's bedroom, the sight of it after so many years knocking the breath from her, but Etta could not stop. She had no time for memories, only action. Only to flee.

The last door hadn't been opened in ages, and she had to shoulder into it hard. Tumbling into the corridor, she glanced frantically toward the entrance to her father's suite farther down.

It was not a kingsman who stared back at her but Gideon, eyes dark, knuckles white with their grip on her father's book. He moved, and Etta ran as fast as her feet would carry her. She reached to hike up the length of her skirts then vaulted over a railing and into a memorial gallery scattered with giant pale sculptures of dead heroes of Westrende.

"Margaretta," Gideon called from behind her, "stop, or I will sound the alarm."

His voice was too close, his footsteps coming too fast. He was going to catch her. If he did, she would never get free. Ducking beneath the carved hooves of a rearing horse, Etta glanced back. Gideon was only paces away. Beyond him, past the gallery rail, strode a line of kingsmen—the general's personal guard.

Etta cursed, spun around a statue of a man holding a sapling and a massive sword, and darted toward the courtyard. Bright light shone on delicate topiaries, and dappled shadows scattered the path. She leapt over a bench, through a trellis of roses... and ran face-first into the chancellor of Westrende.

His arms slammed around her, caging her, and momentum nearly knocked them both to the ground. Too many footsteps sounded on the paths beyond the greenery, their cadence that of soldiers on the run. She was done. It was over.

Etta stared up into Gideon's eyes.

"Margaretta," he said softly.

In reply, Etta whispered the only word she could find. *"Elsher."*

IREEN
CHAU

CHAPTER 19

The fae shimmered into existence through the shifting shadows of a willow tree, his fingers midway through fastening the buttons of a fine silk coat. He glanced up at Etta and cursed. "Must you," he said drearily, "always?"

Gideon was so startled that his grip eased, but only for a moment. He pushed Etta behind him. She did not know what he saw, because the fae in question had been masquerading as the now dead Lord Barrett.

She didn't bother to ask, shoving past Gideon to address the fae. "Help me escape."

Elsher glanced at the flashes of red and black though the trees, uniforms of the soldiers who would soon be upon them. "No."

Etta stepped closer. "Get me to the forest, and I'll relinquish your name." At his narrow look, she added, "If you do not, I vow to call on you every hour of every day. You'll have no more time than to return home before my words will drag you back again."

Beyond the trees, one of the kingsmen barked a command.

"And I'll likely be calling you to a damp, dreary prison cell," Etta said.

"You are a menace," he growled.

"Then end it. Help me."

His gaze roamed the courtyard then briefly shifted to Gideon in his fine uniform coat for a once-over. Etta opened her mouth to refine her terms, to shout, "only me," but Elsher tossed up a hand.

"Done," he said with a self-satisfied smile.

Etta's protests went unheeded, and a heartbeat later, when she was rolling across a bed of moss, the fae man's chuckle vibrated through her despite that he was nowhere to be found. She cursed, coming to a stop flat on her back, limbs splayed. It wasn't a heartbeat more before Gideon tumbled after—thrown a little harder, it seemed, though Etta's body worked well enough as a stop.

She grunted when his form collided with hers, knocking a huff of breath from his chest on impact. He lay atop her for a moment, evidently stunned, before his face rose from its nest among the material of her bodice. His eyes met hers. He blinked.

When his senses returned, he scrambled backward, but Etta only groaned.

He froze, midway to his feet, to stare at her. "Are you hurt?"

She pushed up on her elbows to look at him then purposefully shifted her gaze to the surrounding forest. Gideon, apparently still stunned, took a moment to follow her indication. He stood slowly but did not entirely straighten, perched among the ferns as if in a ready crouch.

"There it is," she muttered at his realization of their surroundings. She shoved up to stand. He would be a minute, processing the idea, she assumed, so she glanced down at herself to check what might be amiss. The gown had come through their tumble well enough, but one foot was bare and sinking into the blanket of soft earth and moss. Searching the ground they'd crossed, Etta moved to fetch her missing slipper. When she picked it up to shake out the hunks of greenery, she glanced again at Gideon. "What did you do about the general's footman, anyway?"

He made no sign of hearing. Etta pulled the folded pages from the pocket of her skirt. Her father's guards had either seen their chancellor running after a faceless girl who'd escaped the general's rooms and had assembled in record time, or they'd been lying in wait for another attempt. She wondered what the general thought of his intruder and whether he had any idea that what Etta had said before was true—she was his daughter—or if he suspected she was just part of another fae ruse, aiming to manipulate whatever bargain he had made. It was very possible she'd avoided both time in a cell and torture. To the last, he would refuse to acknowledge that it might be her.

She supposed the truth would be harder to discern without the gift of sight, but it didn't make forgiving him for what he'd done any easier.

"What... just... happened?"

"Ah," Etta said, not glancing up from the papers. "You're back." She held a hand in the direction of the castle. "You'll need to walk that direction and quickly, and do not stop to touch any animals or trees. Keep your face up, eyes on the sun, and should you find yourself turned around, start again. Do not shout for help until you're clear of the trees. It's important."

Etta felt his stare.

"I'm sorry," she said. "You don't... well, I won't say you don't deserve this, but you have my sympathy nonetheless. Just go, and do it quickly."

"Are we in the greenwood?" Gideon's voice was a croak.

He turned slowly, and Etta could not help but glance up at him.

His tone rose, words slow and wavering. "Is that *the wall*?"

Etta waited until he looked back at her. "Yes."

He rushed to close the distance. "I do not understand what happened, but we need to go. Now."

She sighed. "That's exactly what I was trying to tell you. Go." She gestured in a shooing motion, but Gideon did not move.

"My lady—"

"We have little time, either of us, and you're not going to like anything I'm about to do. Please, my lord, run from these woods and do not look back."

"I can't leave you here."

Her eyes pressed closed for a long moment. She truly wished she had her sword. "Oh," she said, reaching forward to draw Gideon's from the sheath at his side. "This will work."

He stared at her.

She held firm on the sword in case he decided to attempt taking it back. "I'm protected now, and you've some sort of dagger or something on you, I'm sure. Best we part ways and you return to the castle before General Ostwind thinks you're in on the... whatever this is."

He was silent for a long moment. "Have you lost your mind?"

"My face, in fact. Please go."

His expression hardened. "Margaretta, I do not know what is happening, but I refuse to leave you alone *at the wall*."

She strode past him. "I assure you, you do not want to stay at my side."

Standing square with the wall, not near enough to sense its magic, Etta drew out the notebook Gideon had given her. She etched a decent copy of the image beneath the glamour the wall projected—the section where she would make her attempt—then scratched out a hasty note for her father so that he would know what had become of her, should the worst happen. She ripped the page free of its binding, folded it deftly, then passed it to Gideon, who'd moved beside her.

"For General Ostwind."

Gideon had been watching her work, his gaze moving slowly from Etta's profile to the words, and his eyes met hers. Recognition fought with the confusion in his expression. She had forgotten the hours Gideon had spent studying the handwriting of Lady Ostwind.

"It was you," he said. "You forged those letters so that you could— what? Deceive me into handing over the investigations and reports? Are you some sort of foreign agent? Or are you working for someone inside of Westrende?"

"I realize this is a waste of breath, but here it is. Those letters were not a forgery. The face I'm wearing is. It's a curse set upon me by the prince of the fae—" A little rumble of magic swelled beneath Etta's feet, and she swallowed hard, lowering her voice. "You've been deceived, as has the rest of the kingdom. The fae walk among us, and they're closer every day to committing an unspeakable crime." She would not bring the word "unrend" to life, not so near the wall. "If no one else will protect us, then it falls to me."

"Margaretta," he started, but her look cut him off.

"I am not and have never been Margaretta. There is no Margaretta.

I'm Antonetta. An Ostwind, the very one you claimed unfit for the position of marshal. My handwriting looks like Lady Ostwind's because I'm her. And not you, not my father, not one fool person in the entire kingdom will hear me out or come to my aid." She jabbed a finger toward the wall. "I am Lady Antonetta Ostwind, and I'm going to go through that wall to steal back my face. I'm going to end whatever foolishness is keeping the council from recognizing the truth. I'm going to do whatever I can to save myself and this kingdom." She leaned nearer, her grip tightening on the sword. "I dare you to try to stop me."

THE SPEECH HAD DONE LITTLE good to convince Gideon of anything, but Etta felt better for having said it. She turned to face the monstrosity of twisted metal masquerading as a beautiful stone work of art. Behind her, Gideon muttered something, but she had decided to steadfastly ignore him so that he might go away. The moment he was out of sight, she would perform the magic to open the wall.

"An-ton-etta," a low voice spoke in a menacing sort of singsong, and Etta knew right away that something had gone horribly wrong.

Sword raised, she spun to find, standing casually among the brush and briars as if it were the topiary gardens Etta had just left, *him*. The prince of the fae, as real and solid as any man. He gave her a wicked, terrifying grin.

She stepped back, her heart in her throat. "I did not call you."

The words were only a breath, barely more than a whisper, but the prince had heard. "Indeed," he said amicably. A long-fingered hand gestured coolly toward Gideon. "He did."

Etta's gaze snapped to the man in question. Gideon stood, gaping, the note to her father held loosely in his hand. Opened.

"You read my private letter?" she accused, outraged. Had he not been in shock, she imagined he might have said it was evidence in an investigation, that it was his very duty to discover what it said. As it was, she could not help the incredulous question that came out of her instead, because she could not fathom how such a thing had happened in the first place. *"Aloud?"*

The fae prince chuckled. "Fortuitous, was it not?"

"You can't," Etta warned the prince of Gideon. "He'll not bear it." Even as she spoke, it seemed as if the man's very being had been broken, stunned into a monument by what he was witnessing like the figures that rose from the wall. But Gideon was still flesh. Gideon would have to return to Westrende. He would *know*.

The prince shrugged. "It's not for me to decide. The curse was laid upon all of us, Lady Ostwind. He'll have the sight now, same as you."

Hatred ran through Etta at the reminder and at the way he bit out her name, as if the very taste of it... well, as if he found her as distasteful as she did him. He stared back at her, not hiding that distaste in any way. *You*, his look seemed to say, *are the cause of all that has happened. Everything.* He was too spindly, his hair too long and his figure too finely dressed. He seemed to tower over her, just as he had when she'd been a girl on the floor of her room, even though a good bit of forest floor separated them and she'd grown taller. The prince was as powerful as ever, and his sharp features and finely embroidered coat seemed to scream the reminder that he was royalty. His very posture seemed to want to force her to kneel.

Her hand tightened around the grip of Gideon's sword. Etta had not forgotten what the prince had done.

"Will you not ask me of your bargain, then? What trade I would accept to return your precious life?"

Etta gave him precise directions to a dark and torturous abyss.

His jaw flexed. "Very well. Your time will run out soon enough. Until then, I'll have my fun with your..." His gaze shifted to trail over Gideon in his uniform coat. "Oh, I see it's a chancellor. How lovely." To Etta, he spoke the aside, "Haven't collected one of those yet."

She stepped forward, sword at the ready.

"What does he mean?" Gideon's voice was level. Apparently, he'd processed at least some of what had happened. Etta couldn't be certain that was for the best.

"They've been supplanting kingdom officials," Etta said, not taking her eyes off the prince. "Lord Barrett was killed so that the painter could be replaced with a fae. To curse me and—" To the prince, she asked, "What? Why come for me when I had not yet been installed as marshal?"

A hum purred in the prince's throat. "If you do not know the answer to that, then mayhap you shouldn't have been vying for the position after all." He *tsked*. "A competent marshal would have figured us out ages ago, would they not have?"

CHAPTER 20

Etta rushed the fae prince, sword raised to strike. She was going to drive the blade through his heart and be done with their games, once and for all. His slow suffering would gain her nothing. The prince needed to be gone as quickly as possible. It all had to end.

He didn't move to defend himself in the least but let a small smile lift the edge of his lips. Etta swung. The blade glinted.

She was knocked to the dirt with a force that took her breath. Staring up at the sky, sword jarred free of her grip and flung onto the forest floor, out of reach, she could only blink in shock. Her blade had not touched the fae, and his magic had not touched her. She'd been foiled by... saints, she could not believe it.

"What are you doing?" she roared at Gideon, who pinned her bodily to the moss in an expert grip.

A chuckle came from the prince. Gideon said nothing at all.

Etta struggled beneath him but made little progress with anything other than sinking deeper into the soft earth at her back. The prince sauntered closer, his steps slow and easy as he took in the pair of them, candidate for marshal and uniformed chancellor tangled on the ground at his feet like a pair of wild animals. "It seems all of Westrende understands something you do not, Antonetta." He crouched a man's length away from them, forearms resting on his thighs as his gaze burned into hers. "No harm may come to the Rivenwilde prince."

She raised her head to glare at Gideon. His gaze was on hers, decidedly refusing to give it to the prince of the fae. Gideon could see him, though—she knew that. The same sight she had would have been gifted to him the moment he'd called the prince's name, the moment he'd laid eyes on the man. Gideon would know. Gideon would see Etta for who she truly was.

Gideon had still stopped her.

Her head dropped to the earth, and she uttered a groan.

"You're not going to query me," the prince said, "because you know what I will ask in trade."

Etta closed her eyes. She did know. She'd known all along. She knew something else too. The fae could do no harm to a Westrende king. It was why they had kept one from coming into power, the ancient laws only safeguarding those who held a throne.

"The choice is yours, Lady Ostwind. Give me Westrende, and I will return all that you have lost."

Heartbroken, some ignoble part of her buried deep inside wanting to scream "yes, please, anything, just bring her back," Etta told the prince of Rivenwilde, "Not even if it was naught but ash." The prince had spent the better part of her life taking everything that mattered, and he could not be trusted with the one thing she had left. "Westrende will never be yours."

"Well enough," he murmured. "I'll take it on my own." He stood, tossing a speculative gaze toward Gideon. "Should you change your mind, you know how to call me." Then he strode away, whistling as if he'd not a care in the world, the eerie tune still echoing off the trees long after he was gone.

"Get off of me," Etta complained as Gideon watched the wall—through which a man had walked—aghast. She suspected he was seeing the truth of the fabled structure, the way it writhed with magic, the forms rising from its surface as if trapped for all time. His grip loosened in his apparent shock and dismay, and she was finally able to shove him off.

He rolled to his hip beside her, and she wriggled her legs from beneath his.

"Well, you've ruined any chance I had of sneaking in. Thanks for that."

Gideon's attention snapped to hers, roaming her face with an examination so careful it made her feel too seen. She wrapped her arms over her middle. His gaze followed the motion, catching on the gauze that poked from beneath her sleeve, gauze he had beheld on Margaretta's arm only hours before.

"That's right," she muttered. "Still me. It's been me all along."

Gideon was chancellor—he would be clever enough to understand what had transpired. That didn't mean it would be easy or particularly expeditious for him to adjust.

Something shifted in the shadows of a tall oak, and she reached for the sword. "We should go. It will be dark soon."

Gideon dragged his attention from Etta to the woods, where he would be seeing—for the first time—low spiky shapes moving through the shadows with unsettling speed and all-too-eager playfulness. "What is that?" His voice was low, cautious enough to make clear he understood the danger the things posed.

Etta pushed to her feet, readying his sword. "Lesser fae."

"Lesser—" One darted from behind a tree to a bush nearer where they stood, and Gideon reached for his sword.

"No, you don't." Etta jerked it out of range. "You may spar well enough, but these creatures give no quarter. You're not about to learn how they move for the first time in a forest full of them."

Gideon pressed his palms to his eyes then blinked hard, as if he might do away with the sight if he just tried hard enough.

"You'll get used to it," she told him. Used to the sight, but not used to the truth of what he was seeing. That never got any easier. "Now, come on."

She strode forward, and Gideon hurried behind her as if he meant to catch up. With a quick dodge at the last instant, he reached around her and snatched the sword. He did not need to remind her that the weapon was his, but he did anyway. She went for him. He jerked his sword arm from her grasp, so she reached beneath his coat and wrapped her hand around the grip of his dagger. Their gazes held for one long moment before she pulled it free, and for another moment after that, but they did not speak a word.

They made it nearly an hour before the first attack. Gideon, not surprisingly, was unprepared for the unnatural way they moved. It was as if the shadows rose to life, agile forms springing from the dark hollow beneath limbs and brush in one instant then clinging to their victims' chests in another. He swung at the thing stuck to him, trying desperately to get a good strike despite that it was pinned against him, its viciously long claws sunk into fabric and flesh. Two more made their attempt, taking no interest in fighting with honor, and a larger furrier beast hovered just outside of range, his dark gaze on Etta.

She wished she had a sword.

Etta drove Gideon's dagger into a small creature that leapt at her back, rolling out of its path and toward the others that circled his feet. She came up from beneath one, getting a swipe in at its haunch, then missed the other completely. Gideon's boot knocked against a felled tree, and he stumbled, but Etta's outstretched hand reached past the creatures that clung to him just in time. He grabbed hold of her forearm, steading himself, then turned his body so the beasts were not between them. In one swift move, Etta reached around to stab the thing beneath Gideon's raised arm. It screeched and fell, then with two more swipes from Etta's blade and a wide swing of Gideon's sword, the lot of them darted away to regroup with the others in the trees.

Gideon's gaze had followed, and it stayed on the larger beast as it stilled to stare back at him. He and Etta stood, pressed together. When night fell, the forest would come alive, breathing with ill intent, its magic more free in the darkness. If they didn't make it out before then, that hulking thing would be the least of their worries.

"Keeping your distance is key," Etta told him. "Once they're on you, they're too fast and wily to fight."

Gideon stared into the trees, his chest heaving. Wordlessly, he handed Etta his sword.

Her breath came too quickly, in something of a laugh. She passed him the dagger. "Come on. If we don't give them a chance, it raises ours."

"WE'VE ALREADY PASSED this section of forest," Gideon said hours later.

Etta shook her head. "I know how to get us out of here. We can't turn around now."

"Night will fall soon. We need to stop and get our bearings. This cannot be right."

She frowned. It was far later than she liked, but they'd no choice but to go on. "Trust me."

"Trust you? You've done nothing but lie to me from the start."

"Of course I lied to you." She gestured wildly in an attempt to encompass all that had gone wrong. The gesture fell sadly short. "As if you would have accepted any form of the truth."

He could not argue that, despite how clearly he wanted to.

"My apologies that you feel betrayed. It's not as if you haven't called me unfit for office, accused me of a crime I didn't commit, of being a fraud, of being a spy... shall I go on?"

"I was going to have you arrested."

Her gaze snapped to his. "Me and my father both."

Gideon's mouth went hard.

"Right," she said. "Because you still may arrest him."

"You handed me evidence against him."

Etta's own mouth tightened. Her evidence wasn't all Gideon had. There was only one reason he would have possessed her father's signet ring.

They walked in silence for a long moment, their attention on the forest.

"What deal did you make with the fae?"

Etta stopped to face him, her grip tightening on the sword. "None. They set a curse upon me. I gained nothing from it." At his look, she relented. "I have made trades. The last, you saw. The painter who appeared as Lord Barrett. I gave his own name to escape my father's guard." She waved a hand dismissively. "He wasn't meant to drag you along. Before that, I traded another his life in exchange for the painter's true name. That's all."

"That's all," he repeated incredulously. "Only a few trades with the fae and some... existing relationship with the prince of Rivenwilde."

Etta slapped a palm over his mouth. "Do not speak his name."

Gideon narrowed his eyes on her. He reached up, closed his fingers slowly about her wrist, and drew the palm from his lips. They stared at each other.

Something squawked in the trees, too near.

"Go," she told Gideon, and he did, keeping hold of her as they ran.

COVERED in scratches beneath tattered clothes, they came out of the trees just as the sun dipped beneath the horizon. It was fully dark by the time Etta had led Gideon along the routes she'd learned as a girl. He'd given her a speaking look at her ability to bypass castle security, but after she'd saved him from being trapped in the greenwood overnight, he likely would have followed her anywhere.

Once they were inside the castle, Gideon seemed to become aware that their hair was woven with twigs and their clothes shredded to rags.

"Jules is going to murder me," Etta grumbled when she saw him looking. "It will be refreshing for someone pleasant to try for once."

"We can't be seen like this." His words were quiet as his gaze darted around the corridor.

Etta crossed her arms. "You mean you can't. Because it would be unseemly for one of your station." She pointed toward her face. "I'm just a lowly assistant. I'll be fine."

"You won't be fine. You're a fugitive by now, and I at the very least will be wanted for questioning." His worried gaze snagged on a shadow in a doorway down the hall. He rubbed his eyes. "Tell me that's a dog."

"I thought you wanted me to stop lying."

Gideon pressed his eyes closed hard. He sounded a little sick. "How many of them are running around the castle?"

She made a face as she considered whether her breaking it to him there or his finding out on his own would be worse.

Gideon watched her, seeming to take in the direness of the situation for a moment before his expression shifted to into pure mortification. "Is Clara…"

Etta patted his shoulder. "No. She's just habitually wet and unwieldy. But don't trust any that you do not know. Sometimes, if the light is right, they'll catch you off guard."

"This is why—that first day in the chancery, when she leapt on you unsuspecting…" A tremor ran through him, not unlike the shaking Etta had done.

"I'd like to tell you it will get easier. But it won't."

The sound of approaching footsteps echoed down the corridor, and Gideon pulled Etta with him into a darkened alcove. "We can't walk into the chancery like this. Not when the kingsmen were chasing us hours ago."

It had been a bit more than a few hours, and her father had likely posted kingsmen at the chancery entrance, but Etta didn't have the energy to quibble. Instead, she let him lead her through the lesser-used corridors to the courtyard that connected to his rooms.

As he closed the door behind them, he took her hand, guiding her through the darkness to a small study where he placed her atop a settee. She could barely make out his form as he moved through the windowless room, his steps sure in the familiar space. He lit a candle then placed it on a table to retrieve two more. The room came to light to reveal rich polished wood, close walls lined with bookshelves, a small desk, and only the one settee. He moved one candle to the table beside her then the other two opposite the settee. Shrugging out of his ruined coat, he gestured that she wait.

Etta leaned against the cushions with a sigh, kicking off her slippers and vowing never to wear anything but boots until the fae were no longer in existence. She was too tired to go through his things, despite that a fine inlaid box atop his desk promised to hold something interesting and the many books on the side table would reveal what he read in his private hours. She loosened the tie of her dress, just a little, and found a gaping hole down the side. She would have to burn the whole thing before Jules found it.

Gideon returned with a basin and pitcher in one hand, a plate of food in the other, and a bundle of supplies beneath his arm. He spread them out on a low table then scooted it closer to the settee.

Apparently having washed as he retrieved the basin, his shirt sleeves were rolled up to reveal clean forearms and hands. Etta took the soap from him to begin on her own while Gideon retrieved a decanter of water and a finely made cup. Once filled, he held it up.

"I've only the one."

Etta could not be made to care. She dried her hands, drank deeply, then handed the cup back, brushing off her nails and rinsing her arms a second time before drinking again. Gideon had collapsed onto the cushions by then with rye bread and a piece of fruit. When the nectar dribbled into his wounds, he leaned forward to wipe them on a towel.

"Here," Etta said, taking his arm to examine the cuts. "Those need tending."

He tugged it back. "You don't have to."

She drew it to her again. "I do. Elsewise, you'll have to explain them to someone." She turned his palm over, tracing a fingertip up the inside of his forearm with a wince. They did not look pleasant. Leaving his hand resting on her thigh, she leaned forward to riffle through the supplies he'd brought in. Setting several ointments and tonics aside, she chose a small amber pot of salve.

"They'll only burn the first few days," she told him. "But make sure you keep them clean. They've a bad habit of carrying on unless they're tended well."

He watched her, sleeves tugged up to her elbows, carefully applying salve to each of his wounds. "How are you not covered in thousands of these?"

A humorless laugh escaped her. "I learned early." She glanced up at him. "I was very young when I first saw the prince. It seemed to incite something in his beasts whenever I looked at them. I don't recall being attacked once before I saw them for what they truly were. Once I did, though, they were relentless."

"It's part of the curse," Gideon murmured as if remembering what the fae prince had said.

He flinched when she touched a particularly deep cut, and she leaned closer, examining the wound to be certain nothing remained inside. "He calls it a curse. We call it the Rive. The thing that binds the fae, that holds them beyond the wall... it keeps us from seeing them as they truly are."

"Until we set eyes on the prince."

Etta nodded. "Only him. The book we took from my father's vault says the thrones of the Riven Court and that of Westrende were tied in the bargain that created the Rive. It's my belief that the protections he's afforded, the edict that the prince of the fae must not be harmed"—the brief look she shot him was only partially an accusation for what he'd done in the clearing— "is why whatever keeps the others from seeing falls away in his presence. We must know it is him. We have to be given the chance to see the truth." Lest a misstep be made.

"I am not sorry for stopping you," he said of Etta's attempt at skewering the prince. "But I confess, when I opened your letter, it was as if the word called for me to speak it. It was not my intent and I do not do such things, not here."

He was right. Etta had sat across from him in his office for days. He'd never read aloud from anything that had crossed his desk. She shrugged. "I likely would never have made it back through in any case. Desperation rarely leads to success."

Gideon blinked. "You were going through the wall."

"I told you as much."

He swallowed. "I didn't think... I mean, of course I understood that someone might get through. I was aware there was a process of sorts. But I didn't—I don't think I ever believed. Truly." He gave her his gaze. "I would have stopped you."

Etta grinned. "You would have tried."

"Saints," he breathed. "This explains why my new assistant was so good with a sword."

The reminder settled unpleasantly upon Etta's whole being. The curse would end soon. It was time to accept that it was over, that she'd lost her chance and would need either to surrender to it or find someplace to hide until the apple rotted through. Every comfort she'd found since her return would be stolen once more. "I suppose there's no point in returning to Margaretta now."

"I don't know," he said quietly. "Her company was growing on me."

The statement threw Etta so off balance that she stared openly at him.

Glancing up at her through his dark lashes and with a flash of that boyish grin sneaking over his lips, he said, "And Clara seems to enjoy her company a great deal."

Heat swelled in Etta's chest at the timbre of his voice, and she became abruptly aware that she'd been sliding a thumb idly over the skin inside his wrist. She snatched her hand back from his. "Gideon, when I'm gone, there will be no one else who knows. And if you... if it turns out my father..." If the general was guilty of making bargains with the fae...

Gideon reached to take her hand in his, a gesture more comforting than it had been before.

She stared at their intertwined hands where they rested atop their touching knees. She had to tell him. "It was my fault," she said.

"What was your fault?"

She swallowed the lump in her throat. "The first time. When he came for my mother."

Gideon went still. His strong hand remained cradling hers, but she suddenly felt more distance. The shame in Etta's words made the hedged confession clear. Gideon was sharp enough to fill in the rest from their encounter with the fae.

His voice was low. "The prince killed your mother? The general said she was taken by illness. There was a record of it—the entire family isolated for months to prevent its spread. She suffered a great deal. He told me himself."

Etta met his gaze. "She's not dead."

Everything about Gideon's posture seemed to want to bolt to standing, to act on her words. But he held himself there, keeping her hand in his, his thoughts surely recalling every word he'd heard spoken by the general in all the years of their acquaintance and by the fae prince earlier that very day.

"He has her," Gideon said numbly. "He offered to break your curse and to return everything he'd taken from you."

"He has her because of me. I spoke his name. I called him there. She made the trade to keep me safe. The prince thought to take the general's daughter but instead won an official of the kingdom who was also the general's wife."

Gideon's brows shifted. "But you were only a girl." At her tortured expression, he added, "How could you have known?"

Etta pulled her hand from his. "It doesn't matter that I didn't know what would happen. I did it. I caused this. Without my recklessness, she never would have gone. She traded her own safety for mine." It had been horrific. Her mother had made Etta swear never to call the prince and never to come for her, lest the sacrifice be in vain. Etta was to become marshal. She was to grow into the woman who would defeat the prince on his throne, who would do the one thing her father had not.

Etta had failed them all.

"No." Gideon placed a finger beneath her chin to drag her gaze to his. "I mean, how could you have known his name?"

Etta stared at him, opened her mouth to speak, then caught the words. She'd no idea. She had never thought of it. At that age, Etta hadn't the wherewithal to assign blame.

Blame came later and not for anyone but herself and maybe her father, because he had made her hide the truth.

"Antonetta." The word came as natural as any that had slipped off Gideon's tongue, despite how it rumbled through her. "Someone gave you that name. Someone placed it in your hands. The hands of a child."

The same name that had been drawn from a chancellor as if against his will. She'd never considered that the fault may not have been entirely hers to bear. After a moment of stunned silence, Etta said, "Perhaps the prince was right. Perhaps I am not shrewd enough for the position of marshal."

Gideon shifted closer, intensely focusing on her face. He would have been able to see both the truth and the lie, now, the same as she. It was impossible to know which he was after. "You're not telling me everything about the curse. They took something from you. What was it?"

Etta explained what had happened with Lord Barrett, the terms Elsher had left her with, and the details he'd left out.

That the fae had stolen her life.

Gideon Alexander straightened at the words *the painting for your life* then dropped her hands, stood, and strode from the room.

CHAPTER 21

It had to have been past midnight. The chancery was dark. Not a single sound echoed through the chamber. Gideon moved with the grace of a man who could traverse the entire wing in a blindfold—Etta, not so much. She stumbled behind him, trying desperately not to make a sound and to stay at his heels. They were fugitives, after all. The last thing she needed was to get caught.

Her stomach dropped when they came into the records room. Moonlight cast the floor in strips of blue. A candle flared to life at Gideon's hand, illuminating the determination on his face and casting the room in a warmer tone. As she walked farther into the room, his light revealed the thing that had filled Etta with dread.

She wanted to stop him, to prevent him from seeing. Gideon had encountered the prince. He'd gained true sight. He would be able to take in every horrid detail.

He reached up and tugged the drape to drop to the floor. Standing in the dim light before Etta's portrait, holding the single taper aloft, Gideon was transfixed. Etta watched him, the painting and his figure illuminated in the center of a space whose edges fell to shadows and darkness.

Whatever Gideon's thoughts, he did not seem to find the portrait ridiculous. Instead, he appeared to examine with great concern the rotting apple perched delicately in her painted hands. His eyes did not stay long on the carnival behind her, lingering mostly on her image. His attention snagged on the ribbon laced through her lips and, as if the magic drew him closer, Gideon raised his hand to hover above the canvas. His fingertip grazed lightly over the ribbon on her likeness's painted lips, and Etta shivered at the touch.

Gideon clearly felt it, as he turned his face to hers and let his gaze fall to her mouth. He stared for an interminably long moment. Something seemed to come to him, and he glanced at the portrait—specifically the slit in the canvas—then back to Etta's wounded arm.

He went entirely still.

Indeed, Etta thought. No part of what he was realizing was good. The curse had hold of her, and it had nothing but ill intent.

His expression shifted, the change evident even in the light of a single candle. Etta's stomach flipped again.

"You're giving me that look," she said.

His voice was rough. "What look?"

"You think I'm a misfit. One of those souls you'd sacrifice everything to help." Like the ones he'd gathered to chancery, like Etta herself that first day, shaken and bedraggled and begging for a post.

He held her gaze. "They're not misfits. They're exceptional."

Etta swallowed. "But you're going to help me, whether I ask for it or not."

He turned back to the canvas then set the candle aside to reverently lower the drape and cover the cursed portrait from view. When he finally faced Etta again, it was with the most solemn expression she'd ever seen. He sighed, unapologetic. "I'm afraid it's a flaw in my character."

Etta's chest heaved in something painfully close to a sob. She did not cry out but only stood there, silent as Gideon moved to draw her into his arms.

One of his hands wrapped gently to the curve at the back of her neck, his other lower, keeping her close.

When the emotion seizing her chest melted into something less painful, Etta raised her chin to look at him. "Gideon?" she asked.

"Would it be a great crime against the dignity of the chancery office if you were to kiss someone recently on staff?"

He was unbearably near, his answer a soft breath that brushed her lips. "Yes," he said, drifting almost imperceptibly nearer. "A very, very great—"

Etta grabbed the front of his shirt, yanked him to close the distance, and kissed him full on the mouth. Gideon made no hesitation, walking them back to press Etta against the stacks, sliding his hands beneath her arms to lift her the short distance to his height and deepen the kiss. He was relentless, not breaking the contact even as Etta's roving hand knocked the book tucked in the back of his waistband to the floor. A little growl sounded deep in his throat, as if he could not help it, sending warmth through Etta's entire being. She kept one hand still knotted in his shirtfront, refusing to let go, lest he come to his senses and attempt escape. She tilted her head, unable to get close enough, and Gideon shifted to meet her, his palm sliding over her thigh to bring them closer still.

Footsteps sounded outside. Gideon froze. Etta took a heartbeat longer to regain awareness of their situation. The pair of them hung there for a moment in the flickering light of a single candle, motionless, listening.

The night patrol, Etta thought numbly, remembering the muffled thump the book had made when it dropped to the floor. *They heard and are coming to investigate. Gideon will send them away. It will be fine.*

Gideon lowered Etta to the ground, shifting in front of her as he purposefully slid the book beneath a shelf with his boot. They were trapped with nowhere to hide and no exit aside from the door through which they'd entered. He would have to think of an excuse for whatever they were about, the chancellor and his assistant, alone in a dark records room in the small hours before dawn. But it would be all right.

The footfalls neared, and Gideon's gaze flicked toward the portrait. A heartbeat later, he was moving toward the door.

He didn't make it. Two kingsmen blocked the entrance, shouldering inside with a half dozen more at their backs.

They were not chancery patrol. They were her father's men, the private guard of General Ostwind. Etta stepped backward, but there was nowhere to go.

The kingsmen didn't wait. They shoved past Gideon, and the first two snatched hold of Etta by the arms as the others pressed Gideon back from the door. When they lined the small room, a new figure came into view.

The General of Westrende stood in the doorway, his hard stare on Etta's face and form. The kingsmen passed a light forward, and the man near Etta held it high to illuminate her face. Whatever work the glamour was doing, her father knew well enough that not being able to recall his intruder's description, even as he looked directly at it, would mean she was somehow connected to the fae and that she was guilty of being in his rooms.

"That's her." His voice was cold, his expression colder. "Take her." The general's gaze flicked to Gideon. "And you, I'll see stood before council for harboring a fugitive, before the week is done."

Gideon's face had gone hard, the stern, sharp jaw of chancellor back in place. Etta jerked against the soldiers' grip, despite having no chance to defeat eight armed men and her father with nothing more than her fists. Her father would refuse to believe it was Etta—he could only accept that it was a fae trick, that his daughter was gone forever like her mother. "Take me where?"

The first sign of pleasure crossed the general's expression. "To a cell for what's left of the night. But soon, before council, where you'll be tried for treason."

CHAPTER 22

Prisoners of Westrende, it turned out, had no ranking. They were placed in cells in the order in which they'd been arrested. It meant a high-born lord, despite his status and attachment to sundry comforts, could be settled next to a lowly, filth-covered lady of treasonous intent. And it was how the girl previously known as Margaretta was tossed to the damp stone floor of a cool, dim cell next to Nickolas Brigham of the venerable Brigham line.

"Sometimes, in my nightmares, we're attacked by birds," Nickolas said dourly, shoving his arms through the bars so that they dangled into Etta's cell. "And at the end, our clothes look precisely like that dress."

Etta gasped. "Nickolas."

He sighed. "I suppose I knew it was coming. The general's spies spotted us meeting outside the chancery, searched my rooms, and found a stack of parchment concealed beneath my closet floor that apparently detailed closely held state secrets. I can't say for certain because I was never allowed to read them."

Etta groaned. She had not thought she could feel more wretched. "I'll tell them," she vowed. "I swear to you, I will clear your name."

He gave her a level look. "I beg of you, do not do me any more favors. The last thing I need is a treasonous lady with no trace of papers or connections taking up my cause." He frowned. "Are you well? You look miserable, but I don't see any open wounds."

She scooted closer to the bars. Her wrists were pinned in irons, so there was little chance she would be able to wriggle free. "They haven't hurt me yet, but my father is certainly out for blood. First, he caught Margaretta in his office, spying. Then more recently, someone with a similar face broke into his private vault."

Nickolas drew back and took a long breath. "His vault. I have to say, my lady, I did not think you could surprise me." His tone implied the "but here we are."

Etta bit her lip.

"Saints." Nickolas moaned. "There's more?"

"I was being chased, so... well, it didn't seem I had any other choice." She let him have her gaze. "I called a fae to bargain my escape. We disappeared right before the kingsmen's eyes."

"We," Nickolas said slowly.

Etta cleared her throat. "The chancellor and me."

Nickolas was silent for so long that she began to wonder if he'd heard her.

"I was trying to cross the wall without calling the prince—"

"Calling the prince." Nickolas, apparently snapped back to life by insuppressible incredulity, drew his arms back to grip hold of the bars. "You possess the true name of the prince of Rivenwilde?" When Etta only stared back at him, his tone shifted into something more sardonic. "Oh, truly, and why have you just not spoken it all along? Why not call him for tea? Why not have him over for a game of—"

"Nickolas," Etta said calmly. "You seem overset."

"Overset," he repeated with considerable outrage. "Antonetta, you have just seen us—though honestly, I cannot fathom why this comes as a surprise—but you have seen us thrown into a pair of prison cells fit for the lowest of the kingdom's most criminal kind, admitted to bargaining with a fae *while* you are wearing his curse, no less, to revealing all of this to a chancellor who wants you thrown from office before you even take your post, and then casually mention that you might call on the prince of the Riven Court." He glared at her. "Do go on about my delicate emotional state."

"Point taken."

His forehead thunked against the iron bars. "You're not going to get out of this one, are you?"

Her throat felt thick. "No. I won't."

When his eyes rose to hers, they held a question: *won't, not can't?*

Antonetta Ostwind possessed the true name of a fae. She could bargain her way out of anything.

Etta's gaze dropped to her lap, wrists bound and hands limp upon the tattered fabric of a borrowed dress. Her voice was barely above a whisper when she said, "No matter how I might want it, the cost is too high."

CHAPTER 23

Etta stood before the long table where she had, only weeks before, looked on with a heart swollen with hope and pride. The council chamber in all its majesty felt hollow despite the twelve kingdom officials seated at the table's sides.

Her arms were heavy, the manacles at her wrists seeming to weigh even on her soul. Every gaze in the chamber had skimmed over the face she wore, not meeting the familiar bright eyes they'd known since she was a girl.

Not even her father, who should have, above anyone, recognized them as easily as his own. The general stared back at Etta, radiating pure loathing.

"Ostwind," Louis demanded of the general, "why have you called us here for this scrap of a girl?"

"Treason." He gestured to an assistant, who rushed forward to deliver documents to several heads of law and kingdom order. "Conspiring against the kingdom, assuming a fake identity to gain sensitive information regarding the prospects for king, acting against a kingdom official with ill intent"—he waved a hand toward the document— "the list goes on."

Etta noted that he did not mention how she'd broken into his rooms. She gave him a look she hoped would convey that she was onto him. Etta had information he would not want revealed. He had no way of knowing she no longer possessed his book, a surely outlawed collection of pages that detailed the laws of fae magic.

They'd searched her. They'd searched her rooms. The general had found nothing.

His gaze stayed on hers. "The most pressing point," he noted, "is that she evaded capture by way of magic."

Cerys's tone was hard. "Consorting with the fae?"

Stefan's usually warm eyes narrowed on Etta with open disdain. "You think she wears a glamour. That she's one of them."

The general gestured toward Etta. "Decide for yourself. Look away and see that you might list one single attribute once she's out of your sight."

"I have your eyes," Etta murmured. "There's an attribute for you."

The general's hand dropped to the table in a manner so controlled it was more threatening than if he'd slammed a fist. He would remember what she'd said in his office, that she was his daughter, that she was truly Antonetta. He did not believe her. He had decided she was just another fae trickery, one of the like they'd used on him before. "Another word, and you'll be gagged."

"I invoke prisoner's rights."

His tone was level. "You have no rights. You are not a citizen of Westrende."

The council members watching Etta turned their attention to the general.

"What do you want to do with her?" Cerys asked.

General Ostwind's gaze met the cursed magic he'd hated for so long, obscuring Etta's face. His voice held the hint of the satisfaction of a game won. "A filigree cage."

Etta felt as though she'd been struck hard in the chest. Her knees went weak and her heart wild. He had never meant to stick her in a cell, to let her slowly fade in the darkness of a Westrende prison. He meant to bind her inside the magic that made up the wall, a tracery of metal that kept anything fae from passing through. She had been wrong. Her father never could have been guilty of making deals with the fae. He hated them too deeply.

In a filigree cage, she would not linger until her curse came to an end then be spirited away to Rivenwilde. She would be trapped, unable to fulfill the terms of the curse and unable to break free. The flesh would rot on her bones, like the withering apple her likeness held in the portrait. She would be trapped forever inside a curse, neither living nor dead.

The prince would not have his due.

Bile rose from Etta's stomach. Saints, she was going to be sick right there in the council chamber.

Gideon's sentiment that she must have been given the prince's name by someone when she was a girl came back to her. She recalled the dark days that followed, too, with her mother gone and her father severe. *Do not speak their name*, he'd told her. *Speak of them and they will return.*

Next time, he'd told her, *they will take something worse than just you.*

She wanted so badly to scream it at the top of her lungs, to shriek the prince's name to the sky, anything at all to see her mother returned and to see herself set free despite the vow to her mother and the warnings from her father. But she could not—would not. The price was too high.

She met his gaze. "You say a filigree cage yet deny the existence of fae. The public face of Westrende is no less a glamour than what covers my own." She jerked her chin toward the council. "This is all an illusion. The fae threaten our very lives, you know it, and yet you remain. Your silence keeps nothing at bay. The prince is coming, and he means to unrend the world, to break the Rive. And when he does, Westrende will have nothing to save it while you cling to your silence. But I will not give you to him, not even if you deserve the fate more than she."

"Silence!" The general stood, his voice like thunder, his anger like the coming storm.

Etta had no way of knowing whether he understood her words, but he would know soon enough. The prince wanted to break the curse that kept fae from Westrende, and to do so, he needed power over the kingdom. Controlling the general was the closest he could come.

"I call the vote," her father said. "Speak your objections now, for this creature belongs in a cage, and I mean to see it done before the hour is through."

Etta had no more than resigned herself to her fate when the doors to the council chamber banged open. Cerys froze, gavel in hand, only a breath before the mallet met its base to settle the course of Etta's doom.

All eyes turned toward the chamber door as Gideon Alexander strode in.

"Stop him," the general growled. "This is a private trial, and he is connected to the suspect's crime. He shall not be allowed to interfere with this proceeding."

Gideon's steps did not slow even as the kingsmen approached. "I am still chancellor." The calm in his voice was not as level as one might have expected, but Etta could not say whether that owed to the fact that her father meant to arrest him or that he was clearly about to declare something utterly ridiculous in Etta's defense.

Cold dread rose in her, and she prayed he would not attempt to convince the rule of twelve that the fae walked among them, that they gathered outside those very chambers. The council would not tolerate those who spoke freely of the fae and certainly not those who challenged their judgment. Etta had only spoken openly because she was already doomed.

Gideon did not give the general his notice but let his gaze travel the table of men and women who made up Westrende's rule. "Will you deny me the right to submit evidence?"

Louis gestured the kingsmen away. "Lord Alexander is welcome, should he have anything of value to provide."

"I do." Gideon's tone had strengthened, but his gaze never strayed to Etta or her father. It was good, she supposed, that he did not look at her, because she would not have been able to stop herself from frantically waving at him to run away—or worse, that he might show her kindness and cause her to weep in front of everyone present.

He stopped, apparently undecided where to stand, given that the table was occupied on every side, with Etta at one end and her father at the other. One of Gideon's hands was pressed to his midsection, and Etta had a sudden wave of fear that he might be about to reveal the book, that it was hidden beneath his robe and he intended to bring it forth—as evidence against her father. The one person left to defend Westrende against the prince would be thereby removed from his post. It felt a bit like she was standing aboard a ship, with the floor beneath her feet swaying unsteadily.

"I have," Gideon started, still not looking at her. "I have evidence —" He stopped, the hand not pressed to his middle coming up to wipe sweat from his brow. Beneath his breath, he murmured something that sounded a lot like "fates protect us." He let the council have his gaze. "Forgive me for what I'm about to do."

The swaying ship deck beneath Etta's feet plunged into the ocean. She was certain by his tone that he was about to commit an act far worse than presenting evidence against her father. Gideon was going to do something that would cost him more than even his own post. She shouted, "Gideon, no!"

He did not heed her. Instead, Gideon Alexander, chancellor of Westrende and most law-abiding citizen in the history of histories, moved to the center of the council chamber and spoke the prince's name.

CHAPTER 24

Etta stared in shock at the prince of Rivenwilde, who stood in the center of the highest office of Westrende, surrounded by gaping council leaders. He was perched atop their hallowed table, looking down at his oldest enemies as the ancient magic revealed to them the sight.

Cerys cursed, Maura drew a sword, and Louis shoved up from his chair so hard that it crashed to the floor. There was a lot to be said about the amount of force it took, for they were not insignificant chairs.

"Well," the prince said with a careless grin toward Gideon. "Look what you have done."

The fae wore a long-tailed suit of solid black, silky and sleek, fit perfectly to him. Upon his head was a tangled crown of bonelike spikes that rested tidily in a nest of neat dark hair. Every detail on his person was perfectly done, as if he'd dressed for the occasion.

Etta's gaze swung to Gideon, his drab robe and mildly sick expression a stark contrast to the prince's flair. He had done the thing that Etta had never been able to do, the thing her father had threatened her about and that her mother had made her swear never to do. The council could see.

"Gideon," she said breathily, unsure if he understood precisely what he'd done, how he'd tied them all into the dark secret that the prince called a curse. At the sound of her voice, though, eyes turned to Etta, and three more council members shoved out of their chairs.

"You see," Gideon said evenly. "Now that you've encountered the prince, you see what he has done. Lady Ostwind is not guilty. She was acting in the best interest of Westrende, despite being constrained by a curse."

The prince chuckled. "Oh, indeed. Poor Lady Ostwind." He snapped his wrist, and suddenly, a sword was in his hand, which he casually spun so that light flashed on its blade. "As if it were not I who is truly bound."

There was too much happening. Etta could not quite decide where to look. "Cut me free," she murmured to Maura. She settled her gaze on her father at the opposite end of the table, seemingly leagues away with the prince between them.

"Antonetta," her father whispered.

"I know," she replied. She knew he hadn't been able to accept it was her. She knew he was sorry. She understood that his biggest fear had come to life. "There's nothing to be done for it."

"I only wanted—" He stopped, appearing speechless, which Etta was sure she'd never seen. The general swallowed hard, and his voice was rough when he spoke. "I tried to keep you safe."

It was as if Etta's heart had been run through the wash, wrung out, and pinned to the line. She could do nothing but wait until it resumed any shape that was normal. She could not think about what it all meant. Perhaps, he hadn't sent her away to be rid of her but because she mattered too much. Perhaps he couldn't bear to lose her too.

"Heartwarming," the prince said flatly. He glanced at Etta. "Now, what's going on? He was about to pin you in a cage?"

She glared up at him.

"Best leave it," he told Maura, who was fumbling with the locks of Etta's manacles. "If she gets free, she'll have a sword before you know it, and she'll attempt to break the oldest covenant among a long, long list of rules never to be broken"—he shot Etta a look—"again."

Pinning the sword to his side, he loudly clapped his hands once, calling the assembled crowd to order as he faced Gideon. "Let's get to it, shall we? What sort of bargain do you propose?"

"Lift the curse from Antonetta Ostwind."

The prince's smile was slow.

Gideon reached into his robe to withdraw the book. "And call her mother to bear witness."

Etta's knees gave out. She barely caught herself on the edge of the table, gouging the wood with her manacles. It was not her proudest moment. Across the room, her father made some sort of incoherent cry, apparently not faring much better.

Gideon held the book before him like a talisman. "It must be allowed, per Riven Court law."

Saints, he'd read it and had already researched the rules by which the prince must behave. He did seem a bit bedraggled, now that she looked, as if, like her, he'd been up through the night. But Gideon wasn't a prisoner. He had not been in a cell next to Nickolas, knowing his last hours were slipping past. He was chancellor, diligent and meticulous, knowledgeable in nothing so much as the law. He had stayed up pouring over fae rules.

Bless the man's studious soul.

The prince crouched on the table to meet Gideon's confident gaze. "Are you certain you want to play this game?"

"Call her," Gideon said, "by the rules of your code."

The prince's answering tone implied that he was humoring Gideon, as if he'd no other occupation for the day other than to watch how it all played out and that he had no care for the laws that bound him. "So be it."

Gideon moved forward, drawing strips of paper from inside his robe to hand to Cerys and Louis. "As you'll see, Lady Ostwind has committed none of the crimes of which she's been accused. She was acting on behalf of the chancery, pursuing the very task she was assigned in order that her nomination be allowed to return to vote."

He paused as if just realizing that Etta *had* completed his task. The fae had supplanted agents of the kingdom and had meddled in every manner possible relating to the head of Westrende. She had uncovered precisely who'd made attempts on the prospects for king—she just hadn't been able to tell anyone. Because no one would have believed her. He paused as if realizing that she had planned to fight the fae on her own.

"Indeed," Gideon told the council, his gaze caught on Etta's. "I vouch for the lady's character and the very Ostwind name."

Maura seemed distraught that the focus was being drawn away from the very tall, very fae figure atop their table. "The office of marshal is the least of our problems at the moment. Lord Alexander, what are you about?"

Papers delivered, Gideon stepped back, his hands clasped before his waist, where they held the book of fae law. "In fact, my lady, the office of marshal is very much to the point." He let the prince have his gaze. "Rivenwilde has been positioning fae among us, in posts near officers of the kingdom. Their most ardent desire, it seems, is to possess the seat of power. Lacking a king, that position falls to the head of council."

Every gaze in the room, save Gideon and the prince, turned toward the general. He sank into his chair. Etta had not yet reclaimed her heart—she would have to decide later whether she held sympathy for the fact that the secrets the man had so desperately clung to were unraveling before his eyes. As it was, she could not quite grasp the relief she'd anticipated of having it finally out. The council could no longer deny the existence of fae in Westrende, not with their prince strutting before them. And yet, nothing could be done to stop the consequences of it all coming undone.

The lock of the irons at Etta's wrists finally clicked free, and Maura removed them and took one of the papers that had been silently passed through the room. Etta rubbed her flesh. Her fingers itched for a weapon, but Gideon had been correct. She could not run the prince through. What they needed was a filigree cage.

But before Etta could signal her father to set up a trap, his expression melted into something Etta might never have seen. *Might*, she thought, because somewhere, far off in her memory, was the shadow of the same emotion crossing her father's face. When he had discovered they'd taken...

"Marianna." The general's voice was a plea, as if he could not quite believe it was true.

But it was true, and Etta could see it. Atop the long table beside the prince of Rivenwilde, her mother, the lady Ostwind, who'd been stolen when Etta was only a girl, suddenly stood. The same Lady Ostwind the council believed to be dead.

The council members stumbled away from the table—all eleven, save her father—just as Etta tried to climb aboard. Maura and Stefan dragged Etta backward, as if she were the danger. Perhaps she was, she thought, as the prince smiled down at her.

No harm could come to a prince of Rivenwilde, no harm to one who held the throne. The prince believed he was cursed. He blamed Etta for what had become of her mother. He'd said as much when Etta had called his name.

"Lady Ostwind." Gideon bowed deeply toward Etta's mother, as if the room had not broken into utter chaos around him. "You have been called to bear witness. A curse has been laid upon Antonetta, but she has refused to ask the prince for a bargain to win herself free. Today, I will bargain for her, in hopes that what I offer will be valuable enough to return our incoming marshal to fight another day."

Restrained by Stefan and Maura, Etta watched her mother take in the man in chancellor's robes, telling her the prince had cursed her daughter, seeding important hints to their situation into a succinct introduction, and the council members, who appeared as if they'd seen her rise from the dead. Her gaze moved toward Etta, softening with warm affection and pride, bright with unshed tears as her lips shifted into something of a smile. Then, quite deliberately, her focus moved to the other end of the table, where her husband still stood.

There was a frozen moment in which Etta could see nothing but her father's answering expression, the torture and awe melting into steely determination, as if he meant to ride into battle.

Etta's knees felt weak. "Let me go." The two holding her did not listen.

"Bear witness, I will," Marianna said. "But first, I offer a trade of my own."

CHAPTER 25

"No!" Etta shouted just as the prince rammed his blade into the table with a crash of magic, driving a hush through the watching crowd.

Into the silence, the prince said, "There is only one trade I might accept from you, Marianna. Do you offer it now, after so many years of refusal?"

Etta's mother seemed to hesitate, her throat moving in a swallow, her gaze flicking briefly to the general then to Gideon before finally stopping on Etta once more.

"Take me," Etta pled to the fae. "It's what you wanted. Have me and leave them alone."

The prince flicked a hand as if swatting at an insect. "I have a bigger prize in mind, Lady Ostwind." He'd not even looked at her, his focus solely on Etta's mother. They all knew what he wanted, what he'd wanted all along.

The head of Westrende.

Etta's mother was going to give it to him. Marianna's shoulders squared, the simple gray gown she wore somehow suddenly regal. Her amber eyes shifted toward the prince. "I offer, in exchange for my own freedom and for a reprieve of one year in which you vow to never cross the border into Westrende…"

The entire room fell under a disbelieving pall, the gravity of Marianna's words impossible. The future of Westrende hung on the final utterance from a woman they'd thought they would never see in the flesh again and who was about to give it all away.

"My husband, general of Westrende."

The prince had wanted him all along. Etta had refused to be any part of giving him over, though, because her mother had made her swear a vow and her father had threatened to send her away.

Giving him over meant the end of the kingdom.

Etta jerked free, Gideon rushed forward, and nearly every member of the council drew their weapons.

In one instant, the prince raised a hand, triumphantly calling, "Done."

In the next, Etta became aware of the bang that had preceded his decree. It seemed to echo through the chamber.

The prince's gaze fell to Cerys, her hoary eyes on him as a wicked smiled crossed her lips. In one hand, she held the gavel. In the other, the strip of parchment Gideon had given her when he'd first come in, a paper that Etta had believed had detailed her innocence. Etta stared at its twin, the crumped parchment that had been passed to Maura moments before—a parchment, she saw, that had warned of a coming threat.

It asked the council to remove the general before Westrende was taken.

"What have you done?" The prince's voice was ice, his face twisted in fury. He lurched forward, but Etta's mother had hold of the neck of his fine jacket, and no less than half a dozen swords were abruptly aimed at his person.

"What she has done," Marianna whispered menacingly at his back, "is release the general from his post as head of council." Marianna returned Cerys's smile. "And finely so. You always had excellent timing, my friend."

Etta's father pressed through the crowd, stopping when he was face level with the crouching prince. "You do not look pleased. You've won a general and an Ostwind. Is that not enough?"

The prince went for him, but it was too late. The bargain had been struck. The price had not won a head of the kingdom. He grabbed hold of the general's coat, jerking him forward, threats pouring from him with a good deal of oaths and swearing. Etta's father did not seem to care in the least. His attention was only for Marianna, their eyes locked as she stood atop the table, an arm's length out of his reach. What passed between them was hard to say, but Etta could see, even from where she stood, that the look held nothing but vows of duty and devotion—not simply for Westrende but for one another. And for Etta.

The prince tore free of the council members, leaping down to seize his prize. The general appeared unconcerned as his attention turned to Etta. "You have done us proud, Antonetta. Westrende could not ask for a more adept marshal."

It was the first moment for as long as she could recall that Etta cared not a whit about becoming marshal. She rushed forward, trying to reach him before the prince turned and yanked the general away from the crowd.

"Hold!" Gideon ordered.

The look the prince shot him was so filled with contempt that something in Etta wanted to shrink back.

Gideon only moved closer. "The curse."

"You think I would set her free after the betrayal you all have dealt? I would sooner cut off my own hand."

Gideon lifted the book. "You've forgotten, I know the rules."

The prince's jaw pressed so tight that it seemed his teeth might break. "Offer."

Gideon slid the book into his belt then positioned his hands patiently before his waist. "In exchange for the breaking of Antonetta Ostwind's curse, I relinquish your true name."

The prince leaned threateningly toward Gideon.

"If you do not make this trade, I will invoke your name, and you will be drawn across the border, breaking your bargain with Lady Ostwind," Gideon said.

"It does not work that way," the prince snapped. "I may cross without repercussion if called."

The tilt to Gideon's mouth said that he'd only been testing the boundary of their rules. He'd gotten his answer. He drew a breath. "In that case, a counteroffer." He gestured toward the dozen officers of Westrende watching. "Each fae we find on our side of the boundary will be locked inside a filigree cage so that they may not assist you across. Perhaps, knowing this, you'd be willing to trade the breaking of Antonetta's curse for the return of those prisoners to Rivenwilde land, with the agreement, of course, that no additional fae pass through."

"You cannot leave them," Etta said. Without the ability to return to Rivenwilde, the fae would be starved of magic. He would be sentencing them to death. "The law says—"

"I know our own laws." The prince shot her a glare then turned back to Gideon. "The two of you will pay for what you have done." The hand not tangled in the general's coat twisted through the air, and suddenly, in it rested a fresh, bright apple. He tossed it aloft, the breaking of a curse, and vowed, "This isn't over."

By the time the apple landed in Gideon's palm, the prince—and Etta's father—were gone.

CHAPTER 26

The curse was broken. Etta had wanted desperately to win back her life. Her post as marshal. Her mother. She had not expected that it would cost so much.

But the Rive was intact. The prince was gone.

"Darling girl," Marianna said, wrapping her arms around Etta in a hug that made her want to fall to the ground and weep. Etta's mother pulled back to look at her. "I'm so sorry, my love. I'm so sorry for having gone."

Etta nodded, unable to speak past the lump in her throat.

"We'll make it right. I've learned so much while I was away. What your father gained from that book was nothing compared to what I know from being beyond the wall." She pressed her hands to Etta's cheeks. "I've so much to do. It all needs to be dealt with straight away. See me tonight, yes? Come find me once this is settled, and we'll spend hours upon hours tucked before the hearth."

Etta nodded again, turning her face to kiss her mother's palm.

Then her mother tucked a lock of hair behind Etta's ear, wholly present for a frozen moment before she smiled and rushed away. Etta watched fondly as she crossed the room, giving only a quick look back before reaching the members of council. The woman had always been a force, and that hadn't changed. Despite her years away, Marianna took hold of council as if she'd formed it from her own will. She would see everything set to rights. The lady Ostwind would take her place as the new head of council, possibly even as general, and she would see her husband returned.

The lady Ostwind would stand against the fae.

Gideon moved beside Etta and slid his hand into hers, their fingers tangling in the most natural way.

Etta let her gaze travel from face to face as the council members, who had been so adamant in their refusal to change, talked animatedly with her mother. Etta would no longer be forced to stand alone in her fight against the fae. They had the sight, so council could not deny the existence of the creatures. And she was not alone because Gideon would stand with her. They'd created a world where it might be possible to root out the fae, together. She turned to him, closer than propriety might have permitted.

His gaze roamed her face. The curse was broken, and nothing but Antonetta remained. The breath that came out of him was one only of relief.

"You saved me," Etta whispered.

Gideon's hand rose to brush a thumb over her cheek. "You saved Westrende."

"It doesn't feel like it."

"It will, in time. We can make certain it's so."

Then he leaned in to kiss her right there in the council chamber, though the others were so deep into planning they would probably never know. Etta didn't bother looking. She closed her eyes, wrapping her arms around him and feeling as if she might be willing to lie right there on the council floor and take a nap, at least as soon as she'd had enough of Gideon's soft, sweet kisses. He pulled her more deeply into the embrace, pressing his lips into her hair and the base of her ear, to every part of her he touched.

"We should get Nickolas out of his cell," Etta murmured.

Gideon's attentions trailed the line of her jaw until his lips found hers once more.

Etta drew back to ask, "Did you hear me? About Nickolas."

Gideon leaned in to kiss her again. She gave him a look.

"Very well." He took hold of her hand, as if he could not bear to lose contact. "Let us cease this perfectly enjoyable moment that we've both earned dearly to go let the poor cockscomb out of his cell."

Etta let out a helpless laugh. "Thank you for mustering the enthusiasm. I do owe him. It's the least I can do not to leave him locked in a dungeon." She hesitated, glancing back at the council. "Is there not something you need to see to? I'm sure I can manage a jailbreak with just a note from the chancellor, not the chancellor himself."

Gideon shrugged. "I have a clerk to dismiss and a few other concerns to clear up. But it can wait. The rest of this day belongs to you, my lady. If you want to spend it on Lord Brigham—"

Etta gave him a quick elbow to the ribs, smiling as they turned to walk from the room. "Lord Alexander, I was entirely wrong about you."

"Is that so?" he asked.

"Yes. It's going to be a great deal more fun to keep the lord chancellor in check than I anticipated."

EPILOGUE

A week later

"My lady," Gideon murmured, his body only inches from hers while his dark eyes trailed every line of her face. "I fear the worst has happened."

"Has it?" Etta replied.

Gideon hummed gravely in affirmation. "It seems I've become infatuated." He shook his head as his gaze fell to trace her lips. "I may not be able to comport myself."

"This is perhaps not a crime you should be confessing to a law official."

He leaned closer. "Precisely why I thought it best to get it off my chest. Before it's too late."

Etta grabbed hold of his uniform and jerked him near, planting a kiss on his lips as her free hand toyed with the freshly cut hair at the nape of his neck. After a long moment, she drew away to look at him. "Better?"

"Much," he said in a low, rough voice before he leaned in to kiss her again.

"Oh, truly," a sullen voice said from down the hall.

Gideon paused but did not look away.

"Well, well, well. Lord Alexander, look who's unbecoming now. Cavorting in a public corridor with an official of Westrende, the both of you." Nickolas clicked his tongue, his hand waving in some gesture that was probably supposed to imply disappointment.

Etta didn't bother looking away, either, even as Gideon replied, "It's not a public corridor. I cannot fathom how you gained access."

"I have connections." When they still didn't give him their full attention, Nickolas crossed his arms. "I see where I rate now." Gesturing over a shoulder, he asked, "Shall I just tell them you're not coming? That you'd rather stand here and gaze longingly into each other's eyes?"

Etta did look at him then. "You know I'll be able to arrest you by the time this ceremony is over."

"It wouldn't be the first time you've had me thrown in jail." He threw a glance at Gideon then pointed a finger toward his own collar, where Gideon's was out of place. He bit back a smile as the chancellor rushed to put himself into order. "Lady Ostwind," Nickolas said, "I meant to offer to walk you, but I see now that you have someone already fit for your arm. I suppose this means I'll be stuck escorting my mother. Thanks for that. Nothing like being abandoned for a stodgy officer of the court." When Gideon glared up at him, Nickolas shot Etta a wink. "I'll meet you later."

As he turned to go, he glanced back over his shoulder. "I was wrong, by the way. That color suits you perfectly."

Etta tried very hard to wipe the smile from her face as she straightened the sword at her hip, tugged down the hem of her marshal's coat, and took Gideon's proffered arm.

They came into a corridor filled with courtiers, men and women who served Westrende, and not a single one of them fae. Her mother, head of council and by unanimous vote the new General Ostwind, had been swift in her removal of the shadows, and the revelation had scattered many of the lesser fae. Etta had never felt safer, more proud, or more certain that her mother's vows would all be done. She'd sworn to win back the general, and with any luck, it would be done before the next moon. They would be a family again.

"I've a council member to speak to." Gideon's voice was low, sending a shiver through her as it brushed her bare neck. He was right—they were in trouble. "Infatuation" was not a strong enough word. "I'll return to you in a moment."

She nodded then walked the line of portraits to where the final one hung. A new artist had been called to paint over the work the fae had done, the canvas patched, and a plate installed that read Antonetta's full name. Beneath it, engraved in metal: Marshal of Westrende.

Etta came to stand beside Jules, who stared up at it. "It's truly lovely, my lady. Congratulations on gaining the post."

Etta smiled toward the canvas. Jules would not have any idea that Etta had been Margaretta. Gideon had told the chancery staff that their newest assistant had returned home to care for family. Without the glamour, Etta would not be able to thank Jules for all that she had done. Still, she said, "Thank you. I'm grateful for the help I received to get here."

Jules shook her head. "I cannot believe you let them paint over it. But I suppose it's safer on this wall than anywhere else."

Etta's face snapped to look at her. "Do you mean... as evidence in the Lord Barrett crime?"

Jules laughed. "No, my lady, not that. You were right, though. The original was hideous. The swan alone."

Something brushed Etta's arm, and she turned from her gaping to find Gideon, his brow drawn in obvious concern. "Is something amiss?"

Etta looked back to Jules, but the woman was gone. Etta scanned the crowd for any sign of her.

"They're waiting on you," Gideon urged.

Etta shook herself, and when she turned toward Gideon, he was watching her as if to see if all was well. He had said before that Jules was protected. Etta would ask him later what that meant and what he knew of Jules. She nodded, inhaled deeply, then took his arm.

They walked the length of the corridor, courtiers moving from their path, the mood of the hall buoyant. He led her to the dais, where upon the platform, a dozen council members waited. In a matter of moments, Etta would be awarded the band that marked her a Westrende official. She was steps away from becoming marshal.

Beside her, Gideon leaned in. "Ready?"

Etta glanced up at the waiting figures atop the dais with a smile. "Lord Chancellor, you should know by now. An Ostwind is always ready."

WITHIN THE HOLLOW HEART

CHAPTER 1

Nickolas Brigham was going to marry a princess. She would be beautiful and charming and hang on his every word. She would be flawless. Incomparable. Her station would be high enough to place him securely in the ranks of Westrende's most prominent citizens. A princess was indeed the answer to all his problems, and he would marry her posthaste. He just needed to find her first.

"What is the highest rank in the kingdom again?"

His mother glared at him over the rim of her teacup.

"Oh, that's right. I'd forgotten. There is no king, only the council ruling in his stead. No king, no princesses. And among council, the youngest, I believe, is aged around two and forty. So..."

"So the highest-ranking match you'll secure is already beneath us." She made a tsk of disapproval. "Honestly, Nickolas, your great-grandfather dined with a king. Your great-aunt was gifted a horse by another. It should not be so difficult to tie yourself to a woman of station, given the esteem of our family name."

Nickolas gave her a look. She placed her cup on a finely carved side table and glared into the distance as if she'd not noticed his response. Nickolas moved to stare in the same direction, crossing his arms in his finely tailored suit and finding nothing but a finely papered section of

227

wall between a pair of finely painted floral arrangements. He glanced at his mother over a shoulder. Her hair—darker blond than his and just starting to reveal its first strands of silver—was drawn back into a flawless bun, her attire impeccable. *Expensive.* They both knew the Brigham line had fallen well beneath what one might call influential. It was high on the precisely detailed list of reasons she'd pushed him so hard to find an acceptable wife.

He turned to sit in the chair across from her, making certain his feet and elbows were placed in a manner that wouldn't bring a round of censure, although his words surely would.

"Mother, I have doused nearly every woman of high society in my charm since the day I turned two and ten, to no success. They spurn me, every one. They have run off to marry their bakers and their map makers and left me alone in the splendor and finery that the fortitude and fortuitousness of our ancestors bought. There is no one left who meets your standards. I beg you, for the love of all that is tolerable, let this—"

The look she turned on him could have cut glass. In fact, Nickolas felt as if shards of it suddenly lined his spine. He sat straighter, overcome with an urge to check that his vest and cravat were in order.

His mother said coolly, "I have delivered my conditions. You will follow them."

The *or else* was plain in her tone. Nickolas swallowed, knowing full well what the "else" would entail. It wasn't as if he hadn't expected it—they'd been having the same argument for years—but each time he thought of it, the knot inside of him grew tighter. It felt very much as if, if he didn't find a way to stop his mother's plans, the thing that was knotted inside him would become impossible to unbind.

His voice was careful when he told her, "I'm afraid that I cannot do as you've bid." Could not marry. Could not allow himself to be part of her schemes. Could not abide by the underhanded, unpleasant—

The thought cut off at the sound of a knock on the main door. Nickolas's gaze went sharp, but his mother's expression didn't change.

"You speak to me as if I were enfeebled, Nickolas," she said. "I have given you every opportunity to do this on your own. It became clear far before this evening that you cannot."

The knot cinched tighter. He did not know what she'd done. Perhaps the caller was only a lady he was meant to attach himself to. One of his mother's friends, perhaps, in her dotage and desperate for a replacement helpmeet, a stand-in for a dead husband. *Perhaps*. Nickolas stood, wondering if it were too cowardly to leap from the window in escape. His gaze flicked to the balcony. Yes, it would be dangerous and daft and, above all, cowardly. But it would not be the first cowardly thing he'd done.

The light of a bright moon reflecting on the railing brought a sudden, sharp realization of how late it had become. His gaze snapped to his mother. Her face, like that of his eldest sister, was long and slender, her eyes a steely gray. The countenance had been nearly unwavering since the day he'd been born. When the corner of her mouth quirked, he felt his first real shock of fear. It was too late for callers, well past the hour any respectable family would allow themselves presumed not to be abed. And his mother, she had called him there to... Saints, what she had just said.

He did not bother to ask what she had planned; it was too late to attempt any kind of retreat, with dignity or not. He was trapped. Nickolas had known his mother was obstinate, but he had never expected it to go so far. He should have leapt from the window when he'd had the chance.

He straightened, a sense of dread sliding over him as the figures of three hulking men darkened the sitting room door. They were dressed in the livery of castle staff, crisp black suits with very little trim. They were not castle staff. One man met him with a dead-eyed glare. Another's eyes held a concerning amount of twinkle when he rubbed his palms together and said, "Evening, my lord."

"THIS CANNOT BE HAPPENING," Nickolas repeated as they heaved him over a pile of fine silk pillows. It was happening. In fact, most of it already had. The men had hauled him down a darkened corridor, his various attempts at fighting be damned, and into a wing of the castle that held some of the most prominent families in the kingdom, where he'd been unceremoniously dragged through a set of garishly decorated private rooms. His jacket had been torn off in the struggle, his shirt tugged loose over a throbbing side and wrenched shoulder, and now a pair of men with the strength of oxen held him against a sturdy bedpost while a third man tied his hands with his own cravat.

Nickolas hurled a few insults, but he was not quite certain whether they pertained to the henchmen or the woman who had hired them. The men did not seem to care either way. The moment the knot was secure, his captors let go their hold and stepped back to take in their work with the pride only a man of difficult labor could know.

Nickolas let his head drop back against the post, wincing at the pain in his shoulder. "Very well. You've done it. Good job, all of you." He would not tell them what it would cost them, what trusting the lady Brigham would buy them each in the end.

Lashed to the post of a bed in some unnamed lady's room, Nickolas felt they deserved their fate, in any case.

One of the men chuckled. "Aye, a fine job we did. Look at you there, trussed up like a bird."

Another one chimed in, "Fanciest lord I've ever seen, even without his quills."

"Ain't a roasting he's in for." The first one smiled, a row of fine straight teeth flashing in a face that seemed to possess no other symmetry. "Not when Lady Carvell finds him in her bed." The lot of them laughed uproariously, apparently unaware that Nickolas had already begun working the knot.

His mother might have found the men sufficiently brutish and unconcerned with the law to haul him there, but she'd not bothered to make certain they knew their tethering skills. Five more minutes and he would be back in his wing, packing a trunk to leave his mother, his sisters, and if he had to, the entire kingdom of Westrende.

Anything but what she was attempting to set him up for. He would not be forced to marry the Carvell woman, no matter that propriety would demand it.

"There she is now," one of the men whispered as a door in the next room clicked shut. They were gone in an instant, apparently not speaking a word to the woman in the next room on their way out. Beyond the bedchamber door, the sound of light footfalls meandered through the sitting room of the suite. The lady was evidently in no rush, casually about her business before she made her way to the man shackled to her furniture.

In Nickolas's ears was the echo of his mother's words as she'd stood over him while the hired ruffians had prepared to drag him away. "This is for your own good," she had said coldly. "For the good of the family."

Nickolas tore a wrist free of his binds, biting back a curse at the chafing of his skin. He was on his feet, yanking the fabric free, unwilling to leave a single scrap that might be used as evidence against him.

"My lord," a pouting voice called from the doorway. "Don't tell me you're attempting to run away."

Nickolas froze, his back to the woman. He did not turn and did not even look toward the unmistakable sound of Lady Carvell's voice.

Her steps came closer. "My father paid a good deal for this."

There was a low sound in her throat, but it was impossible to guess whether it was anticipation at having him caught or displeasure at his attempted escape. Neither boded well.

"To tie you to me."

Fate save him, the woman had been in on it. She'd not only agreed to the ridiculous plot, but by the sound of it, she'd been eager to marry a man who wanted no part of their scheme. There was a solid chance that when he thought of the scene later, he would be sick. But as he stood, his eyes only scanned the room, searching in the flickering candlelight for any escape.

"Nickolas," she complained. "It's too late for that. By sunrise, everyone will know. You might as well make it easy on all of us."

"My lady," he said, "this will remain, forevermore, between you, me, and that bedpost." His gaze landed on his only recourse. "Predictable," he muttered.

It was the balcony. He should have known; it was always the balcony. Someday, he would be caught in a situation wherein the lady in question lived in a ground-floor room with a dozen windows. Today was not that day.

He rushed toward the doors, thanked every deity he could bring to mind that they weren't locked, and yanked them open to a moonlit night.

A high-pitched scream rent the air behind him. The rush of footsteps that followed was too fast not to have been anticipating the call. He had been right in his guess that a guard waited just outside. It didn't make his choice any easier. Nickolas stared over the balcony railing, his stomach dropping. It wasn't a first-floor room, not even a second. Three stories beneath him waited metal railing, wooden benches, and statuary with more than their fair share of pointy bits. He closed his eyes, vowing to lobby for the installation of more courtyard ponds at the next assembly.

He turned back toward the room, not surprised to find a pair of kingsmen coming through the bedchamber door. What did surprise him, however, was that they were men Nickolas knew—the kingsmen who'd arrested him the last time. Men who had dragged him to a cold, dark cell.

He was done for. The men had thought him guilty of a crime far more dastardly than being in a woman's bed that day and had promised him very bad things. Should they manage to lay hands on him, Nickolas and the Brigham name were through.

He drew a deep breath, swung his legs over the balcony railing, and plummeted into the cool night air.

CHAPTER 2

It was not his finest escape. Nickolas landed unsteadily on a lower stone outcropping, a slanted ledge that, unfortunately, was too slick for proper footing. He slid. He swore.

He fell.

Reaching out, he barely caught hold of a nearby corbel and found his legs swinging with his momentum, then the weight of his body pulled loose his grip. He fell farther, swore again, then crashed against a decorative trellis, where he held on for dear life. It was covered in thorns. Above him, one of the kingsmen shouted.

Below him was a very tall statue of a mostly naked woman atop a rearing horse. He leapt for it and wrapped his arms about the woman's smooth stone neck. He clambered down the rest of her, pausing only briefly to murmur an apology for his grip on her breast. The horse received no such apology. The moment he reached the base, Nickolas threw himself over the surrounding brush and ran full speed out of the garden.

It was late, but the moon was full, illuminating every pale statue and stone barrier. With growing dread, Nickolas spun and ran at every dead end he met in an endless succession of wrong turns. There seemed to be nothing but walls: high walls, low walls, bench walls, topiary walls, and by the Rive, an obscene number of undressed women on horses framed within the surrounding castle walls. He was panting, heart thundering at every sound that might be the kingsmen in pursuit. If they caught him, it was over. All of it, every comfort and freedom he'd ever known.

His life would be ruined. He would have to put on that he'd been in Lady Carvell's bedchamber of his own free will and agree to marry her, or he would be thrown into a cell for breaking into her private suite. He was fairly certain either would bring a special kind of punishment. A woman who would so easily agree to having a man stolen and lashed to her bed against his wishes would certainly not be the sort he would want to bind to his name. But there was more to it than that. Nickolas had encountered the family before; he was acquainted with the woman's father. He knew what the pair were capable of.

A life bound to the Carvell family would be worse than eternity in a dark and lonely cell. At least the kingsmen hadn't jumped down after him. Their lack of senselessness had won Nickolas a momentary opportunity to secure his freedom. While the kingsmen traversed the Carvell rooms to reach the courtyard—avoiding a blind leap into the night like Nickolas—he had one chance to get out.

If only he could find a cursed door.

He stepped on something sharp, swore again, and stumbled forward past a sweetbriar bush. Had he not been looking over his shoulder, he might have noticed the dark metal on the ground in his path. As it was, he did not. Foot tangling in the wires, Nickolas lost his balance and spun, managing to miss falling flat on his face only by taking the packed earth to his back.

A huff of air escaped his chest the same moment that a soft gasp sounded somewhere beyond his head. He glanced up, toward the midnight sky, and whatever breath he'd meant to steal was lost.

Above him, framed by that sky, a face came slowly into view. The creature stared, visage inverted where she knelt over him on the ground. Wisps of rich brown hair curled around a soft, sweet face made pale by the moonlight, her dark eyes impossibly wide. She was a wight, surely, or a statue come to life, some unearthly being that called to mind stories of magic and fae, a being who might capture one's—

"There is no escape."

Her hushed warning cut off whatever his thoughts had been going on about, then the flutter of a dark wing beside Nickolas's head had him bolting to his feet. The woman reached forward to snatch a small gray bird from his path. Her wide, dark eyes traveled up the length of him, his clothes tattered and torn, flesh bared to the night air at his neck and side. Her perusal came to its eventual conclusion when her gaze reached his. Their eyes locked.

The bird flicked a wing, its eyes on him, too, but conveying an eerie level of disdain. Nickolas abruptly recalled the metal that had tripped him and began to yank his foot free of what he realized was a metal cage. He made a sound of annoyed disgust before voices—too near—called him back to the urgency of his flight. His attention snapped to the woman once more. *No escape*, she'd said. Possibly, she'd meant to imply that she would call the guard—though she hadn't yet screamed—but the ominous warning had not precisely landed as a threat.

He said, "I need out."

Footfalls echoed through the garden, and Nickolas scanned the space, his heart in his throat.

"This is a private courtyard. The only door leads into Lady Carvell's rooms," the woman said. "Or to be more precise, her father's."

Nickolas let out a wheezing, horrified groan.

The corner of her lip twitched. She stood, dusting off a plain, serviceable dress with one delicate hand while holding the drab bird in the other. She was not very tall. She whispered, "Perhaps I can help."

He closed the distance, desperation clear in his entire being. "I beg of you." He prayed she might keep him from spending the entirety of his days inside a prison or, barring that, to at least prevent him from being forced into a marriage with the horrid woman inside those rooms. "Get me out."

Her head tipped back to meet his gaze. "I need something from you. A trade."

"Anything."

She frowned. "You should not agree so readily. You've no notion of my terms."

The sound of boots hitting the path came nearer, not two men now but at least four.

"My lady," Nickolas breathed. "It cannot be worse than the fate I'm facing." At her dubious gaze, he vowed, "Anything."

She gave a sharp nod then turned to face the men just as their chase ended. She slid an arm inside Nickolas's, locking their elbows as if to hold him in place. Had she not, he might have run—had he anywhere else to go.

The kingsmen fell to a stop and took in the scene, their prey standing unreasonably—nonsensically—firm against them, having taken up with a petite maiden and her dingy bird.

"My lady." The stoutest of the kingsmen stepped forward, his head dipping in a bow. "Please step away from this offender so that we might bring him to heel."

"How do you mean?" she asked.

Seemingly taken aback by her casual tone, the kingsman gestured toward Nickolas. "This man is a miscreant, my lady. We've been charged with apprehending him in the name of Westrende."

She glanced briefly at Nickolas. "How odd. What could you think he has done?"

The stout man straightened. Behind him, his brethren shifted impatiently. "It's a private matter, my lady. If you would only step aside—"

She laughed. It was a light, careless thing that seemed to echo off the statues then fall dead in the still night air. "A private matter. Sir, you are surely mistaken about how such business is conducted." She tugged Nickolas nearer while he did his best not to flinch at the proximity of the bird. "Lord Brigham and I are the ones managing a private matter. We are here under the authority of Lord Carvell himself. I wonder that you have the gall to interrupt us." She clicked her tongue in a manner that was neither mild nor good-natured but could not precisely be called out as a challenge. "Do go and leave us in peace."

Despite her words, the kingsman stepped forward. Nickolas moved to pull away, but the tiny woman held firm. He wanted to tell her she was going to be hurt if she didn't let go of him, that the men before them wanted blood. He wanted to tell her to forget their bargain, that she should deny she'd ever encountered him.

"Do you doubt my word?" she asked the kingsman. Her tone turned conversational or perhaps as if she were speaking only to herself. "I wouldn't think so, given my position on chancery staff and my relationship to both the marshal and chancellor. But here you are as if I've said nothing at all."

A spike of ice turned Nickolas's spine rigid. He did not dare look at the woman beside him lest his expression give the shock away. *Chancery. Marshal.* By the wall, he was ruined. He couldn't fathom how he'd stepped into a situation with even more perilous stakes. She was tied to officers of the kingdom. All Nickolas needed now was the presence of the general.

But he was not the only one affected by her remark. A nervous glance darted between two of the kingsmen farther back, and the nearest had frozen in his approach. There was a moment of silence.

"What is going on here?" Lord Carvell's voice rang through the courtyard before he was even in view. He took his time, coat half unbuttoned, cravat hanging loosely at his thick, unshaven neck. Beneath an unkempt brow, his eyes raked the scene with a worrying sharpness. He drew up beside the kingsmen, each of whom had adopted a militant posture, hands on their swords.

Nickolas's shoulders sagged in defeat. When he tried to pull away from the woman, she refused to allow it.

"Lord Carvell," she said in greeting. "How lovely of you to have come to shoo off these men." She made a show of gripping the bird tighter, but her grip was not as tight as the one with which she held to Nickolas.

He was only slightly curious what might happen if they dared try to tear him away from her. Whatever it was, Nickolas understood that she meant him to stay quiet.

"Look what a mess they've made of Frederick's cage."

For one long moment, Lord Carvell stared at the woman before his gaze shifted to Nickolas. Something dark passed over his expression, a sort of slimy self-satisfaction at what he'd done and what seemed to be a promise of what was to follow.

Saints but Nickolas hated that man. "Lord Carvell," Nickolas said with no inclination of his head. "You'll forgive me if I'm not forthcoming with delight at your arrival."

The woman dug an elbow into Nickolas's side. "Because, understandably, we expected the privacy I was promised," she said with a meaningful gaze at the men—a gaze that clearly no one present understood the meaning of at all.

Nickolas cleared his throat to speak, but Lord Carvell, evidently done with the baffling midnight games, jabbed a finger toward Nickolas and barked, "That man is going to walk to my study to sign a contract this instant or be hauled to a dungeon cell to await his trial!"

"A contract?" the woman asked brightly. "Whatever for? You know I love contracts, Lord Carvell. You must tell me. I insist. Don't make me wake the chancellor to find out."

The expression on Carvell's face went hard, his tone final. "Lord Brigham is about to marry my daughter."

The laughter came again, impossible amidst the crowd of stern men and still statues. Nickolas had the sense that if the woman's hand were not occupied cradling a sickly bird, it would have gone to her midsection so she might double over with mirth. "He couldn't possibly," she said with a too-genuine smile.

"Why is that?" Carvell bit out.

"Because." She gazed up at Nickolas. "He's already engaged to me."

CHAPTER 3

Nickolas gaped at the woman beside him. *Engaged*, she'd said. *Chancery*, she'd said. By the wall, he had no idea who the creature even was.

He wondered if that had truly been what he'd agreed to—a marriage with her. He shook off the thought before it could take root, because surely anyone, bird-toting stranger or no, was preferable to a Carvell.

Except he didn't even know her name. He would have liked at the very least to have her name. It was probably an adorable one, something short and cute.

"Brigham!" Carvell snapped, apparently not for the first time.

Nickolas's baffled gaze met his.

"Are you going to stand there and gawp at this woman while she speaks for you?"

Nickolas's palm had somehow found its way to rest over his heart. His other hand was tucked neatly against his middle. The arm it was attached to, beneath nothing but a thin shirt, was still latched to the woman in question. He wasn't certain who had possession of his jacket, only that it wasn't him.

"Nickolas," Carvell demanded.

Was he going to let her speak for him? To lay out such a blatant deception to save his skin? Nickolas blinked. "Yes, my lord, I believe I am."

The other man's face flamed, every exposed inch of him twitching with fury. "You will beg off this arrangement and marry my daughter this instant."

Beside Nickolas, the woman lifted a shoulder. "We've already filed the paperwork. You'll have to take it up with the magistrate, I'm afraid." On the surface, her tone was conciliatory, but something in it made clear that the woman meant to crush not only Carvell's plans for a marriage but for the arrest as well. She had connections, apparently, and she was not afraid to use them.

Carvell scoffed, his fiery glare darting between the faces of the woman and Nickolas. He noted their posture, the way her slender arm rested possessively inside the crook of Nickolas's elbow. His eyes narrowed. "Lady Brigham would never allow it."

He was right, entirely. Nickolas had no clue who the woman truly was, but her plain dress alone would be enough to cross her off his mother's list. It didn't stop him from clinging to her as his last hope.

The woman gazed up at Nickolas adoringly. The rapid clip of his pulse stuttered.

"Of course," she said in a soft voice. "Which is why we have kept it a secret." When she turned the force of her gaze back to Carvell, her tone was sharp. "Indeed, my lord, it seems best that you keep our news tucked safely near your chest, lest anyone discover what's happened here tonight. As you may recall, even the magistrate was in earshot when you granted permission for my use of this garden. Now, if you'll excuse us, I believe my dear Fredrick deserves a more peaceful court-yard for his home." Her lips tilted consideringly. "Perhaps Lord Keller's garden."

"Yes," Nickolas heard himself say, recalling that Keller was Lord Carvell's greatest rival. The woman glanced back at him, and Nickolas cleared his throat then shook free of whatever foolishness had come over him to focus on Carvell. "It has ponds."

The statement was both a cut and a threat, and with it, Nickolas reached down to retrieve the mangled cage, then he dipped his head to the unknown lady to indicate he was ready to depart. Without another word, they strode from the courtyard of a sputtering Carvell.

THE PAIR MADE it through a dozen castle corridors before reason returned. Nickolas—disheveled and toting a metal cage—and a small woman cradling a dismal bird were rushing through the halls of Westrende as if they'd not just evaded his arrest and announced a betrothal. "Where are we going?"

The woman didn't even spare him a glance. "Your rooms."

She was pulled to a stop as his steps froze, and Nickolas became aware that he still had hold of her. He let go his grip to straighten his shirt and remove a thorn from his sleeve. The bird fluttered a wing.

"We can't very well go to mine," she explained.

Chancery, she'd said. She worked in chancery. Her rooms would be there, right next to the cursed chancellor and every law official in the kingdom.

He stared at her, his hands stilled in their task of restoring his wardrobe to order.

She gestured toward the long, empty corridor. "It's hardly fitting to discuss here."

"It?" His voice seemed to come from somewhere far away.

"Our bargain."

He kept staring, pinned by those big dark eyes, his words barely above a whisper. "Who *are* you?"

She smiled politely. "You may call me Jules." Then she turned, flapping her fingers and chirping, "Come along."

Saints protect him, he did. When they reached the entrance to his suite, the woman—Jules—waited patiently. Nickolas did not unlock the door. Instead, he leaned forward, placing his palm flat against its finely carved surface to peer at her. "My lady, how is it that you knew precisely which door was mine?"

"I work in chancery."

It was no explanation at all. He waited.

She shrugged. "If you'd rather stand draggle-tailed in the corridor, that's perfectly agreeable to me."

He glanced at her skirts, which did not appear at all as if they'd been dipped in mud, despite that she'd been kneeling in the courtyard. She must have been aiming the remark at him, then. "Right. So I should let an unfamiliar woman and her dubious bird into my suite?"

"Frederick is of good character. And you and I…" She glanced up at him. Those eyes were weapons. "Are betrothed."

Nickolas's forehead thunked against the door. He left it there for a moment then drew a steadying breath. He would do this. If it meant foiling his mother's plans with the Carvells, Nickolas would take the risk of exposing his private life to a stranger with ties to chancery—and her dowdy bird. When he finally straightened to take the key from his pocket, he did not look back at her. "I cannot believe I'm letting fowl enter my sanctuary."

Small cooing sounds came from behind him as Nickolas fired every taper and lamp in the room. He would chase away every shadow in the suite and shed light on every detail of whatever fool bargain he'd agreed to. The woman had warned him, told him not to accept terms he knew nothing of, but he could not fathom how her terms might be worse than what fate had planned for him. He lit the last taper and slid toward the center of his mantel a vase he'd been gifted by a consul, knowing it was time to face her demands.

When he turned, she was standing in the center of his sitting room, her dress the only drab color in the entire brilliant space that was his suite. Well, her dress and that bird. The bird was still glaring at him. He picked up the cage once more, gesturing for Jules to sit while he crossed to a side table to retrieve an ornate letter opener to use as a tool. She chose a low white settee, and he returned to settle across from her, cage in hand. "Tell me about this bargain of yours."

"You don't like birds," she said.

He didn't. He would like very much for one not to be on his furniture. "This isn't about birds. But while we're on the subject, what were you about in Carvell's courtyard?"

"I've been trying to set him free. Frederick, that is."

Prying a wire straight with the letter opener, Nickolas glanced at the bird cradled in her lap. Clearly, it had an injured wing. "He won't be safe if he can't fly."

She seemed as if she couldn't meet his gaze, her slender fingers adjusting the lay of the bird's wing. "I can't keep him in a cage forever."

"He's fed. He seems loved. Is that not enough?"

"No." The word was not exactly sharp, but it came too fast to pass as indifferent. In a quieter voice, she added, "A creature cannot truly feel loved if it is not free. He must be free before it is too late."

When she finally looked up, Nickolas realized he'd gone still, watching her. He made himself focus once more on the cage. "The bargain. You'll keep me from being charged with breaking into Carvell's rooms, keep him from forcing his daughter upon me, and I'm to marry you. Is that the trade?"

She shifted forward on the settee. "No. Not truly. The betrothal is only a pretense until we are each free of the danger we are in."

The opener slipped from a metal wire to knock against the base of the cage. Nickolas looked up at her.

"You, with the Carvells. And me, with a minor legal issue that I need to resolve posthaste." Her lips shifted into what was likely meant to be a reassuring smile. It failed the task. "The whole thing will be over quickly, I'm certain. We'll be free again before the next moon."

"My lady—"

"Jules," she reminded him. "The marriage won't go through. I'll submit the paperwork but prevent it from being filed. We don't have to announce it." Her shoulders lifted in a small shrug. "It won't even be a lie. We *have* agreed to the betrothal. We just won't actually carry it out."

"Legal issue," he repeated.

"A trivial matter, really. I would rather not discuss the details."

"With the man you intend to marry."

"Precisely."

"And yet I'm meant to trust you."

The smile she offered next was less reassuring. "Or marry Lady Carvell instead."

Nickolas pressed his eyes shut and drew another breath. "My lady, I need to know this. Whatever danger you are in, I cannot just pretend it away. You have asked me to tie myself in this bargain. At least allow me the courtesy of being aware of the risks we're meant to avoid."

Her smile fell. She seemed to consider her answer for a long moment, one hand coming up to press thin fingers where a pendant might rest beneath the gray cloth. Nickolas did not take his gaze off her until her eyes finally rose to his.

She said, "I need to break a betrothal contract. One that was taken into agreement without my consent and must be broken by someone other than me."

Her parents, then. Not so unlike Nickolas's situation, except she did not appear to have been trussed up for the matter. Though, to be fair, she might have been tied using only less-literal bindings. "You claimed a relationship with both marshal and chancellor," he pressed.

Jules nodded.

"Why not ask them for help?"

Her expression twisted something inside of Nickolas that wasn't the familiar knot that had been set by his mother.

"I cannot," she admitted. "Because I am not a true citizen of Westrende. They would be required by law to return me home. I'd be asking them to break a vow they've made to their kingdom. It's untenable."

She swallowed, the motion clenching that new spot inside of him. Her impossibly wide eyes met his.

"I need you, Nickolas."

The thing inside of him snapped, his heart pulsing strangely as if it might lift from his chest.

It was grounded like a game bird when Jules said evenly, "And if you don't help me, then your only choice is the lady Carvell or a locked cell."

CHAPTER 4

Jules and her bird had left Nickolas with no more than a brief farewell and a list of demands that included an introduction to Lord Beckett—a man who specialized in interkingdom law—and access to the private library of a Brigham family friend. In exchange, she would handle the threat of Carvell and his daughter.

Nickolas and Jules would keep the engagement to themselves.

"Brigham!" William clapped Nickolas on the back. "You're early. Come, have a seat by the best of your associates before that horrific Lady Mena steals in again. I swear the woman's rose water is strong enough to stave off a raging bear."

"And yet it has remained ineffective against you," Nickolas muttered as he scanned the room for any sign of his family, the kingsmen from the night before, or any threat not theretofore anticipated.

William's hand slid to squeeze Nickolas's shoulder, dragging him along to a high row of seats in view of the rostrum where kingdom officials would hold their forum and hear from the lords and ladies of Westrende.

Nickolas tugged himself from the man's grip, settling between

Ander and Redmahn instead. He did not have the patience for loutish-ness today. "Gentlemen."

Ander offered only a brief nod, his eyes on the gathering crowd. Redmahn gave Nickolas the once-over. "Saints, what happened to you? You look as if you slept in the granary again."

"Late night, Lord Brigham?" William said from Ander's other side, far too loudly for Nickolas's taste.

"What are we campaigning for today, my friends?"

"Avoidance will get you everywhere," Ander murmured with a wink. He gestured toward the floor. "Lord Klein is in an uproar about the uptick in kingdom officials being removed from their posts. That's where my interest lies as well. Not to prevent it, mind you. Only to gain some insight so that I might sneak into one of the vacated posts myself."

Nickolas did not reply, because he knew a thing or two about the situation his peers did not. If anything could be said of Westrende, it was that tradition ruled. And it just so happened that tradition called for the willful denial of the existence of magic. It didn't matter that the Rive was in place to keep the kingdom secure, that the ancient wall surrounding it was said to be a border of the fae realm of Rivenwilde. As far as any citizen was concerned, no magic inside Westrende meant no magic existed at all.

Nickolas had once believed the same. He might give anything to go back.

"I'm here to lobby for naked bathing pools," Redmahn announced as he leaned back into his chair.

William made a grunt of disgust. "Not public ones, please. The last thing we need is a bunch of... Saints, that reminds me of the time Lady Carvell went—"

At Nickolas's sharp look, William's words cut off. "By the wall, Nicky, what have I said to upend you?"

"Don't call me that."

His laugh was loud enough to draw looks from the gathering spec-tators. "Certainly. I'll address you only as the honorable Lord Brigham henceforth. Saints, you're a mess today. What's happened? Some skirt have you riled?"

"Would you *please* keep it down," Nickolas hissed. "A little decorum would not kill you, would it?"

William shrugged. "It might. Best not risk it."

"Speaking of skirts," Ander remarked at a more acceptable volume. "The midsummer ball hits at next week's end. Who can we expect to see on your arm?"

The ball. Nickolas had forgotten. It was a masked affair, another tradition. In days past, a king would mingle with the guests, and not a soul could be certain which was he. No king currently sat on the throne—until one came of age, the council was ruling in his stead—but the ball carried on without him. Every person of status would attend.

It was the perfect chance to introduce Jules to Lord Beckett. The man loathed frippery and never failed to wear the same mask that was no more than a thin strip of fabric barely covering one eye. Nickolas could parade Jules in, right in front of the entire kingdom, and never have to answer about who she truly was.

Redmahn jabbed an elbow into Nickolas's side. "Who is she you're thinking so laboriously of?"

Nickolas's gaze shot to his friend's.

Redmahn laughed. "Oh, a lady has you in her clutches, doesn't she? Whoever she is."

Nickolas shook off the accusation. "I'm only considering the tasks I've to complete this week. Nothing more."

Ander's chuckle was low. "Yes, the contemplation of a busy man. We can all see that."

The gavel banged as the assembly was called to order, and Nickolas was saved from further inquiry. Before him, men and women of the kingdom sat in audience, hearing the concerns and plans that Nickolas was meant to be part of. All he could think of was the ball. He would have to make arrangements quickly, but Jules *had* said the bargain would be over as soon as their complications were sorted. By the next moon, she'd told him. Nickolas could do that. He could take her to a masked gala and let her stay on his arm. His lips drew into a frown, and Nickolas slid his palm over his mouth to keep his friends from noticing. Jules had not appeared to possess the wardrobe for such an event. He could arrange one for her. It would be no trouble.

Besides, the cost of a fine gown would be little expense given that their bargain had saved his hide. The last thing Jules needed to be concerned with was procuring a dress with only days' notice. Being a Brigham afforded him privileges in such matters. He would handle it. He glanced at the grand clock marking the hour. Right after assembly, Nickolas would visit the tailor. And from there, chancery was only a short walk away. She would be thrilled he'd taken initiative, that their bargain would be resolved so expediently.

He needed only to make certain his mother was not aware. Jules would require a particular sort of gown, one that made her seem like the type of lady he might usually have on his arm—but no. She wasn't. He didn't think a gown could do that. Saints, her eyes alone would give her away.

A shout sounded from near the rostrum, snapping Nickolas's attention back to the room, the lords arguing over a tax matter. His gaze roamed the crowd. Far below, across a sea of formal dress, Lord Carvell stared Nickolas down.

Nickolas's lips pressed tighter. The man's look seemed to promise revenge. Nickolas had nothing but the vow of a small woman to save him. Claps and shouts rose through the chamber, but Nickolas and Carvell were still. He would not get up, would not dismiss himself early and let Carvell win.

The Brighams held their ground. That didn't mean they didn't have the sense not to be caught out in an argument before every peer in the realm, though, so the moment the proceedings were through, Nickolas slipped out of the chamber.

NICKOLAS'S TAILOR was a woman sharp only in wit. She had a pleasingly soft manner and person and could be relied upon to dress in a palette of grays that complemented the shade of both her hair and her eyes. She was a woman, he felt, who appeared as if she might pass embraces out as easily as others might offer platitudes. Nickolas adored her.

"Lady Roth." He bowed grandly, despite that she would never fall for such a thing as easy charm. "So lovely of you to meet with me on short notice."

Her smile was wry. "Lord Brigham, I was never notified at all."

He chuckled. "Alas, here I am. Can you spare a moment for me?"

Gesturing that he follow, she led him past a half dozen seamstresses at work on fine suits and gowns. They arrived into a private room scattered with bolts of silk, where she indicated for Nickolas to take a seat on one of the lush fabric chaises. Lady Roth gave him her full attention.

"I need a gown for the midsummer ball." At the frown she gave him, he explained, "I know it's not much time, but I hope you can help me. Something blue, I think. Not too shimmery. And a mask that covers nearly all of a face. No feathers, please. That's merely a personal preference, not owing to any real requirements on your part. It's for a woman about..." He held his hands in an approximation of Jules's width and height.

Lady Roth gave him a flat look.

In return, he offered a wink. "How's this, then? Something with a sash. We'll just"—his hands gestured again—"draw it tight where the narrow bits are. As good as a custom fit."

"My boy, I've no idea how you've made it to this stage in life without a hint as to how women's garments work. Is there some reason she cannot come here for a fitting?"

Several, but Nickolas would not be admitting them aloud. Deciding against the more easily misconstrued, *It's a private matter, I'm afraid, and I think it best not to parade her through the halls where my mother might see,* he said, "A surprise! I want to gift her something stunning and whisk her off her feet."

Lady Roth did not appear moved.

"Perhaps you're familiar with the lady. She's a clerk's assistant. In chancery. Dark hair. The eyes of a harmless forest creature, though perhaps not-so-innocuous teeth."

"Jules," the tailor guessed.

"There you have it."

"Pretty, peculiar girl, that one."

"Precisely."

"Not your usual type."

Electing to ignore the remark, he leaned forward. "Can you help me?"

She pressed her lips. "I realize that most of the charges do not belong to you personally, but there remains the matter of settling the family's account."

Nickolas's palms slid together, not gracefully. "My lady, one more favor, if I might. I'd rather this purchase was settled off the books."

Her gray eyes narrowed. She would know he was hiding it from his mother, but he wasn't certain if she might guess a reasonable excuse as to why. The truth was out of the question, as it was not reasonable at all.

From the pocket of his vest, Nickolas withdrew a fine gold watch, worth a dozen dresses and matching slippers, then passed it to her. "Will this cover it?"

CHAPTER 5

Nickolas's step was a bit livelier on his way to the chancery. He had a plan. Things were looking up. He was going to find Jules and let her know what he'd done so she might be impressed. No, *prepared*. So that she might be *prepared* to make arrangements for the ball.

"My lord," a passing boy greeted.

Nickolas thought the boy was the cousin of a man his sister was acquainted with. It was a chore to keep up with all the lords and ladies who moved within the circles moving about his circles. But as a Brigham, he had to. One needed to be certain, in any case, when one happened across society, which warranted respect and which a healthy distance. Nickolas gave a vague, moderately friendly reply and tucked his hands into his pockets as he continued his stride. Every kingsman in the hallway made him want to twitch, but only four or so actually had it out for him. The odds were low of running across the wrong one by chance.

Two kingsmen very much not on that list waited outside the entrance to the chancery—where its doors rose high and majestic, despite that it was stuffed to the gills with musty documents and kept closed from too much light or, truly, any fresh air. He should have brought the woman a flower or a token to lighten the place up. He was off his game. He'd never courted a lady he was not actually courting. Because he wasn't courting her.

They were engaged.

He missed a step at the thought then straightened, buttoning his coat and smoothing the front before walking through the entryway. Nickolas threw a smile at the kingsman who gave him a look. "New boots."

The man did not reply. Nickolas cleared his throat quietly and walked on, swallowed up along with the brightness of the castle corridors as his steps carried him into the large, dimly lit, shelf-lined chamber that was the chancery office. Document carts and baskets of scrolls littered the space, long worktables positioned haphazardly throughout. One of the figures bustling about stopped to look at him. "May I help you, my lord?"

The boy was wiry with sandy hair and freckled skin, an air of efficiency practically clinging to his person. Nickolas was fairly certain the boy's name was Robert; he and the other young man assisted with sorting and filing.

"Ah yes, I'm here for—" Nickolas's gaze caught on a petite, plainly dressed figure as it froze with the sound of his voice. His lips slid into a wicked smile. "Her."

Jules turned and faced him, the stack of records in her grip lowering before she placed it firmly on a nearby table. The boy glanced from one to the other but said not a word as he continued his work. Jules closed the distance, her eyes darting once across the chamber before returning to him. "What are you doing here?"

Her tone reminded him that their plan was supposed to remain a secret. "I have news," Nickolas said. "An invitation, in fact."

"Could you not have sent a letter?"

His lips pursed, his hand coming to his chest. He had, in fact, not considered it. "There was not much time to spare. I thought it best I let you know right away."

Beyond her, several rooms back, a dark figure paused inside a narrow doorway—Gideon Alexander, chancellor of Westrende. Nickolas dipped his head in a manner that might be taken as recognition or avoidance, whichever the man preferred. In a low voice, he asked Jules, "Perhaps a garden walk? For privacy."

She frowned then glanced toward the chancellor's office herself. Toward Gideon, she made a gesture that, like his own, might have been a wave of acknowledgment or of warning him off. She brushed a lock of hair back from her temple. "Fine. That sounds... fine."

He put out his arm. "Rarely do I receive such an enthusiastic response. Come, let us walk."

She took his arm and did not glance again at those in the chancery, but her posture did not ease, even when they stepped from the outer corridor and into the warm sun.

"Is this your preferred garden?" he asked. "I quite like the gardens on the east walk. My favorites, though, are just outside, past the Baker cottage and bordering the trees. It is a bit overgrown, to be certain, but I hold that is part of the charm."

She stopped and peered up at him. "Why did you come here?"

"Oh. Precisely." He drew a finely penned invitation from an inside pocket of his coat. "Your introduction to Lord Beckett."

She tugged the card from between his two fingers, the tiniest line forming in the center of her brow as she scanned the words. "This is an invitation to a ball."

"A masked ball," he said with only a hint of smugness. "Where we might appear in plain sight with no one the wiser to our ruse."

Her dark eyes rose to his. "You only moments ago strode into the chancery for all to see."

"Well, I'm an important lord. Perhaps I had documents to file."

Her answering look said that was doubtful.

He ignored the insinuation. He wasn't concerned about agents of the kingdom seeing him. He was concerned about his mother and her society connections, and they didn't bother with matters such as being seen before noon. "This ball will be perfect. Just the thing. And all that's left is a visit to the library. How's tomorrow for that? Or do you have a particular day that you prefer?"

She blinked. "I—yes, tomorrow is well enough. Thank you."

Nickolas straightened. "Prime. Then the matter is practically resolved. By the end of next week, you'll be entirely free of me."

Something in her expression shifted, making Nickolas wish he could steal back the words. But he wasn't certain precisely what he'd said wrong. He had been too flippant, perhaps. She had said she was facing a danger. Maybe the cliff she was standing before was steeper than his own.

"I apologize," he told her. "Etta always says I'm a mule. I meant no offense. I'm sure your situation is not something you find humor in, and even now, as I offer my regret, I sound impossibly glib."

"No, I—" She shook her head. "I was only thinking."

"Ah." He held out his arm. "Shall we walk, then, while you think?"

Her hand slid inside the crook of his elbow as if automatically, and Nickolas led them at a sedate pace, unspeaking, over the garden path. It was a good garden, boasting lilies and violets and a curving stream that connected several small pools stocked with pike and trout. The far wall was lined with fruit trees, their leaves providing shade to a row of stone benches that sat bookended by sculpted lions at rest.

Jules glanced sidelong at Nickolas.

"Go on. Ask me," he said.

"I don't—"

"Oh, please. We're betrothed. If there are no secrets between lovers, then there certainly shall not be between us as fellow conspirators." He gave her a playful frown, his tone chagrined. "Saints know you've seen about the worst of my character already."

Her lips twitched.

He groaned. "It's worse, then. Not only have you witnessed my latest downfall, but you've heard something even more reprehensible." He closed his eyes and lifted his face toward the sky. "Don't tell me. Lady Asha? The incident with the pig?"

When she didn't answer, he opened one eye to peer at her. "No? Something older, then. Does it have anything to do with a kerchief and three bread rolls?"

She laughed. "Be assured, I've no interest in the details."

He pressed a palm to his chest in a gesture of thanks, and she added, "But you'll recall I did bunk with Lady Ostwind, if only temporarily."

His step faltered. "You—that was you? This whole time?"

"I will admit that I feel flattered not at all. Your reputation was one of unrestrained charm, my lord, yet you did not even recall my name."

He winced. It was likely that Etta had not shared the name, not if she was fond of Jules. And she was fond of her, he realized, because Etta must have taken great care not to mention Jules by name in all of their conversations about her time at the chancery. It was almost offensive.

Nickolas inclined his head in his most gallant manner. "It is my pledge to you now, this day, beneath the sun of a fine Westrende sky, fair Jules who has yet to reveal to me her surname, that your given name, at least, will never fade from my memory, for I will etch it on the very walls of my heart."

"Is your heart made from stone, Lord Brigham?"

He opened his mouth then pressed it shut. "You realize, my lady, that you're meant to merely swoon, not examine the promises made by a suitor."

"Even once we are betrothed?"

His expression went grave. "Especially then."

"I'll take it under consideration."

"I think it's in the vows." He paused. "You should not examine those, either."

"Sage advice. You realize I work in the chancery office? With records and contracts?"

"Mmm."

"Indeed."

"My lady." He gave her a look. "Jules." When her smile teased *you remembered*, he flashed a grin before letting it melt into something more solemn. "You haven't asked."

They reached the end of the garden, and she turned. Nickolas turned with her. Farther up the path from where they'd come, a dark-haired man sat in the dappled shade of a willow, his gaze on the nearest pond. "You made suit for Antonetta," Jules said.

Nickolas let out a breath. "Not officially, no. But I did think we would suit." They had been friends since they were children. He knew her. Trusted her. If anyone could have stood against his mother, it would have been Etta. But she wouldn't have had to, because her family was among the highest of Westrende. "She would have done well in the position."

"Done well?" Jules asked. "You sound as if you're hiring staff."

She wasn't wrong. The qualification for the position was *satisfy Nickolas's mother without being crushed by the force of it*. He said, "Fortunately for us all, she held not a whit of interest in taking the post." After a moment, he added fondly, "She always was a bit of a bully, so there's that."

"It seems as if you care for her a great deal."

"I do. Antonetta is like the sister I never had."

Jules's brow crinkled. "I was under the impression you had four sisters."

He made a sound of agreement in his throat. He tried not to speak poorly of his sisters, but the truth was they were more his mother's daughters than anything else. They might be Nickolas's blood, but they were certainly not of the same heart.

Nickolas and Jules were silent for a long while as they walked. They would soon be at the edge of the garden, where he would have to return her to the chancery. Voice low, he said, "My lady, you may ask me whatever it is outright."

She glanced up at him.

"The thing that you wished to draw from me by inquiring of Lady Ostwind."

Her expression fell a bit. "You have quite a reputation for trying for a bride, yet you remain unmarried. It is certainly not for lack of status or charm." He pressed his lips, and she asked, "Have you never truly wanted any of them? For yourself?"

For yourself, she'd said. Because Jules understood the situation with Lady Carvell had been created by Nickolas's mother. But she would not know the extent of it. Not even close.

He could not tell her that wanting someone, that caring for them at all, would be precisely the sort of reason that made it impossible to try. He could never tie a decent person to such an indecent situation. He could not allow someone he cared about to be used in his mother's game.

He couldn't make himself tell Jules that, so he asked, "Have you?"

A shadow crossed her expression, unfathomable in its depth. An instant later, the evidence of her grief was gone, but the memory of it remained with Nickolas. It had been like a knife to the heart.

Jules said, "I have great love for... my many..." She shook her head. "I cannot speak of it." She offered him a shaky smile, her free hand lifting to press at what must have been a pendant hidden beneath the fabric of her gown, though he could see only its chain. "I've had too much love in my life. There isn't room, I'm afraid, for more."

They reached the end of the path. Nickolas faced her, laying his hand gently over hers where it rested on his arm. "Allow me to assure you, then, that there is no one you can trust more than I not to intrude on your too-generous heart."

He dipped his head, drawing her hand to his lips to press a soft kiss on her skin. He glanced up at her. "May we both enjoy the safety of our most fitting betrothal yet."

A warning flashed in her gaze, and Nickolas straightened to follow where it held over his shoulder. The man down the path had stood and faced them, his eyes narrowed on the delicate fingers in Nickolas's hand.

"Nickolas," Jules urged. "Come along. It's time to return to the chancery."

CHAPTER 6

Nickolas was still contemplating the man from the path as he walked away from the chancery entrance. It had been strange, but Jules had not seemed afraid. The only urgency, it seemed, was to remove herself from Nickolas's company.

He frowned, disliking the idea, and turned the corner into a connecting corridor, where he was met directly with the worst thing he could possibly imagine—his mother's narrowed gaze. He was not proud when he made a small startled yelp and stumbled backward.

Her jaw was set. "Who was that?"

Internally, Nickolas cursed. Outwardly, he only blinked in confusion. "Who?"

Her tone lowered dangerously. "That chit you just left. Do not try me, boy."

He made to brush past her. "I've no idea what you're on about. I was at the chancery to see Gideon."

She put a hand on his arm as if to stall him. "You loathe Lord Alexander."

"Yes." He made a show of sighing. "But Antonetta has asked that I make the effort. So I have, for her."

A kingsman passed in the connecting corridor, and his mother snapped, "Come with me."

"I do not believe I will."

Her fingers curled into the material of his coat, warning him not to disobey her again.

Nickolas felt his expression go hard. He leaned in. "The Carvells, Mother? Really? Have you entirely lost your mind? To have your own son trussed up like a—"

Another figure passed in the corridor, and Nickolas dropped his voice. "You know what Lord Carvell is capable of. You know the sort of man, the sort of family you were trying to tie us to. Has it truly come to this? Have the Brighams fallen so low?"

"They have fallen precisely so low. And you will bring them back. I do not know how you managed to wrangle out of the arrangement, but mark my words, you will regret this defiance. If you know what is best for you, for the Brigham name, you will make things right with the Carvells." Each word she spoke was bitten off with too-sharp teeth. Carvell might have heeded Jules's warning to keep the incident in the garden private, but it was clear Nickolas was not yet safe.

He tugged his jacket from her considerable grip. "*Right* is evidently the only direction absent from your moral compass. Now, if you'll excuse me, Mother, I have business to attend."

He strode from her, the ire in her gaze tightening the knot in him until he felt rather like he might be sick. He'd made a mistake. He'd been convinced his mother would be nowhere near. She must have heard that he'd escaped her ambush and come to discover how for herself. Nickolas couldn't stand to think of the position he'd put Jules in. If his mother discovered their ruse, if she tried to hurt Jules or to remove her from Nickolas's life...

So help him, he would never marry if he could help it. He hadn't been worried about Etta. She was stubborn and strong-willed, and she possessed a high-enough station that she would have at least had the chance to hold her footing against his mother. But Nickolas could not subject any other woman to his situation or his mother. He needed to sever her attempts to control him. He had to find a way to escape for good.

Whatever Nickolas did, he would have to do it fast. The longer he lingered, the greater the chance he took that someone would get hurt.

NICKOLAS WAS NO MORE than another single corridor away before he was tweaked by the ear and dragged through a nearby doorway. He jerked away from the grip just as the door was slammed shut, closing him in a narrow room with Lady Antonetta Ostwind.

Nickolas rubbed his ear. "That was uncalled for."

Etta leaned toward him. "Was it?" She was in uniform, her hair drawn back and her manner firm.

"Don't you have work to do?" he groused.

She crossed her arms. "Yes, in fact. I was doing it when I caught sight of Lord Nickolas Brigham prancing after a member of chancery staff like a hobbledehoy."

Nickolas drew back. "I was not."

"You were. I cannot believe you, Nickolas. Marriage? To Jules?"

His protestations fell flat. He should have known she would find out. Maybe he had known she would, in truth, though he would have thought it might take a bit longer than a single day.

"It's public record," she reminded him. "Anyone can see it."

"Anyone who looks. And why were you looking? No one reads the records filed with chancery." He narrowed his gaze. "Did Gideon tell you?"

"How I found out is beside the point. What are you thinking?"

He leaned on a small table near the wall. "What's so wrong with it? You think I'm so unfit that I couldn't please a sweet, gentle-mannered lady? That I deserve someone hideous and uncouth?"

"Sweet?" Tone incredulous, Etta lifted her hands to the room as if displaying his statement as evidence. "You clearly know nothing of her at all. Jules has never been one to trifle with. But that's not the issue." Her hands dropped, and she took a calming breath. "She's a stranger to you. She does not belong in your world. It's a bad match, Nickolas, and you know it. Have things become so desperate—"

He straightened. "Don't. Don't pretend you understand what it's like to need a match. You, who spent your entire existence determined to do everything on your own. Honestly, Antonetta. I'm offended." He met her gaze. "I know I'm not good enough for her. I'm certain she knows it as well. Our agreement is temporary. That's all. Just to keep..." He sighed and slumped against the table once more. He was a grown man; he could not bring himself to say *to keep my mother at bay*. "I was caught in Lady Carvell's room. Her father meant to force my hand, and Jules saved me. Nothing more. I'll leave her be, just as soon as I'm able."

Etta flopped down on a bench, fingertips pressing to her temples. "Carvell? Saints, Nickolas, what have you done?"

Lips pressing down, he said, "The usual, I suspect." The thing everyone expected of him. The worst, most rakish and irresponsible thing. He let out a long breath. "I'll make it right with Jules. Then I will leave her alone. I swear it."

CHAPTER 7

After being accosted by both his mother and Antonetta, Nickolas had sent a missive to Jules to arrange their meeting for the following day—at a lesser-used entrance near the mews instead of anywhere they might easily be seen. The Filmore family library, it turned out, was not inside the castle at all but at a private estate near the far walls of the kingdom. It explained why Jules had not been able to secure her own invitation. Their caper—for that was somehow what it felt like—would occupy the entire day.

The early-morning sun was bright and warm and making Nickolas feel quite impatient as he waited for Jules's arrival near the massive stone archway outside the castle. He examined the toe of a boot, straightened his vest for the dozenth time, then forced his hands into his pockets. A fine script was carved into the stone beneath his feet, a motto of the kingdom: *Within these walls, justice.* He'd been taught it as a boy and recited it so often that the words barely meant anything at all. Now he wondered what the motto might mean regarding what waited outside of the kingdom walls.

It had not seemed to keep the fae from attempting to meddle in kingdom affairs. Rivenwilde and its prince were the greatest threat to the kingdom's safety. The desire to deliver justice upon the fae had driven Etta to become marshal. It was also the reason so many Westrende officials had been removed from their posts.

When Nickolas glanced up, Jules was finally walking toward him, her slight form fitted into a dark-gray gown nearly identical to the shade of her bird.

Nickolas's restlessness immediately ceased. She had brought the bird. To visit a library.

Her eyes were on him, watchful.

He dipped into a bow. "My lady Jules." To the bird, he said, "Frederick."

"I hope you don't mind," she said. "I cannot leave him alone, and Robert and Tobias were occupied."

"Not at all." Just beyond the entrance and down a short set of stairs, their carriage waited. There, Nickolas would be trapped inside a confined space for the better part of an hour. With a bird. He cleared his throat. "Any friend of yours and all that." He held out an arm, forcing his gaze away from her bare neck, revealed by hair that was swept up into an intricate knot. A gold chain rested against her skin, whatever hung from it hidden where it dipped into the bodice of her gown. He glanced determinedly toward the sky. "Should be a lovely ride. We have the weather for it."

She made a small hum of agreement.

When they reached the carriage, Nickolas took the cage, Frederick's dark bird-eyes on him as Nickolas climbed in to secure the wire contraption to one of the bench seats. He'd meant to go back for Jules, but she took the footman's hand and stepped up after Nickolas, forcing him backward into a seat. She did not use the bench holding the cage but instead slid in beside Nickolas. He straightened, drawing himself against the wall so that she might have more room. The faint scent of violets rose from her, along with a trace of something that he could not quite make out. Nickolas resisted the urge to lean closer. He was all but pressed against her as it was.

Across the carriage, Frederick glared.

The footman closed the door, and in short order, the carriage juddered to a start. The sound of hoofbeats on cobblestones fell into a rhythm, and Nickolas eased against the cushioned seat back. Outside the window, men on horseback shifted in the shadows of narrow passages, watching the elaborate conveyance roll by. Their gazes slid away one by one at Nickolas's attention.

"What is it that so unsettles you?" Jules asked, drawing his focus from the men. At Nickolas's look, she gestured toward the cage. "About birds."

He regarded Frederick. "Must I have some tangible reason? A horrific accident as a boy or traumatic history involving the creatures that prevents me from enjoying their company? Some very specific incident that tortures me to this day?"

She watched him.

"I do not." He attempted to cross his arms, brushed an elbow against Jules, then dropped his hands to his lap. It should have been enough that the creatures were unsettling. Frederick, in fact, took the act to another level. His eyes were black but not at all hollow. Intelligent, dark, and... oddly judgmental. Focused too sharply on one particular person. Nickolas shuddered. "I reserve my right to the opinion."

Jules's face turned toward the window but not before he'd seen the way she bit her lip.

"What is so great about birds, in any case? Of all the pets from which to choose, why a feathered—" He caught himself before an expletive escaped, then cleared his throat.

She chuckled. "That is a considerable dislike you possess, my lord."

He leaned nearer. It couldn't be helped. "What is your second-favorite pet, then? Perhaps I will like that."

"When I was a girl, I was given a menagerie of sorts."

"A menagerie, was it?" He imagined young Jules with a heap of some small furry things. Mewling kittens, perhaps. Or rabbit kits, whatever noise they made.

She hummed in agreement. "I was denied sweets for a month when I set the lot of them free. It was made quite clear afterward that I would not be allowed a pet until I was of age and under my own care, which I'm afraid illustrates that my father missed the point entirely."

"Ah," Nickolas purred. "A criminal from the start. As I suspected."

"Who is to decide what is criminal? The act was misguided

perhaps, but not the intention behind it. No creature wants for a cage."

"Indeed," Nickolas said. "Compassion is a great virtue. Even if one does choose to bestow it upon a wounded bird."

"Compassion can be bravery when one opens their heart to what they fear."

"I would not go as far as calling it *fear*," he hedged.

"Nor could we call it unflinching."

"Touché. And what of you?" he murmured, trying terribly not to stare at the line of her neck. "Is there nothing that unsettles you?"

She looked back at him, all hint of humor gone from her expression. "Yes. A great many things, Lord Brigham."

Nickolas regretted that he had asked. "Very well," he said, attempting to step back from whatever precipice loomed over their conversation. "Then we shall each have and keep our dislikes."

The edge of her lip shifted but not into a true smile. Nickolas fell silent, hating whatever dark emotion hid behind her reaction, and they both took to watching the kingdom pass outside.

It was warm inside the cabin, and the early sun came bright through the carriage windows. He felt Jules lean into him after a bit, away from the light that shone more heavily on her side. He made no comment, but after a while of silent stillness, he glanced over to find that she'd somehow drifted off to sleep. He stared at her motionless form, the way her limbs seemed to have gone entirely loose and the way her shoulder pressed to his, all hint of distress erased from her features. Her head canted toward him, rocking with every bump and jostle. He wasn't certain whether he should move but knew her position must be uncomfortable. He shifted, only barely, to allow her form to fall further against him, catching her head against the shoulder of his jacket without having to touch her more than she had done on her own.

Satisfied, Nickolas returned his gaze to the seat before them. Frederick perched in his cage, birdy glare intensified. Nickolas resisted the impulse to reply. As if being judged for his behavior with ladies by the entire court was not enough, he was suddenly being outclassed by fowl. He purposefully returned his attention to the carriage window.

The trip carried on, taking them past the many shops and residences, winding through the narrow streets inside Westrende's border, until their way widened with more distance from the kingdom center. Nickolas had loved escaping as a boy, had adored the sense of freedom that came with being outside the castle walls. It was more than simply the expanse of pasture and open sky. It was the space created by the very lack of courtiers.

It was the way it had made him feel as if he might finally breathe.

Etta had held little patience for him then—perhaps not a great deal more than she had in later years—because her entire being was molded around the kingdom and its structure. Her father had been no kinder than Nickolas's mother, but the pair of them had found their contentment in entirely different directions. Nickolas and the other boys had run and screamed and flung caution—and propriety—to the wind when they were away. He'd returned so often without his coat—and on one particularly shameful occasion, his trousers—that Nickolas's mother had punished him by way of making him work off his debt with Lady Roth.

His days mending tools and carrying crates for the tailor had been some of the most enjoyable of his youth. It was the single day he'd been relegated to the bird lady's care that he refused to dwell on. The last thing he would ever do was admit the story to Jules and her censorious bird.

The carriage passed beneath a massive gateway, and Nickolas glanced at Jules. They were nearly at the Filmore estate, and she'd settled quite firmly against him. She was altogether adorable when she was sleeping, not a hint of her sharp, graceful movements in sight. One slippered foot was turned outward, the other tucked beneath the bench. Her hand had curled into the hem of his coat, like a child with a familiar blanket, and her cheek was plastered to his arm. He should wake her. He didn't want to.

He ducked his head toward hers to whisper news of their arrival, but somehow, unfathomably, his lips found their way to brush softly against the crown of her head.

Jules moved.

Nickolas started, straightening, in utter disbelief at what he'd done.

Across the carriage, the bird squawked in outrage then glared what had to be a threat of death.

Nickolas kept his eyes on the creature regardless as, beside him, Jules blinked awake.

Stretching her arms surreptitiously, she glanced out the carriage window. "Here already?"

He cleared his throat, gaze pinned to the unmistakably livid bird. "Yes, just."

Jules ran her delicate fingers over her hair, sweeping back the few strands that had gone astray as she took in the bird. "Good. By the look of it, I don't think Frederick enjoys carriage rides."

"Nickolas!" chirped the tall blond woman who met them in the grand entrance room at the Filmore estate.

Nickolas bowed deeply. "Lady Filmore. Lovely to see you again."

She rushed forward and took his hand in hers before performing a dip that displayed bare arms and a great deal of silk taffeta skirt.

"Compliments on your gown, my lady." He stepped back, but Lady Filmore gave him no distance, keeping hold of his hand while he gestured toward Jules where she stood with her bird. "May I introduce the lady"—he pressed his lips, giving Jules a wink to remind her of his carved-stone heart—"Jules."

Jules dipped briefly. Lady Filmore stared blankly at the cage in Jules's hand.

"And this is Frederick," Nickolas said. "He ranks higher than a mere lord, I believe, though I've yet to gather his full heritage. Has the bearing for royalty. A prince at least."

At his jest, Jules made a choked sound.

Lady Filmore only blinked.

It was progress, he supposed. Nickolas cleared his throat, giving Lady Filmore's hand a little squeeze to remind her that she'd not let go and was not exactly welcoming her guest. "Allow me to extend my gratitude, again, for the favor your family has bestowed upon us today. I assure you that it is most appreciated and will not soon be forgotten."

"Of course," she replied automatically, evidently taking her eyes off the cage only so they might travel over Jules's gown with a no-less-forgiving expression.

Nickolas pulled his hand from Lady Filmore's grip then offered his arm to Jules. "The estate is lovely, as always, Lady Filmore. You must convey my admiration to your father. Such an esteemed property and kept so well by your family."

Lady Filmore's eyes met his, the woman finally taking up his reminders of civility. "Yes. It is lovely. Particularly this time of year. I hope you'll join us for the annual gathering in the gardens, Lord Brigham."

"You must" came another voice from the entrance to the room. Another Filmore sister, dressed nearly identical to the first. "Promise us now before the midsummer ball, where you might be swayed into more lofty pursuits. Rumor has it there will be a handful of all-too-intriguing visitors present. I do so hate to be overshadowed."

"Lady Filmore." Nickolas offered a bow. "We were just headed to the—"

"I know," said the elder sister. "You must permit me to escort you." She also made to reach for his hand, but one glance at Jules—and the cage—and the elder Lady Filmore called for the butler. "Take this contrivance away, please." The sound she made could be classified as nothing but disgust.

Jules drew the cage closer. "Frederick stays with me."

The butler, under direction from his employer by means of a less-than-subtle look, persisted. His hand closed over a bar. The bird drove its beak into the man's fingers. Jules did not let go.

Nickolas moved forward, but neither of the pair spared him a glance. "Lady Filmore," Nickolas said levelly, "kindly instruct your man to remove himself from my lady's presence before I do it for him."

The elder sister laughed, the sound too cheery and overloud in the open chamber. "My lord, surely you do not intend—"

At his look, she apparently understood he *did* intend, because she called the butler down. The lot of them stood in the near silence for one long moment, broken only by the complaints of the aggrieved bird.

Nickolas adjusted his lapel then gave a sharp nod before tugging on Jules's arm, submitting not a moment more to the sisters. Tension remained in Jules's grip on the cage, then they were in the library and safely out of conflict's way. It was the better part of an hour before either spoke another word, and when they did, it was not in regard to how she'd been treated.

"May I help you find whatever it is that you are looking for?" Nickolas finally asked as he watched Jules from where he leaned on a nearby set of shelves.

"I can't—" she started, a tightening in her expression seeming to cut short the words. She shook her head. "I have to do it myself."

He picked up a small ceramic container, halfheartedly examining the painted vines circling its lid. He was fairly certain it was imported, but he'd seen impressive enough imitations. Every summer, there was a little stall set up near the gate with one of the traveling markets, where a family of painters possessed a remarkable talent to mimic nearly any style. Nickolas had always marveled at the courtiers who passed by the youngest child's original gems in favor of lesser works in a popular fashion. "And we are not to ask the Filmore—"

Jules shot him a look.

He could not help but bite back a smile. "Yes, you told me." His fingers twisted at his lips before performing the act of throwing away an invisible key. "They must never know."

Nickolas turned to the shelf, gaze blurring over a dozen embossed titles bound in leather. "It's only that it seems more expeditious to use me. After all, I am here."

Jules stopped in the motion of sliding a slim volume back into its spot to look at him. "Perhaps you should find a diversion to occupy your time."

"Perhaps," he said, chastened. Glancing about the room, he thought that there was not particularly anything more diverting than watching Jules at her work. The thought had him certain it was time to find an alternate occupation. He strode away from her, crossed to an entirely different section of books, drew one from the shelf at random, and took it to the far end of the room, where sunlight fell over a lovely trio of lounges.

He reclined onto one and opened the book. He managed more than an hour of reading before his eyes began to lift once more, catching on Jules where her search had progressed to shelves nearer to him. Restlessness beginning anew, he closed the book, wandered toward the window, then found himself seated at the pianoforte.

He was rarely idle, no matter the reputation he'd earned, and being trapped inside any space for long made a desire to climb the walls rise up in him. He'd had enough wall climbing, he reminded himself, fingers dancing along the keys with a favorite sonata.

When Jules sauntered closer, he glanced sidelong to discover she was watching his hands. He found himself shifting into a more complicated piece, and the set of her mouth shifted with it. He teased, "What have you to say, fair maiden whose name I wear etched on my heart?"

Her dark eyes slid to his. "For one who so dislikes birds, you do a great deal of preening, Lord Brigham."

Nickolas's playing broke off. He turned to her where she stood, too near his perch on the delicate embroidered bench. "You think me displaying my plumage, then."

Her gaze moved meaningfully toward his hands.

He held them up for her inspection. "These?" It felt oddly dangerous, playing this game. He knew precisely what she was implying. He *had* kept on with the playing to impress her. He couldn't seem to stop himself.

"Yes, those. You wave them about as if baiting a fish."

He stared at her.

"Everyone knows what you're about."

Nickolas attempted to appear as innocent as possible. "Ladies have a preference for capable hands?"

She gave him a level look. It was particularly level, as he was sitting and she was standing before him, finally bringing them eye to eye.

He leaned into a more casual stance, one foot sliding forward. Toward her. "Forgive me, my lady, but how else am I meant to catch a wife?"

If color touched her cheeks, he could not see it, because Jules turned away and resumed her perusal of the books. She had not moved far, though, only paces from where he sat. "Perhaps they are not falling for you because your interest is clearly not genuine."

Perhaps he didn't really want to bring them into his life.

"Perhaps," she continued, "you might aim instead for one who doesn't care only for fancy feathers."

He scoffed. Jules did not take the opportunity to say more, despite that he'd crossed a boundary already.

He watched her silently, the sunlight catching on her dark upswept hair before she shifted farther into the shadows. When she reached as if to draw a book from an upper shelf, too far above her, Nickolas stood. He stepped behind her, one hand brushing her waist to still her as his other slipped past hers to draw the book from its place. He lowered the volume, and Jules seemed to hesitate before taking it from his hand.

Saints, she smelled faintly of violets, of sun-warmed books, and the bare skin of that elegant neck was only a breath away from his, from his own breath because he was practically panting on her, for the love of—

He stepped back. Cleared his throat. "A repast," he heard himself say. "We've been inside far too long. Let us take a break, go outdoors, and rest your eyes before returning to work."

Jules glanced back at him, clearly unhappy at the prospect.

"Only for a bit. We can come back straightaway, and if you do not find your answers today, we will return again until you are satisfied." When she looked doubtful, he added, "Think of the bird. Poor Frederick needs some air."

From his cage atop a table by the chaise, the bird squawked in contempt.

Nickolas gave Jules a look to imply her creature was in agreement and felt warmth cut through the knot inside him at the hint of her sardonic smile. "It is agreed, then." He held an arm forward to lead her from the seeming confines of what was, truly, an impressively spacious room.

CHAPTER 8

The Filmore gardens were absolutely lovely, some of the best the kingdom had to offer, and it took no time at all for the fresh air and bright sun to bring a pleasant languor to both Jules and Nickolas. Frederick, however, adopted an even surlier demeanor. Jules had taken the bird from his cage and placed him gently in the grass beside the spot where they had spread their meal. The creature stared on, mostly at Nickolas, refusing both the coddling and bread his mistress offered, wings tucked tightly to his sides and complaints rattling loudly from his chest.

It was evident his discontent weighed on Jules, but no matter her coaxing, the bird refused to move away. She'd been trying to set him free, she'd said before. Nickolas wondered at the pair, as clearly Jules might just leave him should she want badly enough for him to be free, injured wing notwithstanding. But Nickolas did not wish to pry into a situation that seemed so unlikely to end well for either the bird or his caregiver. "The Filmores keep no predators in this garden," Nickolas said. "You may rest easy on that front."

Jules leaned onto an elbow, just as she'd been convening with the bird, then sighed and laid her head on her arm.

"Your eyes are heavy," he said. "You've time to rest."

"I have no time," she told him. "That's the problem. Time is spending faster than I can…"

There was an unmistakable tremble to her words as they trailed off. He wondered why she seemed so weary despite her nap in the carriage. Perhaps her worries had brought sleepless nights. But it seemed nothing should trouble her in such a fine sunlit garden, someone to watch over her while she slumbered. "Come." Nickolas opened an arm so that she might lie against him instead of the ground. "Troubles only grow larger when one's in need of rest. You may tackle it after. Half an hour will not break you."

She eyed him warily. "Ten minutes."

He felt the edge of his lip tilt and gestured her closer with his outstretched arm. "I'll take care to wake you precisely then."

Having Jules snuggled against him in the warm sun untied the knot inside of Nickolas before the first few minutes were up. His own eyes became heavy, his arm gone limp around her, and the small garden sounds a lullaby to his ears. So when, sometime later, Jules shrieked, he startled from sleep like the world had exploded around him.

"Frederick!" she shrieked. "Frederick is gone!"

Chest heaving, Nickolas stared at the display of absolute terror in a person whose manner had seemed nearly unshakable in the face of greater foes. He stood, glancing around the bare spot of green they'd settled upon and landing on an empty cage. A dull-gray feather was all that remained where Frederick had posted himself in his earlier refusal to move. Dread sank in Nickolas's gut.

"We'll search the surrounding vegetation. If he left on his own, he can't have gotten far."

"I've already searched," she said. "And what do you mean *left on his own?* You said there were no predators here!"

He pressed his lips. The bird's wing was too damaged; he could not have flown. There indeed was no sign of any other animal that might have approached. There was, however, a patch of matted grass in a size more like that of a human boot. "I'll request aid from the Filmores." If one of the ladies had played a prank, he would ensure they answered to their father for it, but Nickolas would find that bird.

Jules glanced at the manor, its wide row of high windows overlooking the garden. "There," she said. "It will offer a vantage point of the entire space." She grabbed Nickolas's arm, and they moved toward the house with an urgency that drew attention. From both the upper and lower floors, Nickolas could see figures taking note of their approach. Inside, he gave direction to a member of the staff, and Nickolas and Jules were up the steps in a rush for the high windows. If they didn't see anything of use, he would leave her there and go find Lord Filmore himself.

Nickolas was so set in his course that when they topped the final staircase and turned to find a gathering of figures, he stopped cold, entirely motionless, to stare in shock.

At his mother.

Jules's step faltered a moment later, her gaze trailing from the stately woman centered before a balcony railing to the dark-clothed beast of a man at her left then the dark-clothed brute of a man on her right.

"Mother," Nickolas managed. "What are you doing here?"

She gave him her most haughty countenance. "I might ask the same of you." Her gaze flicked briefly toward Jules, only long enough to convey that the woman was utterly beneath contempt.

Nickolas stiffened. "We do not have time for this." He might have hissed *and on Filmore grounds, no less?* for the woman had clearly lost her senses. She'd taken to kidnapping and trespassing in order to see her wishes fulfilled.

But they truly did not have the time. He took hold of Jules's arm to lead her away. They had to find—

He froze again as his mother flicked a hand. Nickolas recognized the gesture; it was one he'd experienced countless times before. It spoke of retribution, and what swiftly followed was always the punishment for his disobedience. What came instead was far worse than any injury she'd offered before, because it would hurt not only Nickolas.

"I suspected you might say as much." His mother's tone was cold as the man beside her drew an object from inside his coat. "Which was why I have provided incentive."

A chill silence swallowed the room, its bright windows and open space doing nothing to dampen the severity of the threat. Gripped within a cage of the giant man's fingers was the stout feathered mass of a dull-gray bird.

"*Frederick*." The word wheezed out of Nickolas, no disguise to his disbelief. Nickolas's attention snapped to his mother.

Her expression held no remorse. "You will leave off whatever shameful foolishness you're about with this girl and agree to marry Lady Carvell. Or you will both suffer the consequences." Her tone made clear the consequences did not end there.

He took a step forward. The man shifted to hold the bird over the balcony.

Nickolas went rigid. Frederick's wing was broken. He would not survive the fall.

Beside him, Jules stepped forward. "I warn you not to do that," she said. Her words were only for the man, with no hint of acknowledgment for Nickolas's mother.

"Shouldn't have left your man behind," the brute on Lady Brigham's other side said. "Don't think you'll have much luck at stopping us on your own."

Her man. The one who'd approached when he'd kissed Jules's hand must have been a guard. But he didn't understand *why* Jules would have a guard. Nickolas glanced at her, but Jules's attention was only on the beast holding her bird.

"What happens to you as a result will be worse than you can ever imagine," she told the man.

There was such surety in her tone that even Nickolas felt uncertain, but his mother's man was under orders. The beast glanced nervously at Lady Brigham. The lady in question said to Nickolas, "Agree now, or this will be the least of your worries."

"I am your only son."

"And I would never harm you." Her brow lifted as she slid a glance toward Jules.

Nickolas would not stand for it. "This has nothing to do with her, Mother. I will not allow you to hurt her. Understand that she is without fault. Lady Carvell, however—"

His mother's hand flicked again. The three figures at the railing turned.

Before another movement could be made, the beastly man tossed the bird over the balcony rail.

Nickolas lunged just as Jules whispered a single word.

The scene stopped dead, the world gone unnaturally still and Nickolas catching himself mid-dive as a man-shaped shadow shimmered into view. Suddenly, before them, angled away from the turned backs of Lady Brigham and her men and looking on where Nickolas watched with Jules was an unmistakable figure swathed in nebulous black.

The prince of Rivenwilde.

CHAPTER 9

Jules had called upon a fae prince. In the Filmores' manor. Right upon their balcony floor.

Nickolas pressed the base of his palms over his eyes.

He could see the fae, just as the tales had always warned. *Lay eyes upon him, and the shadows will clear.* He wouldn't see only the single man. He would see all fae, every creature. He would be tied to their world. A sad, desperate noise crawled from his chest. He drew his hands away to look accusingly at Jules.

"The prince of the Riven court," he said dreadfully.

She did not answer, despite that it had sounded more a question than anything else. Her eyes were on the prince.

Nickolas turned to look at him as well, never mind that he had in no way wanted to see. That he still wished he could not. Tall and slender, with dark hair and darker eyes, the man seemed elegant, regal, and entirely unnatural. Nickolas took a step in front of Jules. She stepped out from behind him.

Taking in the scene—Nickolas's mother and her lackeys and, *by the wall*, that awful bird, frozen in position in a way that made Nickolas's stomach pitch and senses whirl—the fae prince seemed unsurprised by it all. He turned and looked at Jules, the light catching on the spiky crown of tangled bone upon his head.

It was clear the prince understood what had transpired. To Jules, he asked, "Shall I just—" He made a flicking gesture as if to knock Lady Brigham and her henchmen over the ledge.

Jules shook her head. "No, just save Frederick."

"The bird," the prince said. "That is all?"

"No!" Nickolas shouted, more to the room in general than specifically at Jules. "Have you lost all sense? Don't bargain with him. He's the *prince of Rivenwilde*. You must not be tied to him."

"It's too late for that." There was something hard in Jules's reply, something Nickolas had never heard from her, and it was aimed at the prince.

The prince stared back at her. "I did not set the curse, my lady. Had I wanted, I have people for that. But you can blame neither them nor me." He seemed to consider his words. "It was a rather clever one, as curses go, though. Was it not?"

"Especially cruel. Unnecessarily so, if you ask me," Jules said.

He hummed. "And what price were you given to break it?"

Her look was level. "To marry one who was equal to my station."

They stared at each other for a very long moment. Nickolas, meanwhile, continued in his confusion and gaping.

"And will you pay it?" the prince asked. "That price?"

Jules's voice was ice. "Not if the kingdom depended on it."

The prince gave a swift, decisive nod.

"Hold a moment." Nickolas barely recognized his own voice, let alone Jules's, as he held up a single finger to intercede. When the pair looked at him, he asked, "What the deuce is going on here?"

"A curse," Jules and the prince answered at once, and the prince twitched in irritation. He tapped a long finger to a button on his coat. The button looked, perhaps, to be crafted from solid gemstone. "A curse," the prince said again, his tone making clear he meant to own the pronouncement.

Nickolas glanced from one to the other. "Her or you?"

The prince said, "Both, it would seem. Though mine is the more pressing."

Jules scoffed.

The prince rolled his gaze skyward. "Let us be done with it."

And suddenly, without even a glimmer of warning, the room surrounding them disappeared.

NICKOLAS BLINKED, unsteady on ground that seemed to sway beneath his feet. Ground that was not the polished floor of the Filmore manor but greensward. He took a step backward and bumped against Jules.

She held the bird firmly against her chest, where he grumbled wildly inside a ruffled neck.

"You," Nickolas started. "You made a bargain. For that bird." *With a fae prince* seemed unnecessary to tack on, but he did so regardless.

The prince gave the pair of them a look. "I'll leave you to it," he said, waving a dismissive hand. To Jules, he added, "You know how to find me, should you change your mind."

"Never," she said again.

The prince's expression seemed to imply he was plagued by humans, then he was gone. As easily as he'd transported Nickolas, Jules, and the bird, the prince of Rivenwilde walked through the filigree wall.

Nickolas stared. The Rive, an ancient boundary that surrounded the kingdom, in place to prevent just such a fae from crossing, stood tall and imposing before them in the shape of a finely carved wall.

They were in the hollow heart of the forest. Nickolas had watched the prince walk through the filigree wall.

He stared longer, in wonder, at the sight he'd been granted by laying eyes on the prince. Part of the curse that kept the kingdoms safe had allowed Nickolas to see through fae glamour. The magic that had always hidden such things was suddenly revealed.

Nickolas did not like it. What had appeared as delicately chiseled stone was now writhing with forms in the shapes of man and beast, tangled wire and thorny vines caging them for all eternity. The two sights were layered overtop each other, human and fae, just like the creatures that appeared trapped within the stone. A stone hand reached forward, the barbed metal holding it back pierced through its chiseled forearm, while something vaguely wolflike clawed upward on its carved-stone hind legs, the thing's teeth bared and maw drawn in both directions by iron vine.

Nickolas suddenly yearned instead to be anywhere else, even penned inside Lord Carvell's courtyard.

"Lord Brigham," Jules said gently from beside him. "Perhaps we should go."

He turned on her. "Oh no, you don't. You did not just magically conduct us into the forest by fae bargain and then go on pretending all is well."

Frederick squawked.

"And you!" Nickolas said. "You can stay out of it. This is between me and my *wife*."

Jules slid a step back.

Nickolas advanced on her. "A curse. That was your secret? The trifling little thing you kept from me? *A fae curse?*"

She pressed her lips. "I never used the word *trifling*—"

"Indeed," he shot back. "You said naught of it at all. It's the most untrifling thing it could possibly be. What was it you called it? A minor legal matter? To break a betrothal. To a man of your station, apparently. But oh no, it was best that I find that out now from the *blasted* prince of the *blasted* fae."

"Nickolas, my lord, you seem a bit... overset."

"Over. Set. Truly?" He threw up his hands. "Yes. By all means, set me to rights." He pointed at her. "Tell me the terms of the curse."

She frowned.

"Right," he said. "None of that. Curse can't be spoken. Can't ask for help. One of those, I'm sure." Saints, he couldn't believe it. He should have *known*. He was going to get back to the castle, back to... What had he been doing? Oh, right, he and his clandestine bride-to-be had just disappeared themselves in front of Nickolas's mother and two of her men. Though, to be fair, they'd had their backs turned and had not seen the prince. They might have no idea how he and Jules had escaped. "Etta," he said. "Etta can help us."

But for now, Nickolas realized, he needed to guess the curse. "Sleeping," he tried. "You're always sleeping."

Jules's expression went hard. "Is that a fault, Lord Brigham? Because you did not seem to mind earlier today."

When you dozed off and let your mother's men steal my bird, she meant.

He frowned, lifting his hand between them to wave off her remark. "Bad guess. I'll try again. Your face. It's not... Saints, of course not. How could it be real?"

She glared at him. "What does that mean?"

"Pardon me if it doesn't make sense that your..." His gaze fell from her expression to the way her fingers wrapped possessively around the bird. The bird that was glaring right along with her, dark eyes steely and judgmental. The breath seemed to rush from Nickolas's lungs. He stared at Jules accusingly. "It's... he's cursed. He's a cursed... there is a *person* inside of that bird. A *man*, to put a finer point on it."

"Nickolas," Jules said very carefully, "pray, do not faint inside this forest, as I'll not be able to drag you safely free of the trees."

He laughed, helpless and on edge. "Frederick. Frederick is your..." The laughter trailed away as he looked at her. "Frederick is your..."

"Brother," she answered.

"Brother." He took a deep breath, maybe the first since he'd been thrown to the woods. Something echoed in the trees, bringing him back to his senses. They were in the forest, beside the filigree wall. Beyond it, upon a Riven throne, waited a prince and a curse. "Absolutely," he said in regard to no one in particular, "let us remove to the safety of the castle walls."

CHAPTER 10

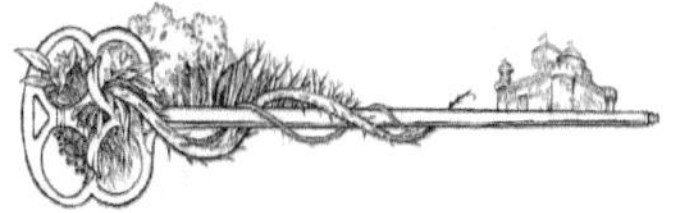

It was nightfall before Nickolas and Jules came out of the forest. With his newly gifted sight, Nickolas experienced the altering of a world he had always considered fairly steady.

He had not taken the change well. With fae creatures shifting in every shadow, watching Jules and her bird with an intensity that put Frederick's glares to shame, Nickolas had, admittedly, handled it badly. It was to be expected. But after Jules had threatened to blindfold him and drag him back to the castle, Nickolas managed to pull himself together. He was not anticipating any particularly restful nights in his near future, though.

Nickolas and Jules stepped over the stones that marked the boundary, a warning that the edge of the forest was near, and something eased inside of him. "What about my mother's men?" he finally asked when they were near enough the castle walls that he felt as if his shoulders could dip beneath the level of his ears.

"I have a guard, and I am housed in the chancery. They will not make an attempt on me there." She glanced up at him, and he nodded. "What of you? Will you be safe in your own rooms?"

"I've a lock on my door, so there's that. But breaking through locks

299

is not typically how the lady Brigham operates. If she means to trap me, she will do so in plain sight."

"Then stay out of sight." Jules's voice was crisp.

"I am not certain how I will ever apologize for what she's done," he started.

Her gaze snapped to his again. "Do not. They were not your actions, and I refuse to hold you responsible."

He opened his mouth to argue, but her attention turned back to their path. "Besides, I knew full well what I was inviting upon myself by making a bargain with you."

"About that," Nickolas said.

She held up a hand. "There's Ian now."

The dark-haired man from their walk in the chancery gardens stood beside a castle outbuilding. He was dressed in neither livery nor finery, only a simple suit, sword at his hip and frown at the ready.

"Has he been watching the forest this entire time?" Nickolas asked.

"Doubtless he heard something was amiss. Or perhaps your carriage returned empty." She stopped and turned toward Nickolas.

She was leaving. Off with her man to the chancery. Something about the idea had him feeling bereft. "Frederick." He gestured toward the bird nestled against her chest. "He needs a cage. I could..." Saints protect him. "Would you like me to pick one up for him at the aviary?"

The bird gave Nickolas a dark look.

"Thank you," Jules said. "But Ian can manage it."

They stood for a moment longer. In his nondescript suit by his nondescript block wall, Ian straightened.

"Right." Nickolas bowed his head. "Good night, my lady."

"Good night, Lord Brigham."

THE FIRST THING Nickolas had done upon returning to his rooms was lock his door. But shortly afterward, he'd written a note for Etta. Nickolas might have been rattled by his encounter with the prince, but though it was the first time he'd witnessed a fae, it was not the first time he'd witnessed foul magic. He understood Jules was in trouble. She had made a bargain with Nickolas because a curse had been laid upon her.

He had to help her break it.

And so, early the next morning, he was in the office of the marshal of Westrende. "Truly," he said, standing in the center of a room that felt palatial and fighting the desire to make a slow spin, head tilted back to take it in. "All this for a marshal?"

The lady Ostwind gave him a level stare from where she sat behind her massive desk. "I'm the head of law and order for the entire kingdom, Nickolas. What did you expect?"

He shook his head. "A bit of modesty, I suppose. Could have at least tried putting some on."

She leaned forward. "I have work to do. Perhaps you could muster sufficient nerve to tell me whatever it is you're avoiding"—her finger tapped irritably on a stack of correspondence atop her desk—"and what it has to do with a late-night order that I send a half-dozen kingsmen to stand watch outside the chancery sleeping quarters."

The chagrin that crossed his face was not put on. "*Order* is a strong word."

Etta shuffled through the stack, drawing out a single page. "... and therefore demand no less than fifteen armed men at all times posted as noted at each of the following locations throughout the chancery—"

"All right. I was under duress. I'd just had a shock." Nickolas bit his lip. "You did send them, did you not?"

She sighed. "I did."

He nodded. "Thank you. That means a great deal."

"And the shock?"

"Right." He settled heavily into the chair that sat opposite her desk. "I saw the prince."

"The prince." Her voice changed, gone as steady as a general. If there was a being who possessed all of the ire inside of Antonetta Ostwind, it was the prince of the Riven Court.

Nickolas leaned back to run a hand over his face. "Yes. That one."

Etta was very quiet, and when he finally looked at her again, he found her expression was as deadly as a general as well.

He owed her an apology, he knew. Etta had the sight. She had seen the prince when she'd been only a girl.

Nickolas had not believed her. Like everyone else, he'd thought Westrende was safe from the fae. "It was horrendous," he said.

"Lady Brigham's men have been sniffing around the chancery. You've asked that guards be placed there. Outside of Jules's rooms," she said.

A long breath fell from his lungs.

Etta nodded slowly. She hadn't earned her position by being a fool. "At your warning, Gideon set his own kingsmen to watch. The chancery will be the safest place for her." She leaned forward, not softly as she might have done as his friend but sharply, the posture of a marshal of Westrende. "What has this to do with your mother?"

Nickolas held back the wild sob that wanted to escape. What came out instead was sort of a helpless laugh. "Nothing at all. She merely wishes me to marry Lady Carvell." To restore the family name.

"Who laid eyes on the prince? Who else has the sight?"

"My mother and her ruffians were turned away. So only me and Jules. But she... Well, Jules has evidently already met him."

"Because of a curse."

Nickolas slid a hand over the fabric covering his knee. "She can't tell me. Each time she starts to speak of it, her words choke off." Or she grabbed at whatever hung from a chain at her neck, he thought. "It's that ridiculous bird of hers. That's part of the curse. Her brother, she says. He's trapped inside the creature. Hates me, by the way. Doesn't spare a chance to let me know it."

He threw up a hand. "And I don't know what it means, how any of it is tied to her curse, or how to stop it. I'm only certain it must have been laid on her ages ago and that the prince and she were aware of one another before being in each other's company yesterday. She needed to get out of a betrothal, so she bargained with me to gain access to places she could not go on her own. Introductions, you know. She wanted to break the curse. And she kept saying..." She had kept saying it would be over soon. He looked up at Etta. "Her time must be almost up."

"The full moon," Etta said. "It's always ending on a full moon with this sort, fae rituals and all. Well, that explains why she's working in the chancery office." At Nickolas's blank look, Etta explained, "To learn the laws of the kingdom so she can unhitch herself from... this other man, whoever he is."

"Laws," Nickolas said. "*Books.*"

Etta's gaze narrowed on him. "Do you need a moment to gather your thoughts? Perhaps before you speak?"

He shook his head. "The library. We were at the Filmore library because she needed to find a book." He went still at her reaction. "What?"

"What?" Etta parroted back.

"You tell me what." He pointed at her. "You've got that look. The one you get when you know something you don't plan to tell me. There! That one. Give it up, Antonetta. This isn't a game."

"I know it's not, you dolt. It's precisely the sort of foolery you should not be messing about with. This is serious kingdom business."

Nickolas leaned forward. "Oh no you don't. I'm in this, just like last time, and you're not going to keep me in the dark until I end up—"

"It was *one* time," Etta snapped. "I got you into trouble *one* time."

"Jail, Antonetta. You got me into *jail.*"

Her lips pressed down. "I may know the book. There was a certain collection of fae laws my father had." At his attempt at rising, she held up a hand as if to stall him. "It's no longer in our possession. Gideon has moved it somewhere safe."

"Can it help her? Does it hold whatever clues she needs to break a curse?"

Etta looked doubtful. "Not without knowing the terms she's bound by. What about the other favor, the introduction?"

"She's asked to meet with Lord Beckett."

Etta hummed. "Beckett specializes in interkingdom law. Perhaps the threat of a betrothal at home is why she's hiding in Westrende, looking for asylum. But it's no wonder she could not ask Gideon to assist her in an introduction to Beckett. The man has ties to his uncle."

"The steward?"

She nodded. "The very one."

Nickolas leaned back in his chair. Jules had said she did not want to put Gideon and Etta at risk. He'd not understood precisely how real that danger was. Fae curses and kingdom officials could not mix. He shook his head. "Well, at least that part, I have covered. I plan to introduce her to Beckett at the midsummer ball."

Etta stared at him. After a moment, she asked, "You're taking her to a ball?"

Nickolas stood abruptly. "I'm helping her. That's all." It was all, truly. She was just a lady who was cursed, and he was taking her to a ball. Etta's eyes still on him, he said defensively, "Find the book. I'll do the rest." Then he turned and walked out the door.

Chelsea Crane 23

Nickolas strode into the wide corridor outside Etta's office just as kingdom business came into full swing. Lords and ladies, kingsmen, officials, and sundry messengers, staff, and scribes filled the imposing space. Nickolas had a list of those lords he was meant to meet with. He needed to review his proposal for the next assembly and, most unfortunately, had run out of excuses not to stop at the exchequer's office to handle some delicate Brigham family business. He would do so today.

"Nicky."

A hand smacked overhard onto Nickolas's shoulder along with the overloud voice. He held back the expression that wanted to claw its way across his face. Lords did not reveal unpleasant tempers in the council's wing of the castle. "William," he said without breaking his stride.

The other man rushed to keep up, not letting go his grip. "Still churlish, I see. Word about Westrende is that you have a new lady on your arm. Giving you trouble, is she?"

Nickolas stopped and turned so abruptly that a scribe knocked into William from behind when he stopped too. "Remove your hand from my person, Lord Adair."

William stepped back. "I see how it is, then."

Something heavy settled in Nickolas's gut. Would that it was only guilt.

William's head tipped closer at his reaction. "Remembering my connections, I see, that a word from me could do more damage than even a Brigham's reputation might bear." His voice had gone smooth, no longer the brash boy he so often pretended to be.

Nickolas said nothing and merely let the cold steadiness of his expression do its work.

The other man's tone dipped in its cajoling. "Come, Nickolas. Our families have been friends for years. I just need a moment of your time. That's all."

Nickolas asked, "What is it that you want, Will?"

His sharp green eyes darted from one direction of the corridor to another. He wore a superfine coat of a shade darker than his eyes, his muddy-hued side-whiskers dipping beneath his shirt points in a pale imitation of his father's. He truly was a menace. "Just a moment of privacy."

Nickolas gave a nod of acquiescence and followed the man to a private meeting room farther down the corridor. Once inside, Nickolas moved away from the darkened alcove, where William latched the door.

Unease crawled up Nickolas's neck, and he couldn't help but snap, "What is it?"

William clicked his tongue. "So that's how it will be, then? Even among old friends?"

"I wasn't under the impression this was a friendly interview, Lord Adair. It smacks of distrain."

A dark chuckle came from behind Nickolas as William moved to face him. "Very well. We'll get to the point. I need something from you, Lord Brigham."

That was nothing new. "I've naught left to give, and you know it."

William's wide mouth slid into an unpleasant grin. "I do. But you have one asset left, do you not? And I intend to use it. You, my fine friend, will do precisely as I ask, or the Brigham name will be turned to muck. No one with a single tie to your family will be spared, least of all your lady mother."

The truth in the threat was plain. The Adairs had information on Nickolas's mother. They'd used it for years to siphon obligations from Nickolas's father. But Nickolas's father was gone.

"Why now? What reason could you possibly have?" Nickolas asked.

The eldest of a long line of Adair heirs leaned a hip against the table and crossed his arms. "Princess Mireille."

Nickolas stared dumbly. "What about her? The woman is three kingdoms away."

"She's coming to the ball. Word is she means to find a husband and strengthen ties with Westrende. I intend to win her."

"Win her? Saints, what are you—" Nickolas's words cut off when he realized what William was planning. The lady was worth a small fortune on her own. But if one could win the support of the lady's father and influence trade from the inside... Nickolas leaned heavily against the nearby wall.

"All I need is a post. To look as if the thing hasn't been set up. A valid title so that, by appearance, I've a different goal. And you, my friend"—a long finger pointed menacingly at Nickolas—"you will get me that spot. Something impressive at the hands of your bosom confidant. And don't tell me the two of you have fallen out. I just saw you leave her."

"You expect a post in the marshal's office?" Nickolas asked, his tone incredulous. "Ostwind would tear you apart."

Will leaned forward. "Let me worry about that."

"It will never work. You have to see that."

William rose to his full height. "You seem to believe this is a favor I'm asking, Lord Brigham. Be assured, it is not. You will secure me a post in the office of marshal by the end of the week, or your four sisters will pay the price."

He dropped a coin onto the table then strode from the room. Nickolas could hear the horrible man's whistle fade into the distance as if he'd not just tossed a threat to the entire Brigham family onto the fine wood table.

Nickolas's mother had never been satisfied. Despite the riches her status provided—the comfort, the security, a lavish lifestyle, and societal respect—there was never enough. Tempted by riffraff, she'd found ways to feed that dissatisfaction. Minor offenses at first, smuggled goods that were not entirely legal, dishonest trades with neighboring kingdoms. But she'd gotten greedy. She became involved with a group who dabbled in more illicit crimes, like forgery. Nickolas's father had chased her debts, ensuring her safety but emptying the coffers even before his death.

The squandering had not stopped. Lady Brigham had driven the family into insolvency beyond repair. She'd betrayed their name for the endless desire for more. And the coin was carved with a reminder of those crimes.

Nickolas stared at it, understanding exactly how dangerous his mother's secret was in the hands of William Adair and unable to stop it.

CHAPTER 12

Nickolas had not laid eyes on Jules since the day she had left him outside of the castle. He'd been thwarted first by his mother's men sniffing around the chancery then again when he'd arrived to find Gideon at odds with some lord who was part of Princess Mireille's entourage attempting to force access to the wing. The risk of being spotted and Nickolas's failed attempts to visit personally had led him to send a message to Jules, which was followed only by a brief conversation with her through a thin panel in a nearby document room.

Ian had stood watch as Nickolas leaned close to the panel, whispering assurances that the masked ball would be Jules's best chance at an introduction to Lord Beckett. "We will find him, and we will sort your troubles. Soon, this will all be only a dark spot in your past."

"I hear your words, Lord Brigham, but I fear they do not ring true. Time is running out for me, and I'm afraid new complications have arisen."

His finger had lifted to trace the thin grooves in the panel that made up a larger pattern of decorative vines. "My lady, let us try."

There was a long moment of stillness. When her voice came again, it was closer, as if she had pressed near the panel on her own side. "We will try," she said. "For it is all there is to do."

Her tone made it evident that she'd given up hope. For his part, Nickolas had not sought out his mother, had not attempted to convince Antonetta that his extortionist associate should be given a post in the marshal's office, and was very much feeling the same sort of resigned despair that he sensed in Jules.

The Brighams would be ruined, come one thing or another. Tying himself to a Carvell or playing into a scheme of the Adairs would only make it worse. Perhaps he should renounce his title and move to the country to take up gardening, or a trade for which he had no skill at all, until their creditors came calling. Perhaps he might strip off his clothes and dance atop the courtyard wall to have it all done with faster.

"You look quite fine," he said dourly to his reflection. "Even if it may be the last time you'll dress in velvet and gilt trim." He'd chosen his finest black coat to wear over the stiff white shirt, with black pants and black shoes. His mask was sleek and dark, shaped to cover him from nose to brow. The only spot of color would be Jules on his arm.

He strode from his suite and toward the grand ballroom, every part of the castle alive with bustle and conversation that only grew as he neared the hall. So much anticipation surrounded the event, and delight at its secrets and masks, that Nickolas had no trouble slipping through unnoticed. He was slowed only when an older man bumped into him, as the man was jostled by the crowd that was gathered where the princess awaited entry. Lords and ladies clamored to catch a glimpse of her court, making the corridor overhot and heavily scented by perfumes.

He steadied the man then adjusted course to walk closer to the wall, weaving around statuary and a man in a deep-blue coat. Nickolas recognized him as the lord who'd attempted access to the chancery. The man had the look of a guard, gaze sharp as it traversed the crowd, and Nickolas wondered how many of Mireille's entourage were not mere courtiers. Surely William was not the only person who had eyes on interkingdom relations, trade or otherwise.

The doors to the ballroom opened, finally allowing the milling guests to go inside, and Nickolas's way became clearer. He glanced over his shoulder before releasing the lever to a small room adjacent to the corridor, where he was to meet Jules. Across the crowded space, the chancellor of Westrende watched from his place beside a pillar. Nickolas could not help the smirk that tipped the edge of his lips upward, as Gideon might be masked and attired in something other than his customary uniform coat, but Nickolas would recognize that stuffy posture anywhere.

Gideon frowned.

The latch clicked open, and Nickolas stepped inside.

Across the space was the familiar figure he'd encountered for the first time only days before in a midnight garden. Everything else in the room fell away. Jules was radiant. Lady Roth had outdone herself with a fine silk gown in the palest shade of blue and topped with a sheer layer dotted with embroidery and jewels. The bodice was trimmed with a delicate strip of lace, cut lower than Jules's usual gowns to reveal a single ring hanging from the end of the familiar golden chain. Her arms were bare above a pair of long white gloves, smooth skin luminous in the candlelight. In the corner of the room, Ian cleared his throat.

Nickolas swallowed hard. His gaze rose to Jules's face. "My lady," he said with his grandest bow, "you are exquisite."

Jules's mouth was in a strange line, her brow knit beneath a delicate mask of white and blue and not a single feather on her person, thank the fates and Lady Roth.

"Lord Brigham," she said.

He stepped closer, unable to prevent the flash of his smile when he added "Enchanting" with a closer look at her mask. Saints, her eyes were wild and dangerous things.

"And you," she said, though he wasn't certain the words were a compliment, given her consternation.

He lifted a gloved hand to take hers. He held it for a moment too long. They both knew it. He said, "Thank you, my lady, for not bringing along your bird."

Her dark eyes narrowed.

"I trust your man has something to occupy him while we are gone."

Jules glanced at Ian. "Oh, he will be attending with us."

"Not *with* us," Nickolas said.

The man's only reply was a speaking glance. The words it spoke were something like *I know well how to perform my duties*, and *I will be watching you precisely as much as I dislike you, which is entirely*.

Nickolas gave him a friendly smile. "Splendid. Happy to have you along. At a substantial distance." Nickolas turned his smile on Jules, who seemed slightly nonplussed. He'd had that effect on women before. He released his charm with full vigor, leaning closer as he moved to her side, and she appeared to force her gaze away. Keeping hold of her hand to press it over his arm, he said, "Come now. The ball awaits."

Jules's evident trepidation did not ease as they entered the ballroom. She held herself stiff, seemingly unmoved by the lights and the music or the midsummer decorations scattered throughout the lavish space. Her gaze stayed on the crowd, as if scanning faces in spite of the masks. Nickolas wondered if she was anxious to see someone in particular. "Shall we attempt to catch a glimpse of the royal Norcliffe party?"

"No," she gasped. "That would be the worst possible thing."

Nickolas had been raised attending Westrende events, and even he found himself dazzled by the grandness of their special occasions from time to time. Perhaps he'd misunderstood her mood and she was uncomfortable. He dipped his head to whisper in her ear, "Would you prefer to leave, my lady?"

A shiver seemed to roll through her, and she drew back to look up at him. He had the sensation of seeing her for the first time, but he was not unaware that every eye in the room was on them. Like Gideon, Nickolas was not a figure a simple mask could disguise.

"No," Jules said determinedly. "We must meet with Lord Beckett."

Nickolas nodded toward the far wall, angling Jules for a better view by gentle pressure on their connected arms. She had not, thus far, let go of him. "That is Lord Beckett there. The tall, handsome fellow in the impeccable black coat. Dark skin, white pants, standing beside the lady in the yellow gown who seems to—saints, yes, that is a half yard of dyed feathers protruding from her wig. Best not to let these ladies near your Frederick. They'd have him plucked and bare before you could say *quill*. Just there, see. Can't miss it."

Jules's gaze no more than landed on Lord Beckett before she started toward the man.

Nickolas held her arm. "My lady, the queue surrounding Beckett looks hours long. Let us enjoy the festivities while we wait for a more opportune moment."

She glanced at him, the mask slipping down a fraction with her brow.

Nickolas reached up to tip it back into place. "I promise, love, you will have your chance at him, even if I have to battle every lord in this room to see it done." He rested his free hand on the hilt of his sword. "But let us take the more decorous route if we can."

"What are we to do for those hours?"

He straightened, humor dancing at the edge of his lips once more. "At a ball? The fates only know. Dreadfully boring things. Everyone says so." When she did not answer, he leaned closer. Nothing was worse than being pressured into something one did not enjoy or had no confidence in before a room full of judgmental peers. But he could not stand to *not* ask her. "How do you feel about dancing, my lady?"

The look she gave him was one of surprise, and she seemed to consider, then to decide she'd nothing else to occupy her wait, before offering her hand. "I suppose that would do well enough."

"Such a flatterer, you. Swooning at my every attention. I'm not certain how much more of this my dignity can take."

"I suspect your pride can bear it," she said as he led her to the dance floor.

He pressed a hand to his heart. "You wound me." The orchestra was without fault, renowned even kingdoms away, and their symphony swelled just as Nickolas turned to face her. He bowed. She dipped into a curtsy, and they fell into step with the teeming crowd around them.

Jules was a better dancer than he was. Far superior, despite all his training. Saints, she moved like a... well, like nothing he'd ever seen.

Her chin was up, eyes forward, flawless form revealing not a hint of concern for the courtiers who might be watching. They would certainly be watching, he remembered, so he forced his gaze away from his partner to perform the dance. Rue throbbed sharp inside his chest, but he ignored it. Jules was betrothed, to someone truly awful from whom she had to escape. He did not know how to help her, and each step of the dance that turned him to face her, each time the light caught on the chain about her slender neck, felt like another plunge of the knife.

The music ended, and they danced again, and because the rules of propriety slackened at a masquerade, Nickolas led them into a third. When it was over, he took her hand, bowing so low before her that he might have kissed it. But he only returned to standing, stealing no more than the slide of his thumb across the back of her hand before letting go.

"What now?" he asked, feeling slightly breathless. It must have been deuced warm in the ballroom. "The refreshment table? Rumor has it there's to be a lavish display of sugared fruit this year and an endless supply of cakes."

When she merely replied, "If you'd like," he led her to the side of the room.

"Perhaps you'll sneak some back for Frederick. Though he likely prefers seeds and grain."

"Bread," she said. When Nickolas glanced at her, she repeated, "I give him bread."

Nickolas stared down at her, her eyes serious beneath the fine mask, her lashes long and dark. He felt himself shift closer, and when Jules's mouth parted, his ears pricked in anticipation of whatever she meant to say.

Then the flock of ladies browsing the dessert table descended and he straightened, increasing the distance between him and Jules. It was poor timing, to say the least.

The ladies fawned and fluttered while Nickolas did his best to politely disengage. He made no formal introduction because Jules was to remain unknown, but when a lady who was the cousin to the stablemaster pressed, "You must, if nothing else, tell us how you met,"

Jules replied for him, the hint of a smile flirting with the edge of her lips.

"Lord Brigham fell into my courtyard." She glanced up at him adoringly. "Like a little baby bird shoved from its nest too soon."

The hem of rebuke in his throat was drowned out by tittering ladies. Annoyed, Nickolas slid an arm possessively around Jules, his gaze on their audience. "If you'll allow me to make my excuses, ladies, I have made promises of cake that I intend to keep."

Once the others were gone and Jules was reaching for a small plate that held a pair of delicate treats, Nickolas leaned in, voice low in the hope of regaining their moment before the interruption. "My apologies. Some days, society simply cannot get enough of my conversation."

She made a snort of incredulity. "I'm surprised you allow yourself such a credit. They seemed not at all concerned with a word that fell from your mouth. Indeed, Lord Brigham, I fear they were trifling with you. If they'd not been busy perusing you in your fine suit, in the way they perused the dessert table, you wouldn't get half so far or even a quarter with most courtiers."

A startled laugh came out of him. "So you *do* believe me handsome."

She bit into a cookie.

"Or delicious, like the desserts," he said. "I'll admit, I suspected as much from the start. 'That Jules,' I said, 'she cannot take her eyes from me.' Like a lodestone, I am. It's a burden, truly, to hold this sort of power over a lady. I worry myself about it day and night."

She dropped her half-eaten ginger cookie to the plate meaningfully.

He pressed his lips together in surrender then offered her a glass of punch.

The moment was gone, but they made a tour of the room, taking in the fine decorations and elegant dress. Nickolas told Jules of some of the oldest Westrende traditions and ushered her to view a particularly stunning landscape, then they made their way to a pair of doors that led out into a courtyard. The space was cool and moonlit, a few flickering candelabra placed around the entrance to the ballroom. The scene reminded him of the night he'd met her. "A baby bird," he muttered as he recalled what she'd said about him falling into her life.

Her expression was solemn with not a twitch of the lip when she looked up at him. "Indeed. Helpless and lost. Poor creature."

Trapped in a cage, he thought, unable to climb the walls Carvell and his mother had built around him. The expectation. The debt. He'd failed to get free, and yet, even now, it was as if Jules was saving him from facing those gallows. He let out a breath, and if it fell across the bare skin above her neckline, he could not be blamed for it. "How fortunate for me that you have a soft spot for pitiable creatures." Music rose from inside the hall, and he had the intense desire to take her into his arms once more. "Dance with me, my lady. Before our time is over."

She took a step closer, dark eyes shining beneath her mask. He suspected she'd heard the lament in his tone, but instead of addressing it, she asked, "And how have you found this evening, my lord?"

He gave Jules a self-deprecating smile as she lifted a hand to take his. They spun gently over the flat stones that bordered the courtyard. Beyond them, masked couples paraded past, gracing the pair with fond smiles and whispering quietly of things best said in moonlit gardens. "Dreadfully dull," Nickolas murmured as Jules twirled in a step that brought her back to him. "Never had such a tedious night of dancing and discussion in my life. And the company..." He shook his head. "This will be the memory I draw forth when I need to appear as if I'm taking an assembly presentation seriously."

Jules laughed, the sound light and musical and carefree.

His heart danced. He wanted to hear it again. He wanted to make her laugh and to—

He froze. The foolish grin that had somehow found its way to his face dropped like a stone in his stomach.

"What's the matter?" she whispered, her steps coming to a halt. "What happened?"

"I—" He shook his head, loosening his grip on her. "Nothing. It's nothing." He swallowed and took a short step back from her. His hand flexed at his waist, palm still warm from the heat of her, wanting to reclaim its grasp. "Perhaps we should—that is, I'm afraid I may no longer be able to—" He cleared his throat, strengthened his resolve.

"I've just recalled another engagement, my lady. Our evening must end here. I regret if I have misled you in any way, but this—"

"There you are." The voice came from the open doorway to the ballroom, slicing through whatever words Nickolas might have said.

Off his guard entirely, he glanced toward the voice, startled to recognize a lord he'd met years before. The lord had been a visiting envoy from Norcliffe. Nickolas straightened automatically before dipping swiftly into a low bow. He felt Jules's hesitation beside him, then came relief when she fell into a curtsy. They both rose, Jules keeping her head bowed, eyes downcast. She had not been introduced, and before them, fate save them, stood the princess of Norcliffe and several members of her court.

The familiar lord came forward. "Lord Brigham. I've been searching for you. You must be introduced to her highness. She's been eager to finally meet you."

The princess stepped gracefully from among the crowd of courtiers, thin silver mask covering only her eyes, embroidered gown trimmed exceptionally well in gold. She was tall and dignified, her manner seeming more affable than prim. Nickolas had not expected her to be so striking. William would have to use every tool and trick at his disposal to win a woman of her status.

Her Highness, Princess Mireille, may I present—"

"Lord Brigham," the princess interrupted smoothly. "Please, let us not stand on ceremony. I feel as if I know you so well by the stories our mutual friends have imparted." Her lips tilted playfully. "You have quite the reputation for misadventure, my lord."

"All lies, I assure you." A crowd had gathered around the doorway, both inside and out of the ballroom. Nickolas inclined his head. "Highness. It is a privilege." Out of the corner of his vision, Nickolas saw Ian moving across the courtyard but could not take his gaze off the courtiers, the elder Lord Adair and his sons among them, and Lord Carvell with his daughter. Nickolas's skin prickled at the nape.

He shifted to introduce Jules, but she no longer stood at his side. She was gone. He cleared his throat.

Princess Mireille reached forward, taking Nickolas's arm. "Come," she said. "Let us stroll through the courtyard. Perhaps you will tell me stories and, afterward, invite me to dance."

Nickolas glanced over his shoulder, searching, but found no sign of Jules. Ian was evidently gone as well, the figures that had been milling about the courtyard now closing in. "I'm afraid I..." He tilted his head for a better look past the moonlit topiary and saw a slip of delicate silvery blue disappear into a far-off doorway before a pair of figures blocked his view.

The princess slid her hand companionably into the crook of Nickolas's arm. "Call me Rei, please."

Nickolas's gaze returned to hers. Saints, up close she was even lovelier. Her features were fine, dark-olive skin glowing in the torchlight, her scent light and flowery instead of the heavier perfumes so many peers wore. She was waiting for him. He knew it. The crowd was waiting for him too. He was meant to take her through the courtyards, to charm her and try to win her with the games courtiers played. He was a Brigham. It was practically his duty.

But he didn't know what had happened to Jules. He glanced once more through the courtyard, finding the lord he'd seen arguing with Gideon outside of the chancery only days before now speaking with Carvell. Nickolas didn't like leaving Jules unattended. His mother's men might be anywhere nearby. At the very least, he should apologize. He should escort her back to her rooms.

The princess gave a gentle squeeze to Nickolas's arm.

"I'm sorry, Highness, but... I must go." He withdrew his arm from hers, to the stunned gasps of the onlookers, and gave a cursory bow. "If you'll forgive me."

Her expression revealed surprise, but she inclined her head courteously.

He stepped forward once more and leaned in to tell her quietly, "Be wary, Your Highness, of suitors with interest in trade." At the edge of the doorway, inside the ballroom, Nickolas caught sight of Lady Brigham's deadly glare. He swore silently, and the moment she was swallowed up by the shifting crowd, he turned to move hastily away.

CHAPTER 13

Nickolas sped through the courtyard, keeping himself hidden from view of the ballroom as best he could. Ornamental shrubs rose around him in tall cones, and the pathway was edged in wisteria, sweet and musky in the still night air. The muffled voices and distant echo of the orchestra faded, replaced by the hollow babble of fountains.

It took three tries to find the door through which Jules had disappeared, and when he finally did, he was only certain it was the right one because the moment he opened it, a hulking man slammed into him and rolled him to the ground. Sword still sheathed—they'd been in a courtyard outside a ballroom, for fate's sake—Nickolas wrapped his hands around the man's coat sleeves and jerked him to the side. The man was stout; he barely moved at all.

Nickolas wedged his elbows between himself and the man's chest and twisted, gaining enough space to free one of his legs. But he was no more than half liberated before he was flat on his back again. Long limbs his only advantage, he slipped an arm over the man's shoulder, wrapped it about his thick head, and pulled in a spin. The man flattened his feet to the ground for leverage, at one point calling Nickolas a beef-witted bamboozler and spitting a bit of what was probably blood—Nickolas was no novice, despite the other man's superior size —before they were rolling again. Finally gaining the upper hand, Nickolas tried to shove away, but formal shoes weren't meant for scuffling, and he slipped in the slime and shattered remnants of a clay pot the pair had knocked to the floor.

Off balance, Nickolas was an easy target, and the man leapt, as quick as a bull, to pin him to the ground once more.

Nickolas drew his fist back, entirely spent of gentlemanly restraint, then froze when a bucket of tepid, reeking plant-water was thrown onto both of them.

Nickolas blinked up to find Jules standing over them, her expression oddly vacant. She let go of the bucket, and it clanged to the floor beside them. When she turned away, Nickolas shoved the man's forearm off his chest with a grunt of disgust. Ian—for Nickolas was finally certain, in the sparse light coming through the room's windows, that that was who his opponent had been—slid to the side, running a hand over his close-cropped hair and flicking the water free.

Jules stepped away then turned and leaned against a long gardening table to remove her soiled gloves. "The two of you are done now."

Wet and thoroughly reprimanded, Nickolas and Ian sat in repentant silence, their chests heaving for breath. Nickolas did not argue that he was not responsible, that *he'd* been the one attacked. Not since he understood what Ian's job was. Nickolas had never seen a man fight in that manner. Ian was meant to be Jules's protector; he might have jumped on anyone who came through the door. "Saints. Where did you train to be a guard? You're deuced awful at it."

The man looked up at him. "I'm not a guard, you daft cad." He ran a thumb over the split on his lip. "I'm her coachman."

"Her…" Nickolas glanced at Jules. Whatever question he'd meant to ask shriveled at the sight of her. It appeared she was, to put it mildly, unsettled. He pushed to his feet, not bothering to brush off the soil and muck he and Ian had rolled in. Something was wrong. "My lady, what is it?"

She shook her head, the distress he'd seen in her expression tinged with grief.

"You can't tell me?" he asked. "Because of the curse."

She nodded.

Nickolas glanced at—well, at her coachman, evidently.

"Ian doesn't know," she said. "He can't give you the details any more than I can."

The man sighed then gathered himself to his feet. "I only know what I saw."

"What did you see?"

He gave Nickolas his full gaze. "That something very bad happened. And she needed my protection."

"Was it the prince of the Riven Court? Did you see him? You would have known—been given the sight."

"Doesn't work like that where we come from. That bird she carries around isn't dressed up to look like a bird. He *is* a bird. Laying eyes on our fae doesn't win you a thing. That's your kingdom's curse, not ours."

"Hold a moment," Nickolas said. "What kingdom is yours, specifically?"

The man's mouth went into a flat line, and Nickolas let out a long breath. "Right. So, she cannot tell me, and you're unwilling. You'll only say that something bad happened, that she needed protection, and..."

At Nickolas's prompt, Ian added, "And I went after her. Whatever it is, whatever was done, I know she had reason. I trust her."

Nickolas's gaze slid to Jules. Her eyes were on him, but her cheeks had gone hot. Ian had said more than she'd meant to have revealed. "Someone is after you," Nickolas guessed. And not just her family to tie her to a betrothal. She'd been accused of a misdeed, some sort of serious offense, so she'd fled to Westrende. "And that someone is from your own kingdom."

There was a muffled scraping sound in the courtyard, and they all glanced toward the narrow window that bordered the door.

The man from Princess Mireille's court—the one who'd been arguing with Gideon outside of the chancery—peered back at them through the thick glass.

Ian stood with a curse, and when Nickolas moved with him, Ian said, "No, stay with her. I'll catch the rotter."

Jules had shrunk back, and Nickolas moved toward her, eyes on the closed door through which Ian had disappeared. "Who was that?"

With no real spirit, she swatted a glove at him, so he turned to face her. "The man I was *hiding* from." Then she burst into tears. Or at least the impression of such. It was a sort of dry, soundless sob, all emotion and none of the wet, unpleasant fluids or noise.

It did not make the whole thing less terrible. In fact, it somehow made it worse. It was like another dagger in his heart—how many was that now, seven? "Jules," he said softly, wrapping his arms around her where she struggled to draw breath. It was not merely a bit of distress. Hers were the motions of pure grief.

Hiding, she'd said. "Why? Because he was from Norcliffe? Is that your home?"

She shook her head, not, he gathered, to indicate it was or was not the kingdom from which she'd escaped but rather that she could not tell him more.

"And I have brought you to him, paraded you at a ball where any one of them might put you in harm's way." He ran a hand lightly over her back. "What if Ian finds the man? Will that sort it?"

She shook her head against his chest. She'd already said she could not involve Gideon, which meant whatever she'd done was serious enough they would be law-bound to send her back.

He slid one hand up to cradle the back of her neck. It was warm and soft, and so was his voice. "Then we will find a way to hide you."

She drew away to look up at him, her face soft in the moonlight, her nose tipped with pink.

He ran a thumb over her cheek. "Does that sound agreeable?"

"They will come for me. It won't matter about the..." Her fingers curled around the ring that hung from her neck as if its chain were choking her.

He placed his hand over hers. "You're afraid they will return you home and you'll be forced to marry, or is it something else? How much trouble are you up against, my lady?"

She swallowed. "They won't force me to marry any man. They'll force me to—he'll be—" Her words choked off again, and she shook her head. "You can't understand. I cannot explain it."

"My lady, it does not matter. Whatever it is, we will face it together. That was our bargain."

Her shoulders eased in his embrace, and her lips parted to speak. But the door to the room slammed open.

Nickolas's gaze shot toward the sound. Just in time, it turned out, to watch Lady Brigham storm in. Behind her, a handful of courtiers and castle staff looked on from the courtyard. She posted herself before the entrance, almost militant in her posture, and faced Nickolas and Jules. Her intent was clear—to punish Nickolas and hurt anyone who held his concern. Nothing particularly new, but Nickolas had met his limit.

"Oh, for the love of—" He stepped out of the embrace to turn on his mother. "Enough." The word split into two, possibly three. He'd never been so angry in his life. "This is it, Mother. I am done. I have tried. I have done my utmost to save this family and preserve our name. But no more." He glared her down. "The Brighams do not *deserve* to be saved."

His mother took a step toward him.

Nickolas turned to the crowd of onlookers who'd gathered outside the open door. "We're cleaned out," he told them. "Done for. Pockets to let, rolled-up, on the rocks. The Brighams have no funds." At the intake of breath from a lady he thought was employed in the kitchens, Nickolas added, "It gets worse. It's not merely destitution. I'm afraid there are unspeakably dishonorable acts to add to the—"

His confession was cut short by the shriek that came from his mother. The entire courtyard went silent, making not a sound aside from the echo of babbling water.

His mother's eyes cut to Jules, and her hand balled into a fist. "Taking up with a clerk's assistant in a dark garden shed at the midsummer ball and you have the nerve to speak to me of dishonorable acts."

Nickolas remembered, quite suddenly, that Jules had been wrapped in his arms when his mother had entered. He resisted the urge to tell the crowd that it was not what it looked like. He edged in front of Jules. "This is not the time, Mother. In fact, it will never be the time again. We are done. It is over. And it's nothing to do with Jules."

"You gave up our chance at a princess. She was practically begging to drag us from the edge of ignobility."

Nickolas felt his brow draw down. He hadn't even considered making suit for the princess. He'd only needed to check on Jules.

When his mother demanded, "Go after her *now*. Tell Mireille you've changed your mind," Nickolas found he could not move.

His mother's air became more dangerous. "I didn't want to do this, but you've given me no choice."

Nickolas did not like her tone. When she spoke again, he knew his impression was right.

His mother, the distinguished Lady Brigham of the renowned Brigham line, committed a crime so heinous no law had even been written to cover it.

She spoke the fae prince's name.

"HAVE YOU LOST YOUR SENSES ENTIRELY?" Nickolas heard himself shout.

His mother had, evidently, because she did not even shy away as the fae prince materialized in the corner of the room. She must have somehow seen the prince at the Filmore estate, or perhaps not. Perhaps she'd only heard Jules whisper his name. But it was clear her action was planned. Nickolas swore.

The fae prince took a look at his surroundings, made an unpleasant face, then stepped from the shadows. He inclined his head to Jules. "My lady."

At his back, Nickolas could feel Jules nod in return.

The prince's gaze trailed briefly over the watching crowd, at least three of whom had fainted, then landed on Lady Brigham. She stood straight and formal as if waiting for an introduction to be made.

Etta was going to kill Nickolas. He would need to make record of everyone standing within view to report to the marshal's office so that she could deal with whatever followed. The paperwork *alone*. What a nightmare. Perhaps he should have danced naked through the court-yard after all and been thrown into the dungeon where he belonged.

"Nickolas," his mother snapped.

"What? You called him. You want to stand on propriety *now*?" At her glare, he turned toward the prince. "May I introduce Lady Brigham, Your Highness?" He gestured vaguely in her direction before grandly rolling his hand toward the prince. "Mother, the prince of Rivenwilde."

The prince's gaze slid from Nickolas to his mother then back.

Nickolas nodded in concession. "I like to think I favor my father." There was nothing he could do to prevent the disaster they all knew was coming. He prayed it would not involve Jules.

"You have called me to bargain, Lady Brigham." The prince's tone was even, but at the doorway, several onlookers stepped back.

If possible, Lady Brigham's spine went straighter. "You shall marry your pick of my daughters. There are four, all exceptionally lovely and accomplished."

"No," Nickolas gasped.

The prince flicked a hand, and Nickolas's words stuck in his throat, just as the scene had frozen on Lord Filmore's balcony. The prince looked evenly at Lady Brigham. "I cannot. An existing betrothal prevents me."

"An exist—" Lady Brigham's lips pressed closed.

Jules leaned against Nickolas's back as she peered past him, and—with a strange sensation—he understood his voice had returned. He demanded, "Leave off with this fool's game, Mother. It will not end well for anyone involved." Particularly not whichever sister was sent to live with the fae, no matter that it might bring his mother a return to the fortune she so desperately wanted. "I will not allow you to harm them. I will not allow you to continue this ploy." He wasn't certain how he might stop her, as a bargain with a fae prince would supersede any power he held, but he would find a way. Her behavior was beyond reprehensible. He should have stopped her long before so it might never have gone this far.

His mother's cold eyes seemed to dare him to try then shifted to Jules and went ten shades colder. "Her," she told the prince. "Remove that chit from this kingdom to never return. Or turn her to ash. I care not which. As long as she's gone forever."

Before Nickolas could lunge at his mother, he was frozen again by the strange fae magic.

"I cannot," the prince repeated.

Lady Brigham's gaze shot to the prince. "What do you mean you cannot? Do away with the girl. She matters to no one."

The prince gave her a level stare, his words loaded with meaning. "As I've told you, an existing betrothal prevents me."

Nickolas felt himself fall back a step, and he bumped against Jules. *Jules, Jules, Jules*, his heart drummed in a panicked staccato. She made not a sound. The ground felt unsteady beneath Nickolas's feet. He could not seem to reconcile the words he'd heard. They did not seem real.

Outside in the courtyard, there was a rush of murmuring and the muffled beat of marching boots on stone. *The marshal*, the watching crowd murmured. The kingsmen were coming.

The prince's expression remained steady. "You have one final offer to make, Lady Brigham. I suggest you consider it well."

Lady Brigham huffed, the sound reeking of smug victory and delight. "I shall save it," she told him.

Because Lady Brigham had won her boon after all. Jules would no longer interfere, not when she was married to someone else. And if she was married to... when she was taken to... Nickolas could not even make himself think it. It could not be real.

Etta darkened the doorway only an instant before the prince was gone. He must have heard the murmurs as well and known she was coming, but he'd waited, watching the doorway for her appearance. One might not have noticed the small quirk to his brow on an other-wise unchanged face—a clear acknowledgment of the challenge scored in his favor—but Etta had.

She cursed, lunged... and drove her sword into empty air. She stood in the space he had been for one long moment, surrounded by shad-ows, then seemed to take a steadying breath. When she turned to face the crowd and her men, she was marshal of Westrende once more. "Take them into custody for questioning. All of them."

She gave a hard look to Lady Brigham. "She can wait in the cells."

Nickolas and Jules had been ushered by a pack of the marshal's men into a small room adjacent to Etta's office. They had been left alone, but guards remained posted just outside.

Nickolas sat on the long bench with a sick, defeated sort of feeling in his gut that he did not like at all, while Jules paced in front of him.

She stopped, finally coming to rest before him. When he did not look up, she slid onto the bench, her fine gown smeared with damp earth.

"You were working in the chancery to learn the laws of the kingdom, so that you might find a way to break the betrothal. It had to be here, because you had to understand *our* laws. You never came for asylum. You came to fight." His words were not a question. He did not know how much she might be able to say since her terms had been revealed by the prince. Because the curse, according to Ian, had not been set by Westrende fae. It didn't matter. Nickolas needed to say it.

Jules's reply was so quiet he felt as if he needed to silence his heartbeat to hear. "I had always heard that fae magic did something to a person. That even their speaking could pluck a string so deep inside you that you could feel it vibrate through your bones. That it might eat you up with wanting."

His heartbeat did freeze. He looked at her. She was so close, face bare and hair starting to escape its updo.

She wet her lips. "It did not feel that way to me."

"You were to marry *one of your station*," he said. "A prince."

Jules did not reply. Nickolas shifted to face her, taking her hand in his, their knees touching. She was not for him. "And what of your crime?"

"Murders that I did not commit. They found me standing in—" She swallowed against words she could not seem to speak. "It was the middle of the night. I was in a room that was not my own. Around me, signs of a struggle, blood, scattered feathers."

"Feathers. No bodies?"

She shook her head. "I was accused of bargaining with the fae against the victims, to steal their... so that I might take their... in order to win a privilege which could not be mine unless they were gone."

"Your brothers. The fae curse turned them into birds, and you were blamed."

She nodded. "I asked for the price and was given a... I cannot say. But the price, you now know. I could not do it. But I could not *not* do it."

To break a curse was always an impossible task, Etta had said. Or a choice in which either option was impossible to permit.

"And your people intended to throw you into a cell when you had a curse to break?"

"It was precisely what they intended. So I escaped. Ian helped me. I never would have made it, otherwise. We rode into the night on horses stolen from the king's stable."

"Murders," he said. "How many brothers do you have?"

"Six in all. The others flew free. As long as I'm... if I agree to the terms... they will be well. But Frederick was injured. He could not fly because he had defended me. I bundled him up, kept him at my side the entire journey." She squeezed Nickolas's hand. "I was granted only the standard betrothal period of the fae. That time is running out. If I do not agree, they will be trapped forever inside their new forms. If I do agree, I will be... it will put..." Her face pinched in determination. "Entire kingdoms will be in danger."

"You've been trying to set Frederick free," Nickolas said. "Because you believe you'll not be able to save him before you're whisked away."

"He won't save himself. He refuses to leave me. Seeing him like this, it makes me... I know that I..." Her hand tightened into a fist.

"You're not afraid that you'll be unable to make him whole," Nickolas guessed. "You want him to leave, because you plan to cross the wall and go through with the betrothal."

Her eyes shone in the candlelight. "Not if I can prevent it. It's only that time is running out, and I see no other answer. If I can save my brothers, if they can be returned to themselves..."

His thumb slid over the back of her hand. He could feel the warmth of her leg where it pressed against his, the touch of her breath over his skin. Unable to stop himself, he reached toward the ring that hung from the chain about her neck, wondering if its magic was what prevented her from speaking freely.

"Nickolas," she said softly. "I must confess something else."

His hand froze.

"My post in the chancery was chosen not simply so that I might have access to research. It allowed me to find those who might be best positioned—or perhaps induced—to help."

His hand lowered to her lap, where his other still cradled hers. He watched her for a long moment. "Why do I have the feeling you're preparing to reveal extortion?"

She did not so much as flinch. "I can help you with your problems. Just as I've promised."

He pulled his hands back. "In exchange for?"

"Not in exchange. You've satisfied our agreement. I can help you, but I need you to help me."

Saints. She *was* extorting him. There was something very wrong with him, because this close, it didn't matter. He wanted to put his lips somewhere on her. Badly. Perhaps the soft bit beneath the corner of her jaw where her pulse jumped. Or an earlobe. Or her mouth. Without a doubt, her mouth. Or, fate save him, that neck.

She's betrothed to the prince of Rivenwilde, he reminded himself. "Still doesn't matter," he mumbled back.

"You're saying you knew my situation," he said. "You mean financially or..." At her level look, he sighed. "What else, then? Did you know I'd be trussed up and—" He sat straighter. "You did know. You knew about the plot against me. That I'd end up in Carvell's courtyard. You—you asked permission to use the man's gardens in front of the *magistrate*."

Her steady gaze never wavered. "There are very few in Westrende who are aware of curses and fae magic. After all, I could not ask Etta or Gideon."

He ran a hand over his face.

She said, "I cannot explain more, but the terms of the bargain are no small thing. I had to use whatever I could to my advantage. I had to find a way out."

Nickolas watched her for a very long moment. Jules was a princess. He should have known. She was too graceful, too clever, too impossibly beautiful to be anything else. He understood what came along with that. Royalty accepted that they must do whatever it took to protect their people. Jules would go to the ends of the earth to see it done. Perhaps she was nearly there already.

Nickolas stood, straightened his torn jacket, and strode to the door. "Gentlemen," he called to the guard outside. "Fetch Lord Beckett, if you please. I have a bargain to uphold."

CHAPTER 15

Jules was in a private room, questioning Lord Beckett about interkingdom law, when Etta and Gideon finally arrived, Frederick's cage in tow.

Nickolas stood. "Did you find the lord from Norcliffe?"

Gideon placed the cage on a table and crossed his arms. "Ian apprehended him. They've both been taken in for questioning."

"He's looking for Jules."

"We gathered," Etta said. "Ian demanded we return the bird to Jules's care and keep her under guard and away from the Norcliffe party until the turn of the moon. What else have you learned?"

"She's betrothed to the prince."

Etta's brows lowered in confusion, but Nickolas did not pause long enough to listen to her remark. "Her brothers were cursed, transformed into birds like Frederick, but there are five more back in her kingdom. No idea where that is yet, as she and Ian won't come clean. She plans to pay the price to break the curse—that is, to marry the prince of Rivenwilde so that her brothers might all live. Apparently, the act will endanger entire kingdoms, but she sees no other way." He tossed up his hands. "And I'm to stay here and cosset her bird."

Etta opened her mouth, closed it, then opened it again. "She means to leave the bird with *you*?"

"Thank you," he said. "For once, a voice of reason. One of you must convince her to change her mind."

Etta straightened. "I can't keep a fae-cursed man-bird. I'm the marshal."

They looked at Gideon.

He said, "I can't do it. I have a dog."

"That doesn't even make sense," Nickolas said. "It should be you most of all. You've proven you can keep an animal alive, for one thing. Two, no one would ever suspect you of breaking the law by harboring an illegal fae-bird-thing." When Gideon only stared at him, Nickolas added, "It should be you. Precisely because you and that bird have identical temperaments."

Gideon narrowed his dark eyes into a glare. Beside him, in the cage, so did Frederick.

"See? There." Nickolas threw up his hands again. "Making my point for me, gentlemen."

The room fell silent for a moment, then Etta asked, "Nickolas, why did you not tell me of your situation?"

He slumped onto the bench with a sigh. "And what? Have you arrest my mother?" He winced. "You *have* arrested her, haven't you?"

"I'm considering it. She did try to sell your sister to the fae. But what about the rest?"

"Adair has information on her. He's been using it to extort funds and favors from the family since before my father's death."

Gideon's demeanor softened. Or at least, he uncrossed his arms.

Nickolas rubbed an earlobe. "It's true, all of it. We're busted. Flat broke. The coffers are bare. Now that I've admitted it to everyone, our debts will be called in. I'm done for. Probably be tossed from my suite before the end of the week."

Etta stepped closer.

Nickolas's hand dropped to his lap. "The worst thing is, she chose me on purpose. Mess of a thing, Lord Brigham. Perfect sort of target for such a lark." He looked up at Etta. "And I can't even help her." He was a failure once more. A failure when it mattered most. He said, "So, what happens now? You'll cart her back to her kingdom, and we will never see her again? Never know what becomes of her?" Nickolas did not ask if they would hand her over to the fae. Etta might be the one person less capable of that than him.

The door to the room opened, and Jules stepped in. Nickolas stood as her gaze swept the space, a hint of relief showing in her posture when she took in the bird.

"Well," Gideon said, "there is a great deal of paperwork involved in deporting a person. Likely it will take some time to sort out."

Jules's dark eyes slid to his, shining with gratitude.

"Particularly if there's an active investigation," Etta added. She cleared her throat as if even speaking such a betrayal of her duty was painful then turned to face Jules more fully. "Was Lord Beckett any help to you?"

Jules shook her head. "There's no precedent for—no record of—" She touched the ring resting against her chest. "Nothing of use."

Nickolas glanced at Etta, who gave him an indiscreet nod. Gideon had a book of fae laws. Gideon would help.

"It's been a long day," Jules said. "I'm afraid I've done all I can." She glanced at the wall, but there were no windows to reveal what must have been a very late, very close to full moon. "I'd like to retire."

Gideon nodded. "You'll both come with us. The chancery is the safest place for you right now. We already have a rotation of kingsmen outside your rooms and patrolling the wing."

Jules nodded, but when they arrived at the chancery office after being escorted by the marshal, the chancellor, Ian carrying the bird cage, and about a dozen men, she looked even more dispirited than before.

Etta and Gideon went on to his private office, but Jules stopped before turning to face Nickolas. "My time is nearly up."

Nickolas took her hand in his. "Shall I walk with you?"

Her mouth tightened as if she were holding back emotion. "I think I would like to be alone for a while."

He lifted her hand, bending forward to press a soft kiss on her skin. "Good night, my lady. Know that we will do all we can to help."

Eyes misty, Jules only nodded. It seemed as if she might want to speak, but she did not, only offering him a weak smile before she drew her hand away and turned to go. Nickolas watched as Ian followed with the bird, down the narrow corridor to her room.

"Nickolas?" Etta called from the doorway of Gideon's office.

He cleared his face of concern then turned to join them.

ETTA HAD SECURED the door to Gideon's private office, and the three of them had huddled around his orderly desk. Gideon was as proper and orderly as a man could be, in Nickolas's estimation, but the chancery was stuffed with shelves and stacks and carts. Records of all kinds were housed in every nook and cranny of the ancient wing, and nothing could be done for the dry, dim environment that smelled of aged parchment and spilled ink. The man probably itched to have it all sorted and filed.

He was, after all, twitching like a schoolboy about to get the rod because of the fae relic centered on his desk.

Nickolas let out a low whistle. "I'm no expert, but that looks extraordinarily old and highly illegal."

"It is," Gideon muttered without looking up. "Don't touch it."

Nickolas reclined farther onto the desk, just to annoy him. "Well, someone has to."

Gideon's jaw tightened, but he carefully opened the cover, its binding making a mild crackle of complaint. Nickolas leaned in. The pages had aged well enough and were marked with symbols and lines that seemed to be translated into print. Color dotted the layout sparingly, bits of gold and vibrant red in a few of the illustrations. Not taking his gaze from the writing, Nickolas asked, "Where did you say your father found this?"

Etta shrugged. "I had always assumed he'd taken it off a prisoner. Now, I'm not so certain."

"I've read to here," Gideon said. "The rest will be new."

"And we're looking for..." Nickolas prompted.

"Marriage contracts."

"Right." Something settled in the pit of Nickolas's stomach. It only grew worse as time went on, because Gideon had turned to a section that illustrated fae ceremonies, a full court in attendance beneath a midnight full moon. He did not want to imagine Jules in place of the fae bride, but he could not look away. Trees rose around a clearing, a stone throne centering the edge of the circle like the finest carved marble. Fae creatures of all kinds stood in witness as a prince knelt before his intended.

The office had fallen quiet. Etta placed a gentle hand on Gideon's shoulder. He turned the page.

Pages later, they found what they'd been looking for. Hours after that, Gideon's desk was scattered with documents and scrolls, the three of them poring over contract wording and ancient rites and cross-checking every single aspect of the law.

Gideon sat straighter. "I think we've got it. We only need to verify these last few details."

There was color in Etta's cheeks, and Nickolas could feel a fluttering excitement inside his chest. He didn't want to hope, but there it was, strewn out in front of them—a loophole that might be used to subvert the bargain's terms.

He stood. "We have to tell Jules."

Etta straightened. "There's no use waking her now. We have to prepare, and she's not had enough rest. We'll tell her in the morning."

Gideon stood as well and wrapped the fae book with a cloth before placing it inside his jacket. When there was a knock at the door, everyone froze.

An instant later, Etta was beside Nickolas, blocking view of the documents on the desk. "Enter," she called.

A soldier stepped in, tall and thin, her dark hair tied into a clean knot above the red-trimmed collar of the uniform of the marshal's office. The soldier gave a practiced salute.

"Report," Etta said.

The soldier glanced at Nickolas and Gideon then hedged, "There's a problem with one of the prisoners."

Etta frowned, hand on her sword hilt. To Gideon and Nickolas, she said, "Best take care of this. I'll meet you both in the morning."

Gideon glanced at the windows, where cockcrow appeared to be less than an hour away.

Etta sighed. "Regardless, I'll return shortly. There's much to do."

At the door, she called over her shoulder, "Get some rest, Nickolas."

Nickolas glanced at Gideon, but Gideon waved him away. "I'll take care of this mess. Do as she says. You'll need it." When Nickolas opened his mouth, Gideon stopped him. "Don't say it."

"You don't even—"

"It doesn't matter. Whatever it is, gratitude or mockery, I don't need it right now. Jules needs saved. That's all I've room for."

At that, Nickolas found his words had slunk away. He only nodded, turning to leave the room as Gideon resumed his work. At the door, though, Nickolas looked back, his fingers wrapping around the heavy oak slab. "Gideon?"

Gideon glanced up, chancellor through and through.

"Did you know she was a princess?"

His tone was subdued. "I only knew she needed help."

Nickolas rapped his knuckles once on the wood then inclined his head and pulled the door shut behind him.

The chancery's main chamber was dark and silent. Dawn would soon light the high windows, but until then, it was very large, very quiet, and despite the many kingsmen posted outside the chancery entrance, Nickolas felt very alone.

He should be sleeping. Etta was right. But he couldn't stop thinking about what she'd said about Jules needing rest. Jules had not seemed especially sleepy when she'd left them, not considering the way he'd seen her nap just about anywhere once she had the notion. She had only seemed subdued. It was the manner, he thought suddenly, of a person saying farewell.

His feet moved toward her corridor of their own accord. The knot in his stomach had hollowed out. She was gone. He was sure of it. She'd done something foolish—something brave and foolish and horrible—and slipped away in the night to the forest.

Jules was going to cross the boundary into fae.

When he was half the distance to her corridor, Nickolas's eye caught a flicker of movement outside. He stopped to squint at the window across the space and made out a lantern light moving through the courtyard. Two men were tugging along something he couldn't quite make out. It was small and dark and... about the size of a woman.

Jules hadn't left. She'd been *taken*.

The thought had no more than registered when a call came from one of the guards in the corridor near the chancery entrance. Nickolas did not wait to hear what followed. He was already running, dodging past a scroll cart and leaping over the long table that separated him and the courtyard. Canisters and jars clattered behind him as they rolled to the floor, then the cool night air hit his skin, and he was gone at a full run.

CHAPTER 16

The courtyard was dark, shifting with shadows. Nickolas ran straight for the men, light on his feet as he drew his sword. One of the men had a familiar stride, the other too bulky to be likely to fight with any grace. He would take the smaller one first with a leg strike then pray the other let go of Jules to face him. She didn't look right, her movements off. He wasn't certain how they'd gotten past her guard, but if she was hurt, if they'd done anything to harm her, Nickolas would not need the kingsmen at his back. He would bring the men to justice himself.

He shot past a topiary, and his step nearly faltered at a niggling thought about where the kingsmen were—because surely there had been three dozen about the chancery—but the familiar figure lifted the lantern and looked back, letting Nickolas see his face.

William Adair.

A nasty word came from Nickolas's lips as he closed the distance, but William kept moving. The men were nearly to the gate on the far side of the courtyard. Nickolas would catch them before they made it. He was only strides away. But when the men reached the shadows cast by a massive arbor, they stopped and turned.

Something was wrong. Very, very wrong. Nickolas fell to a stop, too late and too close. Facing him, opposite William, stood one of Lady Brigham's men. The figure between them could not seem to keep its form.

Dawn light crept over the courtyard, coloring the leaves bronze and tipping the statuary with gold and pink. Surrounded by fruit trees and daffodils, slightly behind the men, stood the figure of a petite woman, her visage flickering between glamour and fae. She was not Jules.

Nickolas was already backing up when the first set of hands grabbed him from behind. He spun, tearing his mangled jacket and striking swords with a fourth man. Nickolas had trained kingsmen, so he knew how to use a weapon. One swing gave him distance, and the second struck an assailant in the thigh. He was moving, eyes on his surroundings, but there was no way out other than to fight.

The men had never been after Jules. They'd come for Nickolas. And he was penned in, led into a trap baited by glamour. His mother's men were working with William, all in league with the Rivenwilde woman.

He had no time to think. A sweep, slash, and dodge, and two men were down. The largest came at him from behind while another tried to pin him between the fae and the trees at sword-point while William watched from a distance, but Nickolas was too fast.

The big man came at him again, and with a crush, the brute was knocked to his knees. One of the wounded rose, without his weapon, and Nickolas caught a blow to the cheek before he was once again down to two opponents. The large man grunted when he was cracked by the hilt of Nickolas's sword and stumbled back for a moment that left Nickolas free to make quick work of the other. A few more clumsy attempts by the final brute, and he was down as well, leaving his mark on Nickolas by way of a few busted knuckles.

Nickolas's knuckles stung and burned as he turned to William, his face hard as his grip tightened on his sword.

Before he'd made a step toward the man, William held up a hand. "Lest you attempt anything dangerous, I should warn you that the lady here has been granted leave to go after Jules, should I not be able to pay her."

Three of the men were rising to their feet, weapons shifting in preparation. The one with longer hair held a rope and a large piece of canvas. Apparently, they meant to haul him away. It truly was a trap. Capture, not kill. He would be used... *For what?* A ransom plot, perhaps. And if he forced William's hand, Jules might be used in the same way. If they'd discovered she was a princess...

"You'll never touch her," Nickolas said.

"And yet, I see that you have ceased your advance." William clicked his tongue. "You should have noticed by now that we've the run of the courtyard. Fae glamour can be a marvelous aid when it's on your side. Why, with this disguise, she'd be in and out before a single soul noticed. She's already managed to evade the entire guard." William gave him his most level tone. "Touch me, and she gets the girl. It's part of our bargain. She wins either way."

The fae woman grinned. Her true form was dark and willowy, long hair loose in disordered strands. She wore the gown of a lady, but Nickolas had no reference to be certain of her status among the fae. He'd only ever seen a prince.

William took in how Nickolas's grip shifted on the sword hilt and said, "Yes. There you go. Now, gentlemen."

Around him, the men drew closer. Nickolas lifted his weapon, but it was clear there was no way out. He could not let Jules be harmed, and even if he killed every man in the courtyard, he could not touch the Adair heir. He never should have left the safety of the chancery. He'd been a fool to step foot where he was not protected. All he was left with was the chance to see the fae woman removed from the castle grounds. The sky was lightening. His racing heart was wearing down.

The big man moved for him.

"Wait!" Nickolas called. The man did wait, and Nickolas took a careful step backward. He held up a hand. "Just, hold a moment." He could not do it. He could not allow himself to be taken into William's custody. But there was no way out. There was no way to gain a true victory.

But he couldn't stomach the idea of being hauled off by henchmen again. And *by the wall*, what if William spread the tale?

Even if his mother found a way to raise the ransom, Nickolas would never be able to show his face at court. His pride would not stand for it.

"All right," he said.

The men looked confused.

"I'll go willingly." He raised a finger to point directly at each of the men. "But I want it known that this is *not* a kidnapping."

They glanced at each other.

Nickolas pointed at the man with the ropes and cloth. "To be clear, I will be voluntarily climbing into that sack."

IN SHORT ORDER, Nickolas had been placed on the rough cloth, his hands and feet tied "just to be safe." Three of the men stood in a straggle around him and William. The fae woman lingered in the shadows. As per Nickolas and William's agreement, she would be paid her due once they arrived outside of the castle.

The fourth man sat nearby, his face pale and palms pressed to a gaping wound on his thigh, breeches soaked with blood.

"Leave him," William said. "He's useless to us now."

"But the kingsmen will find him," the brute argued.

William gave the man a quelling look. "Then he should not have gotten *stabbed*, should he? Next time, he will know better."

The brute parroted the look and the tone. "Then they'll tie the crime to me as his associate, won't they?"

William's jaw clenched. "Have it your way." He pointed at the scraggliest. "You, stay with him. Find a way to get him out of this courtyard before"—he glanced at the sky—"well, I'd say you've about five minutes."

With a grand gesture to the brute, William said, "Now, if you wouldn't mind getting on with it before we're all tied to the crime."

"Getting on with it" evidently entailed wrapping the cloth tightly around Nickolas and throwing a sack over his head. Glamour gone, they had to remove him from the premises without being seen. He was tossed quite unceremoniously over the big man's shoulder.

Bound as he was, he could make out only an estimation of their route. They'd gone through a courtyard gate, over the stone walkways that surrounded the wing, then snaked through a castle corridor that Nickolas guessed must have been lesser used.

Once they were outside, the fae woman paid and gone, Nickolas was thrown over a pack horse. They rode at a solid clip, not nearly as far as Nickolas had expected. When he was pulled down from the horse, he had a sick, sinking sensation in his gut. There was the *snap* and *crunch* of underbrush beneath the men's boots, thick enough that it could not be a courtyard or garden, close enough a ride that it must be the forest that bordered the kingdom.

When they'd traveled some distance, Nickolas was set on his feet onto soft earth. His hands were left bound, but they'd given him his legs to lead him by his elbows through the trees. The way was rough, and a nearby chuckle escaped Adair whenever Nickolas stumbled. The smaller of the two henchmen muttered about their surroundings, and Nickolas thought he made out the words *sinister* and *unnatural*. Eventually, they stopped, and Nickolas was pushed onto the greensward on his rear. A murmur of *Rivenwilde prince* came from the smaller man, and the ground seemed to rumble beneath Nickolas. It sounded as if the men took a wary step back.

The sack was pulled from Nickolas's head. He blinked against the dust and the early morning light, his hair falling about his face. William stood before him, dapper in his finery as if they'd not just traipsed through the woods and evidently unaware of the fae creatures that crawled about his feet.

Nickolas, however, could not seem to take his eyes from them.

Catlike and spiky, the things rolled and hissed, one circling near William's boot with its eyes on the man's watch fob. Nickolas had not been so close to one before. He tried to scoot away but could not, given the cloth tangled around him and the rope tying his hands and feet. He glanced up at William, who seemed confused by the look on his face.

"Are you well, Nicky? It was just a little ride in a sack. You've done much worse on a lark." He swatted at something near his ear. "Was it the fae woman? I know, truly, that was unfair. Very unsporting of me. But I must always hedge my bets. You know that."

"Fae," Nickolas wheezed. William was taking him to the fae. No ransom would be enough. Nickolas's return would require a bargain. His gaze darted to the trees, where glowing eyes stared back at him— much larger, much more dangerous creatures waiting their turn. He was grateful that it was daylight, at least. "You bargained with fae. Just to get back at me?"

William had not yet laid eyes on the prince. Nickolas was sure of it. There was no other way the man would be able to stand so calmly among the creatures. The henchmen had not either. His mother must have only heard Jules's words before the prince had used his magic to still the room. If any of them could see what Nickolas was seeing, they would run.

William lowered into a squat, bringing him close to Nickolas. "Oh," he said. "I'm not doing this to punish you. I'm quite glad you're out of contention. It will make things easier for me. Everyone says Princess Mireille has set her cap at you. Can't hurt not to have you around." His voice lowered, tinged with self-satisfaction. "But this... I'm doing this for your mother. She's promised me a great deal in exchange for the task."

Had Nickolas thought he was beyond surprise, the rogue in a gentleman's jacket had proved him wrong again. Lady Brigham was conspiring with their extortionist. He did not know what she meant to gain, but he realized he should not have been surprised. His mother had tried to trade one of his sisters to the fae only the day before, after all. It did not sting any less. "You know you cannot trust her."

William smiled. "That is the beauty of this deal, my friend. I do not *need* to trust her. Your dear mother has found herself locked, however temporarily, inside a cell." He pointed at himself then the other two men. "We make the trade, return to Westrende, and should your mother not uphold her end of the agreement, all the spoils go to me."

One of the other men grunted, and William added, "And them. Of course, the spoils will also go to them." The wink he gave Nickolas made clear the men would never see a single coin.

William leaned down and shoved the sack roughly over Nickolas's head again. "Take care, old chap."

AFTER NICKOLAS'S captor called the prince's name, low words were spoken between William and the prince, barely skirting the bounds of civility. It was not long before William and the henchmen were dismissed. There was a moment of stillness in which Nickolas thought he heard a sigh, then the prince spoke low words of his own, and a new voice followed.

"Take him," the prince said.

A single hand took hold of Nickolas's arm and led him in the direction that he knew was the wall. His feet dug in automatically, but the hand somehow held more strength than it ought. It drew him forward, unyieldingly, and Nickolas sensed the moment they stepped over the Rive.

When Nickolas was a boy, he'd once leapt into a pond on a dare. It had been the dead of winter, and the moment his skin touched the icy water, shock stole through his entire being. He'd barely made it back to the shore that day, shivering and stiff and uttering nonsense.

That shock was nothing to crossing the boundary. For one instant, it felt as if his body were submerged, overwhelmed with pressure and sensation and the intense desire to reach the surface. Then they were through and the sensation gone. He did feel the urge to utter a few nonsensical noises, but otherwise, it was as if the sensation had never happened at all.

The hand on his arm urged him forward, and the path beneath his feet suddenly had the feel of polished marble. He had the sense he'd been moved by fae magic, as the prince had done when he'd taken Nickolas and Jules from the Filmore balcony. A short flight of stairs followed before Nickolas felt warmth and the still air of indoors. He thought he detected the scent of flowers when the hand leading him stopped, giving a gentle squeeze that Nickolas took as an indicator to stay put.

So there Nickolas stood.

"Get that off." The voice belonged to the prince and was tinged with annoyance.

The cloth covering Nickolas's head was removed, his wrists unbound. He stood in the center of a massive entrance hall, its fine, smooth stone reminiscent of the glamour that obscured the filigree wall, every corner and trim piece impossibly intricate. Opulent and grand, it rose three stories, with carved marble stairs and great open archways overlooking the floor. Thin vines trailed over surfaces like living sculpture, flowering magenta and violet beneath the open ceiling so far above.

Nickolas blinked hard several times in an attempt to make what he was seeing disappear. It did not. He was inside a fae palace. The prince stood before him, evidently waiting for Nickolas to grant his attention. Nickolas held up a single finger while continuing to gape.

He could not quite believe it. His own mother had traded him to the fae. He'd been delivered to the prince himself. He was standing inside a *Rivenwilde* palace.

"Lord Brigham," the prince said dourly. "I do have other matters to attend this afternoon."

Nickolas blinked at the man, realizing his finger was still in the air and that his hands were a bit numb from their bindings. He dropped the finger and rubbed his hands together surreptitiously.

The corner of the prince's eye twitched irritably. "Noal will show you to your rooms and provide a fresh wardrobe. He will be available should you require aught else."

Nickolas glanced from the tall, smartly dressed man who had untied his hands to the prince. "My rooms?"

The twitch appeared again, possibly more intensely. "As I said."

His gaze darting across the space once more, Nickolas said, "I'm not... you'll not put me in a cell?"

A flat expression crossed the prince's face, as if put off by the idea, but he said only, "There is no need to bind you. Should you leave this palace, you will no longer be under my protection. That, I believe you will find, is incentive enough."

Nickolas shot a glance at the other fae, Noal, whose expression was a bit more telling. What it told Nickolas was that he did not want to discover what awaited him in the fae wilds.

The prince waited until his attention returned then said, "I suggest you take dinner in your rooms. You may not find the entire court as welcoming as its prince." He inclined his head before turning to go then disappeared through a massive arched doorway into another room.

It had not been disagreeable advice. Noal led Nickolas—free of bonds and free of mask—through the palace to a suite of rooms. The man was as precise as any of Westrende's top staff and had deftly introduced Nickolas to the suite as his bath and wardrobe were prepared by a few bustling fae.

Nickolas and Noal stood alone in the windowless sitting room. Nickolas ran a hand over his face. A window or balcony would do him no good in any case, not when he could not traverse the wilds on his own. "What happens now?"

"That is for the prince to decide," Noal said.

Nickolas considered the words for a long moment, uncertain of the etiquette for any part of his situation, then asked, "How much did she get for me?"

Noal frowned. "In the end, it is often as much as they deserve."

Sick at the thought, Nickolas only nodded. It did not matter how much his mother received in her bargain, only what dealing with the fae would cost her. And that, he was afraid, was more than she would be willing to pay. "And what's he to do with me, this prince?"

"Feed, clothe, and provide shelter, as per the laws of hospitality."

Nickolas narrowed his gaze. "Any chance I could get a copy of those laws?"

"It would be unnecessary, given that you are bound only by the laws of your kingdom. We, however, are bound by the laws of hospitality, as we are with all laws of Rivenwilde, and by the curse."

"The curse?"

"I cannot answer that. As I suspect you already know that those bound by a curse may not lay out the details of its terms, it should not come as a surprise." Noal's thumb slid over a knuckle, where his gloved hands were held precisely before his waist. "It is not so unlike the terms of the laws of hospitality."

"How so?"

One of Noal's gloved fingers twitched. "Your protection under the laws of hospitality protects the prince as well. You'll not be able to speak a word of what you've seen here."

Nickolas's breath caught in his chest.

The fae inclined his head. "Lord Brigham, if that is all."

"You have my gratitude," Nickolas managed. He bowed slightly, though he wasn't certain how much of a lord he even was in the current situation.

Once Noal and the others had gone, inconceivably leaving the door to his suite unlocked, Nickolas cleaned off the mud and the muck gathered during his journey through the forest and before, when he had rolled around the courtyard building with Ian. It seemed impossible that, having had no chance to change or sleep, he was still wearing his clothes from the ball—the lovely and perfect and entirely ill-conceived ball. Nickolas sat on the edge of a chaise, staring at the finely woven rug beneath his feet. He had not allowed himself to recall the night before, had not dwelt on his last moments with Jules. Her grief and fear when she'd been discovered by the Norcliffe lord, her resignation when she'd left him standing in the chancery.

William and his mother would meet a much worse fate than Nickolas for what they'd done, but he could not fathom the distress his disappearance would cause Etta and the others. He could not guess what they would be asked to sacrifice to see his return. The price would be exorbitant.

He could not expect them to pay it.

The thoughts swirled through his head and tore at his heart, and it was there, on the fae chaise with his head in his hands, that Nickolas succumbed to sleep.

When he woke, it was with the sensation of having lost direction. The remaining candles burned low, and the unfamiliar room took on the eerie glow of half-light. He was still in shirtsleeves, the fae wardrobe laid over an adjacent chair. On a nearby table waited a plate of food along with a decanter. The pitcher and basin had been refreshed, and freshly polished boots rested near the clothes.

Nickolas stood, stumbled over the ragged jacket he'd dropped to the floor, and made his way to the door of the suite. It remained unlocked. He opened it and glanced down the empty corridor before stepping out of his room. At the far end was a set of wide double doors carved with ancient script. As if drawn to it, Nickolas moved through the corridor, careful of every doorway he passed, even though each was closed.

When he stood before the doorway, he could not quite bring his lifted hand to touch the carvings. While much of the palace and its furnishings felt clean and modern, the doors seemed as ancient as the script. Finely shaped vines trailed over the words, a phrase he thought translated to something like *balance must be kept*, though one of the words might instead have been *justice*. Brow furrowed, he studied the design in grain that appeared to be hawthorn, darkened with age. A bit of moss covered one of the symbols, and he reached up to brush it away.

The doors fell open beneath his touch.

Nickolas glanced behind him, but the corridor remained empty. Before him was a room that seemed untouched by time. It was a massive open space, lit dimly by narrow gaps in a style of drapery that had not been fashionable for centuries. On high walls, the paintings and frames were of a similar sort, and centering the room was a hawthorn pedestal carved in a manner that appeared to be rooted to the floor, live vines and flowers reaching up to wrap around the base.

Upon the pedestal sat an hourglass, its sands nearly drained. That same sensation of being drawn forward had Nickolas moving, but one foot forward gave him the sense that the threshold was a boundary— similar to the wall over the Rive, which he had not liked at all.

He stepped backward, leaving the room to its peace. When the doors fell closed once more, Nickolas took two steps farther away. He turned, wiping his damp palm on his trouser leg, and surveyed the space.

At the other end of the corridor was a large open archway, soft with evening light. He traversed the distance just as carefully, passing the still-open door to his own room. He heard no sounds or indications of other occupants, even from the rooms below.

The air was cool through the open archway, its marble smooth where he placed his palm to the frame. He leaned forward, staring into a courtyard three stories below. There were no platforms or trellises, not even a statue or pool. Only the stone and the earth and a fall certain to break a good deal of bone.

His gaze lifted to the opposite wall of the courtyard and beyond, where as far as he could see, sprawling estate houses peeked from a landscape more green and lush than anything Nickolas had ever known. But in the distance, at the edge of the forest, stood a pyre as tall as the trees. Smaller pyres stood scattered around it, and countless indistinct shapes moved through the clearing in a manner that was not unlike the staff at Westrende when preparing for an event.

Dread sank into him as his eyes rose to the sky.

"Moontide," said a voice at his ear.

Nickolas jumped, nearly tumbling through the window before he managed to turn his back against the frame. He had been alone in the corridor, he was sure of it, and yet the fae woman was only inches from him, pressing close enough he could still feel the breath as her words had brushed his skin.

She was unusually tall, her features sharp, the corners of her wide lips and dark eyes tipped upward in a smile. She wore a silk gown and jewels in her hair, but strapped at her side was a double-edged dagger that appeared well-used. When she showed her teeth, he had to still the sudden urge to run.

"Are you lost, little lord?"

Nickolas was not proud of how long it took him to get out "I am a guest of the prince."

She leaned nearer, voice dropping to a whisper. "As am I."

He tried to slide casually along the wall, away from the open archway.

She sauntered in the same direction. Her eyes twinkled like an actual, literal spark of light. Nickolas froze, his elbow brushing where the wall met a corner.

She said, "I can take you closer, little lord. Take you to see the festivities below. Would you like that?"

"I'm afraid I must decline."

"Must you?" Her gaze flicked over his disheveled attire. "You do not look bound to me. Come now. It's not far. Only just outside."

Outside the palace, where he had no protection from the laws of hospitality. Where the prince and Noal had assured him he did not want to go. *Noal.* That was what he should do—call for help. Noal would come, surely, just as others had called on the prince. But Nickolas did not know if calling a fae would indebt him in some way. "I must prepare for dinner. If you'll allow me to make my farewell—"

Before he could even attempt a bow, the fae moved closer. "Give me your name, little lord, so that I might speak it."

"I—"

"My lord," said a voice from down the corridor.

Nickolas and the woman looked up to find Noal standing before the entrance to Nickolas's rooms. Nickolas was unsettled to realize the woman's fingers had curled into a grip on the chest of his shirt, and he'd not even noticed.

Noal said, "It is time to make ready for the evening's event."

Nickolas sagged a little in relief then hurried to slide past the woman and toward Noal, the woman's grip dragging free of him. When he reached the doorway, he glanced back to give a perfunctory dip of the head in case there was some rule of propriety he was unaware he might be breaking, but she was watching him with a long-nailed finger flicking irritably at the tip of her knife.

Inside, Noal tutted at the state of Nickolas's wardrobe.

"Would she have harmed me?" Nickolas asked.

Noal gestured to urge him toward the basin and fresh attire. "You will find not everyone at court is as welcoming as the prince."

"He said that already."

Noal handed Nickolas a fresh shirt. "The prince is not known to lie."

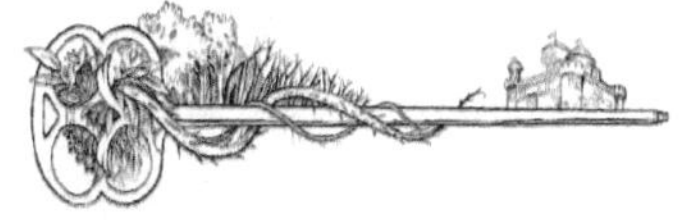

Nickolas was dressed in a fine suit, well-fitting boots, and a too-tight cravat. He had retied the cravat several times, but the sensation of being strangled would not seem to cease. When Noal had deemed him "well enough," they made their way to a private study that was quiet, dimly lit, and painfully impressive. It gave Nickolas a little pang of envy, and he thought he might have preferred the strangled feeling.

Before Noal made their introduction, the prince laid down his quill and looked up at them. He seemed to draw a resigned breath then stood, pulled on his jacket, and slipped the folded parchment into a pocket of his vest. "Lord Brigham."

Nickolas bowed.

The prince came out from behind the large desk then crossed the room and faced him. "It is moontide. The lady Jules and I are to be wed."

There was a long moment of silence, wherein Nickolas was unsure if he'd spoken a word in reply. In his head, many, many words had been spoken. Shouted, even. Words like *no* and *the deuce you will*. But then *moontide* sank in, and Nickolas could only see the illustrations they'd found in Etta's fae book, Gideon's fingers tracing the figure of a bride and groom beneath the light of a full moon. Their potential loophole must not have worked out. She would have to make her impossible choice. *It has nothing to do with you*, he told himself. Because to Jules, Nickolas would be no one. Between his mother's actions, the family debt, and a fae bargain, Nickolas might not even be a lord. He did not understand why the prince was telling him, but Nickolas understood well enough where he stood.

Jules was a princess. She might be marrying a fae, but he was a prince—one equal to her station. Nickolas's entire chest went tight. He could not think of her standing where he was, trapped in Rivenwilde and beholden to fae whims. He didn't know whether she might be locked in a room or paraded about at court events, but it didn't matter. It was all untenable.

The prince said, "She has agreed to the terms on the condition that the ceremony is held in the heart of the forest, near the Rive." His dark gaze slid momentarily away, toward a wall of richly bound books. "And that once the ceremony has concluded, you will be set free."

The weight in Nickolas's stomach felt as if it might drag him to the ground. He was being pulled apart, bit by bit. Jules's terms had already been named, which meant she had sacrificed something new. Something besides the breaking of a curse.

"What did you take from her in return?"

The prince gazed toward the ceiling as he requested, "Noal."

Noal retrieved a draped object from a side table then held it where Nickolas could see. The drape was pulled away to reveal a finely woven enclosure holding a familiar dull-gray bird.

"Frederick," Nickolas breathed.

"Yes." It did not sound as if the prince took any joy in the trade.

Nickolas asked, "Why?"

The prince's gaze came back to Nickolas. "She has no more choice in the matter than I."

"So you set me free but trap her brother..."

"He will only be as trapped as a princess of Rivenwilde."

Nickolas swallowed his response, struck by the bird's wide, dark eyes. Jules would not be alone. She would have a companion. She would hate it, but Frederick had chosen to stay with her time and again. He would likely choose the same outcome himself. It begged the question of why the prince had named it as his price.

"There will be a ceremony, and you are required to attend," the prince explained. "I do not wish to bind you as your people have. Will you give your word to remain under my command?"

Nickolas watched him for a long moment. The prince looked tired and not from lack of sleep. Whatever else he was, whatever deals he'd made with Jules, he was still fae. Nickolas said, "With respect, even I am not fool enough to go willingly into such a bargain."

"Very well." The prince gave his gaze to Noal, and then with the dizzying sensation of falling from an unsafe height, the lot of them were swept away, no longer in the dim study but standing out of doors, near the ancient filigree wall that rose from the Rive.

It was past nightfall, but the clearing was lit with torches and scattered with flowering vines that had not been there before. At the center of the clearing was an altar, standing before a trellis draped with night-blooming flowers. A dozen armed fae men and women waited with their backs to the wall, naked hands at their sides and eyes on the forest. Flickering shadows danced among the trees, where Nickolas could see with his newly gifted sight, and the forms of shadowy creatures appeared to dance as well.

It did not seem the dance of a celebration, he thought, as much as it was like the preparations the king's guard made before contests of skill. But Nickolas was within the Westrende borders, through the wall once more, and his skin felt alight with the desire to act. To run, to fight, to make any attempt at defeating what fate had in store.

Nickolas's hands had no more than tightened into fists before the prince made a gesture that prevented any attempt at all. Roots burst from the ground around him. He leapt back, but the magic surrounded him, shooting upward to weave dark, woody strands into form. When the form was complete, the magic abruptly fell still. A few small clods of dirt fell to the earth with a dull, muffled *thump*.

Nickolas's gaze met the prince's through the tracery. He'd been placed inside a cage, a massive, man-sized enclosure not unlike the ones in Lady Narine's aviary. "What fresh abyss is this?" he whispered.

Beside him, Noal hooked Frederick's cage to a root near Nickolas's head. The bird grunted a similar complaint.

Noal stepped back to stand beside the prince, whose distaste was evident. "I would have much preferred a spoken vow."

Noal's reply was sanguine. "It will encourage them to save him. They'll be far less likely to attempt any deception this way."

The prince's face pinched. "Human trickery does grow tiresome."

Noal hummed in agreement.

"Truly," Nickolas challenged, but his protests went unheard as a call echoed from within the trees. It sounded predatory. Every fae in the clearing looked toward the forest. From the nearby brush, something catlike moved. Nickolas reached through a space in the roots, opened the door to Frederick's cage, and drew the bird to his chest. For once, Frederick was quiet.

What came through the trees was no beast at all but a petite figure wearing a simple muslin dress. Frederick made a croak of protest, and Nickolas realized he'd squeezed the bird too tightly to his chest. Relaxing his grip, he watched with Frederick as Jules came further into view.

She might have been dressed simply, but she held the bearing of a princess, through and through. Shoulders back, head high, she strode with casual purpose toward the prince. She looked impossibly beautiful, features lit by the moon like the first night Nickolas had met her. Behind her walked Ian, his pace steady. He wore a sword at his hip and carried a small valise.

Nickolas did not think Jules had seen him, but when she approached the prince, she disregarded his elegant bow and said, "Release him."

The prince looked up at her mid-bow, glanced at Nickolas, then straightened. "My lady, it is—"

"Release. Him."

The prince cleared his throat.

Jules did not flinch. "It is not as if you should be concerned for his escape. Not when you might move from here to there and snatch him back in an instant. What could you possibly be afraid of? You're the prince of the Riven Court."

The prince's mouth went into a hard line. He flicked a hand, and the roots snapped around Nickolas, falling to the ground in broken bits. His tone was level. "Is that all, or do you wish to lay additional demands upon a prince of the Riven Court?"

She appeared to swallow. She still did not look toward Nickolas or Frederick. "For now, that is all."

The prince's jaw flexed. He turned, proffering his arm so that she might be led to the trellis. Nickolas knew this, because the cursed illustration from Etta's fae book had been reminding him of the scene every few seconds. Frederick made a miserable little sound, but Nickolas could not seem to make a sound at all. Magic prevented him from saying aloud that as the cage around him had broken, thin fingers of vine rose behind the cover of grass to wrap themselves tightly over and around the ankles of Nickolas's borrowed boots.

The prince had not lied. It did not mean he was worthy of trust.

The prince led Jules beneath a radiant moon to stand framed by the trellis. Ian moved toward Nickolas as if merely finding an inconspicuous spot from which to watch. He sat the valise on the ground at his side, without glancing at Nickolas even once. A thin gold chain glinted at the bag's clasp. Two of the fae standing near the wall had never taken their eyes off of Ian, and three more had a solid watch on Nickolas.

The prince withdrew the folded parchment from his vest and laid it on the altar. He picked up the quill and handed it first to Jules. She took it carefully, glancing first at the prince then at the wall. The quill shifted in her hand. She lifted the parchment to read.

"It is accurate," the prince said quietly. "To the letter."

"I'll just... I need to read it first."

The prince gestured that she should proceed but gave a significant glance at the moon. Time was running out.

Jules adjusted the parchment. Shifted the quill. Glanced once more at the wall.

Frederick began to cough.

Jules's gaze shot to the bird. It was nearly time. The moon was high, and Frederick's curse would soon be enduring. The only way to save him was to sign the contract and marry the prince.

"Here," Ian said. "Let me take him." He stepped closer, kicking the valise over as he took Frederick from Nickolas's determined grip.

Jules's gaze brushed Nickolas for one heartbeat, then it was gone. Head down, she pressed quill to paper.

Nickolas went hot. He knelt automatically, unwilling to let a single soul see his face, and made a production of righting the valise. His fingers caught on the chain of the necklace, and a strange sensation rolled through him. He froze, in fear that one of the fae guards might have seen. Then he wrapped his finger twice around the delicate chain and pulled before slipping the ring that hung from it into his palm. Face still hot, he rose to stand, not daring to move his feet.

Because his boots, his voice, and the magic's hold on him was free. The fisted hand at his side held Jules's magic ring.

CHAPTER 18

Eyes on Jules and the prince, Nickolas was gripped by both the intense desire to stop the ceremony and to let it go ahead. Stop it because it was madness to let her marry a fae prince. Let it go ahead because, beside him, Ian held Jules's brother, who would be stuck in the form of a bird forever.

It was just as Etta had said. Neither choice was tenable. They had failed to find a way to break the curse.

A wind picked up in the clearing, whispering through the leaves as if warning of time running out. If Nickolas chose incorrectly, he might condemn Jules and her brother to a lifetime of misery, but it was clear Jules was delaying. Ian had made certain Nickolas had possession of the ring for a reason, and his mistress's hand could not quite seem to make the final stroke on her contract.

Nickolas drew a breath, crushed the ring in his palm, then pulled the sword from the scabbard at Ian's hip in one swift movement. The prince did not even turn around, only flicked his hand in a gesture Nickolas was sure the move was meant to still him. It did not. He was half the distance to the altar when six of the fae guards came off their positions near the wall. He was two strides farther by the time they reached him, and when the prince finally did turn, Jules dipped in a move not unlike a curtsy then rose again with a dagger she'd evidently pulled from beneath her skirts—pressed firmly to the prince's side. Well placed, in fact, to drive upward beneath his ribs.

A sword clashed against Nickolas's—the fae guard not as easily managed as Jules's coachman or his mother's henchmen—and Nickolas was pushed a step backward. He swung again, pivoted, and was nearly struck with a blow that might have severed his arm.

"Stop them," Jules commanded the prince just as Nickolas swung again.

The prince's gaze rolled skyward. Nickolas had the sense that he was not checking the state of the moon.

The prince called, "Halt," and the fae guard drew back but kept Nickolas surrounded. The prince glanced over his shoulder then corrected his gaze lower, at Jules. He said, "No harm may come to the prince of the Riven Court."

Jules stared at him in earnest. "Oh, that warning applies only to citizens of Westrende. As you're aware, I am not a citizen of Westrende."

The prince's eyes pressed closed. The expression put Nickolas in mind of their nanny after she'd been locked with his sisters inside a single room for three days straight. The prince's tone was not a great deal different from the nanny's either when he said, "As you may also be aware, there remains just over a quarter hour before your curse sets its course. If you intend to stab a fae prince, I suggest you choose one you are not meant to marry."

She said, "Let him go. When he and Ian are out of sight, then I will sign, and this will all be over."

"Spoken like the most eager of brides," the prince muttered. He gestured toward Nickolas. "You are as free to leave as you've been this entire time, Lord Brigham."

Nickolas opened his mouth to explain that he had, in fact, not been free at all, when a new voice came from the edge of the clearing.

"Not so fast."

The prince turned away from Jules, who doggedly followed with her well-aimed blade, and glared in the direction of the trees. "Lady Ostwind," he said. "I would like to remind you that this entire affair is none of your concern."

Etta tromped closer, sword in hand, Gideon at her back with an armload of documents and, nonsensically, Princess Mireille with three of her courtiers behind them.

Etta pointed at the filigree wall. "That's where you're wrong, because everything on this side of the Rive is my concern."

The prince's mouth turned down. "We are only on this side of the wall because your..." He cleared his throat. "Because the lady Jules has required it. Had I my preference, we would be nowhere near Westrende."

Etta drew to a stop less than ten paces from the prince, the others fanning out beside her. "Jules is no mere lady, and you know it."

The prince's jaw flexed. "That is her secret to keep. It was never mine to bandy about. And it is her decision whether to proceed with..." His words fell off once more, then he glanced at Jules. "Have you changed your mind about the ceremony or only the terms of Lord Brigham's release?"

Jules adjusted her grip on the dagger. "It is no secret that I do not wish to marry you. But I have no choice in the matter."

"Actually." Gideon stepped forward, every eye in the clearing suddenly on him. He cleared his throat then withdrew the fae book from his jacket.

The prince made a pained sound, but Nickolas found himself stepping closer. The fae surrounding him did not move.

Gideon spoke only to Jules. "The price named was to marry one of your station. It was not specific to the prince of the Riven Court."

The prince said, "While this is all very dramatic, I will remind you that her time is running out." The *there are no other princes present* was heavily implied.

Princess Mireille sidled up to Gideon and gave a little wave to Jules. Jules's color had gone off, but Mireille did not seem to pay it mind. She said, "I heard about what happened at the ball and insisted I be allowed to help. Jules is from a neighboring kingdom to my own, and I told Gideon the stories we had heard regarding her father."

"Namely," Gideon explained, "that the king had fallen under the sway of a fae queen. The very one, I suspect, who cursed each of the king's heirs and left only Jules to escape."

"Frederick was the bravest brother." Princess Mireille's gaze searched the clearing until she found Ian holding the bird. "Oh, is that him? He's darling." Frederick made a chiding hiss, but Mireille's attention had already returned to the prince. "Ian told us that while Frederick managed to save Jules from a similar fate, he was injured. The brothers were presumed dead, and the court blamed Jules, but many among the staff refused to believe it."

The prince said flatly, "Then the palace became plagued by large white birds, five to be precise, determined to ruin every event held at the fae queen's behest."

The princess's grin widened. "Exactly that. Talk began that they were the spirits of the brothers, come to seek revenge. But the sixth brother, it was said, had somehow escaped the queen's curse. Tales began that he would return one day to vanquish the fae queen. As you can imagine, she took no joy in that."

"I need not imagine," the prince replied.

Mireille's right eye pinched in something vaguely wink-like before her gaze flicked back to Jules. "Gideon told me Frederick was well, and I'm so pleased. But I knew there was more to the story. In fact, Lord Holden revealed just recently that he had heard the fae queen had only named the price of wedding a prince. She wanted you forced away from your kingdom, and there would be no remaining heirs. He says it was your father who managed a betrothal bargain with the prince of Rivenwilde so that you would have protection from the queen." At the mention of Lord Holden, Mireille had gestured to one of the men behind her, and at the mention of the prince, she'd casually gestured to him as if there was no difference in the men's stations. To the prince, she said, "It is true, is it not, that you might provide protection from a fae queen?"

The prince's brow lowered, but he said, "Any I name under my protection would be safe inside my home."

Mireille gave a single decisive nod as if the entire mystery was sewn up. Nickolas, however, had a thousand questions, not the least of which was what the fae prince gained by agreeing to harbor Jules. But Mireille had opened her mouth as if to speak again.

"All this to say," Gideon interrupted, "that if Jules renounces her title, she might marry a lord instead. The price would be paid, and the curse broken."

Jules went stock-still, like a statue among the grass in her pale muslin dress.

But Nickolas was moving again, chest bumping against the swords of two fae guards. *To marry one equal to my station*, she had said. Her price. If Gideon was right, Jules only needed a lord. It was all that stood between her and a broken curse. *Just one lord.* Nickolas heard himself say, "I am a lord."

Everyone turned to look at him.

"I am," he said defensively.

"Oh." Mireille's fingers twisted awkwardly at her waist. "I thought —well, I've brought along three of my best courtiers so that she might choose one of them and marry someone close to home."

Etta looked pained. Gideon was frowning. And Nickolas remembered, quite suddenly, that he was about to lose everything. He'd exposed the family's debt, his mother had been thrown into a cell, and Nickolas was a fae prisoner, only released on the condition that Jules wed the prince.

"Right," he said. "Of course. Best that she marries one of..." He glanced at the three men near Princess Mireille, all handsome, well-dressed, and evidently not at all put out by standing in a fae-filled forest or cowed by the prince. He swallowed thickly. "Don't know what I was thinking. Do carry on before it's too late."

"Can you do that?" Jules's voice was barely above a whisper, but it seemed to echo off the trees.

"He's the chancellor," Etta reminded her. "He can. And I can stand as witness. That makes two officials to seal the contract. It is all that is required."

"Renounce my title. Renounce my kingdom. Marry a lord."

Gideon drew one of the papers from the bundle tucked against the crook of his arm, the king's seal glinting in the torchlight. The chancery was guardian of the seal until a king was returned to office. Gideon truly did have the power to save her.

They could break her curse.

The prince clicked his tongue then said flatly, "Noal, seize the lady."

CHAPTER 19

The clearing came alive with movement. Jules was grabbed by Noal, her dagger knocked to the ground. Gideon and Etta rushed forward with swords drawn, Mireille's lords took formation around their princess, and Ian and the bird were suddenly locked inside a cage of fae warriors with Nickolas.

The prince lifted a hand, and Etta and Gideon seemed to slam into a wall of magic in their approach. They each fell a step backward, chests heaving, matching glares trained on the prince. Noal drew a fighting Jules closer to his chest, giving the prince room as he surveyed the crowd.

The prince said, "I was promised a bride, and a bride I shall have." He quirked a brow at Etta. "Unless you would like to war with Riven-wilde this night, Lady Ostwind."

The figures carved into the filigree wall seemed to move as if restless in anticipation. Vines curled outward from the wall, skirting the fae guards as they unfurled, reaching toward Jules and the prince. Noal kicked one of the vines away. The earth beneath Nickolas's feet felt alive with magic. In the shadowy trees, the fae creatures edged closer.

Etta lifted her sword as if she might rush the prince, but a marshal could not declare war—against the fae or anyone else. That responsi-

383

bility would fall only to a general, and it was a keen reminder of previous battles between Westrende and the fae. Etta's jaw flexed. "If you take Jules through that wall, you will pay in ways you never imagined."

The prince's smile made clear he had every intention of doing so. "As she has said, she is not a citizen of Westrende. You have no claim on her, no call to intercede."

If she renounced her title and kingdom and married a Westrende lord, Jules would become a citizen of Westrende. The marshal would have every reason to intervene.

They had to get her out of Noal's hands.

Nickolas glanced at Ian, who had drawn his sword. The bird was tucked neatly inside his vest. Ian inclined his head infinitesimally, and Nickolas's fist tightened around the ring as he gave a small nod back. Together, they surged forward, Ian crashing low into the fae before them while Nickolas leapt through a narrow opening, gaining a cut to the arm and a mere few steps closer to the prince and Jules.

Fae magic surged through the ground, throwing another cage of roots between Nickolas and the prince. But Jules's ring was in his hand, and Nickolas burst through with a single slash of his sword. The prince's calm demeanor shifted to something decidedly more sinister, but Nickolas's step did not falter. An entire wall of roots and vines split the earth, exploding rich soil and greenery over Nickolas, but again, he slashed through with ease.

The prince shifted to face him before turning his palm open, and Noal quickly fumbled with a fighting Jules to hand over a finely made sword. The prince's long fingers curled around the hilt with practiced grace and something that spoke of his eagerness to engage.

"Nickolas, stop!" Gideon called from the sidelines as warnings and chatter rose from the watching crowd, trapped by fae magic.

"I'll renounce my citizenship," Nickolas said, his pace never slowing, attention never leaving the prince. "Do it, Gideon, before I drive my blade through this blackguard and be done with him once and for all."

The prince readied his stance. "Yes," he said. "Do it, Gideon."

Jules shouted, "No!" shoving hard into Noal then slamming a boot to his instep before driving an elbow up to connect with his chin. She lurched forward, half out of Noal's grip, just as Nickolas raised his sword and just as a cloud slid over the moon.

The sky went dark for one moment. In the next, a slow humming built, something beyond the trees drawing nearer. The breeze picked up again, the darkness cleared, and in the silvery light of the moon, five shapes came into view.

Nickolas's approach fell to a stop only paces away from the prince. Ian slammed into Nickolas from behind, jarring a curse out of Ian before his eyes, too, found the sky. They stared up with all the others as the shapes descended. The fae guards took a step back, Etta and Gideon several steps nearer. Mireille let out a sigh of what could only be delight.

Before anyone had even the inclination to throw her a quelling look, five giant birds dove into the clearing, the light glowing off their white wings. They did not slow to glide into a landing but came full force, whooping and grunting, knocking into the trellis, swooping at Noal's head, and crashing the altar to the ground. Two of them rammed into the prince, viciously pummeling until he dropped his sword. Evidently, the fae prince's magic was no match for a curse made by the queen, because he threw no root cages or walls of magic their way.

Jules came to her feet, eyes wet with evident joy. Her gaze met Ian's through the chaos, and in awe, Ian whispered, "They're here."

Had Ian not believed that Jules hadn't harmed her brothers, here was all the evidence he would need. The five elder brothers had returned in the form of birds, wreaking havoc just as Mireille had said.

"They're swans," Nickolas breathed.

Beside him, Frederick narrowed his birdy gaze.

Nickolas put up his hands. "It is neither here nor there. I only meant I was surprised."

Frederick's neck ruffled.

"We must hurry," Jules told the birds. "Time is nearly up."

Four of the birds circled the prince, while one drove its beak repeatedly at Noal until he stepped farther back. The fae guard remained on watch a careful distance away, swords at the ready.

"What's happening?" Nickolas whispered to Ian.

"No one acts against a fae queen" was all Ian said in return. But his eyes stayed on Jules, who had indeed acted against a fae queen's wishes.

Jules, who was about to overcome her curse.

Mireille and the three courtiers rushed forward with Etta and Gideon, and Nickolas's throat went dry. There was a rush of introductions from Mireille, explanations about the contract from Etta and Gideon, and hurried arrangements. Nickolas opened his palm, staring down at the ring laced through the fine golden chain. He glanced up one last time at the prince, who stood watching the commotion with a resigned expression. It was done. Jules was safe. She would marry her lord.

Nickolas handed the ring to Ian then turned to go.

Behind him, the bickering abruptly cut off. "Lord Brigham," Jules called, the sound a bit jostled as if she was shoving through the crowd.

Nickolas stopped, unable to look at her lest she read the expression he was sure was plain on his face. The base of his hand was pressed to his breastbone, he realized, and he dropped it straightaway. "You're nearly out of time, my lady. Please, do not waste it on me."

She took hold of his elbow, tugging gently until he looked down at her. She was so close, her dark eyes shining up at him in the moonlight. Incomparable, that was what she was. And Nickolas did not know how to stop the *wanting* of her.

"Nickolas," she said softly. "You're still a lord."

The knife in his chest went deeper. Surely, there could be little left of the thing that had been his heart. "I'm not certain that's true any longer," he answered. "It's not worth the risk."

"If it was—"

"But it isn't. And you're out of time. Save yourself, my lady. Free your brothers. Please. I couldn't stand it if—I do not wish you to be unhappy."

She tugged him around to face her. "You are a lord, Nickolas. Despite all the rest. Your debt has been answered. The records filed with chancery." At his expression, she explained, "I told you I would uphold my end of the bargain, and I have."

"You—" He swallowed hard. "What?"

"My kingdom is wealthy. *I* am wealthy. I could take none of it with me, but I ensured you and Frederick would be well taken care of, should I have ended up in the hands of the fae."

Nickolas's knees felt unsteady, but he had nowhere to sit. Jules's touch was all he had, and he clung to it with every fiber of his being. "You resolved my debt."

She nodded. "The Brighams are solvent. You remain a lord. I can do nothing to help free your mother, but perhaps that is for the best."

A helpless laugh bubbled up from his hollowed chest. "I am a lord."

"Yes," she said. "Now, would you—is it possible that you would be willing to—" She wet her lips. "Would you like to marry me, Lord Brigham?"

CHAPTER 20

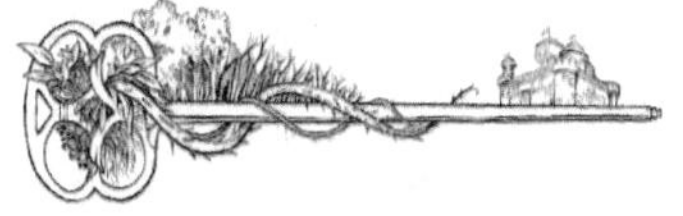

Would you like to marry me? Jules had asked.

Nickolas stared down at her as she waited for an answer, disbelief overpowering his every instinct to shout, "Yes!" But it was no ploy. She was in earnest, and if he said yes, she could truly be his. And he would not be bringing her lower; he would be helping her escape a danger. Jules still had hold of Nickolas, and he slid his hand into hers, locking their thumbs, palms together, so that he might press her fingers to his lips after he carefully, calmly, not at all embarrassingly loudly shouted his *yes*.

He'd only opened his mouth to seal the bargain when Gideon's low voice broke in. "My lady, perhaps this isn't the best—"

Nickolas glared at Gideon before Jules turned to face the man. Etta, Mireille, and the three eligible lords stood at Gideon's back.

"What do you know of her best match?" Nickolas snapped. "Do you think her incapable of deciding that on her own?" He glanced at Jules. "Unless—if it's the coin you've settled upon me, my lady, that can be returned. I won't keep you from your own holdings."

Gideon frowned. "Of course it isn't that. She's never been concerned with a fortune, and even if she was, she might take her pick of the lords present to find ample wealth and stability."

389

"Stability?" Nickolas said. "So you think her incapable of choosing a husband who is stable. Dependable. Levelheaded."

Gideon gave him a look.

Jules stepped between the men. To Gideon, she said, "Lord Alexander, the paperwork is already drawn up, remember? Nickolas and I have both signed the marriage contract. It only needs sealed by your office."

He said, "I don't have time to go back for—"

Ian leaned in to hold a folded parchment he'd drawn from his vest in front of Gideon's face.

"I know you care about my well-being and only want what's best for me, Lord Alexander. But please, know that I go into this arrangement with a full understanding of what it means. Lord Brigham is my choice." She reached back to take Nickolas's hand. "Now, if you'd kindly proceed before the curse has ruined our last chance to save my brothers."

Repentant, Gideon inclined his head. He gestured for Nickolas and Jules to face forward and began an incredibly abridged version of the traditional recital, so swift that Nickolas had no time to panic that Jules might change her mind. Then Gideon asked, "Do each of you willingly enter into this agreement, aware that it is binding and may never be revoked?"

"I do," Jules said with such a lack of hesitation that Nickolas forgot for a moment to breathe. She glanced up at him.

"I do," he said to only her.

"Very well." Gideon pressed the seal onto the contract, and the deed was done.

Frederick coughed up a feather. The dark bit of fluff and barbs flew into the gathering, startling Jules into taking a step backward and causing Ian to fumble the convulsing bird. At the center of the clearing, near the prince and his guard, the swans began to make calls of distress.

One of Jules's hands came up to cover her mouth, the other pressed to her midsection. The moon seemed to glow brighter, not a cloud in sight, and though there was no breeze, Nickolas felt a chill prickle his skin. He slid an arm around Jules's waist, terrified that the magic might somehow take her.

Frederick's body jerked once more, and Ian lowered him to the ground. There was a great deal of unpleasant cracking and popping sounds, but Jules never looked away, didn't bury her face in Nickolas's shoulder, and only watched in horror as she leaned against Nickolas for support. Then a full-sized leg clad in trousers shot from the body of the small gray bird, and everyone jumped a full step backward.

A second leg followed, then two arms, and the chest of the bird seemed to heave into a full set of ribs and shoulders beneath a fine embroidered tunic. Nickolas did not see when the head appeared, but he was grateful when the writhing finally stopped. Frederick—no longer a bird but a weedy young man with a kind, clean-shaven face and eyes very like his sister's—lay sprawled on the greensward, staring up at the sky. A long-fingered hand spread over his chest, adorned with a signet ring. He coughed once more, seemed momentarily on the edge of succumbing to emotion, then rolled onto his stomach before rising to his feet.

Ian reached out to steady him. Frederick appeared to find his balance then patted Ian's hand. His gaze rose to Jules. There was a moment of stillness before both began to weep. The next moment, Jules was in Frederick's arms. Mireille made a cooing sound. Then the group turned toward a commotion near the center of the clearing.

Five men of similar stature and build slapped one another on the arms, grabbing hold of tunics and exclaiming unintelligibly before making their way toward Frederick and Jules. She and Frederick broke through the crowd, rushing to meet their long-lost brothers. They picked Jules up in enthusiastic hugs, spinning her, mussed Frederick's dark hair, and traded embraces between rapid bouts of conversation.

Etta moved to Nickolas's side as they watched. A long breath eased out of her. "I'm glad you have found her."

A small helpless laugh escaped with his reply. "I had nothing to do with it. She found me."

He took in the scene and realized something did not quite sit right with him. Tone lowered, Nickolas asked, "Why is the prince still here?"

Expression grim, Etta did not respond. She remained at one side, sword in hand, as Gideon moved to Nickolas's other side.

"Etta?" Nickolas asked.

The others in the clearing appeared to become aware of the sense of unease, one by one turning toward the prince and his men. The six brothers surrounded Jules, none of them armed. The lords with Mireille resumed their swords.

The prince waited until they all gave him notice, a slow smile tipping up the edge of his lips. "Yes," he finally said. "All is well, the curse broken, and the happy family reunited." It seemed for a moment as if he might turn to go, but he stopped, holding up a single finger. "There remains but one final resolution. A tiny matter, really, of barely any consequence at all."

Nickolas's heart, overfull only moments before, felt on the edge of breaking all over. It was a fragile thing; he was not certain it could take losing Jules, not after all that had happened. He held his breath, waiting for the words to make sense but could not fathom what had been left unanswered. Jules was free, her curse broken. The prince could not want her for a wife, not with the marriage contract signed and sealed.

The prince's gaze connected with Jules's.

"What matter is that?" Jules asked coldly.

His answering grin revealed too many teeth. "Only the matter of an unsettled debt."

Etta and Gideon edged closer to Nickolas as the prince's guard raised their swords.

The prince flicked a glance at Etta before saying, "You all seem to have forgotten that Lord Brigham belongs to me."

CHAPTER 21

Nickolas felt the pronouncement like a blow to his midsection. The prince had planned it all along, had watched as Jules had chosen Nickolas and waited for their contract to be sealed.

The curse was broken, but he owned Jules's husband. Jules and the others moved nearer, surrounding Nickolas in an arc to face the fae guards and the prince. The prince strolled closer.

"You defaulted on our bargain, my lady. Until you pay that price, Lord Brigham will remain in Rivenwilde with me."

Jules reached around her back and pulled a second thin blade from somewhere within her simple dress.

"No!" Gideon and Nickolas called. Gideon, perhaps, because Jules was now a citizen of Westrende and could not harm the Rivenwilde prince per an ancient dictate but Nickolas because he did not want her to be hurt.

The prince reached forward, and Nickolas was pulled across the greensward, half the distance to the prince. Nickolas fumbled for the ring then remembered he'd given it to Ian. Besides, the curse was broken. Whatever magic it held was likely gone. Which meant he and

Jules—and the entire crowd of onlookers—had no protection from fae magic.

Boots hovering just above the tall grass, Nickolas was powerless to do anything at all. "It's all right," he told Jules. "You're safe. You're free. That's what matters." It would be tolerable if he could be certain of at least that much. Whatever the prince did, Nickolas could withstand it, knowing the torment was paid to him instead of Jules.

Jules's lips parted, her eyes glinting in the strange play of moon and torchlight. "I cannot—" she started, but Etta stepped forward.

"Those are your terms, then?" Etta's grip flexed on her sword hilt, making no secret of her desire to drive the villain through. "A princess in exchange for Lord Brigham's release?"

The prince chuckled. "Yes. Only that. A princess for Rivenwilde and you may have your Lord Brigham back."

"Done," Etta said. She snapped a signal, and Gideon came forward.

The prince's brows drew together, seeming more annoyed than confused, and he said, "Jules is married and a mere lady. She does me no good. A titled princess is the price, nothing less."

"Yes," Etta said. "We heard. Gideon has the paperwork here. The princess is yours. Lord Brigham is ours. Release him."

"Lady Ostwind," the prince started, plainly irritated, but his words fell off as Mireille leaned around Etta to give the prince a friendly little wave.

"Mireille?" Jules said. "You can't throw her to the—"

Etta hushed Jules with both a reprimanding hiss and gesture.

Jules straightened as if prepared to argue further, but Mireille stepped past them both to face the prince. "It's me," she said. "Princess Mireille of Norcliffe. I'm certain you know of my family. Most people do." She smiled conspiratorially. "I come to you willingly. Though, if you're agreeable to a small delay, I wouldn't mind a few days to get my affairs in order before I go. The chancellor was kind enough to draw up a contract, guaranteeing my return so that Nickolas may be released without delay—" She glanced at Nickolas, who by now surely looked as pained as he felt, dangling by magic above the clearing. "I would consider it a great favor to me should you let him down. Not that you owe any favors to me, only that it would be so very unkind to keep him from Jules even a heartbeat longer after all she's been through. The poor thing."

The prince blinked.

Gideon crossed the distance to hand him a piece of fine parchment, presumably the aforementioned guarantee, and the prince glanced at it with what could only be aggrieved bewilderment.

"It's all legal," Etta said. "By both your law and ours."

"So, you assume I'll just—" The prince's words cut off when Noal cleared his throat. The prince did not even look at the man. "Yes. Very well." He shoved the contract back at Gideon. "I do not need your paper. I am the prince of the Riven Court."

He flicked a hand, and Nickolas's boots crashed to the earth. "Lord Brigham is free." His lip curled as Jules rushed to Nickolas's side, then his gaze rolled over the six brothers, the three lords, and Ian, Gideon, and Etta. "It would bring me great pleasure should I never see any of you again." Shoulders square, he adjusted his jacket, drew up his chin, and met Mireille's gaze.

He tipped forward in a small bow. When he rose again, he said, "Shall you neglect to call for me, know that I intend to come to collect."

Mireille smiled in that way that shifted her right eye, not so unlike a wink. The prince regarded her for a moment then turned and walked toward the wall. Noal did not acknowledge the crowd before following, then every fae guard disappeared through the ancient wall behind them.

"Well," Mireille said. "It looks like I'll have that adventure after all."

Nickolas and Jules stared at her.

"Come," Etta told them. "We can discuss this all once we're safely outside the forest."

The chittering creatures that had restlessly observed the goings-on paced more eagerly in the spaces between the trees. Gideon handled Nickolas the sword that had been knocked from him when the prince's magic had taken hold then glanced at the six brothers, likely wishing they had weapons of their own.

Jules's hand slid into Nickolas's, palm against palm, and the entire group marched forward through the woods.

It was the small hours before dawn when the group had finally resumed the safety of the castle. Princess Mireille and her men had returned to their suites, Ian was being tended for a minor cut he'd received in their scuffle with the fae guard, and Nickolas and Jules sat nestled between Jules's brothers as Etta and Gideon distributed hot tea and what honey cakes and bread they could find. Jules had not let go of Nickolas's hand.

The moment Etta finally settled—not onto a chair but leaned against a desk across from Nickolas and Jules—she asked, "What can you tell us of Rivenwilde?"

The cake seemed to catch in Nickolas's throat.

Etta crossed her arms. "As I suspected, you are bound from revealing a single of the prince's secrets under the laws of hospitality."

The statement came in such a way that Nickolas guessed it was not the first time the prince had foiled her attempts at information gathering, but the expression on Etta's face made clear it was not the time to question her about it.

"What about Mireille?" Jules asked. "You cannot be planning to actually let her go."

Etta tapped a finger against the sleeve of her marshal's coat. Jules had intended to do just such a thing but evidently could not countenance it for someone else. Etta said, "Mireille offered herself in exchange for Nickolas because she needs protection from a threat much greater than the prince." When Jules started to speak again, Etta held up a hand. "I am not to say more on the matter. But trust that it was done willingly and with utmost consideration."

Jules's mouth snapped shut.

One of the brothers slid a hand over hers. "The fae queen causes a great deal of strife, sister. You have been gone for so long and I fear do not understand the full reach of her influence." His expression was apologetic. "Despite all our efforts, she has managed to corrupt our father past the point of return."

"Is he well?"

Another of the brothers answered, "Not entirely. And worse, he's in grave danger from the queen, and that danger puts the kingdom at risk."

The tea turned in Nickolas's stomach. Jules had said that if she agreed to wed the prince, she would be putting entire kingdoms in danger. And there was her brother, free of his curse, echoing the sentiment once more. Nickolas had no notion of what a fae queen might be capable of, but their tones made clear it was worse than the threat of the Rivenwilde prince.

"The queen is going to marry him," Jules breathed.

The first brother inclined his head. "A date has been set. And once he does... Well, I'm certain we all know her plans for Father."

Jules's hand tightened in Nickolas's as her brother drew away. She asked, "How do we stop it?"

The second brother leaned forward. "We must remove him from the throne before the ceremony is complete."

"I support your decision," she said. "Even though, as I've renounced both title and kingdom, you no longer need my consent."

The brothers glanced at one another.

"What is it?" Jules asked warily.

The one who appeared oldest drew back his shoulders, giving Jules his full attention. It was quite impressive, Nickolas noticed, but Jules did not seem in the least cowed.

The man said, "We have decided to step down. It is not we who deserve this honor. You have broken our curse, defied the fae queen, and sacrificed all in order to preserve the kingdom."

"That's—I can't. I'm no longer even—"

The lot of them stood, moved to face Jules, then knelt on the floor before her as one, heads bowed.

A hush fell over the room before the eldest lifted his gaze to hers. "Julietta Leanna Eleanora Declare, I hereby bestow upon you the right of heir, as my sister, daughter of the king, and honorable servant to the kingdom. Long may you reign."

"Hear, hear," echoed the brothers. "Long may you reign."

"I—" Jules's words seemed to choke off, her hand gone slack in Nickolas's.

For Nickolas's part, he was certain he'd gone at least as pale as Gideon and Etta had. He could not help but ask them, "Why are you looking at me like that?"

Etta opened her mouth, but no words came. Gideon ran a shaky hand across his brow.

"There is no choice," one of the brothers said. "If we do not remove the king now, he will certainly be killed as soon as they're wed."

"And the fae queen will sit upon the throne," said another.

"But—" Jules began.

The oldest stood, reaching forward to place a gentle hand on her shoulder. "We have been touched by the queen's magic, sister. You have not. You are the best hope for this kingdom. Your heart is honest, just, and true, and we have faith in you above all others. Trust that we have not made this decision lightly."

Jules swallowed. "Then I will do my best. You have my word."

The others stood, their mood resolved and decidedly more hopeful.

Nickolas felt as if he'd just stepped off a swaying ship. "I—so this means you'll be queen."

Jules's gaze snapped to his, her brows drawn together. "It does."

He drew a shallow breath, unable to tolerate more, and gave a small nod. "When do you leave?"

"Nickolas, you mustn't—are you saying you won't come with me?"

Nickolas did not know what he was saying, only that it hurt very much to speak, and he felt a bit light-headed. He rubbed a palm over his chest. It must have been the cakes. Honey cakes had never agreed with him.

"You will come, won't you?" Jules asked.

"I—do you want me to come?"

"Of course." She let out a shaky breath. "It is not as if I could do this without you."

"Of course," he repeated. He'd no deuced idea what she meant by not being able to do it without him, but he wasn't about to disagree with her. Wherever it was, whatever she needed, he would be there.

Gideon released a low oath then whispered, "Do we tell him?" before Etta replied just as quietly, "Best let him work it out on his own."

"It's been a very long day," Jules told the room. "Perhaps we should discuss the rest tomorrow." She gave a gentle squeeze to Nickolas's hand. "Lord Brigham, won't you walk with me in the courtyard?"

"Of course," he said again. They stood, then he turned once more to Etta. "What's to happen to my mother?"

Etta rose from her position on the desk. "She will remain a prisoner until the council makes their judgment. If you would like, you may offer a statement in her defense before the trial."

Nickolas nodded. He understood well enough what the council's judgment would be. Lady Brigham would receive no leniency when it was revealed that she'd both committed a crime and made a bargain with the fae, no matter what Nickolas had to say on the matter. "Then, I will have guardianship of my sisters, it seems."

Jules slid her hand through his arm. "They'll be no bother at all. We can find a lovely place for them. Did I tell you, Lord Brigham, of the courtyard gardens I played in as a girl? The most beautiful roses and violets grow there, right around a fishpond stocked with trout. Do you fish? I'm afraid I've never asked you."

He stared down at her as she spoke, aware that he was being drawn from the chancery office and through the unlit corridor, but Nickolas could not make himself care. Not when Jules's arm was locked with his, the pair of them finally safe from harm.

They walked through several corridors before Jules drew him into a lesser-used passage that came out nowhere near where he might have expected. His steps slowed, and she slowed with him.

He said, "This is Carvell's wing."

"As a matter of fact, the Carvells have gone away for a bit." She tugged him back to her. "The marshal's office discovered the family had ties to a crime. Something about forgery and extortion."

"Extortion," Nickolas repeated.

Jules hummed in affirmation. "I believe Lord Keller has already inquired about purchasing the grounds. He plans to install several water features in the courtyard."

A choked laugh came from Nickolas just as they neared the arched doorway outside said courtyard.

Jules reached for the lever, meeting his gaze. "I thought it might be nice to visit once more. This time, without interruptions."

His heart woke again, swelling to the walls of his chest, and when he took a lungful of the cool predawn air, Nickolas felt more like himself. But that was not right, because it was a version of himself that was free from the burdens of debts, secrets, and the sense that time was running out. Nickolas was alone with Jules in a lovely garden, and he did not have a single other place he wanted to be.

She kept hold of his hand, drawing him with her over the stone pathway, through violets and poppies and the statuary he had forgotten was nearly all nude. At a bare spot of grass, she stopped and asked for his jacket. He removed it and spread it over the ground, and the pair of them settled, backs to the low edge wall, to stare up at the stars.

Jules nestled closer, her body warm beneath his arm, and he turned his face toward her as she watched the night sky. "My lady," he said quietly. "Now that you are my wife..."

Her head tilted nearer as if to better hear, though the courtyard was silent.

Nickolas let his voice dip even lower. "Does that mean I can kiss you?"

The curve of her cheek shifted with her smile as she answered, "I'm afraid it means you must. As often as possible. And you should call me Jules."

He leaned in, his lips only a breath from her bare neck when he said, "Jules." She shivered, but when his mouth touched her skin, Jules melted against him. His lips trailed slowly up to her jaw, brushing the sensitive flesh beneath her ear before Nickolas pulled back just enough to let her turn to him. The light in her eyes was playful and content as she came forward to meet him in a kiss. It was soft and sweet, unrushed because there was nothing but this for as long as forever.

"Or at least until tomorrow," Jules murmured.

Nickolas could barely murmur the "What?" that slipped between the brush of their lips, lost again to the unbearable contentment of the moment.

"Nothing," she said. "Never mind."

"Saints," he breathed. "We should have been doing this the entire time we were engaged."

"No idea what you were waiting for," she said as her fist balled into the material of his shirt to drag him back. "Must make up for lost time. Only thing for it."

He slid a thumb against her cheek, fingers at the base of her neck tipping her head toward his. "Noted."

THE ORANGE PINK of sunrise lit the sky when Nickolas's awareness surfaced again. He wasn't certain if he'd dozed off, only that his limbs felt liquid and his eyes heavy. If Jules had meant to watch the sunrise, she'd missed it. Laid against him, her legs sprawled beneath the long skirt, boots canted in opposite directions. She looked impossibly peaceful. One arm was wrapped firmly around him, the other tucked beneath her, hand tangled in the material of his jacket. Her hair had fallen from its pins, long locks of it soft against his skin.

He had the thought that he should wake her but could not quite bring himself to disturb such needed rest. It was followed by the thought that he could carry her, take her back to her rooms where she could stretch comfortably in her own bed.

Then, with a jolt, Nickolas recalled that she was his wife. Her rooms would in fact, be not in the chancery, but his own suite. That was when Nickolas, Lord Brigham, remembered that Jules was a queen. That a queen's husband was...

"Saints," he wheezed. "That's not—"

Jules shifted, snuggling closer to wrap both arms around his waist. Nickolas's words dried up. He could not bear to wake her, only smoothed his hand over her shoulder as he forced himself to relax once more against the wall. He would have to come to terms with what had happened but that was a worry for outside their courtyard garden. There, he was with Jules, and the world was silent, and with her in his arms, he eventually drifted off to sleep.

EPILOGUE

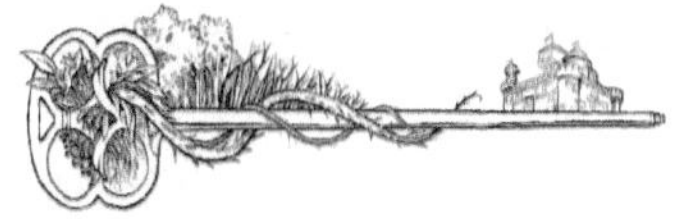

Weeks later, Nickolas stood atop the small knoll overlooking the impossibly grand garden on the palace lawn of the warm and sunny kingdom in which his wife had been named queen. He tried not to think on it too much, because it still hurt his head. Jules's brothers granting the throne to their younger sister had not only illustrated to the kingdom their full support but that she was without fault in her father's dealings with the fae.

The fae queen had been ousted once those bound to her by bargain or loyalty had been removed and any claim on their father or the throne was resolved. No one was certain where she had gone, only that she had given up her ploy far more easily than anticipated. Jules's father had suffered greatly at the hands of the fae queen but seemed more restful once she was gone and his heirs returned.

For her part, Jules had shined. She possessed a calm authority and wielded her easy ability to disregard or focus on the chattering of others like a weapon. Maneuvering courtiers did not stand a chance.

She glanced up at Nickolas from where she stood at his side in a simple gown of the richest fabrics, a thin gold crown woven into her upswept hair. "Will you always look at me in such a manner, or do you suppose it will wear off in time?"

He grinned. "I cannot seem to help it. You are too lovely to look away from, you make me unbearably happy, and, I'm afraid, indecently proud to call you my wife."

On Jules's other side, Frederick rolled his eyes. "One can only hope it wears off soon. I can't fathom what a man would do with more pride than you."

"Someday," Nickolas murmured as his gaze trailed over Jules's skin, "you will find something that satisfies you half as much as this life does me. And that day, you will have to eat your crotchety words."

Frederick scoffed.

The smile in Jules's gaze was only for Nickolas. Then she returned to watching the lawn, where the other five of her brothers idled among the flowers with Nickolas's sisters, Ian, and several members of court. "It seems we've a great many such pairings to look forward to. I can only hope that whomever each of our loved ones find are as well matched."

Nickolas managed to tear his gaze away to take in his sisters, their bare golden locks standing out among a sea of dark top hats and ribboned bonnets. The eldest was speaking closely to one of Jules's brothers. He could not object to her finding a prince, but he did not think he could wish any of his sisters on souls so kind as the Declares. Well, maybe Frederick. But that was where he drew the line.

His youngest sister knelt before a tame rabbit, and Nickolas edged closer to Jules. "Did you say you were once given a menagerie?" His gaze connected with hers once more. "What precisely did you let out of that cage as a girl?"

Jules's lip twitched. "Lions. Among other things."

Nickolas barked a startled laugh, earning a glance from the courtiers who'd engaged Frederick in conversation. "Truly, the heart of a warrior. I am delighted to call you my queen."

She turned to face him, shutting out the entire courtyard with just that bit of attention. "You mustn't," she reminded him. "I am their queen. To you, I am only—"

He leaned in, voice low as he took her hand in his. "It is not as if I could ever forget, love." He lifted their hands to brush a soft kiss over Jules's knuckles. "Your name is etched on the walls of my heart."

409

UPON THE RIVEN THRONE

CHAPTER 1

Once upon a time, in a not terribly far-off kingdom, there lived a king and his daughter who had been so fortunate in all their undertakings that the kingdom was enormously rich. The king and his daughter had everything they fancied and did not find their lives bore much burden at all. But the king stood against an unjust foe—an evil fae queen intent on stealing the kingdom—and soon misfortune befell him, one ill lot after another. And all the splendid furniture, books, and precious goods could not save the kingdom from danger. The king had suddenly lost everything by dint of accident, illness, and disaster. His courtiers betrayed him. His wheat stores turned foul.

The princess tried to stand brave and cheerful in the face of such wretchedness. But both she and the king knew it was not simply a run of bad luck. The evil queen was gathering power. With every kingdom she conquered, their defenses dashed like ships in a storm-tossed sea, her magic grew. Norcliffe was meant to be her next accession, and it was clear Princess Mireille specifically had become her prey. Norcliffe could not be protected by might alone and the king loved his daughter dearly, but the evil queen had to be stopped. Soon she would grow too powerful to be beaten.

When a fae queen was trying to have one murdered, it was usually quick work. So nothing was left for the princess but to take her departure with haste, to escape to a place outside the neighboring kingdom of Westrende where the secrets of fae magic were rooted deep. As the servants could no longer be trusted, she'd brought only her childhood friend Thomas, known to the kingdom as Lord Holden, skilled historian and seasoned bachelor.

One might think that a woman of such desperate fortune must be in want of a well-positioned ally, or at least of refuge. One would be right. But sometimes all that was available was an adversary in the form of a husband. Which was why Princess Mireille of Norcliffe stood in the midst of a dark forest that seemed to be the most dismal place on the face of the earth.

"Are you certain you'd not rather flee to the sea?" Thomas asked from beside her.

Mireille's chuckle was grim. "Would that we could, Thomas. Would that we could."

Before them rose a facade of the wall that marked the Rive—the ancient boundary separating the human kingdom of Westrende from the land of the fae. Beneath its carved stone glamour rested a skeleton of fine filigree metal, iron to be precise, binding the magic of the wilds and meant to keep conflict at bay. The marshal of Westrende stood at the edge of the trees with a company of kingsmen, all watching from a distance to ensure Mireille's safety—at least until she'd made it across.

Law prevented Westrende officials from going any farther, and though the council governing the kingdom was firmly against anything fae, they could not stop Mireille. She was first and foremost a princess of Norcliffe, after all. They had no say in the deal she was about to strike, despite that the fae prince wanted nothing more than to destroy the wall and Westrende's safety, and held kingdom officials ransom in his fight to do so.

The fae had been trapped within the boundary for so long that citizens of Westrende had begun to believe their existence nothing more than tales, that the warnings to never speak their name were only superstition. But the kingdom officials did not want to stop Mireille, not entirely, because the threat of the fae queen was much more dangerous than any human kingdom could face alone.

Which meant an empire of fae kingdoms was the only thing they could fathom that might be worse than the fae lands the princess was about to step into.

Mireille glanced at Thomas. "What about you? Last chance to sprint for freedom. I would not begrudge you any attempt at escape."

His smile was wry. "You'll not be rid of me so easily, Highness. You know how I adore adventure."

Thomas did not adore adventure. But he was loyal, and Mireille knew he wasn't about to let her walk into this mess alone. She turned to face him, brushing a hand over the skirt of her traveling gown. "Very well, no sense in putting it off any longer. How do I look?"

"As if you've trekked through a sinister forest. What about me?"

"As if you could slay a flock of maidens with just a wink."

"That bad?" He frowned. "A lord does generally wish to win hearts without bothering to make eye contact first."

She lifted a shoulder. "They're maidens of very high willpower. I don't make the rules."

Thomas watched her patiently. In truth, the man had always won hearts with less than a glance. He was handsome, fair-haired, square-jawed, and finely dressed, with the sort of smile that felt at once intimate and playful. To Mireille, he had been both courtier and confidant. He was her truest friend, and he knew her well enough to guess that she was delaying.

He tapped the hilt of his sword. "Would you like me to say it for you? I've never called on a fae prince before. It would be a novelty to summon one. You know how I adore novelty."

Thomas did not adore novelty. Mireille flexed her hands and shook out her fingers, then moved to stand beside him. She was about to seal her bargain with a fae—creatures so powerful, so dangerous, that the ancients had long ago built a wall to keep their kind in. She'd be a fool for what she was doing, if not for the *not doing it* being a greater danger still.

She drew her shoulders back and spoke the true name of the fae prince of Rivenwilde. The magic that constrained the prince would force his appearance, but he was not its instrument. He would twist the situation to his advantage. Mireille had no intention of letting him use her for anything besides overcoming the fae queen.

He was there in an instant, stealing into view as if shifting from shadow, donned in black from head to toe, expression cold and magic prickling awareness over Mireille's skin. The tines of his crown rose majestic and feral, his dress impeccable right down to the embroidered waistcoat and finely tied cravat. Too late for Mireille to swallow the words back and flee, she stood firm beneath his scrutiny.

The prince could not possibly be unaware of the kingsmen watching, given the way his jaw ticked, but he pointedly did not look toward their spot near the trees. He had known Mireille was coming, and that was all that truly mattered. He straightened to an impressive height, then dipped into a generous bow. "Your Highness."

"Mireille," she said automatically.

His dark eyes lifted, staying on hers as he rose. His voice was rich and steady, and, most unsettlingly, the forest around them seemed to hold its breath. "Mireille."

She waited for him to return the courtesy, allowing her expectation of it to stand plainly between them.

The edge of his mouth seemed tempted to frown, but evidently he was not above caving to societal pressure. "You may call me Alder."

It was a small win but she would take it. "May I introduce Lord Holden?"

The prince inclined his head, and Thomas said, "Thomas, please."

Thomas only received a brusque nod, no invitation to familiarity.

Prince Alder returned his attention to Mireille. It felt like a great deal of attention, given that he was only one man, but she remained steady. Their agreement had already been settled—Mireille would never have made the trek to the greenwood otherwise—but he evidently thought she needed a reminder of the terms before the bargain was officially sealed, because he said, "Once you cross the boundary, you will be tied by bargain. You will not be released. You will not be allowed to return home."

"I understand."

He was incredibly tall, his dark hair confined by the crown of tangled bone-like spikes. There was a lean elegance about him and despite the crispness of his manner, he did not seem entirely discourteous. He held himself like that of a person of immense power. But there were many kinds of power, and his was the sort that could fell the surrounding trees with the flick of a wrist. An entire kingdom of fae were beneath his rule. Mireille understood that and more.

He said, "If you come at all, you must come willingly."

"I do come willingly." A strange sensation of magic seemed to shift in the soil beneath her feet. She did not look away from the prince, though, in truth, Mireille's willingness was dependent on circumstance. She would not be so inclined without sufficient duress in the form of one very unpleasant fae queen. But the threats to her life and kingdom were more than sufficient, so the words had not been a lie. Even if she had not told the prince of her reasoning.

The prince's attention never wavered. "You will be given one month at my palace under the laws of hospitality. By the next moon, if you mean to stay under my protection, it will be as my bride."

"And if I do not? What then?" What if she did not say the vows that would bind them by law. What if she did not uphold her word.

Bearing unchanged, he said, "Those who have offered themselves under bargain may not be released."

Thomas leaned forward to put in, "Unless they pay the price to break that bargain before time is up."

His statement was roundly ignored. Near the trees, one of the Westrende kingsmen coughed.

For Mireille's part, she had not even asked the price to break their bargain. The due for bargain-breaking was always more than a person could satisfy, and never a matter of petty wealth but one of unthinkable sacrifice. Whatever it was, she would not be able to pay it. The fae did not allow humans into their realm only to let them return to their homeland freely. She asked, "What happens if we are not wed at the turn of the moon? I will no longer be protected by the laws of hospitality. I will not be treated as a guest. But should I go through with the marriage or not..."

The prince's manner seemed to darken. A chill breeze swept the clearing. He said, "Either way, you will belong to me."

His queen or as his captive, that was her choice. Mireille wet her lips. She'd heard many tales regarding how prisoners of the fae were kept. She would be deciding between that uncertain fate or becoming a member of the Riven Court. It may have seemed like an obvious course, but the fae court held dangers of its own. Dangers that might make a person beg for the discomforts of a small, dark cell. And should she marry the prince of Rivenwilde, she could no longer be heir to Norcliffe, not when the entire reason she left was to keep it safe from the fae.

Neither situation would be as unpleasant as the fate that awaited her outside of his protection, though. If she did not find a way to defeat the queen, Norcliffe and everyone Mireille loved would be destroyed. The month she'd been gifted as his guest needed to be enough. Whether she was confined by walls or by vows, Mireille had to get close enough to the prince to discover the secrets of fae magic, but not close enough to risk him discovering her own.

She gave a quick, decisive nod. "I accept your terms. Let us away."

The prince's gaze held a hint of wariness as it flicked toward Thomas, then returned to lock on Mireille's. "Very well." Mireille thought it telling that he would have suspicion of the agreement at all, but he said, "It is agreed." The power beneath her feet swelled, and the prince, the clearing, and Mireille's future all seemed to shift by unknowable degrees.

It was done. Her fate was sealed. Mireille moved to take the prince's arm, and there was a moment of awareness between them that he had not yet offered. More hesitation, it seemed, despite that their bargain was settled. It was a solid reminder that the arrangement was bigger than just the two of them. Mireille gave a farewell glance toward the Westrende marshal, who returned a firm nod. It was unclear whether Westrende had any faith she might succeed.

Head inclined slightly, the prince finally lifted his arm, Mireille slid her hand through, and they walked together toward the wall.

"Thomas," she reminded the prince.

He blinked at her, then, evidently understanding, cleared his throat. "One does not have to be touching a fae to pass through once the gateway is open."

"Oh." She did not let go. "Well, at least, do not forget him."

Behind them, Thomas muffled a chuckle. He was carrying a single small bag, the entirety of both their possessions since their departure from Norcliffe had been executed with as much stealth as possible, and he was the only bit of security and sense of home that Mireille had left. It was calming to hear the hint of levity from him and to know that her friend was at her back.

The prince's jaw flexed but not, it seemed, with shared humor. He did not seem to be having a great deal of fun stealing away a human princess under the watchful gaze of his sworn Westrende enemies, truth be told. But before another breath, they were walking through the wall, its filigree wires uncurling to surround and gather the prince, its magic parting in a manner that Mireille was not quite able to make sense of, even as she was drawn inside the boundary with him. She could see through the wall's glamour to the cage beneath and feel the magic around her, in a way that felt as if it could not be denied, no matter how much power one might possess. It was an insistent pressure not only against her skin but every part of her being, as if gravity, like diving from the cliffs of her home into the icy waters of the sea. Not that a princess would do such a thing. But if she had—very similar.

They came through the other side and the prince pointedly did not glance at her, heaving in breath and clinging to his arm as she was, or at Thomas, who Mireille was grateful to find had made it through and was again at her side. Thomas was a little green and looked as if he might be regretting not taking that last chance to flee but when he met her gaze, he gave a halfhearted nod.

They had made it.

Through the wall, only. The easiest step. Mireille wasn't even certain it counted as a step in her plans. She should have made a list so that she might check off *getting to the forest* and *finding the wall*, lest that was all they would manage. It was always good to feel accomplished.

"Shall we pause for a moment?"

The prince's words brought a huff of helpless laughter from Mireille's chest. "No," she said finally. "That was quite an experience, but I believe Thomas and I have our land legs once more. Do carry on."

His brow pinched. "I thought it best to walk through our domain but that was inconsiderate after the journey you've already made. I shall bring us closer at once."

Mireille opened her mouth to protest but before a word was out, the three of them were transported to a different path entirely. The objection died in her throat. They stood suddenly between an avenue of trees, leaves overhead shifting in the warm afternoon breeze and laying patchy shade over the path. The avenue ended at a splendid palace, but she could not take her eyes off the canopy, made up of orange trees and covered with flowers and fruit.

The prince seemed to notice her gaping, so she explained, "I've only ever seen them in illustrations."

He paused, his gaze flicking between her eyes with something that was not quite so distant before he released her from his arm. He crossed to a low branch at the edge of the path then reached up, and his long, graceful fingers pinched off one of the delicate blossoms. When he returned to offer it to Mireille, their bare skin brushed, and she felt a flutter of his magic once more.

She turned the blossom in her fingers before lifting it to her nose. It smelled sweet and bright over a hint of something bitter, with a trace of other, more familiar fragrances. She quite liked it.

The prince was watching her from where he stood, rather close, Thomas unmistakably looking away from them both.

Mireille tucked the blossom into the collar of her jacket then glanced up at the prince. "Thank you."

His eyes held a strange hint of warmth in the dappled light as they rose from the blossom to trail over her face, the stillness in his form giving Mireille the impression that he was uncertain how to respond. She took hold of his arm once more so that he didn't have to.

The three approached the palace under the distrustful gazes of onlookers who appeared to consist of palace staff and members of court, all of them fae. Mireille held her chin high, eyes forward, and wished she'd chosen a slightly richer gown. She had been unsure what to expect but the opulence of the fae court was impressive, even to one who'd seen a fair share of fine and fancy places.

The lawn was lovely, lush with greenery and blooming flowers, alive with birdsong, and formed in such a way as to create a natural path toward the agate steps leading to the imposing palace. In the distance, trees rose impossibly high, their boughs no doubt obscuring the many dwellings of Rivenwilde's fae. Mireille could not be certain of what lay beyond, though, because illustrations of the kingdom had not been available to anyone outside the wall, and what few sketches Thomas had been able to find were clearly only those of fancy. Fae were secretive, and Rivenwilde fae most of all.

As they reached the top of the steps, the prince's chest rose in a deep breath, and the sensation of magic seemed to rise with it, like the swell of the sea. His gaze stayed forward as they strode through the door, his arm steady beneath hers.

A massive archway opened into the entrance hall, where they were met by a smartly dressed fae man who appeared to be near the prince's age. His skin was the same dark olive as Mireille's, but where her hair was long and light chestnut, his was in short, neat waves of dark mahogany.

"Mireille," the prince said, as if it pained him to speak her name so casually, "may I introduce Noal?"

The man fell into a deep bow.

"Noal will be at your service for any need. You will have all the food and care you want for, at any hour."

"Because of the laws of hospitality," Mireille said.

The prince's jaw flexed. Again, not with humor. "Not because you are a guest of the prince of Rivenwilde. Because you are his betrothed."

She met his gaze. Mireille might not be able to find maps of Rivenwilde, but she knew the laws of hospitality would protect his guests, and until she was thrown into a fae prison for breaking their agreement or thrown into the fae court once she'd followed through, she possessed a title that was equal to his own. A princess would require the highest of care or he would be breaking one of the oldest fae tenets.

He said, "You are under my protection."

"And what of Thomas?" Mireille asked.

"My protection extends to Lord Holden as well." The prince's voice was level. "While you are both within these walls."

"So if we were to leave..."

"Do not leave these walls."

The words felt sharper than Mireille might have expected, and she glanced at Noal to determine if the man seemed to think the reaction out of the ordinary. Noal, however, was staring wide-eyed at the orange blossom tucked into the collar of Mireille's jacket. His gaze slid accusingly toward the prince.

An unspoken message passed between Noal and his sovereign.

"What's this?" Thomas said, edging closer as he gestured between the two. "What's happening there?"

"I do not know what you mean," Noal said, just as the prince said, "Nothing."

The prince did not flick an annoyed glance at his man, but it was clear he wished to. He said, "I must take my leave now."

Mireille asked, "Why?"

The prince froze mid-bow. "I must attend to..."

She suspected he might have been about to answer something like *important prince concerns* when his words dried up.

Instead, he said, "I should allow you to get settled in. You have had a long journey."

She glanced down at her gown, the hem damp and stuck with briars. "Yes, I suppose that's so. I shall dress for our first dinner together, and resume your company then."

When she glanced back up, he was already halfway to the door. He stopped at her words. A moment later, he turned back to face her. "Dinner?"

"We must have dinner together."

"I am... Quite a bit occupies my time."

"Very busy," Noal added helpfully. "Barely an hour free for meals."

The prince shot him a look that promised violence.

"You must have dinner with me," Mireille said. "Every night."

He stared at her, aghast.

"I've only a month to come to know you, to understand what becoming a part of your world will mean." A mere month to uncover his secrets, to safeguard Norcliffe by whatever means necessary to prevent the villainous... villainess from folding it into her malevolent empire. "If you prefer, I could accompany you with whatever you're about. It would be no trouble at all, as I'm to be idle here every moment of every day, unable to leave the palace and unable to plan visits from my friends. A guest must be entertained, after all."

His eyes narrowed infinitesimally. Mireille gave him her most winsome smile. "Alder," she started, and something seemed to roll through him at the word.

He held up a hand, as if to forestall her speaking it again. "Dinner. When it is feasible."

"Every night."

Thomas and Noal stood rapt, no attempt at hiding the looks they were darting between their prince and princess.

The prince's mouth shifted, leaving no doubt he understood her challenge. "As you wish, Mireille. We will dine together, every night. Until the turn of the moon."

CHAPTER 2

Mireille and Thomas were led to their rooms, Mireille's lovely and spacious with his smaller suite adjoining hers. Had she any doubt about the faithfulness of the prince to the laws of hospitality, they would have been thoroughly quashed. Even their wardrobes and chests had been filled with the finest garments, fine gowns for her and a variety of jackets for Thomas. She had a full sitting room, a sewing room, a bathing chamber, and a bed so wide she'd be hard pressed to find the edge of it when she woke in the dark.

There was one other door, which Noal discreetly explained could only be opened by magic, and never would, for it belonged to the prince. Essentials covered, Noal said, "I trust all is to your satisfaction. Should you find yourself wanting, you are only to call."

"I am most appreciative. Thomas and I will try not to be much of a bother," Mireille said.

Noal inclined his head. "After you've rested, I would be pleased to take you on a tour of the palace."

"No." She pressed her lips. "Of course it is generous of you to offer, but I would prefer to be shown by the prince."

"The prince is—"

"Very busy, I know." Her finger slid over the gilt edge of a fine porcelain bowl. "Perhaps while the prince and I are occupied at dinner you could show Thomas the grounds. He will certainly want to find the lay of the land."

Perhaps the pair of them could be kept busy while Mireille tried to make headway with the prince. Perhaps Thomas could gain information from the staff that Mireille could not from their sovereign. Thomas was, after all, an expert in securing delicate—and concealed—information. Despite that he betrayed not a tap of the finger, he was surely itching to discover as much as possible as soon as possible about the palace they'd found their way into.

"As you wish," said Noal. "I will leave you to prepare for dinner."

The moment the man was gone, Thomas and Mireille scoured the room, searching for any traps or trickery, checking beneath the bedclothes, testing the door locks, and peering beneath the rugs.

"I don't see anything," Mireille said, cheek pressed to the plaster as she gave a one-eyed survey of the wall behind a painting. "What if he doesn't want to trick us at all? What if the prince truly is committed to their rules about guests?"

"Alder," Thomas reminded her. "You need to get used to calling him by his name. You know the fae cannot tolerate that sort of thing. Did you see him all but twitch when you said it in the hall?"

It was true. But it was not the magic she had used in the forest. Summoning a prince by name only worked outside of his palace. While she was a guest in his home, she could not expect more than what hospitality required. He would not simply materialize with a word. He was not at her beck and call. "I think he hates it when I say his name."

Thomas chuckled darkly where he was bent over examining the underside of a settee. "I think he does not know what to make of you. And what was with that look that passed between the pair of them regarding the orange blossom?"

Mireille shrugged. "Perhaps it was considered a gift? I know much less about fae traditions than I would like. We will have to find the library soon."

"Before we unintentionally break any laws, you mean."

"Unintentional or not, I prefer to be prepared. See if Noal will show you the dungeon."

He glanced up at her from where he inspected the bowl of fruit resting on the small table near the settee. "You think there's a dungeon beneath the palace?"

"Or cells, at least. It would keep the prince from having to set protections against his secrets. Should the prisoners be released, the laws of hospitality would prevent them from speaking of what they witnessed while under his roof."

Thomas held her gaze. "Prisoners of the fae are not released."

"On occasion. In exchange for someone else, sometimes." Her lips drew down. "It happens."

He shifted his weight to one leg, the lordly equivalent of a disapproving finger-wag. "And a dungeon is not exactly hospitable."

"There's food and a bed. It counts. We both know we're only in a suite because of my station. We are fortunate he's not decided to twist the terms in order to stick us somewhere less pleasant, traps or no." She shook out her hands. "Regardless. We're here now and there doesn't seem to be any immediate risk. Best prepare for dinner. Who knows what time the fae eat meals?"

"Right. You get a bath and I'll lay out your dress."

"You? Pick my wardrobe?"

His nose scrunched. "Are you truly questioning whether I'm the right person for the task? That I would not know the best gown to display a woman's figure?"

"Not my figure."

He rolled his eyes. "I'm your friend, not your brother."

"Thomas!"

"What? I've noticed. As has every other lord who's attended a ball with you, even if their attention is only surreptitious. Trust that I know which gowns brought out the most lecherous leers."

"You think the prince a lecher?"

"Not at all. But I think him a man. I think he has eyes. We will use every tool we might to your advantage."

She crossed her arms. "This may be the single most offensive conversation we've had, Thomas. I think you should know that."

"Highness, if this conversation offends you, you're in no way prepared for fae court." He glanced back at her after he opened the wardrobe door. "Or the cut of their gowns."

THOMAS HAD BEEN RIGHT, Mireille was not prepared for the cut of the provided gown. Deep, shimmering blue with a low-cut square bodice and a thin, slim fitting skirt, the gown left little to the imagination. Worse, Thomas had draped her in jewels, making certain that the candlelight would catch on the bare skin above the gown. She'd been given no gloves, no shawl, and no sense of how, exactly, their dinner was meant to go.

When Noal arrived to her suite, he only gave a vague gesture of approval before conducting her from the room.

A few fae moved silently past them, with no more than the whisper of cloth trailing behind. Noal took Mireille through many long corridors, each so unlike the ones she'd grown up surrounded by in her castle home. Instead of tapestry and portraiture over block, the palace walls were as smooth as polished marble, featuring carved scenes that seemed as alive as the vines that grew at every corner and column. It was nonsensical, as if a courtyard garden had been brought indoors. Mireille adored it.

A dozen questions populated in her mind, impatient for the moment it would be socially acceptable for her to pester Noal for information. His pace slowed as he led her past a music room, then he paused before a pair of finely carved doors, not quite near enough to imply he meant to open them.

Through the narrow gap between wood and stone, the prince's voice carried. It was muffled, but his tone was plainly angry, his words clipped. "...I will not be told how to manage my own affairs."

A feminine voice replied, the sound smooth with fury, though Mireille could not quite make out the words. Clear enough was that it was an argument.

Mireille was no fool. Eavesdropping on royalty was a trespass she was not about to commit in front of a witness. She moved to tug her arm free of Noal's but he stepped forward, as if he'd only paused to release her and open the doors all along. She wasn't fooled by that, either.

At the sound of Noal's entry, the heated confrontation inside the room broke off. Noal released the lever, drawing himself straight as his gloved hands crossed at the wrists. "Her Highness, Princess Mireille," he said.

Mireille stepped forward and the room's two occupants snapped their focus to her. The prince stood near a tall woman with warm skin and bright, tipped-up eyes. She wore a fine silk gown with sleeves to the knuckle and an embroidered train, but there appeared to be several broken twigs stuck through the fabric of the hem. The woman stared at Mireille in an introspective sort of way, while the prince's eyes were narrowed menacingly. It was not entirely surprising that the prince's gaze revealed displeasure, given that he'd done so from the start, but the way it aimed at first her, then Noal in a more accusatory way, did not bode well for the night's event.

Alder crossed the room, his suit no less black than the one in which she'd first encountered him, but certainly more formal. Noal remained steady, shoulders back and hands crossed precisely in the manner of a member of staff, not a hint of the man who'd been impertinent within Mireille's earshot a half dozen times so far.

The prince ended his approach just in front of Mireille and when he leaned forward, taking her hand to bow low over it, she caught the faint scent of bergamot and something more warm and musky. Her hand was bare, as was much of her arm and chest.

His gaze rose. "Highness. So generous of you to grace us with your company."

Though custom demanded no deference, Mireille returned his gesture with a small curtsy. The prince kept hold of her hand, placing it on his arm to lead her farther into the room. He paused before the woman he'd been speaking with. "My sister."

Mireille inclined her head. The woman's lips pursed. Her dark hair was braided through with a delicate jeweled band and, perhaps not intentionally, a thick thorny leaf.

"Nisha is the spare," the prince explained. "You'll find she attends every gathering to protect the throne by preventing threats against my person." There was a brief pause before he added meaningfully, "Lest she have to take my place."

Nisha's mouth twisted in a wry smile as she held his gaze, some unspoken message passing between them, and then the woman glanced purposefully at Mireille, seeming to note her bare hand where it was tucked into Alder's arm. "And what of this one? Does she have claws? Is she a threat against your person?"

The prince gave his sister a quelling look. "*This one,* as you so ineloquently put, is under my protection. You will leave her alone."

He drew his arm—and Mireille's hand with it—closer to his side, then led her from the room. Nisha chuckled as she followed behind them.

When the prince and Mireille stepped through a wide set of doors to the chamber outside the dining hall, two dozen pairs of eyes turned toward them. Fae courtiers stood in their finery, jewels tucked into neatly tied tresses, delicate embroidery trimming dinner jackets, and boots polished to within an inch of their lives. They had clearly been waiting on their prince and, perhaps, on Mireille.

Mireille had no way of knowing to whom the prince had revealed their betrothal, but the gathered fae certainly did not disguise their interest in the pair, paying particular notice to her hand where it was tucked against his arm.

As they walked past the other attendees, the prince not sparing the crowd a glance, Mireille realized none of the others present were wearing a gown cut in the style of her own. In fact, the woman standing nearest wore a garment with extravagant lace shaped so high on the neck that it tipped into a point near her slender ears. Another had a bare throat but full-length gloves and a fur-trimmed drape. The styles were not entirely dissimilar to other royal functions Mireille had attended, but while her wardrobe cabinet had been stocked with sheer gowns and daring cuts, the fae were dressed in sturdier fabrics trimmed with designs resembling vines and branches, their appeal the fine make, not the figure beneath. They seemed not to judge her for it, but as she'd yet to see another human in the palace or on its grounds, they may have simply been distracted by her appearance at all.

The gathered fae stared on, but the prince moved past the lot of them without introduction.

Dinner with the prince, it turned out, was not the private affair Mireille had anticipated. The dining hall was large and elegant, candelabra lining the walls and dozens of serving staff standing in attendance. At the foot of the table, a tall man uniformed in black drew out a finely carved chair, and as Mireille sat, her fingers slid from the prince's arm. He crossed to the opposite end of the exceedingly long table, past an array of fine dishes, and took his seat in an even grander chair at the table's head. The others came in, filling the long row of seats at either side. Nisha settled two chairs down from the prince, and began conversation with a tall, thin man at her side. Nisha did not particularly favor the prince, but Mireille understood that succession in the fae court was not a mirror of her own court. In fact, she suspected very little of their respective traditions overlapped. She would need to remember that.

The service began without a pause or address, indicating a level of informality. To Mireille's right sat a petite fae with copper hair. When the server leaned forward to place a dish of roast vegetables, a comment passed that caused a smile to split the woman's face and drew a quiet chuckle from the man beside her. To Mireille's left, a stout man with dark hair and deep-set eyes poured amber liquid into Mireille's glass, then gave her a friendly nod while the couple beyond him took candied fruit from a long platter. Aside from their unnatural elegance and grace, and the occasional tell of their magic or strength, the fae around her appeared much like any other royal court. But nothing could have been further from the truth.

A bit of dread swam in Mireille's stomach. She had hoped to meet the prince alone. She was not prepared for whatever rules of propriety his court held, even if the dinner did seem less formal. Her gaze lifted to the opposite end of the table, past serving dishes and ornate candelabra, where the prince leaned forward, his head inclined toward a stately, silver-haired woman to his right but his eyes on Mireille. In the high-backed chair among the group of courtiers, it would not take a crown to recognize who held rule. But the crown was there, a stark reminder of just what Mireille had gotten herself into.

She was too deeply in the situation to do anything but see herself through. She lifted her glass toward the prince, then took a cautious sip of a sweet, fruity cordial. His gaze tracked the motion, staying on her until a server leaned forward and blocked him from view.

"Have you toured the gardens?"

The voice of the man at Mireille's side snapped her attention back to her immediate surroundings. She pasted on a pleasant expression. "I have not. We only just arrived this afternoon. Do you recommend them?"

"Without reservation. The lilies alone..." He sighed wistfully. "Would you agree to let me show them to you? It would only require a bit of your time."

"That sounds lovely—"

Mireille's words cut off as a server leaned between the pair to place a dish of pears onto the table, more heavily than required and before the first course was up. The server's dark eyes met hers. She was thin with short, smooth hair and a chin that came to a delicate point. Her expression remained neutral but the act had clearly been a warning.

When the server drew away, the man asked, "It is agreed then?"

"No. As I was saying, that sounds lovely but I must decline."

"Must you?"

Mireille's fingers tightened around the stem of her glass. "It would be foolish, would it not, to agree to any bargain—no matter how trivial—so readily?"

His answering grin was wide and sharp. When he raised his glass, the gesture seemed intended more toward the server and the interruption than toward Mireille. *Right*, she thought. The games hadn't taken long to commence. Her every step would have to remain measured and cautious. For an entire month, regardless of whatever came after, she could be nothing but vigilant. Bargains were dangerous things. It was impossible to guess what the man's offer might have brought—perhaps Mireille would have awoken to the darkness to find herself helplessly striding toward a nighttime rendezvous. Perhaps something worse. It was difficult to know when even the mention of her time could translate to literal days of her life, or her freedom.

Those were things Mireille did not have to spare.

Conversation carried on around her, no further bargains offered but no real interest from the fae placed near her. They spoke to one another about trivial matters, laughing and nattering without bothering to include their guest, which implied Mireille was only truly considered a guest by the prince and his staff. She took another sip of cordial, the entire ordeal seeming to sour her stomach. If the evenings that followed were much the same, she would never get near the prince, and never discover what she needed.

His eyes met hers once more from across the long table, and she could swear they mocked her demand for nightly dinners. Another point for him, another chance at answers lost for her. It was not as if she didn't know the fae could not be trusted, but she desperately needed to win. She had known it would not be easy, that the fae loved toying with humans, and that she would be in danger every step of the way. But if she could not outwit a mere prince, what chance did she have with a queen? Mireille let her gaze slide down the row of fae at each side of the table, careful not to linger long on the details she cataloged. Colors, flowers, symbols, and trim. Who preferred jewels, who had jagged nails, whose garments appeared to be hiding something beneath. She knew what nearly none of it meant, but she would learn.

The server leaned in to take Mireille's final plate, then Alder rose, inviting the court to a connecting chamber where music was to be played. When Mireille made to stand with the others, a dark, spiky shadow skittered out from beneath the table.

Before she had an instant to react, the thing launched itself toward her. Mireille rocked backward but the creature leapt at her chest, swinging a shadowy paw. Long claws caught the fabric of Mireille's gown as she dodged away. The creature was too fast, too unnatural. Mireille stumbled into her chair just as the dark-haired server's tray tumbled to the floor, sending shards of pottery flying. The woman had hold of the shadowy creature before another blink, and the thing shrieked out a horrible cry.

The cry fell silent just as the world went still. Even the echo of shattering glass abated. The shadow creature dropped from the motionless server's hands, but it did not run away. The creature did not move, only stared hungrily at Mireille. Beyond the glamour, it was wholly fae, a thing with too many limbs, a wrongness about it that could not be put to rights. It was a child's drawing of a nightmare, come to life. Mireille's gaze rose to find the prince at the opposite end of the table. He stood, as still as the world around them. Every fae present had risen to their feet—frozen as if time had stopped. A goblet rested on its side, the droplets of wine suspended mid-spill off the edge of the table. Mireille's fingers longed to reach for it, to test the drop. But all of it was real. So very, very real.

The prince stared back at her, his gaze for her alone. She managed not to breathe, which was useful, as it likely would have cut through the silence like a horrified gasp. Alder lifted a hand. The room's occupants remained frozen, but all else seemed to shift. The table, the dishes, every single object that separated the prince from Mireille, slid carelessly aside. A half dozen platters crashed to the ground as the table screeched to a halt, candelabra hit the floor and guttered out, and some of the fae in their fine gowns were splattered with cordial and fruit. The staff at the edge of the room made not a single move. Mireille wasn't certain they could.

The prince strode forward, lit only by the remaining torchlights on the wall.

In the moment, Mireille hadn't had time to realize the shadowy creature may have represented a political attack, that someone may have known she was to be his bride. But if the prince's act in response had been a warning, it was effective. Each fae became unfrozen as their prince moved past, even his sister, and each took a knee, their heads bowed low and eyes downcast, as solemn as death. His slow stride seemed to promise that whoever was responsible for the deed would pay.

Mireille's stomach swam, both from the shock and from the dizzying way the room had shifted. The prince stopped before her, and everything that was frozen resumed once more with the drip of wine echoing in Mireille's ears. Without a word, Alder held forward a hand.

She took it. They would not be enjoying an evening of music, that much was clear. And though she wasn't certain she had a choice in the matter, she let him lead her from the room.

Noal waited in the corridor outside the dining hall. When they strode past, he followed Mireille and the prince through the adjoining room and into a large, open space scattered with statuary.

The prince released Mireille's hand as he turned toward her and inclined his head. He seemed to be restraining a great deal of fury. "Noal will return you safely to your rooms."

"I'd prefer to walk with you. I was hoping for a tour," she said, mildly ill and shaky, and somewhat proud her voice did not reveal either. What she was truly hoping, was to not lose her chance to stay near him so that she might discover anything at all to help her kingdom out of a mess.

He frowned. "I have important tasks that must be completed—"

"Of course. The tour can wait. You may complete your tasks as needed and I'll simply watch while you..." She made a little fluttering gesture with her fingers to indicate his tasks, light and airy, as if they both weren't aware she'd just watched him destroy a dining hall.

He did not seem pleased by either the gesture or the suggestion that she accompany him. "The information I intend to discuss with my staff is privileged. Though you are a guest here, even your own interkingdom policies would not permit an outside presence, regardless of our agreement. If you will allow Noal to return you to your rooms so that he and I may have a private word—"

"That is entirely understandable, and I assure you it's no trouble at all. I'll just wait over here by the sculpture until you're finished with the confidential bit with Noal." She brushed a hand casually over the fabric of her gown, where the lesser fae had left a tear. "I doubt anything will bother me while I wait. If it does, I'll be sure to scream."

His expression darkened.

She did not waver.

The prince flicked a gesture—considerably less carefree than her own—toward Noal, effectively ordering the man into a separate room. The door closed behind Noal and the prince as Mireille wandered nearer the statue, then she lifted her feet out of her slippers and rushed across the room. Ear pressed to the door, she held her breath to hear.

"...whoever did this and deliver them to me personally."

"Of course."

"She is under my protection. We are betrothed. I do not have to tell you the consequences should she be endangered again."

"Of course. I shall see to it straightaway."

"Noal."

"Highness?"

"You cannot possibly believe I will let you walk out that door without answering for the rest of it."

"I am unsure of what you're referring—"

"You know exactly what I'm referring to. But *by the wall*, I cannot understand what you were thinking."

"Of course. The princess's attire. It was entirely my mistake. I was working under the impression such was the fashion in Westrende so I believed it fitting. It is our duty to make guests comfortable, after all, so of course only familiar fashions would do."

"You've been to Westrende," Alder snapped. "Recently. You know their fashion is no such thing. It was clear to me, as well as everyone in attendance, the intent of such a costume."

"I am unsure what—"

"Do not try me."

"Of course," Noal repeated. "Her highness's wardrobe will be remedied. Just as soon as the seamstresses are able."

There was a weighty pause. "*As soon as they are able?* So that is how it is, then? Betrayed in my own house by my own man."

Noal did not answer.

The prince's voice dropped low. "Do you think me so easily persuaded? That a bit of skin would tempt me to fall at her knees?"

A pause. "She is quite striking, is she not?"

There was the sound of something solid settling very heavily onto wood. When the prince spoke again, his resolve was evident. "That seals it. You have proven you cannot be trusted. No more traps for your prince—the prince, I'll remind you, to whom you've sworn allegiance. And from this night forward, no more gatherings. You will not parade her about or take risks with our treacherous court. In fact, dinner will be private, the lady and myself only. Should she attend a gathering, she will be on my arm through the entire event or she shall not attend at all."

Noal said, "I can see how that would be best."

The prince's tone dipped and Mireille had the sense he was leaning in to deliver his threat. "I will not forget whose side you are on."

"We are on the side of Rivenwilde, Highness. With respect."

He huffed. "*We* you say, as if the entire house were against me."

If Noal made a response it was silent. Then footsteps sounded and the prince's voice came nearer to the door. "I am Rivenwilde. You would all do well to remember it."

Mireille stumbled backward then ran as fast as she was able toward her spot by the far wall. When the door came open, she held her gaze on a tall piece of marble statuary in the shape of a woman, a bounty of fruit spilling over the carved arms and a fox curled around the figure's legs so that the tail hung over the base. She could feel the prince's eyes on her as he stood for a moment at the doorway. He closed the door with Noal inside, then strode toward Mireille.

Beneath the long skirt of her own gown, she shoved her feet back into her slippers. She kept her gaze on the statue, specifically the flowers and fruit, which somehow evoked the scent of early summer despite that they were merely cut stone. When Alder reached her side, Mireille said, "This is beautiful."

He did not reply.

"I've noticed a few recurring themes in the works throughout the palace." She glanced at him. "What is the significance of the orange blossom?"

It was the wrong question. His posture, already rigid, went more so, his wide shoulders drawn back and neck taut. "I must return to my tasks."

She straightened to face him, offering a small smile. "Of course. Do, go on. Pretend as if I am not even here."

He muttered, *"Of course,"* then turned to walk down the long corridor.

Mireille hurried to keep pace, concerned she might have pushed him too far by using the words Noal had repeated. But she had to push him enough to keep him at least a little off balance, or she would never find answers.

They traversed several rooms and corridors, passing dozens of closed doors before she said pleasantly, "While I eagerly await the coming tour—I suppose I would do well to be familiar with the expectations of your house in the meantime. Are there rooms that I am not to investigate? Areas that may be forbidden?"

"You are not imprisoned. You may go where you like."

"But not outside the walls of the palace," she said. "And not to court events."

He stopped so abruptly that she nearly stumbled into him. "You agreed to the bargain. Willingly."

"I have not changed my mind. I am only attempting to find my footing."

"There is nothing to find. Until the next moon, you are a guest here."

Afterward, Mireille would be taking on an entirely new role. There was a tiny line at the edge of his brow, as thin as one of his dark lashes. She fought the urge to reach out and touch it.

Something like ire sparked in his gaze. "Perhaps you should focus on ways to take your duties as guest more seriously."

He pointed toward what Mireille realized was a familiar corridor. "At the end of this passage, you will find the door to your suite."

Ignoring the dismissal, she glanced at the set of doors that had to be his. She said quietly, "It's very close to yours."

He went still.

"I suppose they are like our queen's apartments back home. Meant for your bride. So you might—" She made a little walking gesture with her fingers, indicating how a prince might make his way to his wife's room. "I wonder who might have stayed before me."

"Good evening, Your Highness."

"Mireille," she reminded him.

His jaw tensed. "Mireille."

"You said I may go wherever I like."

"You may. I suggest you learn to like your suite." He inclined his head shortly, then turned back the way they had come.

Mireille followed.

Hand on the lever of a door dark with age, the prince stopped to look down at her. Mireille was not a small woman but he managed to tower over her anyway. There was no possible way that he believed she'd misunderstood his dismissals. "This is my study."

"Oh," she said. "So, *anywhere*, but not"—she pointed toward the door—"*there*. Would you call the study forbidden, then?"

His gaze narrowed. She smiled sweetly.

After a moment, he unlatched the door, then held it open as he gestured her past.

She stopped in the center of the dimly lit space. It was exquisitely decorated in rich hues and dark finishes and smelled faintly of something warm and sweet. It was a very personal, intimate sort of space. She was surprised he'd let her in.

His low voice seemed to brush over her skin from where he waited behind her. "I'll remind you that you will not be able to repeat anything you've seen here. Investigations into my rooms will do you no good."

She did not turn to look at him. "I'll remind you that I am not a spy. I'm only interested in becoming acquainted with Rivenwilde." She did not say, *And you are Rivenwilde, after all*, because she had been, in fact, spying when she'd overhead the comment.

The prince walked past her toward his desk and she moved to peruse a wall of books. It was clear that he was endeavoring to stay within the bounds of courtesy and those of the laws of hospitality—he must, given that she was princess and equal to his station—but there was no question he found the entire situation trying.

What was less clear, was why he needed a princess that he did not seem to want.

"Is this your full collection? Or is there a library located elsewhere?"

Head down, hand spread over a document he appeared to read, he said, "I believe I was to pretend you were not here."

She could not help the smile that tugged at her lips. Reaching toward a book on the shelf, she glanced at him over her shoulder. "May I?"

He watched her face, not the finger hovering over a title. "You may take all the privileges due to a guest."

She dropped her hand. "I do not wish to take privileges. I would rather they were granted freely."

His eyes returned to the document. "Read any title you like. You will find no secrets on those shelves. I have nothing to hide that you might find there, nor on any shelf in this palace or its library."

She wandered close to his desk, her gaze tracing the lines of the fine script on the page. "No secrets, then. But I wonder if the tales are true." She leaned nearer to watch as the line of words grew beneath his pen. "Can you lie?"

The nib caught on the page for just an instant before resuming its path. "What is a lie but intent?"

She hummed. "And what is glamour if not a lie?"

The quill stilled. The prince looked up at her. "You have seen through our glamour from the start."

She reached forward, carefully brushing a finger over the edge of his brow where a small scar hid beneath that glamour, invisible to the eye but plain beneath her touch. "Then why does it remain between us?"

His reply was barely above a whisper. "That is not for you."

She drew her hand back, uncertain whether he meant the glamour or the touch. "How thoughtless of me. Of course not everything is meant for me."

In the candlelight, the darkness of his eyes seemed to shift—like pools beneath a night sky that begged to draw her in. She straightened away from him. He was right, the glamour had not been meant for her. It was only another tool of the fae, and if the prince wanted her to be drawn to him, he would not be trying so hard to push her away.

"Forgive me," she said quietly. "I will leave you to your work."

Halfway to the door, she stopped at the sound of his reply.

"Perhaps… a book might help to occupy your time. Feel free to take along whichever were of interest to you."

CHAPTER 4

Mireille had taken a pair of books from the prince's study that appeared well-worn. The first included diagrams of a variety of plants and their root systems, and the second was a thin volume of poetry in a language she was less familiar with. Perhaps it was true that she would not find his secrets, but it might at least bring her some understanding of the man. She could appreciate the responsibilities of a title and the desire to hold distance or withhold trust—the very behaviors she practiced with him—but Mireille could not help but wonder what else might be behind the prince's taciturn manner.

She wished very much that he had not brushed aside her comment regarding any princesses who might have come before her.

Back in her suite, Mireille sat with her feet curled up on the settee while Thomas settled in the chair nearby. Dressed in a dark blue coat and breeches, he appeared as dapper as any of the fae she'd dined with, though considerably more weary. She gave him a brief summary of her evening's events before asking about his own. "You seem to have survived, at least. Did all go well?"

He shrugged his shoulders, adjusting his jacket. "*Well* may be too strong a word, but I was able to gain my bearings a bit and met a few members of staff."

"Anything of use?"

"It seems the palace staff is eager to have you. So that's something. Past that, I'm not certain what either they or the prince gains from the bargain. Noal was keen to assist with anything I asked…"

"But?"

His gaze slid to hers. "I do not believe he's dressed you in the style of court."

Mireille nodded. "So it seems. I overheard the prince giving him a thorough set down. The household may be encouraging the prince in ways he is not comfortable with. Unfortunately, it's impossible to know if this makes them our allies or simply another obstacle to overcome."

He nodded, though his mouth had gone flat. "Evidently staff is also aware that the queen has shown interest in the relationship between Westrende and Rivenwilde. There is speculation as to how it might shape the future of the realm."

When Thomas went quiet, Mireille realized her hand had slid protectively over her throat. She dropped it. "What else?"

Thomas's finger tapped the plush arm of his chair. "It was brought to my attention that there is a lovely piano in the music room. Twice."

She frowned. "I've not played in years. How would they have guessed I once had an attachment to such a thing?"

"They've evidently made inquiries." He gestured to the console table near the door. "And look there."

Mireille followed his indication, finding the table had been set with a bowl heaped with oranges between a pair of orange blossom bouquets. "Well," she said. "We will certainly be looking into the history of oranges."

Thomas hummed in agreement, but it was not the satisfied sort. It was the sort that held an undercurrent of concern. If Mireille had to guess, she would say it was owing to the time they had left, and that it was already dwindling away.

But she did not have to guess. Thomas had told her repeatedly how displeased he was with her plan. He wanted her safe. He wanted her alive.

Fate save her, she was trying. The prince's reserve wasn't helping. He did not trust her, and she couldn't be certain it was merely due to her connection to his enemies in Westrende. That they had looked so deep into her past was worrying. Mireille hoped very much they had not looked as far into Thomas and his skillset, or his access to the palace and its staff might be cut off.

She said, "So, tomorrow night I attend a private dinner and you..."

"Find the dungeons," he finished.

She dropped her head back onto the settee. "Capital. All we need now is to figure out how to thwart a queen who is all-powerful."

"She's not all-powerful. Everyone has a weakness." Thomas stood. "Mine is cheese."

Mireille smiled up at the ceiling as Thomas made his way to the doorway. He sank easily to the floor in front of the door to the corridor, tucked a hand beneath his head, and crossed his legs at the ankles before his eyes slid closed.

IT WAS midnight when Mireille rose from her bed. She had no need of a timepiece; it was always midnight when she rose. Bare feet gliding silently across the cool stone floor, she made her way to the door of her room. She did not step over Thomas, but stood very near his slumbering form. The understanding that he could not be awoken settled within her, and her body shifted. Drawn toward the corner of the room, she pressed her palm flat to the wall where no door should be. A hidden panel opened.

Mireille did not feel the surprise that should have come at her hand finding a panel her mind had not known was there.

She walked into the corridor. If anyone in the palace was present, Mireille was not aware. Her feet continued through the maze of corridors, taking her to an exterior palace wall. The palace was somehow more alive in the darkness, but she could not pause to consider why. She only continued through the corridors, past carvings that seemed to writhe, past gilded decorations and crawling vines. Her steps did not cease until a toe bumped against a tall arched window, open to the world beyond. Cool night air brushed over her skin, seeping through her thin shift. The sickly-sweet scent of hawthorn flowers on the breeze drew her forward. She leaned into the archway, only night air between her and the courtyard three stories below.

Mireille did not feel the fear that should have come.

In the distance, firelight dotted the horizon, the fae courtiers in their costumes and finery, dancing at a moonlit ball. She could hear their laughter, feel their revelry. Wind tugged at the hem of her shift and she swayed with the music, further toward the open air and the nothing below. She had no control.

The song of the fae whispered, beckoning her on. *Mireille*, it sang. *Mireille*.

Her bare foot lifted past the lip of the archway.

Mireille was unable to feel the dread that should have filled her, but she knew what was to come.

She stepped forward.

"Rei!" Strong hands gripped her shoulders, drawing her back just in time. Thomas, chest heaving, hands trembling, murmured, "I have you. There we go." He dragged her farther from the ledge, cursing and muttering about the sort of palace that would have open windows and an utter lack of guards.

Mireille did not feel the relief that seemed to swim through him, though she knew she would. He let go only long enough to wrap a dressing gown around her. "Come on, back to bed," he said, and he tugged the gown tighter before guiding her by the shoulders. "This was a close one. Tomorrow night, we're tying bells to your person."

IT WAS EARLY the next morning, wrapped in her dressing gown beneath several layers of blanket, that Mireille felt everything she should have the night before. It was never pleasant when the feelings returned, never left her unshaken to have lost all control. The hope that a bed inside the palace might be out of the queen's reach was gone.

She had woken to find Thomas's spot by the door empty. A large dresser had been slid across the room, covering the panel they'd missed in their initial inspection. A collection of delicate glassware was placed precariously near its edges, easily crashed to the floor should the dresser be jostled.

They should have found the panel. They had made a mistake.

They would have to do better.

Mireille called for tea, then searched the wardrobe for her most serviceable gown. She found a scrap of fabric to tuck into the low neckline of the bodice like a fichu, and in short order, she was prepared for the day.

Thomas met her near the library as planned, where they intended to scour the shelves for fae tradition, law, and history. Much of the outside world did not credit the existence of magic. To most, fae were only a tale of times past, a danger which had long ago been caged, which was how the fae queen had been so easily able to slip into the kingdoms she'd taken before Norcliffe. Few understood the laws that bound fae, and even less was known about how they spent their time. Mireille knew more than most, but it felt as if she knew nothing at all.

The library rose three stories, open in the center where arched beams draped with tangled ivies cut through the light from a ceiling composed of etched glass. A network of stairs and ladders wove between balconies and levels, and yet, many of the shelves remained bare. Likewise, despite the size of the palace, not a single other soul was present. Mireille's best chance to save her father and their kingdom should be there, within the massive fae library. But the scene was suspect.

Mireille glanced at Thomas, who was biting his lip. "Do you suppose…"

"Let's not suppose." He ran a palm over his neck. "We'll do well to remember we are no longer dealing with the expected. It would be foolish not to check here first."

"Right," she said. "Where shall we start?"

Lips pursed, he gestured vaguely toward the far wall. "You take that section, I'll try the second level."

They spent hours scouring the shelves for any hint of information helpful to their cause. Half the tomes were in languages Mireille had never seen, and what wasn't locked behind glass and marble was entirely useless for her purposes. She was being pursued by the fae queen, a malevolent terror who wished to destroy Norcliffe and all that Mireille held dear, and nothing could be done to prevent the impending disaster. If Mireille did not find a way to subvert fae magic, to save her family and her kingdom, then nothing would be left. The queen would rise in power, gaining more authority with every crown she grasped and every castle she toppled.

Bargaining with the fae prince had been, quite literally, their last chance. And she could not even find a book on the cultural history of fruit trees. It was beginning to appear as if they'd never had a chance at all.

By the time tea was served, Mireille had nearly given up hope of finding information on fae law or tradition. "Perhaps he wasn't lying. Perhaps there's not a secret here among any of the shelves."

"So, where, then?" Thomas popped the last bite of a cucumber sandwich into his mouth. "The prince's suite?"

Mireille's own sandwich stuck in her throat.

He handed her a cup of tea. He said, "Well, *I* can't go in there."

"And you expect I can? That anyone would allow me to dance my way right over the threshold to his private chambers?"

The look he gave her said far more than any remark could have.

Mireille groaned. "Be reasonable, Thomas. It's not as if fae secrets will be bolted to the wall with a finely engraved plaque. *Here lies the knowledge of every fae conundrum known to man. Feel free to browse this register of twelve proven methods to trick a fae.*" The edge of Thomas's mouth twitched and, a bit overtired, Mireille plowed recklessly on. "Perhaps I'll find just the one I need now: A *detailed account for working your way into a fae prince's bedchamb*—"

Mireille squeaked and fumbled her teacup as a throat cleared behind her. There was a flash of surprise in Thomas's expression before it smoothed to something more cordial, revealing that he had been just as unaware that they'd been approached. Mireille set her cup on the small table, then glanced at the fae now standing beside them.

The woman leaned forward as she replenished the tray. It was the dark-haired server who had saved Mireille from the shadow creature, and from the seatmate who had tried to trap her in a bargain, the night before.

"Forgive us," Mireille said. "I'm afraid... well, I'm afraid there's no excuse for it."

The woman offered a closed-lip smile as she worked.

Mireille tried again. "I want to thank you for last night. It can be quite difficult to navigate court life and it means a great deal that you were willing to come to my aid."

The woman only inclined her head. Mireille glanced at Thomas; he gave an infinitesimal shrug. Mireille reached forward, gently touching her fingertips to the woman's hand to still her work. When the woman met her gaze, her dark eyes seemingly free from pretense, Mireille asked, "What may I call you?"

The woman placed the tea pot on the table, then reached up to tap her fingers to her throat.

Mireille gestured with her reply. "In Norcliffe, we were taught a bit of signing. Is this version familiar to you?"

The woman responded with a gesture that appeared to mean, "well enough," then she glanced at Thomas, who held a book over his knee, and indicated for him to pass it over. When Thomas obliged, the woman pointed out the letters of a name.

"Kin," Mireille said.

The woman inclined her head again.

"Well, Kin, I am in your debt."

The sidelong glance she gave Mireille spoke volumes.

"Right," Mireille said. "I will remember not to offer my debts out so easily, as well as not agreeing to any sly bargains."

She gave a curt nod, then dipped her head as if to go.

"Kin." When she turned back, Mireille asked, "Would the law books be on the first level or the third?"

With the smallest upward tilt to the corner of her mouth, Kin indicated her burden of tea pot and tray as if to imply she could not answer.

"I wonder," Mireille said smoothly, "if the fae laws of hospitality would supersede any orders from your prince."

Kin's brow lifted playfully, then she turned to place the tray on a side table.

"Interesting," Thomas murmured.

Mireille grinned. "Indeed."

It was surely no accident that the fae secrets were tucked away. The morning search had been fruitless and frustrating and Mireille had no time to waste. They were going to have to use fae customs they did not entirely understand in order to gain any ground.

They followed Kin up a wide spiral staircase to a second story balcony where only a handful of bound volumes rested on a shelf. A pale stone ledge extended from the wall beneath the shelf, its supports carved into woody vines with wisteria draped over the edge. To one side rested a plush chair, beside it a small table.

Mireille bit her lip, exchanging a glance with Thomas, as they'd already checked the few books on the shelf. She said, "Anything on customs and traditions would be helpful as well, but what we would really like are the older texts. Thomas is a bit of a historian, you see, and this is his favorite pastime. I, on the other hand, could do with a primer on court etiquette and something detailing the royal code."

Kin nodded, tucking her dark hair behind an ear as she stepped closer to where Thomas stood by the ledge, his fingers tracing carved markings that Mireille could only assume were some sort of ancient script.

Shoulder to shoulder, Kin placed her hand over Thomas's. She guided his palm to lie flat against the stone. He started, his hazel eyes flicking to her face, then Mirelle sensed the tingling warmth of magic that rose from their connected hands.

Kin's fingers slid away, and beneath Thomas's palm rested bound linen pages, their script trimmed in red and gold. He went still for one very long moment before his own hand slid reverently down the page.

Kin placed her palm on the ledge beside the first book, and another rose to the surface. Her smile was soft as she crossed her wrists behind her back and strode toward the window, eyes on the distant trees.

Thomas was too still, too quiet. Mireille leaned nearer, glancing briefly at the tome Kin had apparently left for her. "Well?"

His laugh was small and breathless, attention never straying from the page. "I don't have any idea what it says."

Mireille could just make out the corner of Kin's mouth lifting where the woman stood facing the balcony. She had done what they had asked, fulfilled the wishes of the prince's guests. But she had not broken any trust; the fae secrets were just as far away as they had been.

Except that Thomas was no amateur historian. He excelled at breaking codes. Beside her, he said, "Another. Please. Same time period."

Kin turned, expression wary at the change in his tone, but Mireille only smiled and said, "See? He loves this stuff."

Late in the afternoon, after Thomas had exhausted Kin and devoured more texts than Mireille could count, Noal appeared to retrieve the pair. Mireille made a point to grouse about their lack of success.

"Was there something in particular you were searching for?" he asked.

Absently, she ran a thumb over a finely carved vine that edged the table. Every detail of the palace felt intentional, as if nothing had been left out. "Actually, several things. But I was wondering most of all about fae customs. The significance of certain flowers, for instance." The flowers were far less a concern than the stipulations of fae bargaining and the right of rule, but the blossoms seemed her most likely chance to gain Noal's trust, especially given the look he had shared with the prince their first night. When he did not respond, she tapped a fingernail against a small glass urn atop the table. "Can't find anything of the sort, despite all of these references."

Noal's expression remained level. "You wouldn't. They're in our hearts, practiced within our rituals. Our traditions are not bolted to the wall with a finely engraved plaque or listed on a register for all to see."

A small, choked sound came from the corner, where Thomas

attempted to cover his laugh with a cough, likely at the man's reference to her earlier comment.

"Yes," Mireille said. "I can see how listing them out might be a problem. I wonder, then, how one might find the answer to those questions instead."

Noal did not respond.

"I suspect I will not find them with the prince."

Noal's attention seemed to sharpen on her. "Indeed, if one were to discover insight at all it would be with the heart of Rivenwilde. Your dinner with the prince approaches. Shall we return you to your rooms so that you may prepare?"

She leaned nearer, dropping her voice. "Truly? You've nothing to offer but obscure comments?"

"Not in the way of kingdom secrets, no."

Mireille narrowed her gaze. "Because you cannot reveal more or because you will not?"

"Precisely."

"I see," she said. "It appears we are left entirely up to our own devices."

BECAUSE OF THE ATTACK, Alder had changed the rules. Their dinner would be private. He was to meet Mireille at her suite, then walk with her to a secluded dining hall.

Dressed for the occasion in a gown that was far more elegant than the last—and with a much lower neckline, despite the prince's warning to Noal—Mireille stood in the center of her sitting room, watching as the door came open, well past when she was to expect the prince.

It was not the prince who entered, but Noal, dressed in his dark suit and perfectly tied cravat. "The prince has been detained with court business. Perhaps this evening's dinner would be better taken in your rooms. Shall I have it brought up straight away and send your regrets?"

She gave the man a patient smile. "I will wait for him."

Noal's expression did not waver. "It may be quite some time."

"I trust that the prince will keep his word. He will show eventually, and that is all that matters. I have nothing but time, after all." *And nowhere near enough of it.*

"Of course." Noal's hands unclasped to fall to his sides. "I will return when he is—"

"I will wait for him outside of—wherever he is."

That earned her a small twitch at the corner of his lips. "As you wish."

He led her to a gallery that looked out over the kingdom, a wide window before low stone steps that felt very quiet and still. "No one will bother you here. This is a private gallery reserved for His Highness."

Mireille drew her eyes from a view of expansive estates and lush forests. "You do not have to wait with me. I'm certain you've other matters to attend."

Noal inclined his head. "Should you need anything—"

Mireille waved his comment away. "I have it well in hand, though I do appreciate your concern. You'll recall, I am a princess as well. I'm used to waiting for selfish and stodgy royals with no regard for the schedules of others."

He appeared to swallow a sound but Mireille could not quite make out whether it was one of humor or shock. She suspected a man like Noal could not be easily shocked.

"Well, then, I will leave you to it." He gave a bow and walked from the room.

Hours later, Mireille still sat on a finely carved marble step watching as the sun began to set. Far in the distance, the treetops were tipped with a rosy gold. Her slippers were tucked neatly beneath her skirts, and well away from the ledge of the archway that opened into the coming night. Outside in the distance was a festival, its fae music drifting up to her on a jasmine-scented breeze. She would need to return to her rooms before midnight, but no matter how much the sound felt as if it were calling her, Mireille would not go. Not in the light of day when she had any choice in the matter.

Besides, if she stepped foot outside the castle, she would no longer be protected. The prince and his rules were all that was keeping her safe.

She was not certain how long he had been watching from the shadows, but when the sun had finally dipped below the trees, the last of its light a fading haze of color along the horizon, Mireille said, "It is quite a breathtaking view. I can see why you've chosen this as your sanctuary."

A moment of stillness followed in which she was not certain he would reply. Perhaps he had not meant for her to notice him. Perhaps, like her, he had felt the stillness of time, there at the dying of another day, too bittersweet to break. But he came forward, on slow and silent steps, to stand by her side.

Mireille glanced up at him. "Is it a festival to celebrate the change of seasons?"

His gaze remained on the fires in the distance. "A festival, yes. Marking the coming of winter... no."

She ran a hand over her bare arm. "I confess, it seems very strange to have stood in the Westrende forest where leaves seemed ready to fall and to experience that bite of wind, only to step through the wall to find, suddenly, surroundings like that of a hothouse. Will winter come for your lands soon?"

"One way or another, I suppose it will." His dark eyes met hers, and he held forward a hand.

Mireille took it, her bare palm sliding against his glove. They stood for a moment before the balcony. Perhaps Mireille imagined the sense of loneliness from him before he turned, placing her hand inside his arm to guide her to their promised dinner.

He led her to a room that was as spacious as the one in which they'd dined the night before, but instead of a long table lined with seating, there waited only two chairs at a table even longer. And the chairs at opposite ends, no less.

After Mireille was settled into her seat, Alder strode to the taller, more elaborate chair, clearly meant for a prince of the fae, its back a carved tangle of wood that mirrored his crown, its arms wrapping solidly around him before disappearing like roots into the floor.

Mireille examined the table setting as a server poured thick red liquid into her goblet.

"It is... very formal," she said to the prince, feeling the need to raise her voice to reach him at the other end. "This is surely not where you normally dine. Would you prefer to return to your usual dinners, with family and members of your court?"

"Most evenings, I do not dine with my... with anyone. This month, the celebrations, it is an unusual affair."

She cocked her head in interest, but he did not go on. Clearly, he was not going to make it easy to get close to him, even when she had him relatively alone. "Where, precisely, do you dine, then?"

"My study."

"Well, that sounds..."

He flicked a gesture at the wait staff.

"...cozy," Mireille finished.

The prince took a sip from his goblet.

"Can you tell me about your court? I would love to hear how your days are spent—"

The prince's goblet returned to the table. "I will not discuss matters of the court or my duties to the palace. You are not yet privy to kingdom affairs."

Mireille stared at him. He stared back. She said, "Noted. Are there any other topics that are forbidden?"

His expression hardened. She wondered if word had gotten back to him about their search in the library. She wondered if they'd gone too far on only their first day, revealed too much.

Alder waved the servers to proceed. The first two courses did not go any better. By the time they'd progressed to the third, both were speaking curtly, when they spoke at all, and it was clear the prince was itching to escape. He had likely expected her to give up waiting for him to meet her that evening at all. It may have been her fault that he felt pressed, but she could not be sorry for it.

"Dinner was," she started at the same time he said, "Perhaps we should retire—"

He broke off, something like frustration skittering over his expression before it disappeared.

"Yes," Mireille said. "We should absolutely excuse ourselves early." He began to stand and she added, "Best we leave plenty of time for the tour."

He froze midway to his feet, bent awkwardly over the table as he glanced up at her.

He was likely going to hate her before the month was up, but Mireille only smiled. "You have the time, do you not, given that you had planned to spend it here, with me? Per our agreement."

A muscle near his jaw ticked. He straightened to standing.

Mireille waited, his name hovering on the tip of her tongue. She would use it, as often as she must.

"Yes," he finally answered. "The tour."

His tone implied something along the lines of *let us get this over with* but it was not the time to quibble. She'd won a victory, minuscule though it was.

CHAPTER 5

It did not take long to realize the prince intended to give Mireille an abrupt tour. He shared little to no detail or history for each of the many rooms as they walked through the palace. "The blue room," he said. "The conservatory." Past a circular chamber, he gestured vaguely. "The east wing." Then, "Staff quarters."

But when they came to a music room, Mireille stopped, peering through the doorway into a lavish space adorned with rich blue draperies, gold-trimmed furnishings, and filled with instruments that appeared to be of the finest craftsmanship she'd ever seen. Her gaze snagged on the sleek grand piano inlaid with a vining pattern of leaves and blooms, and her heart twisted.

It felt like only a moment, but the prince must have noticed. "Would you like to play?"

"No." Mireille's words were too faint. She forced herself to look away from the instrument—and at him. He had extended an olive branch in the one area she did not wish to venture. She couldn't know if the house staff had told him of her history, or if he'd only seen her response to the instrument. She said, "I haven't played in years," as she tucked her hand into the crook of his elbow. "Come, there must be much more to see."

His dark eyes slid from her face, then he turned, making no comment on her evasion. They passed through several more rooms before a large portrait gallery caught Mireille's attention. "May we?" she asked with a glance toward the prince. He inclined his head, but only drew his arm from hers, freeing her to move as she wished while he waited in the corridor.

Mireille wandered slowly through the room, taking in compositions that revealed very little of fae life. Nowhere in sight was a battle scene, an interior of everyday life, nor even an arrangement of flowers. The works, it seemed, were merely a record of faces, various figures standing in the center of cold spaces, in decidedly austere jackets and trousers or serviceable gowns, a pedestal or seat in a few, the occasional vague archway behind, as if in concession. It did not dampen Mireille's interest in the least.

She strode forward, mesmerized by the unparalleled skill of the artist. The strokes were loose and feathered, and yet hit so perfectly as if to disappear. Her eyes could not stay landed on any particular detail, for every other detail was too fine not to follow to. "Remarkable," she whispered, finding herself drawn closer and closer as she went. The corner of the mouth, the tilt of an eye; they seemed to contain the very soul of the subjects, distilled to their essence.

Her steps froze. She turned to face what may have been the most impressive portrait of all.

In his spot near the entrance, the prince had gone suddenly too still. But Mireille could not be made to look away from the wall.

The figure in the painting stared down at her, as large as life. He stood tall and slender, long, fine hands with elegant fingers that spoke of grace and beauty, and richly dressed despite the wardrobe being carefully nondescript. Dark hair beneath a crown of bone-line tangled spikes framed a face whose expression was that of a man certain he's been done wrong. His posture seemed to judge the viewer, even as his gaze seemed to smolder with intent. He was handsome, as handsome as any man Mireille had ever seen. And yet, the portrait spoke of a terrifying power. It held a dark and deadly weight. A secret.

The portrait was of the prince with whom she'd just sparred over dinner, so well painted that as Mireille studied it, the corner of his lips seemed to tip into the hint of a smile.

She blinked, resisting the urge to step back. But the painting appeared as it had before, unsmiling, foreboding. There was no wicked smile curving at the edge of his lips at all. It was only a portrait, no more than pigment and oil.

At the entrance, its subject waited in the flesh. He had spoken not a word, but watched her with a very particular sort of stillness.

Mireille smoothed a palm over her skirt, thoroughly burying her unease before rejoining him. He was to be her husband if she had any hope of stopping the queen. She would not fear his power when he had not attempted to use it against her.

"Such an interesting collection," she said.

"Does it please you?"

She gave him a shallow smile. "The palace is stunning, all of it. The flowering vines and statuary, grand halls, intimate drawing rooms, and here, a gallery filled with exquisitely skilled work... I would be very hard to please indeed if I could not be happy with a place such as this."

His gaze stayed on her as they walked. "That was an evasion."

She pressed her lips. They passed an open balcony, revealing a starless sky that had darkened to a blue so deep it was nearly black. "It is very beautiful. Leaving behind a family and a kingdom is no easy thing. I suppose it would be easier if one were to be assured those were safe. But I cannot fault your palace, Alder." At her use of his name, a shiver seemed to run through him. Mireille found she did not hate that at all. But it was not the time to put away difficult discussions. "From my perch inside the marble cage, your land seems lovely as well."

His voice was low. "I did not trap you in a cage. You were free. You stepped into it of your own accord."

She hummed her agreement. "And my only way out, it seems, is to marry you."

The prince did not respond. Decidedly so.

"You needed a princess. Had I not come, you would have taken any other with the same title. To overcome your battle with Westrende and destroy the barrier that is the wall? To unrend the kingdoms, unbind your power, and crush them beneath the terrible weight of fae magic. Is that why I am here?"

"You are here because you chose it." Then, as if he could not quite seem to help himself, he snapped, "You think me incapable of any act but destruction? That I am as corrupt as the tales say?"

One of her brows lifted. "Would you want me to admit such a thing?"

"When I ask a question of you, I would want that you could say yes or no without fear."

"You do not trust me. You shut me out the moment I inquire about the slightest detail. You want something, need something from me owning to my station, but you do not want to marry me."

His jaw flexed.

"I did come willingly, as you say. And yet, you accepted the bargain. A bargain in which I have only the choice to become your bride or to break our agreement and end up your prize." His eye twitched. "There," she said. "I see you, Alder. I understand that you do not want me. Not as your prisoner and not as your wife. You will not tell me why. So how do I win in such a situation? How, before the next moon, do I choose correctly?"

He straightened, the action drawing him away from her in a way that made her aware just how near they'd become. "There is no winning. You have already chosen. When moontide comes, the wedding ceremony will take place."

So, he thought making the bargain was where she'd gone wrong. Perhaps it was true. But Alder did not know that outside the protection of his palace waited a fate far worse than any she might face with him.

THEY WERE quiet as they walked back to the wing that held their suites. Unwilling to reveal their hands, unable to back down, they were resigned to their situation, and possibly a little sheepish about the weaknesses they'd just revealed. At least, Mireille knew she was.

It was time for a change in tactic if she had any hope of breaking through his façade.

There were no footmen, no courtiers, no other present in the corridors aside from Mireille and the prince. She wasn't certain if the others were in another part of the castle, or out for the festival, but the halls felt strangely quiet and still. If she had her bearings correct, the walls they strode between laid directly below the corridor outside the prince's rooms. She glanced at the prince.

"Ask." His tone was polite, and after a few strides without a reply, he gave her his gaze.

Her cheeks did not flush to be caught staring so openly, but it was a near thing. She held his gaze. "I was wondering whether these rooms lay beneath my suite."

"They do," he said.

"Then, likewise, yours, since they are connect—"

"One final stop?"

She blinked. Bringing up their connecting chambers more than once may have come across as an all-too-eager interest in his suite, or perhaps his staff had shared what they'd overheard in the library. But Mireille suspected she was being shut down anytime she strayed near the subject of the women whose betrothals had surely come before her own.

The prince only drew them toward a pair of tall, elaborately-carved doors. There was a moment of hesitation before he stepped away from her to push wide the door. It opened into a massive ballroom. The sight took her breath. Outside, the moon had risen. Pale marble limned by moonlight from a row of arched doorways on the far wall covered the entire space. The opposite walls were lined with tall mirrors, creating a silvery glow that shifted with Mireille's every step.

Faint music rose over the balcony like a whisper carried on the cool night air. She walked forward, her reflection keeping pace on every side, and she was helpless to prevent the grin that parted her lips. She spun, a bit giddy with the delight of it. The moment was so perfect, so lovely, that it did not seem real. Of all the beauty she'd experienced in his palace so far, this was the finest, made ethereal by the light and the music and the mirrors in the night air.

She remembered she was not alone, and paused her swaying to ask, "It is breathtaking, is it not?"

The prince's dark eyes stayed on hers, and though he did not answer, he moved slowly toward her.

"Come, won't you dance with me, here in the moonlight while the palace sleeps?" she dared to ask.

"The palace is not asleep."

Her smile widened. "Pretend. Imagine with me that we are not a prince and princess, that there is no bargain and that we have never been at odds."

He frowned. It did not make him any less handsome.

Mireille held her hand forward, and he took it, if reluctantly. She drew him nearer, her voice dropping. "Do you never relish a private moment? With every day surrounded by courtiers, by structure and formality, rarely alone to just..."

"Dance in the moonlight?" His voice was even, but not cold. He did not seem to find the moment unpleasant, and a bit of his surliness faded away as they stood, fingers entwined.

"No," she said softly. "I suppose you do not." She bit her lip. "But tonight, with me, you will."

Mireille guided his hand to her waist, taking position. For a heartbeat, she only stared up at him, unsure whether he would play along. But the music rose far in the distance, and he took the first step in rhythm with the soft, sweet fae melody.

He was a fine dancer. Graceful and fluid, seemingly aware of her in a way that made her own steps easy. His grip was steady against her waist, his other hand a practiced lead. They spun through the ballroom, gliding over the polished floor like seabirds skimming smooth waters.

She had not danced in ages, her kingdom under threat and her people in fear. She had not stood close to a man who was not her guard, or her friend, or her father. Alder was very a much a man, despite that he was fae. Tall, strong, and competent, and not quite so prickly once he'd relaxed into the motions. His gaze fixed on her, and the ballroom seemed to fade away. The song came to an end but Mireille did not want to let go. She did not want to return to the way things were, to thinking about what was to come, the worry about her people and her family. When he began to pull away, she held fast, not stepping backward, her hand remaining clasped in his. She needed him. She needed this.

Their eyes locked. "Stay with me," she whispered, though certainly she must have meant to add *for one more dance*.

Something shifted in his gaze. Magic perhaps, some hint of glamour or power, flickering beneath the influence of fae music and moonlight. His expression did not change, but his attention was on her so thoroughly that the atmosphere did.

In the distance, a new song swelled, carried to them on sweetly scented air. Alder's gaze remained on Mireille as his hand slid up to her shoulder blade, in preparation, she thought, for the new dance position. The cut of her dress was low, and a shiver ran through her as his gloved fingers grazed her bare skin. His lips parted, as if to speak her name, and Mireille felt herself tipping her head toward him. They were so close that the breath he released brushed over her skin.

"Your Highness."

The voice from the doorway broke whatever spell had come over them, and Alder went suddenly stiff. He dropped his hands. "What is it?"

The uniformed fae bowed deeply, in a move that spoke of regret. "Apologies, Your Highness, but there is in issue that requires your attention."

"I'll be right there." He seemed to shake himself before taking a step back from Mireille. Tone gone tetchy, he said, "I shall return you to your rooms, Your Highness."

At first Mireille chalked his tone up to the shock of interruption. But his conversation was noticeably curt as they made their way to her suite, and the rigid posture and obvious distance he held between them felt more like a rebuke. Mireille had been so close to... *something*.

Her time was running out. She needed to uncover the prince's secrets, and the secrets of his people, to find a way to save her own.

She needed him to need *her*. And not merely because she was a princess.

But Alder was protecting himself and his secrets. It was clear he hadn't meant to slip. He must have realized he had nearly let her in, and he likely had no intention of dropping his guard again.

It was clear that Mireille had just lost any footing she'd gained.

CHAPTER 6

At midnight, Mireille rose from the wide, plush bed once more. Her booted foot slipped between the scattering of metal and glass trinkets Thomas had spread over the floor without a whisper of noise. With nothing in her wardrobe but flimsy night dresses and elaborate gowns, she had taken a pair of his trousers, rolled at the waist, and a knotted-up shirt. Still, they had been certain there was no means for her escape.

She stood in the darkness of the still room. She could feel the soft weave of the rug beneath her toes, could hear the slow steady breath of Thomas in his spot by the door.

Thomas was thorough. After the panel had been discovered, there were no other exits he hadn't blocked. None aside from the passage meant for a queen—the door between Mireille's suite and the prince's that had been sealed by powerful fae magic. Magic a human princess could not break.

She moved soundlessly toward the door anyway. It was tall, half again her size, and carved with intricate vines and leaves. She placed a palm to the wood. Her pulse beat against its grain. For one beat of her heart, Mireille's awareness of the room disappeared, then she was back, trapped in the state of semi-consciousness she'd been in before. The leaves seemed to have shifted beneath her palm, and the door fell open into a short, dark passage. Mireille's feet drew her forward.

Mireille had not felt the fear that should have come when she'd nearly stepped into the night air off a balcony, and she did not feel the fear of stepping over the threshold into the room of the most powerful fae in Rivenwilde. She should have, she knew that, but it changed not a thing.

The room was finished in dark wood and trimmed in shades of green. Tapestries lined the walls, embroidered with deep green and gold, blue-green draperies hung loose over finely carved windows open to the night sky, and a pair of settees were scattered with velvet pillows. A single bed centered the far wall, empty of occupants. A plush chair rested in the corner, a bright strip of silk draped over the arm. Near the door through which Mireille had entered, halfway between her and a wide fireplace, sat a writing desk. Atop its surface, the flickering light of a single taper glinted off a glass inkwell and the silver blade of a paper knife. The taper was the only light aside from the blue-silver glow of the moon.

The prince sat in a chair near the empty hearth. Dressed in trousers and a loose shirt, the sleeves rolled up his forearms where he held a leather-bound book, he glanced up distractedly.

His gaze went dark.

Mireille could not decipher whether it was owing to the sight of the woman who was to be his wife in such a manner of apparel greeting him like a wight in the small hours or something more along the lines of a suspected assassination attempt, but the prince seemed to take either outcome as an a threat. He stood, the book he'd held sliding quietly onto the padded chair. He spoke not a word, but the warning in his gaze said volumes.

He was the prince of Rivenwilde. His power was so great that it could crumble the palace beneath Mireille's feet.

Against every scrap of her will, all while knowing it would be her end, she felt herself press forward. In a few short steps, near the edge of the desk, her hand reached past the inkwell.

Her fingers curled around the handle of the paper knife.

The grip was slim, cool against her flesh.

The prince's dark gaze tracked the movement, his own fingers curling tighter in tandem with hers. He held no weapon in his fist. Only magic. Fathomless power.

Mireille would lose.

But Mireille was not willingly playing the game. Her movements were decided by the fae queen. The queen's magic had drawn her from bed, had opened the sealed door, and had brought her to stand before a prince. It would see Mireille done in just as efficiently.

Before Alder made a single step forward, as he watched and waited as if to see how she might attack, her fisted hand raised. The knife did not aim for the prince, as he might have expected. The knife stabbed toward Mireille's own chest.

There was an instant in which time seemed to slow, the flash of realization coming to Alder's dark eyes that it was not, in fact, an attempt on his life. Then he lunged.

In the space of a heartbeat, Mireille was flat on the floor. The blade was knocked from her hand, clattering to the plank before it had hit its mark. The prince of Rivenwilde splayed over her, his magic and his body a heavy weight pinning her down, pinning down the magic running through her. It was as if she were buried beneath the earth itself, as if she could not find her body or her will. Neither Mireille nor the prince had spoken a word.

One side of her face was pressed to the floor. His cheek brushed the other. Against her ear, he whispered her name.

A shiver ran through her, deep and rich, and not at all reassuring, as it was suffuse with fae power.

Mireille snapped back to herself with a gasp, the queen's hold upon her broken. Her hands began to tremble, her heart to race. She had nearly met her end, at the invisible will of the fae queen, or at the very real, very tangible hands of a fae prince. It had been that close. And with it, the end for all of Norcliffe.

Overtop her, the prince exhaled roughly. Mireille managed to make a sound, not a particularly dignified one, and his grip on her slid from irons into something more like an embrace.

But his hold was not precisely what one might call gentle. "*Can you lie*, you ask me," he said, low against her ear. "*Can you lie?*" His fingers tightened for one instant against her bare arm then disappeared from her skin entirely. "As you masquerade before me, nothing but lies and deceit tied to a wire crown."

She barely had time for confusion to settle in before he was standing over her, staring down like she had betrayed both the man himself and his kingdom.

"This entire time, the bargain, the storytelling, all of it a ruse to get beneath my roof. And for what? To buy favor from the queen? Did you think I would not know? The seal on that door was formed by my own magic. Not a single fae might break through, except one as powerful as I, a royal. Did you think I would never guess? That by merely walking through that boundary you would not reveal your ties to *her*?"

Her, Mireille's mind repeated. *A royal.* He thought her in league with the queen. It was no wonder had offered her no trust.

Mireille rolled smoothly onto her feet, the way she'd been taught as a girl, ready to defend herself, to fight her way out of whatever sort of tussle she was about to be in. Because if her frantic heart and panicked limbs wanted anything, it was to act, to release the fear and emotion that had been trapped within. It did not matter that it was not the prince who had caused her situation. "A ruse?" she said. "You think this was a jape? A little lark for a bored princess with nothing else to do?"

"Clearly I do not think it a jest. I think it an act of treason."

Her hands balled into fists as her voice raised, any hint at discretion having deserted. "Treason? This has naught to do with you, or your kingdom. My only desire has been to save myself and my own people."

He leaned forward, voice a dagger. "Her magic is all over you."

Mireille's mouth came open to explain, to reveal what a monster the queen truly was, but before a word could escape, Thomas burst into the room.

Hair disheveled and collar askew, one arm braced against the door frame, the other positioned in a way that may have appeared it was securing his breeches, Thomas stood, his wide eyes darting from Mireille to the prince, then the blade on the floor.

The prince shot a look at Mireille that held something of shock and, possibly, accusation. It was then, she thought, that he realized what she was wearing.

Mireille flicked a meaningful glance at Thomas but he apparently had no intention of quitting the room. "He guards my door," she said defensively. "To prevent... nighttime wandering."

"Well, it was certainly well done of you," the prince snapped.

Thomas straightened.

"Don't—" Mireille started but before she was able to speak further, to describe the magic that came over anyone while the spellbound Mireille was in the room and how Thomas had done all he could in such a situation, the prince was well into another tirade.

"Coming here to trespass and what—rummage through our libraries? Is that what you looked for? An answer to some riddle of hers? And what choice do I have in the matter? I must, against my wishes, entertain these bargains—these utterly foolish offers— endlessly. All because of a single curse. Because of one fool act in one fool court." He carried on, his fury a rumble of power through the room. "I knew not to trust it. So eager to wed a prince. And now here you stand, your ties to her as clear as that fetching smile and capti- vating gaze my court goes on and on about. As if I cannot see with my own eyes. As if I need reminding." Mireille resisted the impulse to feel even remotely flattered. The prince shook his head once, swift and sharp. "All of you, Westrende and beyond, inventing your stories to scare children, warnings of how the fae are so scheming and devious, nothing but trickery. When it is you, in every single instance, every opportunity made or stolen, doing wrong by *us*." His gaze snapped to hers, angry and expectant.

She crossed her arms, realized it was not the thing to do in a thin shirt, then dropped them again. "I bargained with you as fairly as any fae. I have not once told a lie." At his incredulous look, she amended, "To you." And then, "About this."

He scoffed.

Her voice dipped. "Had I any other choice, trust that I would have taken it." When he showed no sign of relenting, no interest her explanations, she could not help but add a sharp, "You speak to me of your innocence while you hold Westrende prisoners under your very roof."

He moved toward her like the snap of a sail in storm winds. "You speak to me of captives as you gave yourself to us willingly."

"You."

His face pinched. "What?"

"I gave myself to *you*."

He drew back, a fraction of the heat seeming to drain from his posture. His throat moved in a swallow, but his tone did not entirely gentle. "Why was I not told of your connection to her?"

"It is not what you think. I have no bargain with the queen. I am here only to save my people. She wants Norcliffe." And she wanted Mireille.

His expression darkened. "You expect me to trust you. Knowing you walked through that door and—and—" He glanced at the paper knife in evident disgust. "You brought her into my palace."

Mireille ran a hand over her arm, then glanced at Thomas, who stood in silent support. "It was my hope that she could not reach me here. And I never suspected a door secured by magic could be opened by my own hands, so I certainly did not expect that she... that we would end up in your suite. She's never... I didn't realize her power ran so deep. I believed it was only the other entrances we needed to worry about, ones not sealed by magic. We covered the hidden panel as soon as we discovered it the night before."

The prince's reply swift, his words for Mireille but a good deal of his anger aimed unfairly at Thomas. "This has happened before?" When she didn't answer, he leaned in, voice low. "You are under my protection."

It was not simply her trespass, but his vow that had him so angry, then. If his guest was not kept safe, he would be breaking an ancient fae tenant. Mireille did not think that could be helped, but if she was able, she would give him an out. "This is my burden. It has nothing to do with you and I will not ask another to bear it."

He straightened, his manner never so princely as in that moment. "If the burden was truly yours alone, then your man need not sleep at your feet like a dog."

Mireille flinched.

Thomas moved forward, clearly prepared to defend his position, but Alder raised a hand in warning. The prince said, "This discussion is over. I will oversee these... nighttime wanderings myself." His fingers flicked a dismissal and, without another word, he turned his back on the pair.

481

CHAPTER 7

The prince's words had felt like a slap. It hadn't mattered that Thomas had vowed to protect her of his own free will, that protecting her was a step toward protecting their kingdom. It was that Thomas and every other person who cared for Mireille and for Norcliffe were made to suffer because of what the fae queen was trying to do. It was that nothing could be done to stop it.

Alder did not owe Mireille kindness or understanding. She knew that. She'd entered his bedchamber, kept her secret from him and, though she hadn't realized it possible, had put him at risk from the queen's magic. But she could not let go of the fact that Alder, too, was fae. Fae, like the queen who had destroyed everything, mercilessly tearing the future from everyone Mireille loved.

He could not be trusted. No fae could. And yet, she felt ill at her own part in all of it. She tossed and turned, sending Thomas back to his own rooms, and by the time morning came, Mireille was a wretched mess. She had to make it work, had to find a way past their distrust, to melt his defenses. And she had a mere month to do it.

She'd managed only to don a gown and get her hair in decent order when there was a sharp knock at her chamber door. It was not the knock she'd grown accustomed to from Noal, so she crossed to the entrance to open it instead of calling out. When she did, the prince stared back at her.

He did not appear to have weathered the night as poorly. He was just as handsome and put together as always.

Mireille inclined her head. "Your Highness."

His jaw ticked, presumably at her formality. He bowed, then held forward his arm.

Mireille only looked at the proffered limb.

He cleared his throat. "I am willing to answer at least one of the many concerns you have brought to my attention. If it pleases you."

His tone made clear he meant something more along the lines of *that you have badgered me with incessantly since you arrived, and in fact, on several occasions, used to doubt my character* instead of *brought to my attention.* Or some such intimation, Mireille wasn't certain.

She straightened. "It does please me." In fact, she would have liked answers to all her concerns, but more than that, she needed any time he would give her. Grabbing a shawl Thomas had managed to obtain from a member of the staff, Mireille tucked her hand into the crook of the prince's arm and closed the door behind them.

At the end of the corridor, he led her down a wide flight of stairs that opened into a massive chamber, then through several more corridors cooled by the shade of endless creeping vines. The walk carried on for so long that she was sure it must be as far as possible from the entrance to the palace. When they finally slowed at a large archway that opened into an atrium, Mireille had the unsettling sensation of realizing her assumptions were in fact very, very wrong.

She stared across the space at a figure that appeared to be dressed in the uniform jacket of Westrende red and gold. The man's legs were stretched out before him, boots polished to a shine. There was a thick book in his hand, and a glass of amber liquid resting on the small table beside him.

Mireille's gaze shot to the prince.

"Go on," he said. "Speak with him."

The words were plain enough. Mireille was meant to satisfy her concerns so that she might never accuse him again. She swallowed down her reply, stepping forward into the open room.

As she approached, she took in the scene. Sunlight streaming through a tall window was cut by palm leaves, throwing long lines of shadow across the man and the plush golden chair. His hair was golden as well, bright and clean, the trim of his silk suit straight and fine, his flesh appearing not only undamaged but full with health. All of this came as a surprise, not because she'd come across the man in a fine fae palace, but because the man in question was *human*. A prisoner.

He was a Westrende official. Mireille had met the man at a long ago function. She stopped before his chair, her breath caught in her chest, and he glanced up distractedly from his book.

"Lord Cadby."

"Princess," he said with a shocked smile. "What a joy it is to see you!" He began to stand, but his expression fell. He glanced anxiously through the room. "No," he said, "it would not be a joy, would it? Has Norcliffe been taken? Are your people well?"

Mireille knelt at his feet. "Cadby, how long have you been here?"

His bright brown eyes returned to her. "Two years now? I'm afraid it's hard to say. Things were a bit fuzzy for a while. Got into trouble, made some bad trades."

"A fae bargain? That's why you're here?"

Lord Cadby frowned. "It is, Highness. And there are more of us, still. Lords and ladies of Westrende, officers of the court, anyone of noble blood or with ties to a would-be king. I pray that is not how it happened for you."

"Something of the sort." She glanced toward the archway, but Alder's face was too shadowed to clearly make out. "I have an arrangement with the prince. I must become his bride by the turn of the moon, or break our agreement and join you and the others as a prisoner."

Lord Cadby breathed out a curse and leaned forward to take her hand. "Oh, Highness."

"Norcliffe has been under siege from a greater foe than him. And I'm afraid, my lord, that should our venture fail, it will not be my life alone at risk."

He whispered, "What can I do?"

"I need whatever information you can provide of the workings of fae bargains, any weakness of the prince, how we can use the magic that holds together the Rive in a way that might help protect our own kingdom. We are desperate for any scrap of knowledge that might break the fae's hold on Norcliffe."

He squeezed her hand. "I fear it is not so simple. The prince is tied by the Rive, and his kingdom is tied to him. The fae are divided as much as any kingdom. His court trapped, and the queen's court working to keep them that way." He shot a glance through the room, then leaned closer. "If the Rive comes down, the court of Rivenwilde will be in danger. It protects them as much as it keeps them caged."

"But that is what he wants. The prince has claimed to desire nothing more than to be set free."

"No," he said. In the archway, Alder stepped from the shadows, and Lord Cadby released Mireille's hand. "I don't trust him, Highness, I don't. But there is more going on than we've been told. Something else binds him as well."

Mireille had the same feeling, because despite their betrothal, the prince did not seem to want her too near. Mireille recalled his words from the night before, how one fool act in one fool court evidently led to him having to entertain offers of marriage. She wondered how many princesses were being held within the palace. She wondered whether they sat in sunshine reading books, or if they had met a fate far worse.

She stood. "Thomas is with me. I will send him to you. We will see what might be done to return you home."

Lord Cadby shook his head. "It's too late for that. And, though I don't deserve your kindness, I hope that you'll grant me leave to offer my support."

Mireille drew a steadying breath. "I would count myself lucky to have it."

MIREILLE HAD, perhaps, discovered the prince was not as ruthless as he seemed, but she did not say so on their return. He was still holding citizens of Westrende captive, bargain or no. He was still fae.

She still had to marry him.

He left to attend court business and Mireille, alone while Thomas did his best to investigate the goings on with the palace staff, wandered through the palace.

She traversed the corridors and climbed the grand stair, feeling turned around and out of sorts by the palace's layout. It was as if the rooms shifted about her, and she could never quite place where she was meant to be. When she turned the corner into a wide hall scattered with columns, Mireille's steps faltered.

Across the hall rose a pair of massive doors, seemingly carved out of the same strange stone that made up the filigree wall. Unlike the boundary wall, the doors revealed no glamour, only a pale polished surface carved into scenes from what Mireille could only imagine was very long ago. Their beauty drew her nearer, but with an undeniable sense of unease. There was something terrible about the carved figures; while a marvel of craftsmanship, their subjects were too real, their torment and anger palpable.

A rearing horse rose tall, its foreleg reaching off the surface and its eyes rolled wide. The man on its back was barely visible, but he, at least appeared human, face a rictus, longsword in hand. Fae warriors surrounded him, their magic seeming to tingle over Mireille's skin. She did not want to touch the doors, exactly, but she could not seem to prevent her hand from lifting, her palm expecting cool stone but finding only warmth.

The door eased open beneath her touch. Mireille swallowed and drew her hand free. Her tingling fingers curled into her palms, and her heart beat a warning in her ears. Still, her feet moved forward, into the darkness waiting on the other side.

A shaft of light cut through the space, leading her onward. The echo of her footfalls sounded far away, and the focus of the room was farther than any palace ballroom or hall Mireille had yet seen.

She did not cross it. Because over the dark stone floor was a fracture that rent the room. Stones rose beside it, jagged and uneven, their edges sharp. Blackness was all that could be seen in the space between, like a chasm despite that, surely, there would be rooms below. On the other side of the room, at the end of the split, was the Riven Court throne. It, too, was jagged and broken, its majestic spires incongruent and off-kilter, the light and shadows only making the scene worse.

A prickle ran down her spine. Very little was known of the magic that had split the kingdom of Westrende from that of the fae. Mireille was a royal, and as such usually afforded more details, but even she had been able to uncover aught else. It was said that the thrones of Westrende and Rivenwilde were tied, and while rumor vowed ill-luck was all that had prevented a new king from rising to power in Westrende, Mireille's friends seemed to think it was something more.

In Westrende, investigations into the illnesses and accidents that had stalled eligible bloodlines from coming into power had led only to dead ends. Lord Cadby had told her other royals were being held, anyone with bloodlines related to the king, and Thomas had reported hints from the fae that the prince was bound by more than simply bargains.

Alder had said he was trapped. Westrende was quietly losing kingdom officials.

Mireille ran a sweat-slicked palm over her skirt. She had witnessed very much the same sort of events in her own kingdom, at the hands of a fae queen. Perhaps she had misjudged much more than she knew.

A far-off bang echoed through the room, recalling Mireille of the dangers of exploring a fae palace. She backed toward the door, then let herself out, willing her pulse to steady.

Hours later, Mireille sat alone before a wide balcony with a luncheon of pastries worrying her lip. It was unlikely that Lord Cadby's warning and the information Thomas had discovered were unrelated. But she would have to uncover the missing connections herself. She had decided to attempt the library once more when a slender mink leapt onto the balcony railing. Mireille let out a small, startled sound, certain the creature had not been there before..

It was a great distance to the ground below the balcony. Perhaps it had had been hiding near one of the water features. The mink stared back at her. Mireille sighed. "Never mind me. I feel as if I'm losing my senses, the way the décor seems to shift and creatures appear from nowhere around here."

The mink gave Mireille the sort of a look that might have been an eye roll from another creature. It raised onto its hindquarters and licked its paw as if it had no further interest in her, but when Mireille made to stand, the air shimmered around the creature. In the next blink, the mink was gone. In its spot stood the prince's sister.

Mireille sat heavily back into her seat. She lifted a hand, but it sort of hovered there, unsure what action might make the event she just witnessed disappear from existence as Nisha watched her. Mireille wasn't certain she'd understood such a transformation was possible, even if she knew the immense power of the fae.

The prince's sister crossed the space, the diaphanous hem of her ivory gown swirling in her wake, then, giving the tray of almond pastries an unimpressed glance, took the seat opposite Mireille. Though she had been fur-covered only moments before, her fae hair was perfectly coifed, held back from her face by a series of small braids laced with silver wire and tiny gems. There were no twigs or leaves clinging to her as had in their last meeting, nor any sign of the outrage she had expressed toward her brother.

In fact, she seemed entirely at ease. Brushing a bit of fluff from her fingernail, she picked up the slender table knife from the tray and began to tool at the edge of it. "I can see you're surprised. Not every fae walks through shadows." She blew a puff of breath on the nail. "That's more of a Riven Court talent, and my mother was of the Storm Court."

Mireille attempted composure. "Is every fae of the Storm Court able to shift as you do?"

Nisha's dark eyes rose to Mireille in an unflattering manner that reminded Mireille far too much of the prince. "Do you know nothing of the fae? Truly?"

"How would I?"

She lowered the utensil. "Are we to believe you are entirely unaware of the fae who glamour their way into Westrende?"

"No," Mireille said. "Indeed, I was aware of glamour. But those are human forms. Only a trick of the light." Mireille startled at the bark of laughter that escaped her companion. She took up her cup for a careful sip of tea, and a moment to think, before settling the cup back onto its saucer. "So, fae can alter their forms as well as use glamour."

Nisha leaned forward, gesturing loosely with the knife while she spoke. "You are from a royal family. You must understand power. Yet, you bargain yourself away to a prince and know nothing of his magic." She shook her head and speared the knife into a block of cheese.

Mireille's gaze drifted toward the knife. She found she did not like that it remained within reach. "It is not as if you make it easy. I have done nothing but search for knowledge of that very kind."

"In books?" Nisha scoffed. "In Rivenwilde's own library?" She eased back against her chair. "I thought better of you, Princess. Truly."

"Strange that you would think of me at all."

The corner of Nisha's lip rose slightly. "You are a princess, are you not? Perhaps with the aim of becoming a queen." Her tone made it clear she did not regard Mireille's title as it was, let alone the absurd notion she might become queen.

"The prince is your brother. Is your situation so dissimilar to mine?"

Nisha took up a pastry and tore it in half, but didn't eat it. "Fae titles are bestowed by the land, not the people. A prince of Rivenwilde may only ever be prince while his lands are torn apart. The boundary prevents his power from reaching past the walls. Why do you think the Rive was created in the first place? Why do you think we so badly want it down?"

Mireille fought to keep her expression neutral. Nisha had given her more answers in a moment's conversation than she and Thomas had been able to secure in days. The prince was caged, the Rive keeping his power in check. He could never be king while the boundary still stood, never access the full power of the land. While he had been trapped, the fae queen had been snatching up the surrounding lands, doing her best to steal and conquer. She had only grown in power, all while the prince was confined... and searching for a princess, one he did not seem to want to marry.

Mireille wondered what would happen if he ever got free. She wondered if it was already too late.

Nisha wrinkled her nose and dropped the pastry onto a plate without having taken a bite.

"What will happen when the Rive falls?" Mireille dared to ask.

Nisha's lips curled coyly. Mireille found she liked the woman much better as a mink. "Now, Princess, fae affairs are not within your purview. I would advise you to think twice before making such inquiries." As she stood, her gaze swept over Mireille. "I will leave you with one last morsel of advice. Whatever game you are trying to play in the Riven Court, you will lose. I suggest you play no games at all, particularly where my brother is concerned." Then the air shimmered and Nisha was once again animal. She turned, her sleek body gliding out of sight the way she had come.

Mireille stared at the space the fae had occupied, thoughts swimming. Every conversation since she'd arrived left her with more questions than answers. And answers were the reason she had come.

CHAPTER 8

Mireille's dinners with the prince had not gone as she had hoped. As he sat silent and stony at the far end of the long table, unreceptive to conversation, the time slipping away weighed on Mireille's every decision. If she could reclaim the moment they'd had in the ballroom, she might have a chance, but it seemed to have only served to fuel his determination to avoid her.

There had been no further mention of the incident in his quarters, though she had noticed when she'd changed for dinner that someone had removed her own paper knife and anything else pointy from her room.

She considered Nisha's warning about playing games. Such had never been her intention, but she supposed it was not so different than the games of any court. Except Mireille had no idea what the opposing party actually wanted. It was a considerable disadvantage.

Alder's every action made clear he had no intention of encouraging a wife. At the rate things were going, she suspected he might prefer she choose to break their bargain instead.

It felt impossible, and yet she could not surrender.

"Tell me about the marriage ceremony."

At her abrupt statement, Alder's gaze shot up to meet hers. Even across the distance, long table between them, his full attention made Mireille feel exposed. He said, "What matter are the details?"

She lowered her chin. "Should I not be concerned with the potentialities of my future?"

A muscle jumped in his neck beneath his high collar. It seemed she had hit another nerve. The man must be entirely made of nerves. "Any information you require will be provided before the ceremony." His attention returned to his plate, a clear dismissal.

She pursed her lips. If they were playing a game, she was losing. "About tonight, when I am sleeping—"

"I will see to it, as I've said."

Given that the *it* he referred to was her being puppeted by a fae queen's magic, Mireille found she could not so easily accept its dismissal. "Exactly how do you intend *to see to it*?"

She managed to keep her tone even, but the prince's fingers flexed where he held a fork. His dark eyes slowly lifted, pinning her to the spot. "If you wander, I will *see to it* that you are contained."

Mireille's lips parted. "Contained?"

He dropped his gaze. Again.

"Is there some part of you that truly believes I will let such a comment go unchallenged?"

"You will be protected."

"I am asking you how." She pressed her palms flat on the table, aware that she was not entirely gaining ground in her plans to melt the prince's heart. "Can you not imagine why I would be concerned with the details, what it is like to have your will stolen, to know that that any moment you might be walked through a window into the open night air and unable to stop it?" She shook her head. "You'll forgive me if your offer of containment is no great comfort."

When his gaze lifted again, it tracked her posture, her flushed cheeks, and his expression softened. His words, however, remained a disappointment. "You are protected. I will protect you. There is no further explanation I can offer."

She let out a light huff of laughter, spurring him where she might since he was not willing to give. "If you want to forgo sleep to watch my every movement, then so be it. At least Thomas will finally be allowed a night's rest."

MIREILLE LAY awake in the center of her massive bed, dreading midnight. The queen would come for her, the way she always did, but this time, the prince would be waiting. She told herself it couldn't be worse than what had happened in the prince's rooms, her own hand driving a blade toward her heart then the prince knocking her to the ground to hold her there, but she knew it wasn't true. It could be far, far worse.

Despite those fears and against her will, when the weight of the queen's magic drifted into the room, Mireille sank into sleep. Her last thoughts were that Thomas, who had refused to leave her room, would keep her safe. There was no need for Alder's protection. All would be well.

At first, she slept fitfully, hovering on the edge of wakefulness and plagued by scenes she could not quite grasp. Flashes of her mother, her father, memories from when she'd been only a girl. Then she dreamed of walking outside the Rivenwilde palace, in the lane bordered with orange trees. The soft scent tickled her throat, reminding her of the white blossom Alder had gifted her in a rare moment of kindness. But had it truly been kindness? She was trapped in an impossible position, and he seemed intent on keeping his secrets.

Dream Mireille studied the night-darkened blossoms, lamenting her fate, when a low whisper sounded in her ear. "My princess, things are not so unfortunate as you suppose. All you have suffered will be answered for, your every wish gratified."

She spun to face the source. It was a woman's voice, softly accented, and somehow an assurance. Nothing like the wicked queen. Then another voice, one like the prince's, a caress against her skin, though he was nowhere in sight. "Do not try to find me out, no matter how I may be disguised, for what you find will be your undoing."

In the dream, Mireille shot up in bed, a warning in the woman's voice echoing in her mind as true as the beat of her heart. "Do not trust your eyes. Do not let yourself be deceived." The words seemed to beg her to save the prince from cruel misery, shadows woven through every one.

The door to the prince's room was closed, but midnight was near. He would be listening on the other side, waiting for her to roam. Thomas stretched out on the floor in front of the main door, and furniture was blocking the hidden panel. She was safe, safer than she had been in a long while. So why did the pounding of her heart disagree?

Midnight had come, and Mireille had not risen from her bed.

Something was wrong, though. As the shadows cleared, the room felt suddenly eerie and unfamiliar. The entire space was lit with the dim glow of moonlight, too bright, as if the moon had lowered itself to peer through her window.

Thomas was not in his spot by the door, it was only a lump of fabric. Mireille's fingers curled into the bedding, only to release when she realized they were clad in soft gloves. She wore a sage gown, one that might have been appropriate in Westrende were she playing the part of a proper princess in search of a husband.

Attention so thoroughly on her state of dress, Mireille startled when she became aware Alder had appeared beside her bed. She flinched back from his proffered hand, unsure if it was some new trick by the fae queen. The unnatural moonlight gilded his sharp features, his expression impassive, more like himself and less of the version that had appeared in her earlier dream.

"Mireille," he said, hand still extended.

Her eyes narrowed at the gentle way he said her name, but the fine line above his brow was plain to see. There was no indication that it was not truly the prince. He seemed so very tired.

Fighting the tremble in her fingers, she placed her gloved hand into his, then climbed from her bed, sliding her feet into silk slippers that matched the dress. Whatever was happening, she would soon find out.

Alder led her from the room, and she went with him silently. Had she wanted to question him, she was not certain she could. For the first time, the queen had not come for her. A fae prince had instead.

"HOW ARE YOU DOING THIS?"

Mireille watched as Alder's long fingers traced the leaves of a wisteria tree, its trailing blooms quaking in the soft night breeze. He had led her there through a maze of gardens that surely would not be safe for her to journey alone. The unnatural glow of moonlight had followed, allowing her to see more clearly than true night might allow.

Alder brushed a purple blossom with the tip of a finger. "She can only reach you while you are sleeping because your subconscious is unoccupied. Here, however, I may influence you as well."

"And where is here?"

He didn't look at her. "In your dreams."

"Well, that is terrifically unsettling." She felt her brow furrow. "And while you are with me..."

"She is not."

So the prince must occupy her dreams to keep the queen at bay. *Contained*, he had said. She supposed it was preferable to anything else she might have imagined. But she wondered at the broken way she'd drifted at first, and how much of a battle it might have been.

"She cannot reach us here?"

"Not when I am present."

Mireille nodded, hoping it was true. "Then I must tell you."

He turned to her.

"It is not just I under the thrall of the queen. It began slowly, with messengers, courtiers, kitchen staff. Every night, citizens of Norcliffe fell under her spell. Every night, someone or something becomes a risk." She did not add, *to me*. She swallowed, hating the way the words tasted, hating that she was helpless to stop it. "The queen desires to end me and end my kingdom. I came here to find a way to save myself and to save Norcliffe. The truth of the matter is, we had nowhere else to turn."

Alder stared at her for a long moment, as if weighing her words. They were sincere, even if she had not told him everything, even if she *could* not.

He said, "I gave my vow. You are under my protection and will remain so as long as you remain inside these walls."

He did not offer to extend that protection to her kingdom, but she would take what she could get. She glanced at the surrounding garden, the wisteria tree at its center. If the entire court felt alive, the garden was its beating heart. Every bloom and leaf breathed with magic, their stems seeming to dance, pulsing with the power that was Rivenwilde. The power that lived through its prince. "Why bring me here?"

Transfixed by their surroundings, she again started when Alder gently gripped her wrist. He led her beneath the wisteria tree, only stopping at its base. Alder slid the glove from Mireille's hand, then guided it to trace the rough patterns of the ancient bark, another maze, but one to be walked with fingertips. Her heart thundered at his gentle touch, so much more real than anything she had felt in a dream before, then his touch was gone, leaving her to continue tracing the aged trunk alone. Warmth seeped into her fingertips, but she could not bring herself to draw them away. It was unquestionably fae magic, but not like she'd ever experienced before. The tree felt, impossibly, like Norcliffe.

Like home.

She released a breath, and the prince said, "The wisteria is a direct connection to one's kin." He was so close behind her that his chest brushed her shoulder, his words a feather against her ear. "You said you were worried about your family. All you must do is touch this tree, and you will know that they are well."

Mireille did not know if the prince was offering her a kindness or simply bowing to the rules of hospitality after she mentioned her unhappiness. But the tree felt so much of home, providing a sensation of comfort that, somehow, she truly believed her kingdom had not yet fallen.

"Does it please you?" He had shifted away from her, his words more distant.

"Yes," Mireille said, her palm against the tree, heart swelling with warmth. Norcliffe and her father were running out of time, she knew, in danger because of the very fae queen that Alder had believed Mireille had willingly allied with, the one who had followed her to Rivenwilde.

But while he might still be fae, Mireille could not fault him for what the queen had done. She began to turn, getting out only the word, "Thank—" before she gasped, sitting up in bed.

Thomas was stretched out on the floor before the main door, asleep. The doorway to the prince's chamber was sealed. Mireille swiped a gloveless palm across her forehead, then let out a shaky breath. It had only been a dream; she'd never left the bed at all. And yet, the memory of bark beneath her fingertips and Alder's whispered words lingered on her skin.

CHAPTER 9

Mireille spent the next morning peering out every window of the palace. If she could spot the purple of wisteria blossoms, or even the path they had taken to find it, then she could be certain the dream had been real. Never mind how real it felt, when the queen had come for her, it was always only to direct her actions. Alder had somehow reached Mireille more deeply, but he had not taken her thoughts or her will.

For his part, Thomas had slept the night through and could offer no additional clues. But the staff had been helpful in other areas of their search, revealing scraps of information regarding previous kings and queens and how they had been bound, so he hoped to gain more as the fae prepared for the week's events. She'd had to swear to Thomas that she would not leave the castle in search of proof before he left to seek out more members of the staff.

Deciding she might have better luck from a higher vantage, Mireille climbed a narrow flight of stairs at the end of the corridor. Her stomach sank when she crested the stairs only to find the double doors that she'd encountered the day before. She spun, certain it was not possible that the corridor where she stood connected to the staircase she'd used the previous day, but where the narrow stairwell that she had just climbed had been, was a different one—one she had not climbed. Mireille ran to the bottom, finding the entrance hall, its elaborate carvings seeming to peer down at her, more threatening than they had been before. Feet light on the marble floor, she ran toward the west wing until she was breathless, then took another stair to the next floor. The massive doors loomed in front of her once more. She ran again, to the third floor, and higher. But every staircase she topped, every corridor she turned, led her back to the throne room, as if the palace meant to send her a message.

Mireille stepped back, nearly falling on the top step of the grand staircase. A fae woman watched her from the hall, taking a bite of a small, misshapen apple. The wet crunch echoed through the space.

Abandoning entirely her plan to find the wisteria tree or any single thing on the upper floors, Mireille came down the staircase, striding past the fae woman without a word. At her back, laughter echoed over the marble. Mireille did not care.

Safely away long enough to catch her breath, her heart resuming its pulse, Mireille perched on a stone windowsill. The large glass pane revealed a flower garden, its bright blooms playing host to abundant butterflies. The sun was beginning to set, casting warm color across the greenery. It was a picturesque sight, but not one she had seen in the dream the night before.

A throat cleared behind her. Mireille turned, half dread at the prospect of another encounter with a fae, but it was only Noal.

Her shoulders relaxed, and she resumed her study of the garden's butterflies. "It is beautiful here. I quite regret not being able to explore the grounds and the kingdom farther."

"That is precisely why I've found you," Noal said. When her attention returned to him, he explained, "Because you cannot attend our festivals outside his protection, the prince would like Rivenwilde brought to you."

She eyed him skeptically. "This was the prince's request?"

Noal's lips parted. He smiled. "The actions of the palace staff reflect directly on the prince, Your Highness. Our job is to anticipate his wishes. All we do is at his request, in a manner of speaking."

· · ·

THEY WALKED through several corridors that did not seem to shift, and Mireille resisted the urge to glance back to be certain they remained once she had passed. But when Noal led her into the courtyard, all her unease was forgotten. She gasped, and she could not be ashamed of it.

From the center of a massive archway draped in vining roses, their blooms as big as her outstretched hand, Mireille took in a scene that might have come out of a fanciful painting. Fae in colorful gowns danced among the foliage, playing games and acting out melodramas and enjoying general revelries. A small orchestra performed the most beautiful melody, and the scents of flowers and food filled the air. Sculptures rose through the greenery between a maze of pathways, colored ribbons strung from column to column, and laughter echoed from beyond the shrubbery where a picnic had been laid over the ground.

It was a delight. A festival on palace grounds.

"There you are," Nisha said, suddenly beside them. "What took so long? We had to start dancing without her."

"She was exploring the palace."

Noal's reply held no particular tone, but Nisha's attention shifted consideringly to Mireille. She took Mireille's arm. "Come, Princess. Let us introduce you to the best of the Riven Court before my brother finds out. Do you sing, perchance?"

THAT EVENING, after Mireille had been returned to her room and had washed the fruit from her hands and paint from her cheeks, Noal appeared at her door.

"I suppose you are here to inform me of some pressing business of the prince, and that it would perhaps be best that I dine alone in my room?"

His chin dipped in acknowledgement. "The prince is indeed very busy and has sent me to inform you of such." No hint of the afternoon's festivities remained on his person, but something mischievous danced in his eyes. "I find, in fact, that I would be remiss in my duty should I not encourage you to avoid his highness's study at all costs."

"At all costs, you say?"

He laced his arms behind his back, rocking a bit on his heels. "Truly, the prince's study would be the last place he would want you to dine."

She narrowed her eyes. "Acting in anticipation of his wishes, I see." Mireille wasn't certain why Noal was making such attempts to bring her and the prince closer, but she could use all the help she could get, even if she didn't trust anything that brought joy to the expression of a fae.

"I am sure I do not know what you mean," he said.

Mireille nodded. "Very well. I agree it would be the height of presumption to invade the prince's study when he's in such great need of privacy. I thank you for your advice."

He inclined his head before turning to walk the corridor. Mireille thought she heard the echo of a whistled tune when he rounded the corner, but she was already up from her seat and on the way to her wardrobe to prepare. The prince had raised the stakes the night before, bringing her safety in her dreams. She needed to prove she was worth his efforts.

She needed to be certain he would let her in.

AT PRECISELY NINE, Mireille surprised Alder by knocking on his study door.

"Since you've been so reluctant to abandon your princely obligations, which is honorable, truly, I thought I should make it as effortless as possible for you to fulfill your duties as host." She strode past him into the room.

Alder stared at her, frozen in his place at the doorway. He made no mention of the dream, but she did not think he would, real or not. He had come to her in her bedchamber and imagined her a Westrende gown. Mireille suspected those were things a prince of Rivenwilde would not admit even upon the threat of death.

Safely inside and a good distance past, she turned to face him. "So, I will take dinner here, with you." Her tone brooked no argument, but he did appear as if he had one at the ready. Mireille smiled. "Alder."

His brow lowered. "Why do I imagine Noal will not need to be ordered to bring a second plate?"

"He is very clever, I'm certain he'll sort it out." She glanced around the room, looking for something, *anything* to redirect their conversation. She refused to let one more night go by without learning something useful or breaking down his walls. Her gaze caught on a stack of books atop a side table. "Do you read often?" The beginnings of a civil conversation, at the least, even if she felt a bit like a ninny asking in the middle of his personal library.

"When necessary."

Her gaze shot back to him, where he stood suddenly close. Not menacingly, exactly, but her pulse picked up a beat. She said, "Surely you enjoy at least some activities that aren't strictly necessary. Or do you only find satisfaction brooding alone in your dark study?"

A look of genuine surprise crossed his face. It did not last long. "I do not *brood*. I have never."

She had to bite down a smile. "Highness, I daresay it is one of your most finely honed talents."

"What would you know of my talents?"

He was baiting her, she knew it. She shrugged. "If you have any others, they have not been demonstrated thus far."

A noise came from deep within his throat. "And what talents have you to speak of?"

Mireille had sparred with nobles before, and she knew the prince was quick, but a long-buried ember lit in her at his smug expression. She found she would like very much to wipe it from, at the very least, those lips.

There was a talent she could show him, one of her finest, and though it bore a high price, the game she was attempting had even higher stakes. She lifted her chin, swallowing the familiar sensation of grief tickling her throat. "I will show you, if you like. But I cannot do it here."

There was no disguising the surprise that flitted across his features.

She would have given nearly anything for Noal to interrupt them with dinner that very moment and relieve her from a show of boldness, but the corridor outside the study remained stubbornly silent.

The tickle in her throat grew to a lump as Alder offered his arm. Her hand nestled in the crook of his elbow, Alder gestured toward the door. "Lead the way."

His tone gave her courage. It was a dare, and if Mireille knew anything, it was that men on a gamble always had their tell.

SHE SAT at the piano she had discovered during their palace tour—the very one she had avoided. Gleaming instruments stood around them in silent witness, the blue and gold draperies nearly black in the moonlight. Looking down at the keys before her, Mireille took a shuddering breath. But Alder stood at her back, waiting, and she placed her fingers on the heavy ivory keys.

She could do it. It was only a simple song. She had done far more dangerous and daring things. Deciding on one she had played a hundred times before, she closed her eyes, but her fingers made a different choice.

Mireille nearly missed a note at the unexpected tune, one of the last songs she had played for her mother. It had been a favorite. But she did not falter, letting herself sink into the music, her fingers moving without thought, always just where they should be. The instrument was impeccable and her notes built to a devastating crescendo that echoed through the dark hall. She had needed this, she realized, so lost in the fae world with only Thomas to anchor her to everything she had left behind. She had needed the reminder of who she was, of what she had endured before and why it was so important to give her all. The song tapered off, its final notes a receding tide.

Swallowing back tears, she managed a casual, "There, do you still find me so talentless?"

When Alder did not reply, she looked back at him. He held her gaze, his dark eyes searching. He said not a word, but lifted his hand. She slid hers into it, their gazes locked. Moonlight cut a sharp line across his features, a stark reminder that he was wholly fae. But he only stood, keeping hold of her hand, his expression soft. She rose from the bench, her body seemingly drawn to his of its own will, her heart hammering in her throat. They were very close. They were very alone.

"Extraordinary," he breathed.

Her lips parted, and his eyes tracked the motion. Then, as if suddenly remembering himself, he turned and precisely tucked her hand into the crook of his arm.

Heat rose up Mireille's neck as he led her from the room without a word.

In the study, Noal and Kin hovered near a table perfecting two place settings.

Alder released Mireille from his arm, stiffly gesturing for her to enter. She no more than took a step inside, having given up discovering anything from the man after their encounter, when he cleared his throat, leaned in, and said, "I enjoy sculpture. And, it must be said, I am not terribly unskilled at it."

She spun to ask him more, but he was already disappearing down the corridor, leaving Mireille to dine alone.

She let him go.

Noal approached, his interest plain.

Forcing a smile, Mireille said, "I believe I will take my meal in my rooms after all." Eyes on the open doorway, she added, "But moving forward, this is where I will spend my evenings."

THOMAS EYED HER SKEPTICALLY. "He likes to *sculpt?*"

"Keep your voice down," she hissed, glancing at the sealed door into the prince's rooms, even though she doubted he was there.

Thomas whispered, "I don't see how we can use this."

"I will take anything at this point." If Alder could only soften to her, to open up a bit, she might feel able to reveal precisely what she needed.

Thomas lifted a brow. "Fortunately, I have learned something a little more helpful."

She sat forward. "Tell me."

"I persuaded Kin to attain a proper wardrobe for you."

Mireille glanced at the wardrobe, but her mind was on the sage green gown that Alder had, possibly, dreamed for her.

"But that is not the interesting part. Mid-undertaking, Kin hinted that the prince has bindings placed on him, and I do not mean by the existence of the Rive. Bindings separate from the curse, not on the land, but on the prince himself."

"Are you certain that was her meaning?"

"Yes, because she was vehemently reluctant to reveal more, and I believe it's connected to the fae queen herself."

"Our fae queen?"

"The very one. It must have something to do with why he accepts any willing princess into his kingdom. It cannot be a coincidence one queen is entangled with you both."

She straightened. "But that makes no sense. He cannot become king while the Rive stands. The boundary has him trapped. How would marrying a human princess change that?" If it could, he would have married long ago.

A hint of the confidence she hadn't seen in so long slid across Thomas's features. "Precisely. So what are the terms of the binding and how are they connected to the wedding bargain?"

Mireille stood to pace. Thomas was right. She should have been less worried about discovering their rules and law, and more worried about why the prince had agreed at all. "He said something about being forced to entertain the bargains. But if he has no true desire for a wife, why bring her into his home?"

Thomas leaned back into his chair.

The prince had vowed to protect Mireille. He had shared the wisteria tree. There must be a reason, something he stood to gain.

She just needed to discover what it was.

CHAPTER 10

The familiar weight of the fae queen's magic settled upon her once again and Mireille felt her body begin to rise from the bed. Then the heavy sensation suddenly disappeared, along with the sickly-sweet scent of hawthorn flower, and Mireille's eyes blinked open to the glow of unnatural moonlight that filled her room.

Alder stood over her, as if he'd been waiting.

Taking his proffered hand, Mireille swung her feet toward the edge of the bed, and realized the dress she wore was far different than the night before. Her free hand came up to the lace that curled at her neck, matching the butterfly sleeves and the lace that nearly covered her hands. It felt like... A wedding gown.

Had she conjured such a thing, or had it been him? Aghast, she met the prince's gaze, unsure which might be worse.

He made no comment, only turned to lead her from the room. They followed the same path as before, through the maze of gardens that surrounded the wisteria tree, but though her room was roughly the same in the dream as when awake, the corridors and paths never were.

The night air was warm, and fireflies danced amid the swaying greenery. In the distance, soft rain pattered against leaves. The gentle scent of wisteria clung to everything, its presence alone working to ease Mireille's distress. She said, "It is beautiful here."

Alder glanced down at her. "It is."

Mireille recalled that she had a purpose. No matter how seductive the idea of sinking into the peace the garden brought, she had to find her course. "Why do you wish to be free of it?" His brow lowered in confusion, and she asked, "Are these lands not enough for you?"

His lips tightened and it appeared he would not respond, then he turned abruptly to face her. "The land chooses its ruler. There is no *enough*. The land does not wish to be divided, and so I, as its prince, must find a way to unrend it, to destroy the curse that holds us within its walls."

She stepped closer, his figure in the moonlight somehow more imposing, yet he was not as icy and closed off as before. Mireille wasn't certain what had changed, but she had no interest in pretense. "What happens when the boundary falls? You will rise to king and the land will be satisfied? Or will it want more?" It was hard to imagine the Rive coming down as anything good, not when she had seen what an unbound queen was capable of. Part of her, a part she understood may not be entirely virtuous, wanted to keep them caged.

Alder's expression darkened. "You think me so power hungry?"

His tone sent a chill down her spine. Her shoulders drew back. It was only a dream. She would speak as she pleased. "You accepted my bargain with no apparent desire to have me as a wife. I was given to believe we would be wed, but it seems as if you only wish for me to break the bargain, so that you might add me to your collection of prisoners."

He stepped nearer. "What makes you think I have no intention of marrying you? Do you truly believe I would not honor my word?"

She craned her neck to look up at him. "You're evading the point. You have done nothing but attempt to keep distance between us. You want my choice to be a prisoner. Why else bring me to Lord Cadby and make clear that I would be choosing relative comfort? Why else not show me a single consideration above what is required by law of hospitality?"

He leaned in so that he looked her directly in the eye. "If being a prisoner of Rivenwilde sounds so preferable to being my wife, then perhaps your decision has already been made."

She released a growl of frustration. "Would you please cease answering my concerns with accusations."

The corner of his lips twisted in a manner that made Mireille uncomfortably aware of how churlish she was being. After a moment, he released a resigned breath. "I felt the fae queen's magic on you. That was why I agreed to the bargain. That is why I... held myself in reserve."

Mireille's own breath caught.

"I was not wrong," he added. "I will admit I never expected you to allow her into my home. But even before you entered my chambers, it was evident you had ties to her. As an ally, or a pawn, or a victim. I believed you the former."

The subtle swaying of the flora seemed to shift, as if agitated. Mireille asked, "And what is it that you believe now?"

He did not answer. It was answer enough. Alder believed she could be conspiring with the creature who had entirely destroyed her life. The one who had threatened her kingdom so thoroughly that she'd been left with no choice but to abandon her family and secure a bargain with a fae prince.

Her fists clenched tighter. "I am no ally or pawn, and though some have given it their best attempt, I am *no one's* victim. I have told you before, and I will say it again. Norcliffe is under threat. I stand before you now, in this—whatever this is—because of her."

He studied her face, then lifted a hand to pluck a leaf from her hair. She jolted when he reached toward her, and they both knew it. The bravado of her speech didn't change what a fae was capable of. But he was not the queen. He held the leaf for a moment between his fingertips, then let it fall to the ground.

He was using her as a tool to unbind his kingdom. She was using him to save her own. She could not have one without the other.

"Is any of this even real?" she asked.

"That depends how you define what is real. The garden is true, but we linger now in your dream. Your mind conjured the way your hair is styled, the gown you wear. Will it not persist in your memory? Does it not become part of your existence?"

Heat flushed her cheeks. The wedding gown certainly felt more significant knowing she was responsible for it. She would have somehow preferred it had been his conjuring. She said, "I suppose if it does not exist in the morning, then it is not truly real."

His fingers trailed across the lace covering her arm, and her traitorous body reacted to the touch, leaning nearer.

He said softly, "It feels real enough to me." But his gaze never met hers, instead shifting toward the moon in what was most certainly not a sky Mireille had imagined. "The midnight hour is far beyond us. Good night, Mireille."

She opened her mouth to protest, but darkness took her instead.

Mireille jolted; someone was standing over her where she lay in her bed. Her eyes flew open, her heart racing, but it was not the unnatural glow of a dream that lit her room, only lamplight.

Noal stared down at her, his dark eyes narrowed consideringly. He held a silver tray, its contents smelling of tea and freshly buttered toast. He said, "Forgive the intrusion but it's onto midday. If we were to wait any longer, you would not have time to prepare."

From his spot on the settee, Thomas lifted a toast point. "I told him to let you sleep."

She swiped a palm across her face. She could not remember ever lying in so long when she wasn't ill. She looked back to Noal. "And what am I to prepare for?"

"There's to be a ball," he explained. "Kin is here to assist you."

Mireille only then noticed the woman standing near the bathing chamber door. "So you were all three just... waiting for me to wake?"

Noal set the tray on a bedside table and gave her a meaningful look. "You'll need to be rested for what's to come."

When he quit the room, Mireille looked to Thomas, who only shrugged. "You know as much as I."

Kin frowned at them both, but made no effort to communicate additional information.

Mireille picked up a piece of toast, but her stomach turned, still haunted by the dream. The prince had thought she'd been in league with the queen and had still brought her into his home. For what, she didn't know. Perhaps to get closer to the queen. Perhaps something darker. Her gaze lifted to meet Thomas's, desperate to share what she had learned. But his gaze was on Kin. And Kin's was on Mireille's hand where it clutched her dressing gown.

A quarter hour later, Thomas was gone and Mireille was chin-deep in a hot bath, the prince's words running through her mind again and again. Kin placed a stack of towels and a jar of oil on the small table beside the tub. The door to the bathing chamber eased open and Kin absently lifted a foot to press it closed. Something low and dark wandered in, vaguely catlike, but before Mireille could even register it was not feline, the creature shifted to a woman around six feet tall. Kin fell back, knocking into the table and overturning its contents. Mireille darted up to help, slipped on the oil that had coated the tub edge, and splashed water across Kin and the floor. She cursed, wiping at her stinging eyes.

Nisha sneered down at both of them. In a simple cream gown that draped her body perfectly, she looked every bit a princess of fae, even if she had only moments before been a mink. The entire weight of her distaste turned on Mireille. "Why aren't you ready? I need time to work."

"You?" Mireille choked.

Nisha rolled her eyes, then made a gesture at Kin. "Get her dried off." She gave Kin a full once-over and shook her head. "The both of you." With a flick of her skirts, she strode out of the bathing chamber, making a feline-like huff of disgust.

Mireille locked gazes with Kin. Whatever was happening with the ball, it seemed Mireille was not the only one uninformed.

A quarter hour later, Mireille sat before a vanity table and small gilt-trimmed mirror, her silk dressing gown decorated with a delicate pattern of swirling vines and flowers. Kin ran a brush through Mireille's long locks as three fae women in simple staff garb looked on. One held a comb and assorted hair pins, another a sewing kit, and the third was apparently in charge of gowns.

Nisha snapped her slender fingers, then pointed at the gowns. The woman rushed to grab the first where it had been draped over a rack, then held it forward for Mireille's inspection. She repeated the process twice more, each of the gowns deep cerulean and soft, supple fabric, but varying styles.

Nisha said into her ear, "It's his favorite color." She backed away and gave Mireille an appraising but somewhat disappointed look. "I'm not certain it will suit your hair. How do you feel about feathers? No? Understandable." She patted her shoulder. "We will figure something out."

In the end, Mireille was forced to try on all three gowns, and the group eventually settled on one sewn of the softest silk, with a high neck and detailed with delicate vines in a slightly darker shade of blue. The same vines crawled down the sleeves of the dress, ending in embroidered foliage near the wrists. It was a fae gown, through and through. Mireille had never worn anything like it, but even Kin nodded her approval.

The dress was removed, adjustments made, and Mireille was bustled back to the vanity where her hair was pinned and twisted into an elaborate form. Mireille met Nisha's gaze in the curved mirror. "Are you going to tell me what you're up to?"

Nisha's grin was wicked. "If anyone knows how to truly tempt a fae male, it is me." She held a palm out, and the woman with the hair pins handed another over.

"Why would I need to temp a fae?"

Kin dusted color onto Mireille's cheek, distinctly not meeting her eyes.

"And why are all of you conspiring against him?"

Nisha made a sound in her throat, not unlike the dismissive sound her brother favored. "Careful, princess, for you're making it sound as if falling for you might be to his detriment."

Mireille caught the gleam in Nisha's eyes, but Kin's fingers trembled as she applied lotions and creams. The two seemed to be working toward the same goal but, possibly, possessed entirely different motivations. Nisha, Mireille thought, was giving her the appraisal of someone taking pride in their well-trained pet.

"There," she said. "Just one final touch." And Mireille was dabbed with the light, fresh scent of orange oil.

CHAPTER 11

Nisha and the fae ladies departed, and Thomas was finally returned to Mireille. He slid his hands into his pockets and stared openly at what they had done. "Well," he said. "That's quite a statement."

She raised a hand to her hair, delicate gold vines woven through, and lifted a softly curled tress away from her face. "I look like a queen."

"No question."

"It's the prince's favorite color, apparently."

"Solid choice."

She fiddled with the accents on the high neck of the gown. "Should we leap out a window and run for the hills?"

He grinned. "Probably. But you know how I love a ball."

Thomas did not love a ball, particularly, she suspected, not a fae one. "Quite," she said. She drew a deep breath. "So, we stay for you."

He raised a hand to his chest. "I am grateful, as ever."

She shrugged, the bulk of the gown shifting around her. "Least I can do."

His grin shifted into something more genuine. "Indeed."

They turned in unison at a knock on the door, and Mireille called for Noal to enter, as it was all she could expect, given that Nisha would never deign to knock. But it was Alder who stood on her threshold.

He was dressed in black, the fabric of his coat embroidered with silver thread shaped into thin, twisting branches. If her gown was the color of the sky in deep spring, his clothing was like night in the heart of winter, the effect only emphasized by the sharp bone crown atop his dark hair. His eyes stayed on her for a heartbeat longer than was generally considered proper in polite society. Wordlessly, he offered her his arm.

Mireille cast a glance at Thomas, who gave her a firm nod. "I will be waiting right here."

She returned the nod, then slid her arm through Alder's, his warm, crisp scent sending a strange sensation through her belly. The prince did not acknowledge Thomas's vow, only led her from the room. They traversed a long corridor in tense silence. Mireille had overheard the prince make his own vow, telling Noal that she would attend no fae event lest she be on his arm, but she was not certain why he'd chosen to bring her at all. Perhaps, she thought, he was only afraid she'd show up unannounced mid-ball to surprise him for dinner.

Something shifted in an alcove, catching Mireille's attention. She kept her face forward but could not help but smile. It was Kin, likely waiting to meet Thomas. She could not begrudge the pair for not attending; they would probably have a much more agreeable time searching out clues to fae bargains than being shuffled on a gameboard by the likes of Alder and Nisha.

When they passed no one else in the corridor, Mireille's nerves got the better of her. "Are there any particular customs I should know to observe? Will there be formal introductions?"

The question seemed to make Alder uncomfortable, though his stride did not falter. "It is simply a ball. You need only eat, if you like, and dance."

"Dance with you?"

His expression tightened.

"It's only that I was under the impression you wished me to stay away from fae gatherings."

"You have made clear you will read hidden intentions in my every action. Attend any such gatherings if you wish."

She doubted that meant he would not be right at her side, but she didn't argue, because they had reached the ballroom. Two fae men in long-tailed suits opened a set of double doors and the abrupt chaos of music and conversation filled the corridor.

"The doors are enchanted," Alder explained. "Guests enter through the main hall to lights and decoration, to encourage joyous celebrations."

"Wouldn't want such a thing echoing through the palace," she murmured.

He hummed in agreement, evidently missing her point. Alder guided her inside. Fae in fine silks, lace, and jewels swept gracefully across the marble floor, in perfect time with the music. Their wardrobes were far more elaborate than she might have guessed, their number overwhelming. Glittering chandeliers and tabletop candles shone golden light over the entire affair. It was warm and lively and distressingly unlike any ball she had attended before.

Alder glanced down at her, and she realized her grip on his arm was a little too tight. Curious glances followed their movement across the floor as he led her toward an impossibly long table bedecked with every type of sweet and sustenance imaginable. Alder released her arm to lift two long-stemmed glasses filled with something pink and sparkling, but his eyes were not on his task, instead scanning the ballroom, which seemed strange given that they'd just arrived.

No one dared approach, despite the throng, and there was something very urgent and wary about his look, sentiments she did not normally associate with the prince. She surveyed the crowd as well, but other than the entire hall being filled with powerful and potentially dangerous fae, found nothing that seemed amiss.

A moment later, as she lifted the glass to her lips, Mireille had her answer. A shiver seemed to go through every fae in the room. The crowd turned toward the main entrance. The double doors swung outward, revealing the fae queen of Mireille's nightmares. Maeve.

She was in the one place she should not be. The one place Mireille had thought herself safe.

Mireille took a step back and bumped into Alder. His hand slid over the small of her back, holding her in place.

Across the ballroom, Queen Maeve's sinister gaze fell upon Mireille, then lowered to Alder's steadying hand. Long auburn hair fell in glistening waves over the queen's gown, the flowing fabric glimmering in the light and sliding over her tall form like a living thing. "Bow," she commanded.

Every fae in the room except Alder dropped into a bow, the music cutting off with a clatter. Beside Mireille, the prince stood tall, anger radiating from him more like ice than fire. Maeve's laughter was the tinkle of bells. "Rise. For I am a guest, here to enjoy the festivities." She lifted her hand, and with it, the fae moved as one, rising awkwardly to face her.

There was no question they had moved by her hand, her magic, like the way Alder had frozen the dining room when Mireille had been attacked.

The queen's gaze met Alder's. She said, "I was invited by your prince, after all."

Mireille went cold. She made to run, certain she'd been snared, but Alder's touch had turned into a grip. There was no escape. Murmurs slid through the crowd, but Maeve gestured, and the music started up once more. Fae parted around her like the tides as she glided across the room. Her vibrant green eyes danced with amusement as she approached. "Prince," she said, no disguise to her pleasure. "I might have been insulted by the last-minute invitation, but it seems even your court was unaware of the ball until quite recently."

Alder was rigid, more so than any statue in the palace, and just as imposing as the day Mireille had met him. He said, "These are my lands. Here, we do as I wish."

Maeve inclined her head, a smile playing across her lips. Beyond them, the fae danced cautiously, their liveliness from earlier gone. The queen said coyly, "And would you wish to offer your guest a dance?"

The queen extended an arm, clad in a long silver glove, and Mireille tensed, every part of her wanting to jerk away. But Alder held her firm.

He said, "As you can see, my arm is already taken."

Maeve's bright eyes slid to Mireille. "Why, yes, Princess Mireille." She drew a fan from thin air, snapping it open in clear insult. Given the power she'd just displayed, it was unforgivably petty. "What a surprise to find you so far from home. Have you left your dear father?" She clicked her tongue. "I do worry about the poor man. Let us hope he fares well without you."

Heat flared through Mireille. She drew herself up, wanting nothing more than to strike the woman with that cursed fan, and possibly Alder, too. She had come to find protection, he had made a vow, and there stood the queen, invited by Alder himself and delivering barely veiled threats. "The kingdom of Norcliffe's fate does not rest on my shoulders alone."

Maeve lifted a brow meaningfully at Mireille's slender shoulders. "I should hope not."

In that moment, had she a weapon, Mireille could not have been trusted not to use it.

Alder shifted, the first he'd moved since the queen arrived, and Mireille's gaze flicked to him. "If you will excuse us," he told the queen, "I owe my betrothed a dance."

Maeve's expression remained unchanged, but her fury was a tangible thing that bit at the air around them. It felt as dangerous as standing in a lightning storm, and Mireille was a good deal certain one of them was about to meet their end, but Alder only swept past, pressing Mireille forward and toward the dance floor, with himself bewteen her and the queen. He took the drink from Mireille's hand, which she had quite forgotten she was holding but now bubbled thick and black, and deposited it on the tray of a passing server.

Then his hand was in hers, the other positioned at her waist, and he was leading her through the steps of an unfamiliar dance. Her cheeks were hot, her chest was tight, and hundreds of fae swirled around them in a dizzying blur.

"You are angry," he said.

She found focus, narrowing her gaze on his and stilling her trembling limbs. "Livid."

He drew her body tighter to his.

"How could you?" she hissed. "I told you what she has done. You understood that I was here for your protection, that my kingdom, my father, everything I hold dear is in danger from *her*."

His movements were steady and sure as he spun them in another turn, as if the entire world was not spinning out of control around them. "I had to be certain."

"Certain of what?"

He met her gaze.

"Certain that I was not her ally? That I was not here on her behalf?" She felt sick. "If I am a pawn in anyone's game, it is yours. I was a fool to trust you. And what care you for my allegiances? Why claim me as your betrothed?"

His eyes darkened. "You never trusted me." The music changed and Alder brought their dance to a stop in the center of the ballroom, his hand firm on her waist. He leaned forward, his breath hot on her cheek. He was very tall, and very imposing, and there was so very much of him right there in her space. "Maeve is gathering power. She has come for your lands. What makes you think she would not come for mine? The stakes are higher than you can understand. I had to be certain."

"Our enemy is the same. You knew all along."

"You have not been honest."

She glared back at him. "Nor have you. And not even solely with me. Your staff has done nothing but push us together, while even they are left in the dark. The curse you speak of is the Rive, but there is a binding on you that is more personal still."

His expression hardened. He did not like that she'd found out, that much was clear. She said, "You have done everything in your power to drive me away. Why do they encourage you closer?"

Around them, the dancing fae began to take notice of their scene. Alder leaned near, his lips brushing the shell of her ear. "They do not know everything."

She wasn't certain it was a confession, but across the room, drink in hand and ire simmering for all to see, Maeve watched with a strange tilt to her head. Mireille held the woman's gaze, lifting onto her toes to whisper into Alder's ear, her hand pressed to his broad chest. A spark of something hot shot through her at his closeness, and she was unsure whether it was fear, or something worse. "We need to move this discussion somewhere private."

The look he gave her was pure heat and, again, Mireille was unsure exactly how to process it. But the hand at her waist spun her to his side, and before she could summon even a second thought, she was ushered from the room.

CHAPTER 12

They stood alone in the night-darkened music room, and Mireille had to force her gaze away from the piano. There was a part of her that could not believe she had actually played for him. She wasn't certain what had come over her since she'd agreed to a bargain with a fae prince. Desperation, that was all.

Alder peered down at her, his face half in shadow and half in moonlight. He had let go his hold but had not stepped away. "What do you know of my bindings?"

The words were emotionless, but Mireille flinched nonetheless. "You need a princess to bring down the Rive."

He felt more dangerous in the moonlight, but when his words came, they were not in the tone he'd used before. If anything, they seemed pained. "I do need a princess."

"But not me. Why? What is it that I cannot offer you?" He turned away, and her hands balled into fists. "This is absurd. You said yourself we have a common enemy, and she's out there, right now, in your own ballroom."

Alder's shoulders sagged, a weight like the one she'd watched her father carry for years. He said, "It must be a princess of Westrende.

The Rive split the land, but we are bound still. Our kingdoms can only be united with a union of the two."

After a moment, he turned to face her. "There is more, but I am bound from discussing the details." He pressed a palm to his chest, one of his long fingers tapping slowly over his heart. "Suffice it to say, a match of convenience would do me no good."

A very unpleasant sensation danced in Mireille's belly, writhing dread and nervous energy, and a strange sort of anticipation. She began to pace. "Then you refuse me because you are certain I cannot break it. Yet, you agreed to entertain the offer because you are required. And as a fae, you cannot break your vow, so your wish must be that I will terminate our agreement before the ceremony. You must have some plan in place, some way to prevent it, otherwise you would have been wed by now." Pacing ceased, she turned toward him, slowly lifting a hand to her collar. "Except, that choice surely belongs to me."

His eyes narrowed. "You would trap me in a curse? Knowing what that means?"

She shrugged. "Why, who's to say I would not prefer a life at court? What if I spirit my father away and we let her have Norcliffe?" It was evident that much, at least, he did not believe her capable of. Her voice dropped. "The queen has threatened my kingdom. I am my father's heir. If she is to take control, she will need me dead."

"Or married to a prince from another kingdom."

The terrible sensations inside her belly flipped. "Yes, or that. I would become queen of my husband's kingdom and would relinquish my claim to Norcliffe." And she could never become queen of Riven-wilde if the Rive held.

He asked, "Whose decision was it to bargain you to me?"

"Mine. Maeve had no hand in this. We would not have been fool enough to trust anything we had not devised ourselves, not after she infiltrated the council and the royal advisors. I knew no one could protect me from a fae queen but a fae from another court. And the only place I might find a way to beat her was within your court, your library, your home. I had connections to Westrende—" She swallowed. "Friends who knew of the fae. But even then..."

"Your options were few."

She nodded, but guilt and shame had her glancing toward the window as she did. "There was nothing noble about it."

He was suddenly close behind her.

"Am I to understand you planned to find a way to defeat her first? That you hoped to never have to marry me?"

She forced herself to look at him. "I would do anything to save my kingdom."

"And to turn the Riven Court against your enemy queen?"

Mireille hesitated. She had not thought that far ahead. Throwing herself to Rivenwilde had been an act of desperation, likely a fool's errand that would only buy more time. She supposed she never believed, truly, that she could overcome the queen. But Norcliffe was worth the risk. "Yes. Whatever it took. Even that."

His chin dipped. "I will not pretend any of this was done for the safety of your kingdom, only mine. But I spoke the truth. Our enemy is the same. And I have every intention of besting her."

Mireille's lips parted. "Are you suggesting a truce?"

"Agree not to marry me. We will find a way to defeat her before the next moon."

The breath that huffed out of her may have sounded like a laugh. It was not. "I will agree to ally with you. Until then." She held a hand forward to seal the agreement and Alder took it. They stood, studying one another, the unlikeliest of partners, hand in hand.

A distant scream sounded, reverberating off the music room walls, and Alder's hand pulled from hers. He ran and it was all Mireille could do to catch up.

When he realized Mireille was chasing after him, he came back to her, a firm grip on her arms. "Stay far away from this. Find a room to hide in and lock the door. If you are in danger, just speak my name."

"But—"

Another scream sounded and Alder pressed her a step back. "Go. If you call me, I will come." He released her and rushed away.

He was right, and she knew it. Mireille had no power to fight against the fae. She hurried in the opposite direction, searching for a place to hide. As before, the palace layout seemed to shift, and she was not certain which way to run. But a landing of narrow stone steps led upward, and the scream had echoed from the lower floor.

Lifting her skirts to her knees, she sped to the higher level and down another long corridor. She gripped the lever of the door at the end of the corridor, but it would not turn. Words were carved into the wood in a language in which Mireille was not fluent, something about balance being kept—or possibly paid. Another distant scream rang through the palace and she moved to release the lever, but something sparked through her palm. Her hand yanked back, and the door creaked inward. When footfalls sounded on the stairs, Mireille hurried inside.

The moment the door swung shut behind her, she knew she'd made a mistake.

The only light in the room came from its center, the same unnatural glow of her moonlit dreams. But it was not a dream. She was awake, the floor solid beneath her feet, and before her stood an hourglass atop a table that was nearly as tall as her. The room smelled of hawthorn flower, thick, and sticky, and sweet. Dread rose through her, every fiber of her being begging her to step away, but Mireille's slippered feet drew her forward.

Roots grew through the floorboards, winding and tangling into one large mass that held the hourglass. Cradled by hawthorn branches, twisted into unnatural shapes and studded with dagger-like thorns, the glass seeped familiar magic, the magic Mireille had felt settling over her room every night the fae queen had come.

As she watched, a single glowing grain of sand dropped slowly through the narrow waist, as if settling in a sea. There was far more at the bottom of the glass than the top, though with the rate it fell she wagered it had been there a *very* long time. She reached one trembling hand forward but stopped short of touching it.

The fae queen's magic was emanating from an hourglass inside Alder's palace, as if the magic had intertwined with that of Rivenwilde. Mireille stepped back. The room was empty, other than the timepiece. The entire space seemed ancient and untouched. Perhaps as old as the Rive.

A common enemy, he had said. From a queen determined to gather lands. For the first time, Mireille wondered if Alder had more to lose than even she.

He would not want her there, she was sure of it. He would not want her to even know. She crept toward the door, keeping an eye on the table, then listened for any movement outside. The screams had gone silent. Mireille escaped into the corridor and hurried back in the direction she had come.

As she neared the foot of the stairs, she caught sight of Thomas running through a crossing corridor. She hissed out his name and he backtracked, peering up at her.

"I've been looking everywhere for you!" He reached out a hand. "Shadow creatures have attacked the ball. Let's get you back to your room."

She took the last few steps two at a time, then grasped his hand. "How did you know where to search?"

"Kin and I were in the library when the creatures attacked. We found a member of staff who saw you leave with Alder, before he came back alone."

As he tugged her along, Mireille could not bring herself to share what Alder had revealed. That he believed he'd taken an ally of his enemy into his court was proof enough that he was desperate. But the sand, well that proved that Mireille was not the only who was running out of time.

ALDER DID NOT COME to her room, and late into the night, Mireille finally climbed into bed. There was no way to know if the queen would find her, if the prince would intervene, or if the queen, so close, could overpower his will. Surely, he would not have invited such a danger into his own palace, but he was fae. There were no guarantees.

Thomas was in his post by the door, lying on his back, a hand behind his head and boots crossed at the ankle. The door to her room was locked. But as midnight neared, it was the prince's magic that settled heavily around her.

She sensed his presence, and the rich smell of bergamot, and opened her eyes.

Alder stood over her, offering his hand. When he helped her from the bed, her gown was revealed to be the deepest black. She was unsure if it was a gown of mourning, or simply that her slumbering imaginings had wanted to match the prince. She looked up at him.

He said, "I have a plan."

CHAPTER 13

Mireille reluctantly withdrew her hand from the wisteria tree. Norcliffe was well enough for the time being, particularly given that the queen was in Rivenwilde, and though the tree gave her comfort, she could not afford to linger. She turned back to Alder, his tall form limned in the strange moonlight. He no longer seemed quite so imposing, but she could not say whether that was owing to the dream, or that she knew his secret.

He had ambushed her with the queen's presence at the ball, but each night, he'd given her the gift of knowing her father was safe, and that Norcliffe still stood. She asked, "You said you have a plan?"

He stepped forward, his dark eyes searching her face. "It will require your cooperation."

"You want me to agree blindly when the last move you made was to invite my mortal enemy to dance alongside us. I may have agreed to an alliance, but I will not hand you indiscriminate trust."

His mouth tightened. "Because you believe me a monster out to conquer human lands. Yet you would expect me to trust you when you would do the same as I."

"The same? I hardly think—"

He took another step forward. "I would do anything to protect my people."

Well, he had her there. She folded her hands neatly at her waist. Around them, the garden swayed in an imagined breeze. There was something calming about the rhythm, though, and Mireille tried to steady herself in its pace. She said, "You witnessed our encounter, besides that she sent me every night to walk to my death—" Her eyes shot up to meet his. "She drew me into your chamber, but given the chance, she chose to drive the blade into me." Not Alder, the prince who she had somehow bound.

"It was not the first time."

"She sends women into your chambers?"

His expression shifted. "No, that's—" He shook his head. "She merely taunts me. In my cage."

"Oh."

He stepped closer, and she shifted, too, her body reacting as if they were still in a dance. "Not an ally," he said. "Not a pawn." His last words were barely above a whisper. "But no victim."

One corner of her mouth ticked up. She couldn't help it. "Not a monster, not a conqueror, but not..." The hourglass rose again in her thoughts, and she could not say the words. Alder was trapped. He was bound by the Rive and bound by the queen and her curse. But he was still a fae.

He watched, waiting for her to finish, but when she did not, his shoulders relaxed and he moved to place his hand on either side of her waist.

"And what of this plan?" she asked against his chest, staring at the spot his finger had tapped during his confession.

He released a breath, then turned her with him to walk from beneath the wisteria and down a narrow path. Ancient stone pillars rose through the greenery, less alive than the ones in the palace, and Mireille wondered if they belonged to her memory or Alder's. He said, "The creature that attacked you on that first night was a miscalculation by my sister."

Mireille tensed, ready to pull away from him, but his next words stopped her short.

"The creatures let loose tonight were a miscalculation by the queen."

"Miscalculation?"

He kept his eyes forward. "Nisha wanted to be rid of you. She believed I had made the bargain against my will, like the others. That it would prevent the breaking of the Rive."

Mireille wondered how many times she had been watched unaware, not giving second thought to the many open windows and balconies that could be concealing a small dark mink. "She no longer seems to feel that way."

Alder's laugh surprised her. "No, I fear she does not. She's impulsive, sometimes recklessly so, but after a time, she believed our arrangement could come to benefit her."

"Has she confessed all this?"

His voice darkened. "She has not. But her schemes are transparent. She cares very little for covering her tracks. And any other fae would not have sent a message merely meant to frighten you off."

Mireille tried not to think about what the *merely* meant, but she knew enough of the fae to understand the gravity of her situation.

Alder paused before at a bench beneath a trellis of climbing roses, gesturing for her to sit. When she did, he settled beside her, the space small and quiet, and shaded from the dreamlight's glow. "Nisha's motives are not difficult to guess. If I were to marry anyone not from Westrende, the only way to bring down the Rive would be to bring down me."

If he married Mireille, his life and his kingdom would be at risk, the same as she. And yet, they were tied by the threat of a ruthless queen. "I still cannot reconcile your choice to invite the queen in. It seems a great deal of risk only to confirm her intentions and mine."

"That was not why she was invited." His tone was off, his attention on the moon through the canopy of leaves. "Tonight, once we returned to the ball, I intended to announce our betrothal to the court. She needed to be present. She will remain as guest and as witness."

Mireille stood abruptly, nearly knocking into him. "I did not agree to this." In fact, she'd agreed *not* to agree to the ceremony at all.

He gave her a speaking glance.

"This is your plan? To announce we've settled on giving up our kingdoms?" She paced only steps away, then immediately back. "You called me your betrothed to the queen. So you invited her to, what, test me first? Before the announcement? To test her?" She resumed her place on the bench. He did not shift over, only watched as she worked it out. "Because if we were to marry, I would be forfeiting my right as heir. You think she would no longer have reason to do away with me, that she would simply take Norcliffe and be on her merry way. But Rivenwilde would still be bound and under threat."

"It is more complicated than that."

He had no idea. But Mireille did not say so, she could not and still have any chance of coming out of the ordeal alive.

"I need Maeve to believe we intend to go through with the marriage, need her to act. That is what I needed to be certain of—that she will make an attempt before the turn of the moon." He leaned back. "And when she does, I will be ready for her."

"So we are to feint, to... pretend a marriage."

"Right up until the ceremony."

She watched him for a very long moment. "And I? What do I stand to gain from this?"

His expression was grim. "This is the price for breaking your bargain. Aid in my scheme and you will be free."

If the queen could be defeated, Mireille could return to Norcliffe. Their kingdoms could be saved. But how was she to believe he could do it?

"What if I do not trust that you can overcome her?" The marshal's words echoed through Mireille's mind. The price of breaking a bargain with the fae was always one too costly. No one would give it willingly. It had to be a trick. Escaping could not be so easy.

"That is the price you must pay."

She blinked. "You planned this from the start."

"I had considered my options. It could have gone other ways."

"Indeed," Mireille whispered. "For I was not even the first princess to agree."

His expression went hard. She did not care. She was not the only princess under threat by the queen, she was simply the last who had managed her way into his palace. There were more, surely, perhaps in the wing with Lord Cadby. Perhaps many more. It was apparent that her wince did not go unnoticed. Every moment, the possibility of preserving her kingdom felt further away. She said, "Then I have no choice at all. The only way to save Norcliffe is to agree to your ruse."

He leaned closer, voice low. "Had you another choice, would you take it?"

She bit back her initial response, because of course the safety of her kingdom, freedom for herself, and the defeat of the fae queen would be worth it. But it seemed unlikely that he would see it done. After all, he hadn't in all the time he'd spent cursed. The boundary wall was ancient, just like the Rive. No one had yet restored it. "I prefer to be told why and how our engagement will force her to act."

"As I've said, I am unable to reveal details. But know that my history with her is long, and you and I are not the only ones with something to lose."

She drew a shuddering breath. If she could not have his confession, then she would not give him hers. They would merely have to work together, doing all they could do drive the wicked queen off a cliff of her own making.

"Then let us bring her down, once and for all,"—she gave him her gaze— "husband."

CHAPTER 14

When Mireille opened her eyes, it was not to a moonlit canopy of leaves. It was to Thomas, staring down at her with a perplexed expression.

She groaned and rolled to her side. "Why must everyone suddenly stand over me in my sleep?"

"You are sleeping half the morning away, that is why." He poked her shoulder. "Tell me, for the household will not."

Mireille pressed her eyes closed very tight. She did not want to know what Thomas had heard. She did, however, have a very good idea. And it was a problem, because she'd vowed—been forced to vow—not to tell Thomas, or anyone else, of the prince's plan. And the prince's plan was very different from the one Thomas and Mireille had arrived with. "What do you mean?"

He spoke slowly, carefully enunciating each word. "Engaged to be wed."

She drew the blanket over her head.

"It was my understanding that you could barely tolerate him. And yet, one night, one dance, and the entire palace has practically broken into song. They're hanging decorations, I hope you know that."

She mumbled a reply under her breath and could feel Thomas lean in. "What was that?" he said. "Didn't quite hear you, what with all the cowering in shame."

Mireille flipped the blankets down. "I said it wasn't only one dance."

The shock that crossed Thomas's expression was not put on. He rocked back onto his heels, ran a palm over his chest. "So, it's true."

"The prince and I have come to an understanding. It seems, unfortunately, that this is our best course of action."

He sank down on the bed and then, abruptly, appeared to recall she was no longer merely his friend. She was betrothed to another man. A fae prince. He stood, sidling awkwardly toward the foot of the bed. "What happened between last night and this morning to change your mind?"

She pressed up on the massive pile of pillows. "Honestly, Thomas, I told you about the dreams."

"Yes," he drew out the word. "And what, precisely, happened in last night's dream to alter your course so thoroughly?"

She could not tell him the truth. Not because he could not be trusted, but because Alder had told her that the only place that was truly safe to speak of secrets was in her dreams. They could not allow their plan to be foiled. It was too great a risk.

Guilt twisted inside her. But it would not be forever. Thomas would understand everything soon. Whether they managed it, or not. "He convinced me. We share a common goal. We both care about our people. And once she sees we are to be wed, the queen will turn her attention elsewhere."

Thomas's brow pinched. "Will she? Or will she go after your father?" He crossed his arms. "And Alder? What about him? What does a prince stand to gain when he doesn't even know—"

She cut him off with a raised hand. "That is enough, Lord Holden. I've made my choice."

He slid his hands into his pockets. "I see. Very well, then."

It felt horrible. Cruel. Unconscionable. She was definitely going to live with regret for eternity.

He said, "What shall I do today? For the cause."

She swallowed against the shaky feeling in her throat. "The engagement was meant to be announced last night, but the ball was cut short. It will be announced instead at a formal gathering this afternoon."

"Last night," he repeated. "Before your dream walk."

She stood. "I'll need to get dressed for the gathering. You're welcome to attend. If you'd like." She crossed to the bathing chamber, then closed the door behind her, bracing against it to catch her breath. Through the finely carved wood, she heard Thomas wait for her to take it all back, to tell him the truth, and then, she heard him leave.

Kin, evidently assigned as a lady's maid to assist Mireille before the event, came later. Mireille did not mind the company. After pinning her hair, Kin held forward a gown of jet-black silk. Mireille smoothed a finger across the silver embroidery of wicked bare branches, likely a match for the coat Alder would wear. It was not a gown suited for the balls of Westrende, but one only fit for a fae court.

Kin frowned and Mireille clumsily signed, *What troubles you?* The woman looked a bit as if she'd swallowed a small poisonous toad.

Do you love him? Kin signed back.

Mireille suddenly felt as if she had swallowed a similar, if larger and more lethal, toad. Thomas had not been exaggerating, then. The entire household must have been abuzz. And her concern was that the prince was *loved*.

Mireille could not recall the sign for *engagement*, so she replied, *I have chosen willingly.* It may not have been the answer Kin wanted, but it would have to do. Alder was exasperating, brooding, and stubborn. But he had kept his word. He had protected her. It was all she had.

It should not matter if her stomach grew alight when he stood too close. It should be of no consequence if she imagined, even for a moment, that he saw through everything to who Mireille really was. He considered it an arrangement only. There would never be more, because... well, because to him, it wasn't real.

She cleared her throat, returning her attention to the dress and its laced bodice. "Help me, will you?" Kin might ask of love and things uncomfortable to consider, but answering those questions was preferable to lying to Thomas, who was far more likely to accuse her of being rash or foolish. Because she was. Not as a rule, but certainly of late.

Kin kept her eyes lowered, attention pointedly on task, apparently dissatisfied with Mireille's reply. Or perhaps she was unable to convey what she wished for reasons of loyalty or magic, bound by the same rules as Alder. By the time Mireille had slipped on the long black gloves, she could take it no longer. She ducked forward, meeting Kin's gaze before signing. *Do you not trust in your prince to choose correctly?*

Kin's dark eyes were steady, but Mireille could not guess at precisely why. A knock sounded at the door, and Kin turned to answer it.

Noal, dressed in matching black with a white cravat tied so firmly against his olive skin that she wondered if he could properly breathe, studied her. "You look well."

"For a human about to dine with a fae queen intent on her murder, you mean?" She adjusted her gloves. "I am under the prince's protection, am I not? Is there any reason for concern?"

According to the prince, Noal was unaware of his plot, but the look in the man's eyes said he understood far more than he let on. He inclined his head. "I am to escort you to the study."

"I am ready," she said, though she was most certainly not.

Then Thomas came through the door in a manner that might fairly be called *bursting in*, before stopping in his tracks to take in Mireille's resplendent black gown.

"Truly," he said. "There is no rush. The moon has not yet turned. There is still time."

Real fear rested beneath his tone, and Mireille's heart pinched. That Thomas would have done anything so nearly an outburst revealed how dire he believed the situation was. Perhaps he thought her under some sort of thrall, like the spell that came over her in sleep. Closing the distance, she gripped his arms through his coat. "Thomas, please trust me."

His mouth sealed into a grim line. He had known the possibilities when they had come, that she might truly be bound to the prince, but Mireille hadn't realized just how deeply he had hoped to find information that might defeat the fae queen, to somehow free Mireille from her impossible situation.

"I do not need you to save me, Thomas. I will save myself, and we, fate willing, will save Norcliffe."

For a dizzying moment, the image of a different future than either would have ever planned swam before her, but she pressed it down. Mireille would uphold her part of the bargain, and if it worked, they would save Norcliffe. She and Thomas would return home. They would leave all of this—the fae prince and his magical court—behind. There would be no midnight walks in moonlit gardens, no sculpture that seemed to come alive, no Kin, no Noal, no dinners over well-worn books in a dimly lit study.

She would never again find Alder, eyes dark and jaw ticking, meeting her gaze across a long table, never again catch the stray twist to his lips that hinted he might own a true smile.

Thomas must have seen something in her expression that convinced him, because finally, he raised a hand to pat hers where it still gripped his arm. "I am here. All you need do is ask."

His words were not the comfort either of them may have wanted, because Mireille did need to ask something of him, and he wasn't going to like it one whit. Before they left, she leaned forward to whisper it into Thomas's ear.

CHAPTER 15

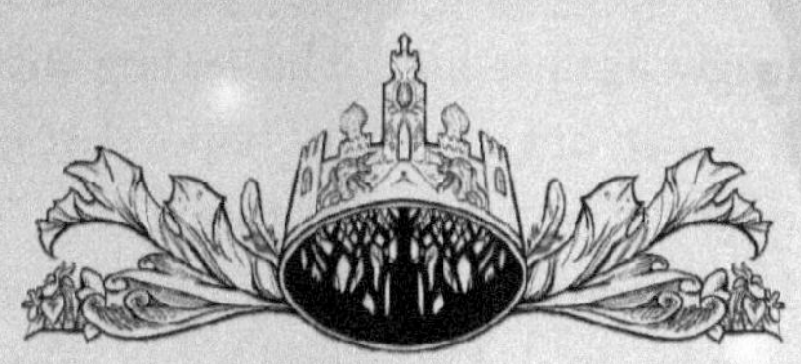

"We gave you what help we could," Noal said as he walked at Mireille's side, the halls empty of any other fae.

She managed a small smile as they approached the study. "I will repay you all the same courtesy."

The edge of his mouth tightened with a hint of concern as he reached for the door. Before it opened, he said, "I do hope you're as clever as you are confident, Highness."

"As do I," Mireille breathed. She gave the man a small curtsy, then strode into the study as if already a queen.

Alder stood behind his desk, dressed, unsurprisingly, in solid black, the embroidery on his coat a match to Mireille's gown. Only his crown broke the inky blackness, resting low on his head as he watched her with eyes like flecks of obsidian.

Noal darted a glance between the pair of them, and Mireille became aware they'd been staring at each other for a bit too long.

Noal cleared his throat and turned toward the prince. "Have you any further need of me?"

The prince's gaze had not strayed from Mireille. "Only to remind you of your duty to secure the perimeter."

Noal flinched. Mireille had to bite down the rebuke she wanted to snap at the prince. It had not been Noal's fault, and they both knew it. The prince had said he was certain the queen had been responsible, even though she could not break the laws of hospitality directly. It was clear that even far from her own court and bound by ancient tenets, she was a threat.

But the prince could not let on that he was not falling for her traps.

Alder stepped around the desk, offering Mireille his arm. She took it, lifting her chin to hide her apprehension. He must have noticed regardless, because he lightly gripped her wrist and shifted her arm to draw her more snuggly against him. The feeling that bloomed in her chest was not merely fear, but a sense of hope. Partnership. They both needed rid of the queen. They were in it together.

And afterward... Afterward she would be freed from her bargain. She would return home, and Alder could find whatever princess he wanted. If she felt a tremble of unease at the idea, she could not be blamed for it, or whatever dark and frenzied thoughts chased after.

Because, after all, the princess was about to lower herself to the role of *bait*.

THE HALL that Mireille had first encountered on her palace tour had transformed, its long row of arched windows draped with sheer curtains that dampened the midday sun. Long tables were bedecked with tiny sandwiches, tarts, cheeses, and platters mounded with fruit that looked plump and ripe enough to burst. Mireille's stomach tightened. She could not quite recall when she'd last eaten, but did not think she could steady herself enough to do it now.

Servers in crisp blue livery with polished buttons walked between the tables offering punch to those seated. It was a relief to find not half as many fae as had been present at the ball. Perhaps only certain members of the court had been invited. The fae present did not seem especially reluctant to attend, despite the previous night's attack.

Mireille was escorted toward a narrow table upon a raised dais.

Nisha was already seated, her posture that of a cat considering play, her gown pale lavender with jeweled buttons up long cuffs that met billowing sleeves. A sudden sensation of being watched came over Mireille, despite that the entire gathering had their eyes on her, and she turned to find the queen swanning in through the main entrance, her gaze daggers. The collar of her crimson dress rose high in an artful swirl of red embroidery, her matching red lips in a contemptuous line.

Mireille could not wait to wipe the expression from her face. Alder had not explained precisely why the betrothal would be such a blow to the queen, aside from it ending her game, but Mireille suspected there was more to it, and that the *more* was tied to his curse. For her part, Mireille understood exactly why the queen would not want it to be her.

She hoped she'd been right to trust the prince. She hoped that while she had agreed to act as bait, she would not be left to become prey.

Mireille's chair was pulled out, and she sat stiffly, keeping her head high and her slippered feet flat on the floor. The crowd of fae were seated or standing near the line of windows, attention on the actions of their prince. A human dressed in fae garb was holding a position of honor at his side, in the presence of an enemy queen.

Nisha leaned close to murmur, "I did not believe you would truly manage it, Princess. Well done."

Alder twitched irritably, evidently having heard the remark. He lifted a glass and the room fell silent. It was a chilling reminder of the dinner at which he'd seemed to arrest time, but he had not used magic to still this room, only the power of his station. He said, "A soul's greatest desire is to find its match. One wishes, in their deepest depths, to marry not for duty or honor, but for that which is the incomparable prize,"—he looked at Mireille— "the bond that is love."

It took everything in Mireille's being to not react. She had expected a more politic announcement, not... sentiment. But she supposed they had been joined by a shared bond, the love for their people, their land, and their kingdoms. She raised her glass toward him.

"Two souls, bound together in a shared intent, equal in all and cherished above all else." His head inclined infinitesimally, then turned back toward the crowd. "So it is, with great pleasure, that I announce my engagement to Princess Mireille of Norcliffe."

He offered a gloved hand and she took it to stand. He had not said that he loved her, not truly. And she wasn't certain Alder couldn't lie. He had said *what is a lie but intent*. But if his intention had been to convince Maeve that he was serious, the words seemed to have done the trick. The fae queen's eyes were wide, her jaw agape, and the color had drained out of her cheeks.

Nisha was the first to break the silence, squawking out a sharp cheer that had the crowd joining in in surprise, even if scattered murmurs of confusion lingered. It was not clear if they understood that she was not a princess of Westrende and could not bring down the Rive, only that Nisha beamed at the pair. Nisha, who would take Alder's place if something were to happen to him.

Alder raised Mireille's hand to his lips, meeting her gaze as he laid a gentle kiss on her knuckles. She couldn't quite look away, and in the moment, on a dais in front of a crowd, her imaginings again went places they should not, places that could never become true.

It was a foolish thing to believe you might best your enemies when they had handed you the knife.

Nisha stood. "Let the celebrations begin!" She raised a glass, then glanced at it in disappointment. "Bring out something with a bit more kick!"

Servers leapt into motion and the chatter among the crowd became something that felt more genuinely of delight. Alder snaked an arm around Mireille's waist, drew her close, and lowered his lips to her ear. "You've done well, but we still must make her believe."

Feigning a chuckle at his words, Mireille slid her gaze toward where Maeve sat with a half-empty wine flute in hand. Her eyes were narrowed, scrutinizing the pair. Mireille quickly turned back to Alder. She had to stand on her toes, resting one palm on his chest to reach his ear. "I will do what must be done," she whispered.

"So accommodating," he rumbled with no small hint of irony. "Perhaps, at least, you could appear as if,"—he drew back to look at her, and his gaze darkened— "as if in the blush of new love."

Her smile was shaky. "Indeed, I have not blushed easily since I was a girl. Only when taken off guard."

A hum slipped out of him, then he leaned closer, voice low. "If I were to confess that I find you impossibly beautiful, that when you entered this room, head held high, in that dress..." his gaze trailed lower, then met hers once more. "You are every bit a queen, Mireille, and not a soul in this room would fault me for wanting—"

She pressed a single finger over his lips. "I fear, dear prince, that you are about to deliver insult with that line of supposed flattery."

His jaw flexed.

She let her fingertip trail slowly off his lips, then whispered. "If you'd like, you may try again. But I warn you, a princess does not blush easily."

Alder's gaze never left hers as he slid a hand over hers where it rested on his chest. Then he lowered his mouth to hers.

Mireille's heart thundered, all thoughts of pretense abandoning her. His lips were real, and warm, and drowning out every sense of the crowd around them. She was kissing the Prince of Rivenwilde, an unquestionably deadly fae in possession of ancient power and, fate help her, she liked it. Bergamot filled her senses, her fingers curled into the material of his jacket, and Mireille melted against him. He had managed to bring heat to her skin, that much was certain, but worse, he'd brought it to her chest, where her fool heart lived in an ocean of hope.

When he broke the kiss, drawing back with an unsteady emotion that may have been surprise, Mireille had no notion of what he might find in her own expression. An instant later though, he seemed to remember himself, and it was all erased by a charming smile. A smile meant, surely, for the fae queen alone.

They returned to their seats, and Mireille's flute was the first to be filled. A pungent liquor scent rose from the glass, and when Alder leaned toward her, his nearness sent an awareness through her she was not quite prepared to face.

"I don't recommend you drink that," he said against her ear.

Bait, she remembered. She was meant to drag the queen from her perch. And with the lingering sensation of Alder's kiss still upon her lips and the terrible sensation of having softened toward the fae, she would need to keep her wits about her more than ever.

CHAPTER 16

The festivities wore on past nightfall, with Maeve's agitation seeming to increase by the hour. By the time Alder stood to escort Mireille to her chambers on the pretense of her needing rest—not entirely a fabrication as she was utterly exhausted from the day's nerves—Maeve was watching the pair with open hunger. She would most certainly take the bait.

Mireille took Alder's arm, avoiding Maeve's sharp gaze as they walked past. Beyond the enchanted doors that shut out the sounds of revelry, they walked in silence until they reached the entrance to Mireille's suite. "Do you think she'll—"

Alder held a finger to her lips, and it immediately recalled when she'd done the same to him, and the kiss that followed. She had to bite down a curse at her foolish heart, picking up pace in her chest. He did not care about her. He needed her only to trap the queen.

He said, "I vowed to protect you. You are safe."

She stared up at him, aware they were standing far closer than was necessary. None of it was real; it was only a pretense, a show for the queen. "Of course."

His brow furrowed at her curt reply, but she stepped back, slipping into her room and closing the door behind her.

Despite asking Thomas to trust in her judgement, she hadn't been certain he would give way easily until she found the room empty. Suddenly, Alder's plan seemed like a terrible idea. She glanced at the closed door. *Safe*, the prince had said. As safe as she could be, under the circumstances. Midnight would come, and perhaps she would visit the tree. Perhaps she would once again know her father and their people were safe as well.

Or perhaps the queen would come to call instead.

Removing the formal gown, she wrapped herself not only in a nightshift, but a thick silk dressing gown, then crawled into bed. The land and its law and the prince's vow might protect her in the waking world, but the safety of dreams was not as faithful. Heaviness fell over her.

Mireille walked barefoot down a corridor she recognized, only it was not quite the same as it had been before. The walls seemed to breathe with the pulse of magic and the silver embroidery of her black gown shone unnaturally bright in the moonlight that streaked the stone floor. It was a dream, not the mindless midnight wandering she'd done under the queen's power. But Alder was nowhere in sight. And weren't they supposed to be laying a trap for the queen? She could not quite remember.

Her feet continued forward despite her concern, compelled to bring her to the familiar door at the end of the hallway. Unlike the other wanderings, Mireille was entirely aware of the fear gripping her heart, and yet, she pushed open the heavy door.

The hourglass that centered the room seemed brighter than before, and there, in the dream, Mireille understood it was a curse clock, counting down until the terms would end. Less sand rested at the top than when she'd last seen it, and as she watched, another grain fell. It glowed, ethereal in the shadowed room, like a shell dropped through water, sunlight catching on its nacre. The fall of sand had sped. The prince was running out of time.

"Perhaps I *should* have made you my spy."

The queen's voice was playful, but it turned Mireille's blood to ice.

Maeve stepped from the shadows, still wearing the crimson gown. Foxglove and lilac clung to the scent of her magic, as if trying to hide the power that pricked Mireille's skin. Maeve said, "You already know this room, else you would not have found the way." Her gaze turned speculative. "But Alder would not have shown it to you."

"You cursed him." Mireille's voice revealed no hint of tremor, though her body felt sick with fear. It was true, she could feel it. The queen's magic was everywhere, but it centered on the clock.

Maeve tilted her head, one corner of her wide mouth tipping up. "No." Then she leaned forward. "Let me tell you a story, Princess, like they do in Westrende. Once upon a time, a handsome prince of the fae was trapped in a curse he did not create. The land was broken, his father was dead, and the prince was desperate. Tragic, really. Suffering all around. You know the way. But one day, a beautiful queen appeared with an offer. And that poor prince, well he had nothing left to lose, so he gambled it all. Twice the cost of the curse for a slim nothing chance to break it."

The queen straightened. "You humans love to believe that the noble-born are noble of character, but the fae never do. You see, pet, he was not cursed by me. He accepted my bargain of his own free will."

Her gaze traveled over Mireille. "For a time, he held out hope that he would beat me, but he has obviously grown desperate with this—" she waved her hand disdainfully in Mireille's direction, "charade."

Mireille swallowed hard, at both the explanation and the accusation. She knew well enough why the queen had come for her. It was not simply to win Norcliffe. "There is no charade. We will wed, and he will win."

"Oh truly? You expect me to believe that he has fallen in love with you, and you him?" She snorted. "Absurd. You come all the way from Norcliffe, show up on his steps like a lost pup, innocent and meek, and he's supposed to fall for your ruse?" Her voice dipped dangerously. "He will never love you."

Mireille's palms broke into sweat and she did not know if the sensation was real or conjured by the queen. She only knew that both Alder and the queen had mentioned love, as if it were a term of their bargain.

Two bindings, a curse and a bargain. Two requirements to break them.

Maeve grinned at Mireille's shifting expression. "I see he has not told you the full truth. And yet, you trusted him, fool that you are. You would not be the first to fall for it, I assure you. The prince does have a certain," she rolled her hand again in that dismissive gesture, "*charm*, but I had thought you cleverer than that. Cleverer than the others." She edged closer, and Mireille had to fight her every instinct in order to remain still. It was only a dream. Maeve wasn't controlling her. She could not be harmed, not there.

Maeve whispered, "But I can offer you a way out."

Mireille gritted her teeth. "I do not wish to escape. I have made my choice."

"Princess, there *is* no choice." Maeve lifted her hands as she approached the curse clock. "Your wish is to save your kingdom, and I am the only one who can grant it."

Mireille's hands curled into fists. "You are the very danger it faces."

Maeve shot her a self-satisfied grin. "Precisely. And so, if you would like to save your kingdom, you will do exactly as I say." She stroked the hourglass, expression gone dark. "You will let Alder believe you are his accomplice until the last moment, but you will keep your distance, treat him as coldly as a viper, for that is what he is to you. You will tell not a soul of your plans. And when time is nearly up, when he believes he has won and outwitted us both, you will forsake him. When the moon is high, all of Rivenwilde gathered round, triumph will finally be mine."

When it was too late for Alder to find someone new. But Mireille understood there was no one else. Only she was left as a threat to the queen.

And the prince's time would be out. The price of breaking Mireille's bargain with the prince was her cooperation. If she turned against him, chose her kingdom over defeating the queen, it would be to spend eternity in Rivenwilde. Not as Alder's wife, but his prisoner. But the safety of Norcliffe would rely solely on the promises of a treacherous queen.

Maeve lifted a finely arched brow. "I see that you are concerned. If your fear is in regard to your bargain to marry the prince, do not fret. Once Rivenwilde is mine, I can set you free. You would not remain a prisoner of the prince for long. And I will never bother Norcliffe again. You would have my word."

Mireille's heart pounded in her ears. Surely, the queen meant that she would merely be *her* prisoner instead. And if she refused, well Maeve had proven what she wanted for Mireille. It was of no consequence how: a dagger, a fall, at the hands of her guard. Alder had wanted the queen near to win the protection provided by the laws of hospitality, and perhaps that was all that was preventing Maeve from ending Mireille right then.

With Alder's plan, Mireille was walking a dangerous line, balanced on the edge of a blade. Now the blade itself offered a promise. She stood tall. "I will make my choice on the altar."

"And what choice will that be? The false promises of a broken prince, doomed to lose all, or the vow of a clever queen who only grows in power?" Her magic swelled through the room. "It is not often I make such a generous offer to one such as you. I assure you, it will be the last."

"I would be a fool not to take it."

Maeve's grin was full of teeth. "I see we understand each other."

CHAPTER 17

The next morning, Mireille was dead on her feet. Alder had not come for her in dreams. He had expected Mireille would rise from her bed under Maeve's control. He would have been waiting nearby to save her, silently listening at the door, or watching her sleep from the shadows. They had bet on the queen breaking the rules of hospitality while a guest under his roof. Without Mireille having left the bed, he would have assumed the queen had not visited her at all.

But Maeve had broken no rules. Mireille had not been harmed. She had opened the door to the room that held the queen of her own free will. They had not trapped the queen. So, Mireille would make a choice—give in to Maeve's demands, or trust that Alder would defeat her.

The prince's plan still had merit. It had made the queen desperate enough to vow to give up Norcliffe. Mireille might never know the details of her bargain with the prince. It was the reason, after all, that they could not be spoken. If one could simply ask for help, curse-breaking would be far less complicated.

Would that Mireille's own problems might be managed so easily, when the queen had twisted even Norcliffe's most loyal against the

563

kingdom itself. The only person who might have a chance to help was Alder.

A brief knock sounded at the door before Thomas let himself in. He looked as bad as Mireille felt, his blue coat wrinkled and his golden hair mussed. "Still alive, I see." The playfulness she knew he intended fell a bit flat. Thomas was tired, and not just from lack of sleep.

"Have faith, Thomas."

He raised a brow. "You look as if you've tussled a bear."

She ran a hand over her hair, and it snagged on the cuff of her gown. "I am perfectly well. I have no other choice; there's a long day of wedding planning ahead of us."

Thomas stepped closer, lowering his voice. "Rei, talk to me. Let me help."

She turned toward the mirror, making a show of sorting her hair.

To her back, Thomas said, "The queen herself is in this very palace, and you are acting as if it's of little consequence. He betrayed you, before the month was even up."

She dropped her arms. "Coming apart at the seams would do no good. Once the ceremony is over, I can quail about however I like." One way or the other, it would be decided.

He reached up to flick a fingernail against a fresh orange blossom in the tabletop vase. "And our kingdom will be left without its heir."

She flinched, she couldn't help it. In the mirror, she met his gaze. "You know me, Thomas. Please, just this once, I need you to not ask questions."

"You brought me here as your advisor. My entire purpose is to ask questions."

Mireille crossed the distance to face him. "For now, I only need you to be my friend."

He studied her for a long, tense moment. Just when she thought he might turn his back on her, he sighed. "I will always be your friend. Even if it means planning a wedding to a pompous, conniving fae."

She chuckled, feeling able to truly breathe for the first time in days. "He is rather pompous, is he not?"

THE DAYS PASSED QUICKLY, planning for a wedding that, if either the queen or Alder had their wish, would not truly be, and the turning of the moon loomed ever closer. Mireille had Alder's vow that if she participated in his scheme, she would fulfill the price of breaking their bargain and he would set her free. But she would only truly be free if he succeeded in vanquishing the queen, and of that she had no guarantee. Maeve's magic had not visited Mireille again, and without the threat of the queen, Alder had not come to her in dreams.

With any luck neither would have to see the queen until the wedding. The wedding at which Mireille was meant to betray the prince.

A dark part of Mireille wanted to accept the queen's offer, to grasp onto the slender chance that she might truly leave Norcliffe alone. Outside of the bargain, she owed no allegiance to Alder. But sometimes, when midnight brewed and memories rose, the remembered sands of the hourglass landed like stones in her heart. She did not know what losing his bargain to the queen would cost Alder, or the kingdom of Rivenwilde. Saving her own people was one thing, allowing evil to prey upon others was something else entirely.

The tip of her finger welled with blood and she cursed, pressing it into her mouth. She'd been picking at tattered threads from an embroidery piece, hoping it would clear her mind. It hadn't worked. Now she was agitated *and* bleeding.

When a knock sounded at her door, she tossed the tangled mess aside and hurried to answer. Kin swept into the room wearing a deep blue day dress and a broad grin. Mireille stared at the gown she displayed, emotions fighting inside her chest. Kin nodded, shifting the gown for better view, and Mireille walked slowly closer, approaching the creation as if it were a predator.

It was the dream gown. Every piece of lace, the flowing train, all of it exactly as her mind had conjured. "How?" she breathed.

Kin's brow furrowed, but Mireille could not explain that she had dreamed the dress—a wedding gown, to her horror—and suddenly it was real and true before her.

Mireille ran a fingertip carefully over the material. It was exactly her taste, the lace soft as flower petals, and the cut like something from an earlier century. Romantic, like a maiden in the paintings she'd adored as a girl, the women from tales who escaped a medieval keep to run away with the hero of their dreams. Fates, was that where she had taken inspiration? Mireille would have never admitted to longing for such a garment in the waking world, not to anyone. And yet, there it was.

He had it made for you, Kin signed. *The seamstress said he was very specific.*

Had she a shell, Mireille might have crawled into it. But her finger continued to trace the soft lace. *It's beautiful,* she signed, the motions coming more smoothly given her practice with Kin. *Thank you for bringing it.*

Kin curtseyed, but there was something hesitant in her expression.

What is it? Mireille signed.

The woman chewed her lip, but only shook her head. She gestured for Mireille to try it on.

Well, look at that, Mireille thought at her reflection. *He* can *make you blush.* It did not bode well for the coming ceremony, the closest she might get to a marriage with the prince.

Whatever choice she made, whatever bargain she placed her fate in, neither involved completing the ceremony. If what she suspected was true, Alder would not be merely giving up on his kingdom if he married her, but far more. Because it must be someone he loved, someone who loved him in return. Not Mireille.

Not that it mattered. She was a princess of Norcliffe. She would always choose what was best for her kingdom. It just... it didn't make sense that he would go to the trouble of designing the dress. Maeve had never seen it. No one but Mireille and Alder would ever know.

She could ask him. He may not be able to tell her details of his curse, but he could tell her that.

But gowns did not matter. They hoped to trap for the queen before the ceremony. All that mattered was that. Mireille had come to Rivenwilde to find a way to save her kingdom, and every step they took was closer to her last chance.

She stood numbly as Kin laced the bodice. In stockinged feet, she moved closer to the tall mirror, taking it in. He had remembered every detail, after only seeing it only once. Mireille remembered too. It was how she knew the dress was perfect. Kin beamed in the reflection behind her, and Mireille forced a smile in return. Dinner with Alder was only hours away, as they had been doing their best to keep up appearances. If she had begun to look forward to their quiet evenings in his study, reading in companionable silence or laughing over something Noal had said, if she had found herself anxious to return to the dreams, it was only that time was so close. That so much was on the line.

It could be nothing more.

CHAPTER 18

That evening, Mireille strolled through the palace in search of a quiet place to sit, open to the night air. Wandering in the direction she believed to be where she'd seen the butterflies before, she came across a towering archway carved with foxes and rabbits chasing through the marble foliage. She passed beneath the archway, staring up at a scene with squirrels scampering over an apple tree, branches twining in shapes reminiscent of ancient knots and leaves. Head tilted back, spinning slowly in place to take it all in, Mireille caught the scent of wisteria blossoms.

Focus snapping toward the garden beyond, she tracked the scent, on the hunt herself, passing through vine-covered trellises and over a small stone bridge. Tall statues rose from the garden, maidens like the ones inside the palace. All seemed to point her toward the center of the courtyard, where stood the wisteria tree of her dreams.

Strange emotions rolled through her as she stared on, each as unsettling as the last. The tree had been real, and inside her dreams. Alder had taken her to the heart of Rivenwilde. She moved closer, taking in the scene in the light of a lowering sun. The boughs hung heavy, brushing her shoulders as she walked beneath, her palm itching to touch the bark. It might be devastating if it were only a tree, if the magic had been only a dream, but she had no choice but to try.

When her hand brushed the bark, its warmth spread through her, and with it, emotions even sharper than she'd felt during her dreams. Norcliffe was there, safe and stable, and her father, too. But while sensing him offered the comfort that he was well, she could feel that he worried for Mireille. He worried for her, and for Thomas, for his kingdom, and for so much more.

He prayed they'd done right to send her away. His wished Mireille's mother was still alive.

"Oh, Papa," she whispered, and it was as if, somehow, he heard her speak. A spark of joy snapped through the tree, feeling of relief and confusion and the fear that came with the unfamiliar. "Papa," she said again. "It's me. I'm in the fae lands and I am safe. I wish you could see it. I wish I could see you. But I will one day, and all will be well." Her fingers curled against the bark, and her chest tightened with the desire to weep. "I miss you, Papa. And I love you. Please do not worry over me."

The tree seemed to sigh, then the warmth slipped away, and all that remained beneath Mireille's palm was the smooth bark of a tree she was fairly certain was a type used to concoct poisons. She drew her hand free, stepping back with a chest so tight she felt as if she could not get enough air. Uncertain she would be able to find it again, she tore the ribbons from her gown and tied them along the path until she reached the palace walls.

But the archway she'd entered before was gone. All that stood in its place was a pair of plain tall columns. The ribbons fell from her hands.

When she turned again, the garden was gone, and only an empty lawn stretched before her.

NOAL ARRIVED PRECISELY on time to escort Mireille to Alder's study. There was no talk of the prince being too busy, or of her taking her meal in her rooms. It had become routine. Until Nisha stormed out of the study door, nearly barreling into them.

She was dressed like springtime, pale pink satin with trailing violet ribbons and what might have been actual, living flowers attached at the hem. Her focus narrowed on Mireille and Noal. "You, the pair of you. Talk sense into him. The proper rites must be observed." Her tone dipped. "I will not be robbed of this." She marched off, leaving Mireille and Noal to stare after.

Noal said, "I'll just... Fetch your meals, shall I?" then turned and walked the other direction.

"Traitor," Mireille hissed at his back.

Straightening her spine, she strode into the study.

Alder stood behind his desk, pinching the bridge of his nose, face downcast. He lifted his gaze upon her entry, then crossed the room to shut the door, sealing them alone inside. "My sister."

She turned to him. "Your sister."

He stepped closer, letting out a tired breath as his dark eyes met hers. "My sister is insisting on ceremonial rites. Traditionally, three nights before a Riven Court marriage ceremony, the bride is taken to a sacred pool where ancient fae rites are performed."

"Oh." Her hand wanted to clutch at the fabric of her dress, but she forced it to still. "I'm not certain I like the sound of that." Pools were excellent places to drown.

"The rite must be completed by another female," Alder continued. "Nisha has decided it will be her. She has vowed your protection, and she will do as she's vowed. She would not misstep when it would cost her title."

"You make it sound as if it's already decided."

His expression was pained. "It is your choice. But, as it's sacred tradition among all of court, it would look especially suspicious for the bride of a prince to not participate."

Mireille crossed her arms over her waist, feeling suddenly vulnerable. She had agreed to cooperate with Alder's plan. Suspicion would not do. But there was still one issue. "Three nights before the ceremony is—"

"Tonight," Alder finished.

A sacred rite at some fae pool with only Nisha to keep her safe. The queen had ceased her attempts at stealing into Mireille's sleep, and Nisha would not be bent by the fae magic the way it came over Thomas. But they would be outside the protections of the palace. "Is there another reason this ritual so important to Nisha?"

Mireille must have said something wrong, because he straightened. "She may be scheming and duplicitous, but she is still my sister. And she will regard you as a sister the moment we are wed."

The words hung heavy between them. It did not matter that there would be no marriage, because Nisha did not know Alder's plan. It mattered that she believed, the same as the queen. Mireille nodded. "And what of protections once I leave the palace?"

Alder's posture eased, hinting that the ritual was not important only to his sister, but to him as well. "Nisha has given her vow. It is a bond that can be trusted nearly as much as my own." Chin dipping, he gave her an especially dark look. "But I will be near, nonetheless."

"It sounded as if you were not invited."

"I am, as of yet, still the prince of Rivenwilde. I may go where I choose."

She didn't like that it felt as if Nisha would not be aware of his proximity, or that she would be forced to rely so thoroughly on trust, or that she did not seem to have a choice in the matter. There was a great deal not to like about the entire ordeal. "Very well," she said. "The matter is decided."

He seemed at once relieved and on edge. On impulse, Mireille touched his arm. Her mouth opened to ask him why he'd ever agreed to bargain with the queen in the first place. She wanted to ask if the terms had been twisted, if he had thought to marry a princess of Westrende, to fall in love. She wanted to ask about the curse clock, and why it seemed he no longer believed he might fulfill the queen's price.

But she could not, for Mireille understood both that the queen was listening, and that she, and her father, and everyone she loved had nearly given up on defeating the queen, too. There was no room for notions of romance. Their only hope was the same sort of trickery the queen used against them. Their only hope was to work together to end her reign.

Hand still on his arm, she said, "Just tell me what I need to do."

His gaze was searching, but she did not reveal more. She would give Alder's plan a chance, and if it seemed it would fail, she would be forced to betray him, to choose the offer presented by the enemy queen.

Princesses did not have the luxury of following their hearts. And neither did fae princes. They had both proven as much already.

NISHA'S MOOD was radiant as she guided Mireille through a dark and eerie wood. They both wore flowing white gowns, as did the flock of fae courtiers trailing after them.

Thomas had thought Mireille mad for agreeing to any of it, and she could not argue that. But it had been Noal who convinced Thomas of Mireille's safety. A fae vow meant more than either had understood. It was not merely the binds of a reputation or the value of a person's word, it had to do with the very magic they possessed. Evidently, fae magic was not one-sided. It could punish those who broke the rules.

A low growl sounded from the spiky bushes ahead, but none of the fae women paid it mind. Mireille suspected, as Nisha tugged her hand, urging her to keep up in the thick growth, that nothing in the forest was as feral as the fae princess she'd agreed to follow.

Nisha's sigh sounded of anticipation. "My mother would have loved this. She never had a chance to perform the rite, and she was particularly fond of Alder."

"Is she residing at the Storm Court?" Mireille asked weakly, barely navigating the roots jutting up through the path.

Nisha lifted her free hand to her chest. "I'm touched you remembered. But no, she passed on long ago. Alder and I only share a father. We are glad at least that he's long gone." She glanced sidelong at

Mireille, not having to say aloud that she was surprised he'd not mentioned their family history.

The path widened, leading to a large mere, its surface glimmering in the moonlight. Nisha came to a stop, as if taking in the scene, a wide smile changing her face. She looked younger somehow, full of magic and mischief. It was not an entirely comforting idea.

The rest of the group hurried around them, lighting torches and candles, and arranging a stunning array of food on cloth spread over the ground. In all her wildest imaginings, Mireille would never have guessed that her bargain would lead there, a moonlit picnic in a deadly forest.

And then there was the pool, magical waters in which she would be submerged, a symbol of her acceptance of the land and its power as her life merged with its prince. She resisted the urge to look for Alder, who had promised he would be near, watching on should any of it go sideways.

Nisha squeezed the hand she'd been holding, then released it. "I'll fetch us something to drink."

When she returned with two long-stemmed glasses, the rest of the preparations seemed nearly done. Mireille took a sip of the sharp, citrusy punch then drew a breath of crisp night air. A fire had been built near the edge of the mere, a relief, given that she was meant to step into water, but she was beginning to doubt her bravery.

She had vowed to do anything for her kingdom. Surely walking into an ominous midnight pool would be the least of it. And as vexing as Nisha could be, the prince clearly cared about her and about the ritual. It must have been important, and in the end, they plainly expected her to remain safe.

Nisha led Mireille to one of the cloths bedecked with silver tureens of roast venison, bright steamed vegetables, and sourdough bread. It smelled as wonderful as any feast she'd ever attended, though that may have been owing to the arduous trek. Settling onto the ground, wine in one hand and plate in the other, Mireille finally felt the return of warmth.

"Now," Nisha said. "Tell us exactly how you and my brother came to fall in love."

Mireille nearly choked. The others watched with interest.

"Go on," Nisha pressed. "Declare your intentions to us and to the moon. Your words will not leave this circle."

To be sure, the circle was not Mireille's chief concern, it was Alder, possibly listening nearby from the shadows. Clearing her throat, she set aside her plate.

Nisha frowned. "You do love him, do you not? At the announcement, he implied it was a love match."

Mireille had watched fae slide a lie cleverly around the truth, certainly by now she could do it too. She forced a shaky laugh. "Well, I am marrying him and giving up my kingdom, after all. It would be absurd not to love him, all things considered."

Nisha's posture eased, but her clear expectation did not.

"I suppose my feelings for him changed from the first night we danced. We were alone in a moonlit ballroom, soft music coming in through the windows..." She sighed at the memory, because it seemed so long ago, and was not unaware that her audience had taken it as wistful longing. "It was just the two of us, no thought of responsibility, only the melody and the steps. It's such a rare thing as the head of a kingdom. As a girl, I cherished such moments when my father gave them to me." Lips pursed, she tried to recall what else she might share. "And then later, again when we found ourselves alone, walking through such beautiful gardens, speaking low of the things that matter most to us. You can tell a lot about a person when there are no crowds, no courtiers to impress."

The fae women leaned in, hanging on her every word, and Mireille struggled to find more that was safe to share. At the very least, she could toy with the man at bit, should he be listening. She said, "At the outset, he seemed so gruff, but it turns out he was never surly at all. He's quite gentle under all that starch and frippery. Like a sugarplum." That drew a chuckle from the group, but they did not seem sated. "Of course, he has a great many duties, and would never succumb to idle pleasures, but he's, well he can be generous and giving. So entirely thoughtful that he—"

Mireille's words cut off, her face gone hot. She'd nearly detailed the dream gown for an audience. Perhaps she'd had too much punch. The women seemed too close, but so did the moon. Or, perhaps it was the influence of fae magic, because she had surely not just been going on about the prince in front of both him and a crowd. She glanced at the prince's sister.

Nisha's grin was wicked, and more than a little satisfied. She stood, offering Mireille her hand. "Come. It's time."

AT THE WATER'S EDGE, they removed their boots. Nisha stood beside Mireille, and barefoot, they walked together toward the pool, the rest of the fae watching from the bank.

The water was so cold Mireille gasped. She spared a moment to think of Thomas, warm by the fire in his chambers but probably worried sick. She hoped they'd been right to tell him she was safe, and she hoped their time away had given him a chance to complete the favor she'd asked of him.

Water closed around her legs, filling her with the sensation of movement. If it was magic, it was a gentle sort, like the wisteria tree. It seemed to promise it would not harm her, even if it smelled a bit of bad cabbage.

And she had just gone and blindly trusted it, the way she had trusted everything Alder said.

The crash of breaking glass was followed by female shouts and screams. Nisha spun, grabbing hold of Mireille's wrist. A monstrous shadow with strange glimmering eyes flung one of the fae ladies aside, then another as the woman rushed it with a violent cry.

It was a thing of nightmares, nothing like the creature that had attacked Mireille on her first night. It stood taller than any man, its claws formed entirely of darkness. The thing's eyes never came off Mireille. There was no question it was there for her as it released a hungry growl and lunged toward the pool.

Nisha shoved Mireille behind her, then leapt toward the creature, transforming mid-air not into a slender mink, but a sleek and massive beast, as large as a lion and jaws spread wide. The shadow creature shrieked. Nisha's cat-like claws sunk into its chest, and they both splashed down into the water.

The force of their impact shoved Mireille back and into a deeper pool. She tried to kick out but could no longer reach the earth beneath. Unseen hands pressed her suddenly down, beneath the surface and into complete darkness. Body spinning, she couldn't find which way was up. She inhaled a lungful of earthy water. She'd always been a strong swimmer, but her limbs floated uselessly, the weight pressing around her somehow far more than any sea.

A hand closed around her wrist.

She was jerked to the surface, gasping and choking the instant they broke through. She felt Alder behind her, one arm wrapped around her waist as she heaved out water.

When the heaving subsided, he brought her to the water's edge. Throat burning, eyes blurry, Mireille searched out the creature that had attacked. It was nowhere on the bank. Nisha, in her human form and dripping with both water and something thick and dark, scowled at Alder. "I had it under control."

Mireille glanced back at the water, and saw, finally, the shadow creature unmoving, its skin smooth and onyx, the magic that had surrounded it gone.

"She nearly drowned." Alder's voice was cold, the rumble of it flush against Mireille's back, his arms still around her.

"I was handling it," Nisha repeated.

"We will argue at the palace."

Nisha appeared to want to argue right then and there, but with one look at Mireille, hanging wet and limp in Alder's grip, she nodded sharply instead.

CHAPTER 19

ireille's stomach turned as the scenery shifted around them, then they were in Alder's study. He braced her while she tried to regain equilibrium, but there was no use. Drenched and with her lungs burning, she slumped against him. He lifted her effortlessly, carrying her toward a cushioned chair in the corner. After settling her gently upon it, he knelt at her feet, his dark eyes more earnest than she had ever seen. His jacket and crown were absent, his shirt soaked through. "Are you injured?"

She shook her head. "There was something in the water, but it only pressed me down." She pushed a strand of wet hair away from her face with a trembling hand.

His own hand lifted, as if to help, then stopped short. "You have my sincerest apologies that she was able to get that far. The queen was securely inside the palace, but her influence has clearly reached further than any of us knew." He stood. "This proves she believes our ruse, if nothing else. She is terrified we may go through with the ceremony, and that means she will try again."

Mireille's throat was raw. She felt as if she'd heaved up a great deal more water than she had swallowed. "How many times does she have to attempt to kill me before we catch her?"

His gaze shot to hers. "The attempt must be hers, and then, only once. But she has bought her way to you, likely with bargains or threats. There will be no proving that she sent that creature tonight."

"Then how can you be certain that it was her? Surely there are more than a few from your own court who would see me dead."

His shoulder flexed beneath the damp shirt, and he jerked loose his cravat. "Because if it was a member of my court, I would have sensed it sooner. There was no warning before the creature attacked. He may have appeared to you the same as the shadow creatures that reside on our lands, but those loyal to the queen are a species entirely aside."

Mireille slumped into the cushions, aware that she was likely ruining a lovely piece of furniture, but unable to summon the energy to move. She'd made a mistake. She should have taken the queen's offer. "We didn't complete the rite."

He rolled a shoulder. "Nisha had her moment. She won't push again, especially after what happened. It's not as if—" He shook his head and Mireille had the sense he could not say what he'd wanted, that it did not matter whether the ceremony was complete, because she would never truly be his wife. He finished, "If the land accepts you, it will tell you itself. It will show you in its own way."

She picked a rogue leaf off the skirt of her gown, trying very hard not to think about the fact that the land had shown her its heart, the wisteria tree. "You were watching the entire time?"

"You played your part well."

Played her part. Because she had been acting, because none of it was real. She did not meet his gaze.

"You're shivering." Alder lightly touched her cheek. "How careless of me." Flames burst to life in the fireplace, licking across fresh logs as if they had been burning all night.

Sometimes, Mireille could almost forget he possessed bottomless magic, that he was just as fae as the queen. As if pulling her from that pool and transporting her to his study in the space of a breath wasn't reminder enough.

"I will take you to your chambers and have Kin draw a bath."

Mireille leaned closer to the hearth, her shivering nearly subsided. "I would like to stay for a bit, if you do not mind." At his pinched brow, she explained, "Thomas will be waiting in my chambers. I'd rather not let him see how wrongly tonight has gone."

"Ah. In that case..." A thick woven blanket appeared in his hand, another reminder of his magic, then he stepped forward, lightly draping it over her.

She drew the blanket closer. "Thank you for saving me."

"You were there at my request. I will not forget it."

"If it is a favor I'm owed, I fear I must ask it sooner rather than later." She bit her lip at the concern in his expression. "Show me your sculpture. I want to see the room where you work."

He ran a hand over his middle. "I was hoping you would not remember that."

"Highness, I have thought of little else."

He smiled softly at the comment, and it was maybe the most genuine one she'd seen. "Very well," he said finally. "Whenever you ask it of me."

"Now."

He frowned. "You are weak and wet and—"

"More of your flattery? Do stop, I've had all I can take. A woman might swoon at any moment with such adulation." She stood, wrapping the blanket tightly around her, aware that the hem of her gown was still far too wet to drag over palace carpets. But at that moment, Mireille wanted nothing more than to discover what the prince of Rivenwilde would choose to immortalize with chisel and stone.

MIREILLE WAS SURPRISED to find herself transported to Alder's chamber. Had she known, she might have given the entire notion a second thought. As it was, she made a concerted effort not to stare at the spot by the writing desk where she'd picked up the paper knife weeks before. She glanced through the space, mostly unchanged from her last visit, but there were no sculptures to be found.

Shaking his head, he crossed in front of her to press his palm to the wood paneling. A portion swung open, and the prince gestured for Mireille to enter. As she did, candles lit one by one, their light flickering along the walls of another, larger chamber.

The space was scattered with countless workbenches, and bins holding rods, boards, and tools. It smelled of clay and oils, and of the dust that clung to every surface. She moved slowly forward, past blocks of stone, tables scattered with sketches, and the half-formed lines carved into pillars of marble and bronze. She could not be made to stop and consider them all, her gaze intent on a cluster of smaller works near the far wall. When she reached the wall, she gazed up, awestricken.

It was not many pieces, but one massive composition, flowers and creatures wound as intricately into the design as she'd seen in the archway that had led her to the wisteria tree, so lifelike she felt as though she might reach out to find petals and fur soft instead of stone.

Hand pressed to her chest, Mireille could only imagine Alder alone in the large open room, recreating every flower and form that touched the land, biding his time until the curse was broken. Trapped. Stripped of his full power. Beholden to the queen.

She nearly jumped when he spoke close behind her.

"It was unfair of me to goad you into playing for me, when it was obviously so painful."

She stiffened. His thoughts had evidently run perilously close to hers. She said, "I did so willingly."

"Still, I should have repaid you this favor then."

Stepping toward a large, canvas-covered piece, she said, "You have now." She could almost feel his discomfort when she neared it.

He said, "There are some interesting studies over here, you need not trouble with that older work."

Mireille reached forward to drag the canvas aside. Orange blossoms. So real she could smell their gentle scent. The white petals were rimmed with the finest grooves, their stamens molded in bronze. She glanced over her shoulder at Alder. She had yet to uncover the significance of the blossoms, and it was clear this piece had a significance of its own.

He moved close to her side. "They did not always exist here. My mother planted them when she arrived. They were her favorite, a reminder of her home, and she spent a great deal of time guiding them into what they are today. The avenue is a sacred place. Forbidden to those who walk the grounds." His gaze met hers. "I'm afraid I was showing off a bit when I allowed you and Thomas to approach the palace through that lane."

There was true sadness behind his words. It was not the secret she had expected, but she understood it well. "My mother taught me the piano. When she grew weak, I played for her, every day until she was gone. I had not played again until—"

"Until I asked you to."

"You did not ask. I volunteered."

"Regardless, I cannot regret hearing you play. It was... I feel honored to have experienced it." His gaze was steady, even as color rose to her cheeks. "You miss her."

"Every day." Mireille's words were soft, barely a whisper.

"Tell me about her. Did she cherish growing up in Norcliffe as dearly as you?"

Candlelight glinted in his dark hair, still damp from the pond. The answer danced on the tip of her tongue, eager to share in the stories of her mother, stories she had rarely been able to reveal, but there were things she must keep to herself. Things that could be used against her. Things that might slam shut the narrow door that they'd opened. "Speaking of her is painful." The words were not exactly a lie, she had truly wanted to tell him, but that was a danger in itself.

"Of course. Forgive me." Expression suddenly guarded, Alder offered his arm. It was as if he had forgotten, as if he had been there only for her. And it was over once more. "I should escort you to your chamber. Surely Thomas is asleep by now."

He wouldn't be, but Mireille took the prince's arm anyway, casting one last longing glance at the sculpture as he led her from the room. The orange blossoms weren't some ancient magic, nor did they bear hidden symbolism. They simply revealed what Alder cherished, and the memories that kept him company in the long hours of the night.

CHAPTER 20

The following evening's dinner conversations with Alder had been noticeably stilted. Mireille had the sense the sands of his curse clock would run out as they stood before an altar beneath the moon—the fae were a theatrical sort—which meant that time was nearly up for both of them, as well as for their kingdoms. And if the queen obtained so much more power, she would be impossible to stop.

Maeve's offered bargain had clearly only been a precaution in the event that her assassination attempts failed. The queen must have believed Mireille and Alder could fall in love. If she had not, she would have nothing to fear. How strange that love was the thing a monster feared most.

Alder, for his part, had ordered Mireille watched almost *too* closely. Her first moment of peace came when Thomas had gone to the kitchens to fetch a snack. Alone in her chambers, she leaned back into the settee. But she'd no more than let out a sigh before the door opened to Noal, pushing a small, wheeled cart bedecked with cake.

Mireille frowned. "I thought we'd decided on the ceremony menu already."

Noal wheeled the cart to her, then took a step back. "Apparently the others have been deemed out of fashion. Princess Nisha awaits your opinion on this new selection."

She picked up a fork, examining the assortment. Strange little leaves and flowers adorned one, sugar sculptures of varying subjects topped the others. Perhaps she should have requested orange blossoms.

"There is a saying about throwing rocks at feeding lions," Noal said. When Mireille glanced up at him, he added, "Don't. That's the saying. Don't throw rocks at feeding lions."

"Lest you get eaten yourself?"

"Just that." He cleared his throat. "I suspect such a game is afoot, and I would be remiss to not say it seems a great folly, what the pair of you are about." He crossed his hands at the wrists, and for the first time, it came across less as a habitual gesture and one that felt as if he were performing a duty. "Mayhap, laying down arms would bring you far greater strength."

Noal was no fool. The man watched everything. She lifted a bite of cake to her lips, refusing to acknowledge the bit about her and Alder surrendering to each other. "I see no lion, only a spider, tangling her web tighter and tighter. And the only good way to be rid of spiders is to set their webs aflame."

"As long as the entire house doesn't burn down in the process."

"Noted," Mireille said.

"Shall I tell Nisha that you have made your choice?" He gestured toward the tray, though she had only tasted a sliver of one. It did not taste well, but they would all taste of ash in her mouth, given the circumstances. "Raspberry, I think." At least it looked pretty.

She cleared her throat against a tickle and reached for a glass. Her tongue felt a bit thick, and she coughed. By the time she lifted the glass to her lips, her airway had constricted.

Noal leaned forward, his eyes gone wide, posture stiff. Mireille stood, the glass fell from her hands, and with not a single word, she collapsed. He caught her just before she hit the ground. Fingers clawed into the material of his vest, she struggled to breathe, and her gaze met his. *Poison.* She'd been poisoned.

That was when she remembered. Nisha had not even been in the kitchens—she'd said she was going to the forest to collect some rare... *something* she'd meant to use in the decorations. Mireille let go of Noal, scrambled backwards, and knocked into the cart, porcelain shattering around her and tea pooling around her limp arms as blackness overtook her.

MIREILLE STARED up at a strange dark ceiling. She blinked, too exhausted to lift her hands and rub her bleary eyes. It was not her bed, not her chamber. Dragging every ounce of her will to shove down the emerald coverlet, she tried to sit up.

"You should not attempt to move." Alder's voice was thick. His shadowed form seemed to block out the rest of the room. A memory swam to the surface, and Mireille was unsure if it was real or a dream, Alders voice, *I shouldn't have let you out of my sight. Not even for a moment.*

"The cakes..." Her throat was raw. Her mouth tasted of medicinal herbs.

He stepped closer. "The queen has grown in power. Noal has been questioned extensively and, it seems, she was somehow able to influence him. The palace was swept, the staff interrogated, no stone left unturned." His jaw flexed. "She has more spies among us than I ever could have imagined. They are inside the palace. Our *home*."

Just as she had done in Norcliffe. Except that Noal had not been asleep. Mireille should have told Alder about the queen calling her to the room with the hourglass, when her magic had felt different and she had not taken full control. She fumbled to grab hold of his wrist; her fingers felt puffy and clumsy. "I am still here. She has failed. Tomorrow night is the ceremony."

He shook his head. "It was only because you tasted so little, else we would not have saved you." He let out an angry breath. "Even here, in my own kingdom, her influence has become insidious."

She attempted to push herself to sitting, her arms so weak they trembled. "Tell me what happens during the ceremony."

He sat gingerly on the bed, pressing her back down. "There are things we should not speak of outside of dreams."

Mireille's fingers found his forearm, bare below rolled-up sleeves. She tugged. "Come, then. Let us dream. "

Alder hesitated, but Mireille's heavy eyes were taking longer and longer blinks, and he finally lowered himself onto the bed beside her, letting her draw his arm around her as she shifted to her side, her breath uneasy and slow.

MIREILLE WOKE IN A MOONLIT GARDEN, fireflies dancing overhead, her unbound hair woven through tall grass and the scents of wisteria and honeysuckle all around her. She flexed her fingers, feeling well once more. She turned her face toward Alder who, inexplicably, lay on his side in the grass beside her.

Or not inexplicably, she supposed, because the dream was hers.

She ran a fingertip over the mark on his temple as his dark eyes traced the lines of her face. When she pressed up to sitting, he did as well. Her fingers entwined with his. "Tell me."

"When she attacks, I will be free to destroy her. I am more than an even match for her, but the bindings on my power must be broken." He drew his hand from hers. "But I cannot ask it of you. I will not risk your life further."

"I am at risk every moment. That risk is the very reason I am here."

"You came here for protection. I have nearly failed, time and again. If I fail once more, if you are harmed—" His words cut off, bitten back with something like rage and despair.

He would lose everything. His lands. His title. The bargain. Because he'd pinned all his hopes on Mireille. "I cannot break your bargain."

Alder went utterly still.

"I saw the enchanted hourglass. You needed her to believe that you loved me, and I you. You needed her to because you cannot marry for anything less." But he had no intention of falling for Mireille. He only meant to trick the queen.

His expression was a mask. "You saw the clock."

"The night of the ball. I was not certain of the details, but it felt of her magic. And there were hints, indications that you were bound by something more." What a fool she was to admit it, because he would know how she had discovered the truth. There was only one other person aware of the details, and that person was the queen.

"She got to you."

The words hurt, and more than they should. "She attempted to call it a ruse, certain that you could not be in love with me."

Alder was silent for a long while. He did not accuse her of betrayal, though surely the thought crossed his mind. He was clever enough to know what Maeve would offer. When he finally spoke, it was to say, "It seems she is no longer certain. She would not have risked coming for you again if she were." He looked at her, his gaze darkening with remembered anger, possibly of the real Mireille, feeble in his bed, barely able to sit up. "If you wish to continue, you will remain at my side. You will not be out of my sight again."

Something in her chest tightened. "And if I do not wish to continue?"

He looked away, brushing a shiny ladybird from his sleeve. "You have done everything I have asked. I will consider your promise fulfilled and your price paid. You will be free to go."

The queen would kill her in an instant without Alder. Norcliffe would be lost. And still... "You would truly set me free, when I am your only chance of beating her?"

His jaw shifted. "I can never truly beat her. She has removed any chance. My only hope was a default, to spur her into breaking our laws —had she openly and intentionally violated hospitality, I could move against her. But she has proved too canny to be baited into such a violation."

Mireille met his eyes, finding only truth in them. He would let his last opportunity slip through his fingers. He was trapped. He could not marry without love. It was the same as her friends in Westrende had always said, the price of breaking a bargain would be too dear to pay.

Mireille found, when she searched deep within her heart, that she did not truly have any other choice. She only hoped Norcliffe would survive her decision.

"We will go through with your plan."

CHAPTER 21

Mireille rested as the day wore into night. Thomas visited her, as did Kin and Noal—the latter of whom had taken the queen's act as a personal slight and was possibly plotting his own private revenge. Mireille made clear that she held no ill will toward the man, and that she herself had been under the queen's spell.

She did not admit it had happened in Alder's chamber.

The strength of the queen's influence continued to surprise them all, but they seemed more angered than unsettled, made worse by Maeve attempting to use the fae closest to Alder to see her work done.

Throughout Mireille's visits, Alder had stayed seated in a corner of the room, book in hand. His eyes remained on the page, but his fingers never lifted to turn one. Seeing her ready to drift off to sleep, Thomas had collected the playing cards he'd brought—a favored pastime of their youth—and had departed with a promise to remain only one room away. All had agreed that while Maeve was after Mireille, it would be unwise for Thomas to roam the palace on his own, so Kin had been assigned as his protector.

Alone again, eyes heavy, Mireille found her attention lingering on

Alder. The sun dipped below the horizon, but he'd made clear she was not to leave his room. "Where will you sleep?"

His eyes did not leave the page. "I shall not."

"You should rest," he said.

Mireille wanted to argue, but the remedies continuously forced upon her had made her drowsy. Against her will, her eyes drifted closed, and sleep came swiftly.

Alder did not come to her dreams.

When she woke, morning light shone through the tall carved marble windows and he remained in his chair, though the book was no longer in his lap. He said, "Kin will draw you a bath, if you are ready."

She rubbed her puffy eyes but felt worlds better. "You trust me alone again?"

He stood. "No."

She gave him a look. He only approached the bed to offer his hand.

"I am steady," she promised, but took it nonetheless. Neither were wearing gloves, and the feeling of his bare skin on hers sent a jolt of awareness through her. He pulled her to her feet and she peered up at him, her thumb sliding across the back of his hand. "Thank you for watching over me."

"Perhaps you would have fared better as my prisoner after all. It seems I've done a poor job of it as your betrothed."

She asked, "Is it not bad luck for the groom to see the bride on their wedding day?"

"Only if the groom finds her displeasing." Then, seeming to realize what he'd said, his voice went gruff. "That is a human tradition."

Mireille suppressed a smile. "And what is fae tradition?"

Lifting her hand, he turned it, placing a light kiss on the center of her palm. "You will soon find out."

A jolt went through her, and she let out a shaky breath. Certainly, that had not been a show for the queen. Alder's eyes rose to hers. Her cheeks were hot, her pulse fluttering in her chest like a trapped bird.

There was a moment of stillness before his lips parted, as if to speak, and she wanted him to, desperately so. But a knock interrupted whatever he might have said. He released her hand, the door came open, and Kin stepped inside carrying a stack of towels. She glanced between them, then ducked her head, beginning to back away.

Alder cleared this throat, and Kin froze. "Please," he said. "Go ahead."

Kin crossed the room, head still dipped, then disappeared into an adjoining chamber. Alder gestured for Mireille to follow. She did, rather gratefully.

Mireille closed the door, bracing herself against it. The thrum of her heart was frantic, a rabbit's before prey. *Do you love him*, Kin had once asked. Fate help her, she did.

She was not certain what had happened, but she felt a bit betrayed. Her heart had always been strong. Sensible. Not a fool to chase a dream off a cliff.

There was only one thing she could do.

Straightening away from the wall, she signed to Kin, *I need your help*.

Kin's smile was warm and open; clearly the woman had no idea what a mess she might be taking on. She signed, *Anything*.

PLAN IN PLACE, Mireille had nearly steadied herself by the time she dressed and returned to Alder's company. He had not resumed his usual state, however, testing her lunch himself before she'd been allowed a single bite. As the minutes ticked by and the ceremony drew nearer, he grew even more cautious, and she was only permitted to return to her chambers to prepare with Kin, Nisha, and Thomas watching her every move.

Draped in the delicate wedding gown, Mireille did a slow turn before the mirror. Kin's anxious smile had Mireille wiping her palms. It would work. It had to.

She gave one final glance at her reflection, then nearly shrieked when Maeve's reflection peered back. It had been the queen's first opportunity to contact Mireille, and she had taken it. Behind her,

Mireille could see Kin had noticed and, as she'd been warned, rushed to distract Nisha and the other fae ladies.

"Have you made your choice?"

Maeve's voice rang in Mireille's head, a knowing not unlike she had experienced in the dreams. Alder had been right, the connection felt stronger, and Mireille hoped she had not miscalculated her chances. The queen wore crimson once more, a celebration of her triumph.

But she had not won yet.

Mireille met her steely gaze. "I have."

"What is she on about?" Nisha said from across the room. Kin must have made a sign, because it was followed by an incredulous, "Practicing her speech? It is not a state dinner. She doesn't—what? Fine, yes, I'm listening. Stop grabbing at me like I'm a basket of scones."

Mireille leaned closer to the mirror. "He will escort me to the ceremony. I will announce to the entire court that we planned a ruse and our betrothal was never intended to go through."

Maeve's eyes lit with dark satisfaction. If Mireille would do such a thing, if she cared so little for Alder that she might humiliate him, then he would never go through with the ceremony, lest he forfeit his kingdom. "Of course it was a ruse," the queen purred.

"In exchange, you agree to never harm me, to leave my father, my kingdom, and the people of Norcliffe alone. You will bring no harm to those I love."

Maeve considered the words. It was asking a lot for a simple proclamation from Mireille, but the proclamation would mean Alder had lost his bargain with the queen. He must marry for love or Rivenwilde would be Maeve's. Mireille was willing to bet she wanted the fae lands more than she wanted Norcliffe. But lately, Mireille was betting on a great deal.

Maeve's lips curled. "It is a nice touch, announcing your ruse publicly. Adds to the disgrace. I like it."

"Well," Mireille said. "You know how I feel about fae who trap me in bargains."

Maeve laughed, the sound light and genuine. "To be sure." She lifted a hand, as if signing their contract in empty air. "Let our bargain be struck. You will make the agreed upon announcement, humiliate the prince, and I will leave your sad little kingdom and its people alone. *And* I vow to not so much as touch a single hair on your pretty little head, or anyone you truly love."

Heart thundering, Mireille could only nod. "I agree to your terms."

"What was that?" Nisha called from the connecting room, just as Maeve flashed a final wicked grin and disappeared from the glass. "Did you just say something about *terms?*"

Mireille turned to find Nisha striding back into the main chamber, Kin at her back, fingers twined anxiously together. Mireille gave the group a baffled smile, shoving her hands behind her back where a gold bracelet now hung at one wrist, its clasp heavy against her palm. "Are those not the ceremonial words?"

Nisha's gaze narrowed.

Mireille shrugged. "Well, it was certainly how Alder initiated our first bargain. Perhaps someone could let me know so that I won't do it wrong." She lifted the braceletless hand to tuck a lock of hair behind her ear.

Nisha did not seem convinced, but the room was empty of evil queens. Kin had fulfilled the favor Mireille had asked. All that was left, was for Mireille to pretend she was about to not get married.

CHAPTER 22

Mireille clung to Alder's arm as he escorted her down a torchlit path lined with flowering vines, moths fluttering near mounds of night-blooming honeysuckle, and blossoms trailing on a chill breeze. The sun was just beginning to set, casting everything it touched in an amber glow. A stole had been added to her dress for warmth, but she found being close to Alder's side was of much more comfort. It did not stop the anguish that twisted in her gut, but the look he had given her when he'd come to retrieve her had certainly helped.

Alder leaned near as a beautiful archway of orange blossoms came into view. They were being married in the lane. He had not told her.

His lips brushed her ear. "I will keep you safe, this time I swear it."

Mireille's chest swelled with warmth. And then, suddenly, a strange, fluttery panic. "Wait." She gripped his arm, and he stopped, turning to look at her. "I—" She could not tell him. She could say nothing she wanted to. She could only ask, "I must know. If this dress was truly my imagining, then how did it come to exist here, outside the dream, with every detail exact?"

"I remembered," he said simply.

"Every detail."

His brow pinched. "Of course."

Mireille drew a deep breath, then let it out with a shaky smile. "I am ready." She turned to face the path, arm in his.

He gave her a sidelong glance but continued on. As they reached the lane, the fae lining each side and dressed their finest turned their attention to the pair. Each held a tall taper, the flames defense against the dark.

Queen Maeve stood toward the end of the path in a place of honor as her station demanded, near a stone dais beneath the grandest orange tree of all. Delicate white blossoms draped low enough that they nearly brushed the dark hair of the fae officiant standing in wait.

Thomas stood near the front of the crowd with Kin by his side. Thomas was noticeably more anxious than Kin, which spoke volumes given that the fae woman knew a great deal more about what was to happen than him, but he gave Mireille a small nod.

Her chest squeezed. They were so very, very close to either victory or utter failure.

Soft music accompanied their walk, and as Alder and Mireille moved past the fae, their candles lifted skyward. Mireille was shocked to see her Westrende friends tucked into the crowd beside Nisha and her feral grin, and worried what bargain must have been struck to bring them there while securing both the fae kingdom's secrets and the safety of Westrende officials. She shot Alder an anxious glance. He whispered, "They were transported to the lane and shown nothing else. It seemed wise to permit them to witness our interaction with the queen, besides that Lord Holden demanded as much on your behalf."

It was not wise, but Alder had done it anyway. For her. She felt her mouth go soft and shaky.

"They are safe," he vowed. "No matter what."

She nodded, swallowing back what he evidently assumed was fear. He reached across his chest, squeezing Mireille's hand where it rested on his arm, then turned to face her before the dais. He took both of her hands in his. She could feel his magic, ancient and powerful, and truly could not believe what she was about to do.

As the officiant cleared his throat to speak, Alder tugged her a fraction closer, as if he could tell she might be about to do something rash —or, possibly, to bolt.

Voice low, she said, "You have asked me to trust you with much. I need you to trust me now, even more. At least for the next few minutes." She squeezed his hands then pulled free, and something that might have been fear flashed in his expression. Or, perhaps, he had been certain she would betray him all along.

Mireille stepped forward to address the crowd, trembling with nerves. The gathered fae stirred at the break in ritual, some appearing only intrigued while others seemed ready to act. She could feel the queen's magic, biting at her as if in anticipation, the bracelet's clasp hot on her wrist.

So much rode on this one thing. It had to work. She swallowed hard, curling the fingers of that hand into a fist.

"Regretfully, I must inform you all that this engagement has been a ruse." Gasps and excited murmurs broke out immediately, forcing Mireille to raise her voice. Evidence that at least part of those in attendance hadn't believed the ceremony would play through had her prickling in cold sweat. Pressing down the thought, she announced, "You have all been misled, and for that, I am sorry only that it may hurt those I truly love. The prince and I never intended to complete the ceremony."

Maeve grinned triumphantly from her spot beside the dais, as if the chaos of the crowd gave her strength, then the sharp sting of magic clawed up Mireille's body and down to her wrist.

The clasp snapped. The bracelet fell to the ground.

Mireille had done as the queen's terms had asked. The bargain had been sealed, as easily as that. Norcliffe and her father were safe, but only from direct attacks. And Mireille knew how those terms could be subverted, which meant they were not truly safe unless... Well, all that was left was to make Alder choose.

She turned to him, and the crowd hushed. His gaze lifted from the chain at her feet. There was something a bit feral in his expression, his posture seeming to want to act but unsure exactly what to do. He would not surrender, even when he believed all was lost.

Neither would she.

She stepped closer. "It was a ruse, a bargain, and you are the most brooding, confusing, and utterly vexing man I have ever known. All of those things are true."

The queen was gleeful, her magic dancing at Mireille's back, ready to devour all of Rivenwilde once the last sand dropped on her deal with Alder. Mireille did not spare her a glance. In fact, she was afraid her expression might give her away.

"Despite all of it, the danger, and the misery, and certainty that every day in this beautiful palace was wasted on me... for, you see, I understood that everything that mattered would soon be gone." She swallowed. "Despite all that, I fell in love."

Alder's jaw went slack. He looked for a moment as if unsure he'd heard her right, and then, all at once, like he had never quite seen her before. It pleased some deep part of Mireille that she had surprised him so thoroughly. And also, not a small amount, that he did not seem disappointed by her confession. The magic bit at her harder, painful fingers that wanted to lash at her.

She took another step toward him, her voice dropping. "I love you enough to break your curse, but only if at least some small part of you could love me in return."

He was silent for so long that Mireille worried she had judged the situation disastrously wrong. Perhaps his care and attention over her was truly only his vow, or that he merely needed her to draw the queen to the ceremony for his plans. Perhaps she would be the one to stand humiliated.

Perhaps she had cost them their chance at the queen.

She said weakly, "The curse surely does not require that you fall madly, head over heels. Even just a little bit, a small amount. If you loved me at all, it could work. We could be free of your bargain with the queen, before the last sands fall." Desperate, she pleaded, "I know that you need a princess of Westrende to break the Rive. I am sorry that I have kept—"

The bite to Mireille's skin went sharp, a rumble of power passed through the dais, and before she could get the words out, the queen laughed, loud and squawking, like carrion on a carcass, ready to claim her prey. It could be no accident the confession had been stopped. It was the single advantage Mireille had.

A pillar dropped to the earth. The queen stepped forward. "He will never marry you, fool. He would lose everything. Nothing matters more to the prince than this land. After all, it is all that he is." Maeve's voice dipped, and another pillar fell, crumbling before it even touched the ground. "He could *never* love you."

Mireille had lost her chance. The queen would act, and Alder would attack, and they would no longer be fighting bargains. They would be fighting the sands of time. She opened her mouth to shout the truth but before a word escaped, Maeve lifted her skirts to move, her magic rising through the space.

It was over.

Alder dropped to his knees.

"Mireille," he said, grasping both her hands in his. "I do. I do love you. Like a fool, for all of it—my kingdom, my title—I would give it up, if you would be my wife."

Behind them, Nisha let out a loud whistle, and at least one other fae in the crowd cheered. With the queen in attendance, it was an act of bravery, but very few understood what was truly at stake. It was not if Alder could find a true princess of Westrende on such short notice, if that was what he thought. He had assumed they had lost. And he was taking her as his bride on their way down.

He loved her. Genuinely. And they were nearly out of time to break the curse.

The queen surged forward, her fingers seeming too long for her hands. There was a darkness about her edges, and heat rolled off her, and though her voice turned cruel and hard, it somehow felt persuasive. "Adorable, truly. But, prince, she has betrayed you. She's all but admitted she's been in league with me this whole time." She held forward a hand and the chain lifted from the dais to settle in her palm. "We had a bargain, she and I. And look at you, down on your knees. *She vowed to betray you.*"

Alder stood, drawing Mireille near him as he stared at the queen. "I no longer care what you have to say. I will break our bargain, and the law will protect me. You intend to take Rivenwilde either way, but you cannot prevent our union."

A loud, harsh breath came out of the queen. Her arms had shifted wide, but Alder was right, she could not attack him or Mireille. They were all under bargain. And as for the people they cared about, well, the queen was a guest on Rivenwilde land. She was as bound as Alder.

He turned to the officiant, a tall man in ceremonial robes who did not appear in the least ruffled by the goings on. "Wed us."

The officiant nodded, placing one hand on his chest and raising the other where Alder and Mireille's were joined. The dais cracked in half.

"You cannot marry her!" Maeve screeched.

It was an actual, literal screech, and the entire crowd lurched backward.

Something changed in Alder's expression; he looked from Maeve to Mireille. She squeezed his hands tighter; there did not seem to be time to explain before the curse clock ran out, and Maeve had no intention of allowing Mireille to say it. Alder might not understand why the queen was so angry, but he was certainly clever enough to see that if that if she wanted to prevent the ceremony so badly, he should complete it, even if it only meant it might force her to act against him and break fae law.

He pulled Mireille against his chest, eyes on the queen, and ordered, "Do it."

The officiant began to speak but Maeve shrieked, "Cease, you fools!"

They did not cease. The ceremony carried on.

Maeve's chest heaved in a great wave.

Alder shoved Mireille behind him, commanding the officiant not to stop for anything.

With every word, Maeve breathed harder, until her body began to thrash. A screech tore through the air, and in the crowd several candles dropped to the ground, guttering out as fae scattered, some to safety, others to stand by their prince. Nisha herded Thomas and the other humans behind her, swords drawn, as Kin frantically signed toward the courtiers near the dais.

Noal calmly released the buttons of his coat.

Maeve's form warped and grew, twisting itself into a shadow creature like the one that had attacked at the sacred pond, but far, far worse. The remaining fae spread out into fighting stances while others watched from the shelter of the trees.

Mireille wasn't certain even the trees were safe. They swayed with the rumblings of magic, their tall trunks creaking and groaning in an unearthly way.

The creature that was Maeve stood twice as high as any in the crowd and knocked two of the largest fae near the dais aside with such force they landed in the distant shadows. The thing charged, and Alder moved for it.

Mireille had to stop him; they needed to finish the ceremony.

Too fast, the creature rose on its unfathomable haunches, long, knife-sharp talons bursting from its shadow hands. Alder's own hands drew back, but he was too close. The beast would tear him to shreds.

Mireille moved without thought, throwing herself between Maeve and the prince. A roar tore through the air, echoing off the trees bordering the lane. Shadowy claws rested a hair's breadth from Mireille's throat.

She stared up at the monster. "The laws of your land may allow you to act first, be punished later, but you and I have an agreement sealed by bargain. I have done exactly what you asked of me. You cannot harm me, nor can you harm my father, my kingdom, or the people of Norcliffe."

Mireille took hold of Alder's arm where he stood at her back, his chest rising and falling in angry, violent breaths. Her jaw tightened. "You may bring no harm to those I love. And I love the prince." She felt Alder melt against her, the way his body and his magic seemed purr in welcome and regard. He might believe his reign was about to come to an end, but it was clear he treasured the moment nonetheless. He was barely touching her, but she had never felt more embraced.

Mireille vowed, "Soon, the Rive will come down, and Rivenwilde will ally itself with Norcliffe, and Westrende, and even the kingdom of Nordhelle."

The statement was not truly hers to make, but no one called her bluff, so she went on. "When the officiant finishes the binding and we are wed, what price must you pay to Alder?"

"Her lands will be forfeit," Nisha said from the steps of the dais. "They will belong to Alder, but Rivenwilde will remain severed due to the curse, so those lands cannot be joined with ours."

"She will be queen of nothing," Alder said with disgust. He slid a hand over Mireille's waist. "And it would be worth my crown to see that alone come to fruition."

Mireille felt sick. She'd seen how close the sands were to running out. She did not know how much longer the prince and Rivenwilde had left. It had truly been his last chance. The fae had not known the details of the curse, that the Rive would not fall unless he married someone of noble Westrende blood, only that if the Rive did not fall, Alder would never be king. Rivenwilde could never be free.

Nisha and several others stepped slowly closer, and the beast that was Maeve breathed its rattling breath.

Alder's grip drew Mireille against his chest. "So the question remains," he asked Maeve. "Why is it so important to that you prevent us from becoming wed, when to break fae law would cost you even more?"

A voice rose from the crowd. "I think I can answer that."

The creature whirled, baring its teeth and releasing a ragged snarl. Nisha flipped a sword forward, seemingly from thin air, and waggled it toward the beast. "It might not kill you, but it will certainly hurt."

Magic rose from the earth, stronger than Mireille had ever felt, shaking the entire platform and warming her to the core. "It might not kill you," Alder said. "But I am still Prince of Rivenwilde, and I will."

The creature's shadowy, malformed muzzle twitched, but it did not attack. Mireille wondered precisely how torturous being torn apart by fae magic was, given how even Maeve reacted to threat of it.

She tore her gaze away long enough to peer into the crowd, lit by flickering torchlight. The voice had come from the marshal of Westrende.

The marshal gave a little wave of acknowledgement. "You said he must marry a princess of Westrende."

"Yes," Mireille started. "He doesn't know."

"Ah," said the marshal.

Mireille turned to face her prince. "I hope you can forgive me. It was the only way we could think to keep me safe. You see, at first, we did not understand why a fae queen would be so set on ruining our kingdom, why she cared so much about the heir of a castle by the sea."

The creature gave a snarly little huff of air. Its skin was shifting into something like the bark of a hawthorn tree.

"The assault was relentless, and it cost—" Mireille swallowed hard. "It cost so much. When it became clear that her true target was me, Thomas and the others began an investigation. It seemed the queen had attacked neighboring kingdoms in recent years, all with one thing in common. But we had no way to defeat her. Clear was that she would not stop, even when Norcliffe was destroyed. So, we had to come. We had to find answers. We had to hope." She gave him her most earnest gaze. "My mother was not born in Norcliffe. She was from Westrende. A distant line, yes, but, well, there has been no one closer to throne for ages, given the misfortunes that have befallen nearly everyone of a royal line."

Alder's expression was one of true shock and, inexplicably, his gaze found the Westrende officials in the crowd.

"It's true," the marshal said. "You know they make officials study all the lineage and trade agreements. Perhaps I not as much as the magistrate here, but between us, we do have to have a thorough grasp of the law." The dark-haired man beside her stared on and the marshal said, "So that is your answer. The fae have kept a king from coming to power since long before Mireille's mother left for Norcliffe. She is the last Westrende princess, now that the others have been married off."

The prince stood in silence. The other humans present, representatives of Nordhelle and friends of the marshal, gave him a little wave.

The marshal crossed her arms, a bit smug that the prince hadn't sorted it all out. "Well, who's the clever one now?"

The blond-haired man beside the marshal tipped his chin toward the queen. "That's why she doesn't want you to go through with it. The wall will come down. The Rive will heal. She won't merely be the queen of nothing. You'll be the king of..." He gestured vaguely. "Everything."

The prince stared at the man, then the marshal, clearly in shock, but his hand did not loosen from around Mireille. His voice dripped with distrust. "And Westrende would allow that? You would cede its lands to me?"

The marshal's stance shifted, her hand resting on the hilt of her sword. "No." A breath came out of Alder, as if he had known it was too good to be true, but the marshal's gaze fell on Mireille. "We would cede it to her."

Thomas had clearly been able to get Mireille's message to Westrende—the favor she'd asked of him before—and though she had hoped their council would vote to support the union, and grant the marshal and magistrate leave to negotiate on their behalf, given that the Rive would fall regardless, it was in their best interest to have an ally in the fae and their new queen.

A noise came from Alder, seemingly rusty and disused, and Mireille glanced back to find that it was laughter. He had lifted his face to the canopy of sweet blossoms, letting the surprised, buoyant sound free. The crumbled pillars shook into dust as moonlight slid into the opening of the canopy, lighting the broken dais in a silvery blue glow.

Then his face turned down toward Mireille, still alight with a joy she could not truly believe, and he swung her around, arms locking her to him, and kissed her, long and deep. Beneath them, Rivenwilde sang, its magic humming through the earth and into every blossom and tree.

When the kiss finally broke, leaving Mireille breathless and wondering, the truth of their situation finally started to sink in. They were free. There were no more bargains, no more curses. Only her, and Alder, and safety for all their people.

On the dais behind them, Maeve had shifted back to her previous form, gown torn, crown askew. She was on her knees, no longer a queen, as the officiant had finished his declaration and the vows had been sealed with a kiss. Behind her, dagger in one hand, Noal reached forward and removed the woven crown with such satisfaction that Mireille had a sort of dastardly desire to watch him do it again.

The corner of his lips twitched, and he tossed the crown. Alder caught it with one hand, giving it a long, silent glance, before returning his gaze to Mireille. "Highness," he whispered, then placed the circle gently on her head, and leaned forward to kiss her again.

EPILOGUE

The prince had not agreed to allow the Westrende marshal and magistrate into the palace until Mireille threatened to offer both all the hospitality she might as queen of Rivenwilde. Because it was true, now that the curse was broken, the lands would be restored and Alder would be raised to his rightful place as king. He was the one who had married her after all, she reminded him.

Certainly, he could not have thought that she might suddenly grow meek.

The pair from Nordhelle, however, Alder treated with much greater courtesy and respect, which was to say, likely as much as he could offer a human—excluding Mireille, of course.

As her friends observed the interior of the palace awestricken, Mireille realized it had begun to feel comfortable and familiar to her. She briefly squeezed Thomas's hand, who had, of course, immediately forgiven her, even if he did seem slightly baffled and overwhelmed by the entire ordeal. Thomas had never been fond of ordeals.

They settled into a large sitting room, Alder, Mireille and her allies from Westrende and Nordhelle, who happened, happily, to be just as well-titled as she and legally able to negotiate on behalf of their kingdoms, plus Thomas, and Nisha. Noal and Kin stood to the side of the room, proprietary in their duties to their soon-to-be king and queen.

Mireille would need to write a letter to her father. The first of so, so many letters and documents to come.

The magistrate pointed to a line of text on a thick stack of contracts they had brought along and had been marking up for hours. "This section will outline the new border laws. Any fae bargains struck outside the of these marcations"—he gestured to a well-sketched map — "will be null and void."

"And your council will agree to this?" Alder's tone was once again that of a royal, sharp and dry and demanding respect.

He shot Mireille a look. "What are you grinning about?"

She only shook her head. It was not very queen-like to be giddy, to be sure. It would take all of them to restore their law, their lands, and bring down the wall without breaking something else. There was much work ahead.

The alliance was necessary, and there would be many compromises on both sides.

"And you truly will not allow the Rive to fall unless I sign this?" He lifted an eyebrow.

Mireille nodded curtly. "Truly." She loved him, but she would do what was necessary to protect their kingdoms. He was still fae, after all. It was not exactly a balance of power unless Mireille held her ground.

"Take her at her word, Alder," Nisha said from where she leaned against the wall, arms crossed. "My new sister knows how to get exactly what she wants."

Her eyes sparkled as she said it and Mireille gave her a smile. Nisha's first act once she'd learned that the Rive would finally come down, was to announce her plan to roam the twelve kingdoms.

The pair from Nordhelle shared a private smile; Mireille didn't think she'd seen them stop holding hands.

The marshal said, "And of course we have stipulated the release of every single Westrende prisoner, with recompense."

"Oh," said Mireille. "I think I should tell you. I suspect the prince kept those royals and officers prisoner because the queen was going to..." She made a little neck slashing gesture.

The prince stared at her, as if mortally offended.

She said, "And from what Thomas and I saw, they were kept in reasonable comfort. I can't help but imagine it was an act of kindness, as terrible as that sounds." She smiled up at him. "Comfort is not the sort of thing one offers when merely attempting to thwart an enemy queen. He's really quite soft beneath that stern exterior."

He glanced at the marshal, then Noal, before his gaze went back to the contracts. "You have no proof of that." She thought she heard him mutter *ruthless* and *indefensible* under his breath.

"I believe the proof lies with the shadow creatures." Mireille leaned toward the marshal. "Do you know that the ones in Westrende are not Rivenwilde fae? Evidently, the queen had a legion of them, tied to her magic and her lands."

The marshal went still. "They were beholden to the queen? The ones that attacked Westrende?" Her focus narrowed on the prince, accusatory. "Not from Rivenwilde?"

"May we please get on with it?" he snapped. "I've had valets less difficult to negotiate with."

Noal took that moment to set a tray onto the table beside the prince. It held a silver dish loaded with sugarplums. "Majesty."

Nisha snorted a laugh.

The magistrate tapped another line in the contract, seemingly oblivious to the conversational diversion. "This will need signed by Mireille's father. Given that the king is well and there may be time for future heirs on Mireille's behalf—"

"All right. Enough."

The room went still at Alder's words, then he shifted, shoving the tray aside and dragging the last pages of the contract toward him. With a heavy sigh, he scanned through the details, lifted a quill, dipped it into an elaborately carved ink pot, then scrawled his name across the page.

Mireille's chest felt as if a flock of birds might burst free. The queen was defeated. Norcliffe was safe. And she... She was in love with her prince.

She looked to Thomas, and he offered her the steadiest of grins. He had, of course, agreed to remain in Rivenwilde as her advisor. He still wore the fine suit tailored for the wedding, but now there was a ribbon tied around his wrist, in exact same shade as Kin's dress. Mireille took in the woman and the other occupants of the room, finding that, though she was eager to visit her father and her kingdom, she had already found a new home. And even though it might prove daunting, for the first time in a long while, she wasn't scared at all.

"Noal," the prince said. "Show these guests to the," he made a shooing gesture, "somewhere with some sort of refreshments." He turned toward Mireille, his hand finding hers as if he'd done it a thousand times. "I have a desire to take to the gardens with my wife."

As the others ambled from the room, Mireille turned to face him. "The gardens?"

He made a short, satisfied sort of hum.

"It is nearly sunrise. Are we to visit the wisteria tree?" She laid a hand on his chest. "I find I've grown quite fond of Rivenwilde and its heart."

He placed his hand over hers, expression solemn, and Mireille could feel his magic in a way she had not before. Soon, the land would heal, he would take his throne, and that power would increase by untold measures. He said, "Majesty, the heart of Rivenwilde now beats for you."

"Truly," she whispered. "I could ask for nothing more." And then she kissed him.

ALSO BY MELISSA WRIGHT

- STANDALONE FANTASY -

Seven Ways to Kill a King

RIVENWILDE STANDALONES

Beyond the Filigree Wall

Within the Hollow Heart

Upon the Riven Throne

- SERIES -

BETWEEN INK AND SHADOWS

Between Ink and Shadows

Before Crown and Kingdom

Beneath Stone and Sacrifice

THE FREY SAGA

Frey

Pieces of Eight

Molly (a short story)

Rise of the Seven

Venom and Steel

Shadow and Stone

Feather and Bone

DESCENDANTS SERIES

Bound by Prophecy

Shifting Fate

Reign of Shadows

SHATTERED REALMS

King of Ash and Bone
Queen of Iron and Blood

- WITCHY PNR -

HAVENWOOD FALLS
Toil and Trouble

BAD MEDICINE

Blood & Brute & Ginger Root

Visit the author on the web at

https://melissa-wright.com